# *Beneath Black Clouds and White*

**CROWVUS**

i

First Published in 2019
Crowvus, 53 Argyle Square, Wick, KW1 5AJ

Copyright © Text Virginia Crow 2019
Copyright © Cover Image Crowvus 2019

ISBN 978-1-913182-00-7

For comments and questions about
"Beneath Black Clouds and White"
contact the author directly at daysdyingglory@gmail.com

www.crowvus.com

## Chapter One

*Christmas at Chanter's House*

In a country at peace, men of war are confined to their homes and families. To some this can create a suffocating world where they can only dream about the freedom of distant lands and the camaraderie of the army. To Captain Josiah Tenterchilt there was no better way to spend Christmas than with his wife of nine years. It would be incorrect to suggest the captain did not enjoy his work, for there was nothing he regarded as highly as the British army, but he loved his wife beyond anything else.

He lived in a large town house which he had received upon making Miss Elizabeth Jenkyns into Mrs Tenterchilt. It had tall railings before a grand driveway, with two imposing sycamore trees growing at either side, and a large Jacobean front with enormous windows overlooking the drive, railings and the road beyond. While Captain Tenterchilt was a fiercely proud man, he did not see this place as anything more than his home. Inside, Chanter's House was filled with lavish marbled floors, high ceilings and strong coloured walls that gave the rooms warmth, even in the cold of winter.

He and his wife did not live alone in the great building for they also shared its opulence with their three young daughters, Arabella, Imogen and Catherine. Each of the three girls appeared now, decked in their most beautiful dresses, sitting at the table to share the Christmas meal with their parents. Ordinarily on a Tuesday the family would not sit down together for a meal, but Christmas day held a special dispensation. The five of them would sit together for dinner on Sunday, but on other days only the eldest daughter would share the table with her parents, for Captain Tenterchilt did not believe it was right for a child younger than seven to eat with their parents.

Now, all three girls watched excitedly as a large joint of beef, tureens of vegetables and the plate that housed the plum pudding were brought through from the kitchens downstairs. Arabella brushed a loose stand of hair from her face as she indicated to one of the footmen the food she would like. She was a lady in miniature, having learnt a great deal from her mother in her eight years, studying each movement that she made and trying to learn from the answers and instruction she gave. This great house would one day be her own, Arabella knew, and she wished to be prepared for such a day whenever it might appear. Imogen sat with her hands on her lap as she knew she should, having been taught ready for her seventh birthday next year, but her eyes sparkled as she took in the splendour of the spread before her. Catherine covered her mouth trying to hide the excited smile she felt creep across her face and she giggled into her fingers as her father stood to carve the meat. Being only four she had a long time to wait before she would be able to share this experience daily with her parents, and to be given an opportunity midweek seemed almost as exciting as the gifts waiting in the Drawing Room.

Captain Tenterchilt, who sat at the head of the table, looked at his gathered family and smiled slightly to himself. Elizabeth, whose eyes never strayed from her husband's, followed his gaze and felt a similar smile catch her own features as she took his hand in her own. Arabella watched on from the other side of the table, unsure whether she should take her father's other hand but deciding against it.

"Catherine," Imogen hissed as her younger sister picked up one of the potatoes in her hand.

"It is alright, Imogen," her father said gently, while Elizabeth helped her youngest daughter with her cutlery. Generally, their mother would not do such a thing, but Christmas brought great acceptance and leniency within the family hierarchy.

"My dear ladies," Captain Tenterchilt said, rising to his feet. "A very happy Christmas to you all. I shall not make a long toast, or Cat may not be able to contain her excitement." Imogen watched as her mother frowned slightly, but her father continued. "But with the events that brew overseas this might be our last Christmas together for a time."

"Josiah, please," Elizabeth whispered as Imogen's eyes filled with tears.

"War is in a man's nature, Elizabeth," he replied, looking around the table. Imogen kept her eyes fixed on her father as he continued speaking.

"I do not mean that I shall die, my dears, only that war does not know the holy days and festivals which we observe."

"But, Papa," Arabella whispered. "You have missed our last two Christmases."

"It is the price military men must pay, my dears."

"I hope that my Christmas miracle might be that you are returned to us for next Christmas, Papa," Imogen whispered with great earnest. Catherine looked across at her father and nodded, unable to say anything with her mouth full of plum pudding.

"You could not wait, my little Cat," Josiah smiled across at his youngest daughter who shook her head, giggling into her hands once more.

"Her name is Catherine," Elizabeth whispered, looking at her own plate but seeing nothing. She loved Josiah so overwhelmingly, but she had been forced to acknowledge that, while she held the highest position in his heart, he still belonged very much to the army. Her husband had only just returned to her from his exploits in India, where he had fought in the Kingdom of Mysore. That he was already planning and anticipating his return to conflict left a bitter taste.

"Then, here is a health to my beautiful ladies," Josiah continued, lifting his glass to them all. Arabella and Imogen copied him while Elizabeth begrudgingly lifted her glass and encouraged young Catherine to do the same. "Merry Christmas, my dears."

"Merry Christmas, Papa," the three girls chimed as one before Elizabeth set her own glass on the table, untouched. At once the children began eating and their mother watched as the three of them, with varying manners, enjoyed their dinner. She tried to recall the celebration of the day, and smiled at each one of her family, but could not bring herself to engage in conversation.

Afterwards, the family withdrew to the Drawing Room and presents were handed out to each of the daughters. Arabella received a beautiful family of dolls, each wearing clothes which were embroidered with her initials, and she traced the stitches with her fingers, appreciating the fine needlework. Imogen, a keen scholar, received a writing set with its own inkwell and a pen into which her name had been engraved.

Catherine, who had no interest in dolls and wrote as little as she could, received a collection of toy horses and riders. But, while their gifts were each so well matched to the individual daughter, their favourite gift was one they were given to share. Elizabeth watched as her three daughters gathered around a small wicker basket and both Imogen and Catherine gave an excited squeal, while Arabella whispered,

"Oh, Mama, is he ours?"

"Of course he is, my little lady," Elizabeth replied. "But he belongs to all three of you. You must share him."

Catherine wasted no time but picked up the sleeping puppy and held it close to her chest as she had seen people do with children.

"What is his name?" she asked. The small spaniel twisted in her arms but, with a gentle firmness which surprised her parents she safely kept hold of him.

"You must name him, all three of you together," her father replied.

"Gulliver," Imogen announced as she traced her finger along the white line on his nose.

"Arabella? Cat?" Josiah asked. "Do you like the name Gulliver?"

"It is a very exciting story." Imogen began to defend her choice, but her two sisters just nodded.

"Then Gulliver it is," Josiah announced, watching as Catherine set the small animal down on the floor and at once it began snuffling around the room. All three of the children followed Gulliver's every move.

Christmas Day concluded with the children taking their new friend upstairs and placing him in the wicker basket once more. Arabella did not wish to have Gulliver in her room so Catherine and Imogen took the little dog into the nursery with them, much to the annoyance of their nurse. Downstairs, Josiah sat in the Drawing Room with a glass of wine in one hand and the bottle in his other.

"Why did you talk to the children of returning to war?" Elizabeth asked as she walked over to the window and looked out across the lawn at the front of the house. "I thought you had hopes to stay a while longer."

"Elizabeth," Josiah said flatly, pouring the remaining wine from the bottle into his glass. "I have a duty to the army. You know that I must go where I am sent."

"Why did you not take the job you were offered at Horse Guards? You will not get an opportunity like that again, I know it. Your children are growing up without you. You have a duty to them, too."

"I am quite certain that Arabella learns all she needs from you," Josiah replied. "And Imogen? What other six-year-old could recite Jonathan Swift? No, Elizabeth, they do not need anything from me."

"And Catherine?" Elizabeth demanded. "The poor child has yet to find anything she might excel at."

"Little Cat," Josiah laughed. "She has a fire that the other two have not."

"Your temper, you mean. She is lost without you. I am lost without you," she conceded.

"You married me knowing I was a military man, my dear." Josiah rose to his feet and walked over to his wife.

"And, in that time, I have had only one full year with you by my side." She turned to face him and allowed him to kiss her cheek. "I know that I have not delivered you the son you so desperately want, but your three daughters love you as much as any son could."

"My beautiful Elizabeth," Josiah sighed. "I could not hold against you that our three children have been female."

"Is it something you must lament?"

"I do wish I had a son," he admitted with a little reluctance. "But not at the expense of any one of my daughters. Only, a son might understand what it is to be a soldier and would not be reduced to tears at the mere mention."

"Is it so bad that your children are sad to hear you will not be with them?"

"You outsmart me at every turn."

"You married me knowing I was a parliamentarian's daughter," she responded, watching as her husband nodded.

"And so, I accept that you will win any war of words. Now you must accept that I will always respond to the call of the army. You have a beautiful house here," Josiah remarked, his voice becoming frayed with impatience, "and when you become tired of life here you have an estate in the north to enjoy summer."

"They are both yours, my dear," she replied, taking the bottle out of his hand. "Signed over on marriage."

"Do you believe I married you for your property?" Josiah demanded.

"I believe I married you for love, so I do not care, my dear. But I wish you were here long enough so that we might share that love." She set the bottle down on the table and walked toward the door. "Happy Christmas, Josiah," she added, closing the door behind her.

The new year arrived at Chanter's House in much the same way as the old year had ended. The three children were so delighted with Gulliver that he would escort them on all their outings and accompany them all the way through the house. The pup had learnt to climb the stairs now and chased through the house tripping up the servants and causing mayhem.

"Do they mind too greatly?" Elizabeth asked her maid one evening.

"Not at all, my lady," the maid replied. "It is so nice to see young Miss Catherine looking after something. Sarah said that Miss Catherine has already turned her Christmas gift into cavalry brigades and she is making them battle one another."

"Penny," Elizabeth sighed, "perhaps I was wrong to suggest that the captain's influence was needed."

"Miss Tenterchilt is a gem, though, my lady. She will have London at her feet when she comes out."

"My little lady," Elizabeth laughed. "She picks up so much simply by watching me. But Catherine watches her father and is too like him."

"She will mature to a lady, same as Miss Tenterchilt," Penny said softly, unfastening the gold chain from Elizabeth's neck. She turned as Josiah walked into the room and she bobbed a curtsy before leaving.

"I can assume that there were no words shared in my favour with her."

"That is not fair," Elizabeth chided. "I was discussing Gulliver."

Josiah stepped over and kissed her cheek. "They all love him, do they not?"

"The girls do, yes. I am less certain about the household staff." She turned to face him and held his hand in hers. "You have been a little late returning these past few days."

"We have been given our orders to the continent. It is the French again."

"When must you go?" Elizabeth asked, feeling tears stinging in her eyes. "How long can you stay for?"

"No time at all. The French have murdered their king."

"Dear God!" Elizabeth whispered. "I did not think they would actually do it. How awful!"

"So, I am called away to war once more. I leave in a matter of weeks."

Josiah held his wife to him while she tried to take in the brutality of the news she had just heard, and the devastation of her small family being pulled once more apart. While her husband acknowledged the shocking nature of the king's death, he felt a certain relief to be returning to the regiment. Despite feeling torn between his duty to the army and his love for his wife, he could not have guessed the words that Elizabeth was to speak the following Sunday at the dinner table.

"Papa has been called to war again, my dears," she began. All three of her daughters looked from their mother to their father and back again.

"Where to this time, Papa?" Imogen asked.

"The Low Countries, my dear Imogen," Josiah replied. "Holland."

"Is it because the French killed King Louis?" Arabella asked, her usual composure ebbing as her lip trembled.

"Yes, my little lady," Elizabeth replied. "It is because of that, and because I do not like the thought of dear Papa fighting and no one there to look after him, I have decided I shall go and look after him."

Josiah opened his mouth but Elizabeth held out her hand to stop him.

"Enough," she said firmly. "I have already written to our uncle and aunt and they are to come and look after you all and will be in charge of Chanter's House while Papa and I are away."

"What are you doing?" Josiah demanded. "You cannot travel to the continent."

"The children, my dear. Hold your tongue for their sakes."

Three pairs of eyes studied him as their mother spoke but, for her own part, Elizabeth only ate on in silence until the three girls had left the table at which time she turned a defiant face to her husband. Her dark eyes studied him as he poured a third glass of wine from which he drank heavily, his eyes never straying from hers.

"You hate war, you hate the army. Why are you doing this?"

"Because I love you, my dear," she whispered. "I know that other ladies of high degree have followed the flag of the army. Your friend, Elias Pottinger, his wife travels to war does she not? And their children are of a similar age to ours."

"She is the daughter of a general, Elizabeth. She has been surrounded by battle and death every year of her life. You have not, nor would I wish you to see the horrors she takes for granted." He rose from his seat and stood behind his wife, hugging her to him. "You might never recover from the sight of such things. You are a lady, my dear Elizabeth. A lady of far greater standing than I had ever hoped to marry. Ladies do not belong in battle."

"My mind is resolute," Elizabeth whispered, in a tone that sounded contradictory to her words. "I do not feel that this campaign will end well, and I shall not be separated from you for what might be our family's end."

"You cannot know the outcome. Even our generals do not."

"The French will stop at nothing, as the Americans would not."

"So, it would be better if we did not fight?" Josiah demanded. "Is that what you mean?"

"I mean what I say," Elizabeth retorted. Shrugging out of her husband's embrace she rose to her feet and turned to face him. "I shall be accompanying you. I do not believe any amount of conflict will put Louis back on the throne."

"It would take a surgeon beyond compare," Josiah remarked cuttingly. "For he fell in two places."

"And so, you see I was right," she responded, her face paling at the words he had spoken. He had said them for that reason alone, she knew. Keen not to incur his anger, she walked out of the room and stepped up the stairs and into her bedroom. Here she watched over the garden where, despite the bitter wind that blew though the city, heralding war, her two youngest children played happily with young Gulliver, who was already twice the size he had been when he arrived at Chanter's House. She placed her hand on the glass of the window, wishing to capture the moment before her and remember forever the beautiful innocence of the picture.

## Chapter Two

*The Journey To War*

Arrangements were made with the regiment that Captain Tenterchilt's wife would share the journey to war with the men. There was little doubt in Elizabeth's mind that they would be, for her father, although ailing in his old age, remained one of the principal parliamentarians in the country. However, he had visited the couple in Chanter's House, two days before the regiment sailed, to try and dissuade her.

"My beloved daughter," he said, sitting by the fireplace and thanking Josiah as he handed him a glass of claret, "we are not suited to war, you and I. We fight our war with words and reason, not guns and bayonets."

"I am tired of having my husband taken from me by the army," Elizabeth began. "It is not right, Papa."

"You have the heart to go," her father continued, "but you have not the stomach. Besides, what of the children? They need at least one of their parents here for them."

"They shall be well cared for, Papa. And though I know that every word you speak is the truth, I am tired of living this way. I have made up my mind and I am resolute." She turned to her husband who stood by the window. "You are unusually quiet, Josiah."

"Because I agree with your father," came the reply. "It is never a safe place to be, against you, my dear."

The conversation had turned then and the three children were brought into the room to see the grandfather who doted on them. Elizabeth watched as Imogen proceeded to tell the old man about a new song her nurse had taught her, while Arabella curtsied delicately as he kissed her outstretched hand. Catherine presented Gulliver to her grandfather.

"I had a dog just like Gulliver when I was Arabella's age," her grandfather said softly. "He will be the best friend you will ever have."

"That is not true, Grandpapa," Arabella announced. "For we have each other and sisters have the strongest friendship."

All three girls remained oblivious to the reason that their grandfather had visited that day, only happy to see him, but, as Elizabeth saw her father to the door, he once again pleaded with her not to journey to the continent.

"Papa, I know you have never approved of my marrying Josiah," she whispered, "but you must see that he agrees with you on this matter."

"Your mother gifted you your estate to throw at the feet of whoever you married. After nine years, why should it matter what I think of your husband? You are happy and have three wonderful daughters. That is all I care. But consider how it would be if neither one of you returned."

"I shall not be fighting, Papa," she laughed, but sobered as he shook his head.

"There are so many reasons you may not return, and conflict is the least of them."

"I love Josiah, Papa. I knew he had no money when I married him, and he had few prospects to further his position, but I love him and, in his duty to the army, he may achieve promotion and climb in society. I want to help him do that."

"The way to do that is not to travel with him, but to give him a wonderful home to return to."

"I know, in my heart I know, Papa, this conflict will tear my family apart and I cannot sit here waiting for that to happen. I shall travel and do my best to ensure my fear does not manifest itself."

"Then God bless you, my dear Elizabeth. I pray you are spared any hurt or harm, for you are my most dear daughter."

"I am your only daughter, Papa." She leaned forward and kissed him before watching as her father left her house. She knew he was right, but she could not bear to wait for her husband while he went to war. She was determined to maintain her little family at any cost, including her own discomfort in travelling over to the continent. She turned and found that her husband stood before her.

"I am ready to embark, my dear. Are you?"

Elizabeth set her face and nodded before she whispered, "I just have to say goodbye to the children."

Elizabeth oversaw the children going to bed herself and she sat a while holding Imogen's thin hand in one of her own and gripping Catherine's chubby hand in her other. Imogen's eyes were filled with tears, but she fought to keep them from falling. Catherine, however, had her face set in annoyance.

"Why can I not go with you and Papa?" she demanded.

"Who would look after Gulliver if you joined us?" Elizabeth answered softly. "No, my dear, sweet Catherine, you must stay here. Imogen, you will be a good girl for Uncle Rupert and Aunt Camilla?"

"You have my word, Mama. And I shall make sure that Cat works on her letters while you are gone."

"Imogen," Elizabeth said firmly, about to correct her daughter with regard to her sister's name but, as one of the tears trickled down the child's face, Elizabeth softened her tone. "I shall leave Catherine's tutelage for you to oversee."

"I do not want you to go, Mama," Imogen whispered.

"Nor do I want to go, my dear. But I am going to look after Papa and ensure that he does not meet the same end as the poor king of France."

"He had his head cut off," Catherine remarked as she chuckled, causing her mother's face to pale.

"That shall not happen to Papa," Elizabeth said firmly and leaned over Imogen and Catherine, kissing each of them. She walked out of the room and closed the door, feeling tears pull at her eyes. Forcing them away she walked to the next door along the hall and knocked lightly.

"Come in," commanded a clear voice, and Elizabeth walked in to see her eldest child sitting before a mirror brushing her hair. "I give it fifty brush strokes every night, Mama," Arabella explained. "Papa says that is what ladies in India do, and that their hair is so radiant it shines." She turned now to her mother.

"I have come to say goodbye, my little lady."

"Must you really go, Mama?"

"Yes. But you shall be well looked after while I am away."

"I know," Arabella said stoically. "It is strange that Grandpapa and Uncle Rupert are brothers, is it not? Uncle Rupert is so young."

"There were a good number of other uncles and aunts between them, my dear, but they are gone now. Either across the world or to heaven." Elizabeth stepped over to her daughter and plaited her long hair as she continued talking. "You must be strong, Arabella, and look after your sisters."

"And so I shall. I shall see that the house is run as you would have it, Mama, and I shall not let you down."

"Good." Elizabeth smiled to herself. "I have told Penny that you are to be in charge of anything your uncle and aunt are too busy to oversee."

"Thank you, Mama."

"Goodbye, my little lady," Elizabeth whispered, kissing Arabella's cheek.

"Goodbye, Mama. Bring Papa back safely."

"I shall," Elizabeth promised and turned from the room.

The heartbreak she felt at these two conversations only grew as she departed early the next morning, looking up to see the faces of her three daughters watching down on her from the upstairs windows. She climbed into the carriage and sat beside her husband, waving to her young children until they turned out of the drive and Chanter's House was hidden from her sight. Josiah remained silent as they journeyed on through the city. Elizabeth could not understand how her husband could remain so detached when his three children had just been left behind but, if anything, his spirits seemed to lift as they travelled on until they left London behind and journeyed to the docks.

For the following days as they boarded the ship and travelled across to the low country where they lay at anchor until they could be carried ashore, Elizabeth saw no one save her husband. The boat's movements made her feel sick and, whenever she tried to stand, the world about her would toss and spin. Josiah was unconcerned about this and left her on her own. He watched as England faded and felt once more the giddy excitement of the campaign as Holland came into view.

"I hear your wife has accompanied us on this trip, Josiah."

Captain Tenterchilt turned from where he stood watching the lights of the dock from the deck of the ship, his gaze resting on Captain Elias Pottinger.

"That is true. But she does not travel well and has confined herself to her cabin."

"I am surprised she has come at all," Elias muttered. He had a candid approach to all subjects so the blunt delivery of this statement did not offend his friend. "She has no knowledge or concept of war."

"That is true," Josiah sighed. "I tried, as her father tried, to dissuade her. But once an idea has taken hold in her head, she will not sway."

"I trust her presence will not sway your own judgement in battle."

"I believe Elizabeth has journeyed here for no other purpose. She is adamant this war will not be won."

"It is wonderful to have such supportive confidence, is it not?" Elias remarked, sarcasm dripping from each word. "She should not be here."

"But Anne journeys everywhere with you," Josiah remarked, feeling that he had to defend his wife against this man, who had not met her on more than four occasions. "She is the one who gave Elizabeth her idea."

"Elizabeth is not like Anne, Josiah. I can see that you know what I am talking of, for your expression speaks louder than your words."

"Could Anne not teach Elizabeth what it is to be an officer's wife in war?" Josiah pleaded. "She wants to be a good wife but, as you say, she has no concept of what that means in war."

"I shall talk to Anne."

This brief conversation on the eve of the regiment's landing helped to put Josiah's mind a little more at rest over the presence of his wife. As the soldiers travelled south toward France, Elizabeth began to feel more settled in her new environment. She did not travel with her husband, who led a column of men, but rode in the centre of the regiment, protected on all sides by the red coated men. She had not ridden since she was married and, at first, had been somewhat nervous about returning to horseback, but the horse was calm and sedate. She rode alongside Anne Pottinger who explained to her what each rank of soldier was and who performed each task within the regiment. There was a curious air to her new friend, for she was both detached and interested at the same time. Each night Elizabeth and Anne would rejoin their husbands and each night Josiah felt more and more relieved by his wife's acceptance of that life which he loved. Elizabeth never allowed a day to pass without ensuring her husband would consider each of his three daughters and, for her part, she missed them painfully and prayed for her safe return to them.

It was not until the end of May that the troops finally had the chance to engage in the bloody sport of combat, but thick fog and great fatigue postponed the British troops' attack so that, by the time they walked out, the French had already retreated. This was met with contrasting receptions amongst the ranks, some claiming it as a great victory while others announced that it could not be a victory when there was no fighting to be done. For his part, Josiah was growing weary of journeying without aim or goal, but each evening he walked amongst the men of his company, ensuring his presence was noted by them all, although he talked to very few of them.

As the siege of Valenciennes took hold in June, the change in Captain Tenterchilt's approach, and the continued presence of Mrs Tenterchilt, became a topic of conversation for idle minds. It was one such discussion that was taking place in a tent a little further through the camp, where Elias and Anne Pottinger discussed the Tenterchilts.

"She is an impossible woman," Anne began, freeing her hair from the band that held it. "Have you noticed how the colonel welcomes her each time she walks into his presence?"

"You sound a little jealous, my dear."

"And so I am," she admitted reluctantly. "I was the light of this battalion, the regiment even. Now common soldiers overlook me to find favour with her."

"Josiah is a fine soldier, my dear. I do not want him hurt."

"Your love of the army has blinded you to what is true here. Do you not see that he will be promoted before you? How will that further your cause in this beloved army?"

"He is my friend, my dear," Elias replied firmly. "I do not want him to come to any harm."

Anne sniffed indignantly and turned from him. "What would my father say to such a lack of ambition?"

"Enough," Elias said, an air of anger in his voice. But he knew his wife well enough to know that she would not leave this idea. Indeed, the following day, Anne emerged from her tent determined to redress the injustice that Elizabeth's very presence caused.

Elizabeth was standing, shielding her eyes from the early sun, and looking off in the direction that her husband had just left. She smiled across at Anne as she recognised her and Anne returned the gesture.

"You seem to have a great purpose this morning, Mrs Pottinger," Elizabeth remarked softly.

"And indeed I do, Mrs Tenterchilt," Anne replied with a winning smile. "But where is Captain Tenterchilt going in such haste?"

"He leaves every morning to assemble his company, hoping that today His Highness The Duke will allow him the chance to lead his company into Valenciennes."

"He is indeed committed to his men. It is a shame, is it not, that it is at the expense of their wives that these military men can be so committed to their duty?" Anne sighed, emphasising her point. "Still, I do wish Elias would be as diligent in his devotion to his company as Josiah is to his own."

Elizabeth smiled slightly as she turned to look once more in the direction in which her husband had gone, feeling the implication of Anne's words strike her. "I am proud of him," she whispered, wishing that she could contradict the woman before her, but feeling that Josiah's highest devotion did, indeed, rest with his men.

"But of course," Anne remarked sweetly. "I must go, I promised my husband I would discuss a matter with the colonel for him."

This brief conversation was to haunt Elizabeth's thoughts as the day wore on. She began to suspect that it was not through care for his wife that her husband had no wish for her to be there, but through fear she detracted from his love of the army. As the warm summer days stretched out she continued to try and support Josiah, who remained oblivious to her concerns, but she became wearied by such pretence. More and more of her time she would spend thinking about her three young daughters and increasingly she wished she had remained home with them. For what role had a wife in such a stalemate as this siege had become? And surely a mother belonged with her children?

"My dear Mrs Tenterchilt," Anne remarked one evening as the two women and their husbands sat down together. "You seem to be fading in the endless sunshine. What is it that ails you?"

"I am well, Mrs Pottinger," Elizabeth replied meekly, but Josiah took her hands and looked across at his wife.

"Anne is right, my dear," Josiah whispered. "You have seemed only a shadow of yourself since we travelled here. Perhaps you would be better suited to return home. I am certain I can arrange your journey."

"And leave you? No, Captain Tenterchilt, my place is here while yours is."

Josiah frowned slightly but nodded as he released his wife's hands. Elias spared a sideward glance at his wife but the gesture was overlooked by the Tenterchilts, although Anne felt its full worth.

The sun continued to beat down on the northern edge of France, scorching the ground and turning the lush green grass into burnt yellow blades that stabbed into Elizabeth's hand as she plucked them from the ground. Her head throbbed and she rubbed her eyes constantly, trying to dispel the pain that seized her. This was not how she had imagined the war to be run. Captain Tenterchilt was as remote from her as he would have been if she had remained at home, more so perhaps. She was conscious that she was little more than a distraction to her husband and she hated this fact.

"You seem distracted, Mrs Tenterchilt," she heard Anne say as the other woman walked over to her, straightening the waistline of her dress as she sat down beside Elizabeth.

"I am plagued by headaches," Elizabeth muttered, sparing the woman the briefest of smiles. "It is the sunlight, I believe."

"And this incessant waiting," Anne agreed. "If we might only be able to fight the French out of their garrison we could move forward. I declare that, without these Austrians, we should have reached Paris already."

"Indeed, it is tiresome," Elizabeth muttered, still unsure that she trusted the woman beside her.

"But you must go and see Peters, my dear Mrs Tenterchilt. Of course, why did I not think of it before?"

"Peters? But who is Peters?"

"Captain Jonathan Peters. He is the regiment's medic. I am sure that he will be able to assist you with your headaches."

"An army medic?" Elizabeth whispered. She felt unsure that such a man might know a cure for the ailment that she suffered under.

"Go to see him, my dear. He will give you valuable advice, I am certain."

"Very well," Elizabeth responded, still in a voice so quiet it was barely audible.

Anne rose to her feet and offered her hand to Elizabeth who, after a moment's consideration, took it.

The older lady guided her through the camp and pointed to a large tent, close to the trench that had been dug. There were people walking in and out of it, all manner of men from privates through to commissioned officers. Indeed, here rank meant very little, for an affliction made men of all birth equal.

"I shall leave you here, Mrs Tenterchilt," Anne announced. "Captain Peters is the man to ask for. It is his tent and he would not take kindly to you usurping him in his own hospital."

"Thank you, Mrs Pottinger," Elizabeth said, watching as the other woman only smiled and walked away in the direction from which they had just come, never turning to look back. Elizabeth envied her. She was so comfortable in her surroundings, almost as though she were one of the soldiers herself. More than anything, Elizabeth wanted to support Josiah, but her presence seemed instead to accomplish the opposite.

She walked over to the tent and stood back as she met a man leaving, scratching at a rash that covered the left side of his neck. He mumbled something to her that she took to be either a greeting or an apology before he hurried away. With an air of great nervousness, she pulled aside the flap and walked into the tent. If it had been scorching in the sunlight outside, how much hotter it was beneath the canvas sun trap, and she felt her breath catch, becoming arid as she inhaled. The tent was remarkably empty considering the number of people who she had seen coming and going. There were two young men in the corner near her, one of the low stretchers was taken by a man who weakly coughed occasionally and whose eyes wandered about the room, but saw nothing. Another man, perhaps of her own age was seated at a desk talking to a soldier who was at the front of a row of four men and presently, as she stood taking all of this in, a fifth soldier came to join the queue. The only other person was seated on a chair with his back to her, playing cards at a table that was filled with implements that made her stomach turn.

Unsure who Captain Peters was she stepped over to the nearest person to enquire as to his identity, but the two young men were talking to one another. Not wishing to interrupt them, she hung back a little way, listening to their words while she waited to share her own.

"Are you sure that you have done this before?" the man who sat on the chair asked as he looked doubtfully down at his forearm, as the other man wrung out a cloth over a basin and wiped the blood away.

"Do I question you on your fighting?" came the reply. "Or how you even came by this wound?"

"I told you," the first replied, gritting his teeth as his surgeon picked up a large circular needle. "One of the men slipped."

"And I believe you as much as I did the last time you told me." He placed the needle aside and picked up a roll of cloth bandage. "It is not deep enough to stitch, but if I were you, I should warn your men not to slip again. My needlework is not good."

"But you are a doctor," came the bemused response. "Are you not?"

"Not yet," the second man replied, a slight smile catching his features as he applied the bandage. For the first time he looked up from the job he was doing and saw Elizabeth standing a short distance away. "Pardon, ma'am," he whispered. "Are you injured?"

"Not exactly," she replied, relieved to look into this man's face, for the sight of the blood on the other man's arm had caused a chill within her. "It is another ailment."

"Lieutenant Kitson is dealing with ailments, ma'am," he replied. "I get wounds."

"But he is a lieutenant," the young man with the injured arm began. "Why could I not be seen by him?"

"Because you were foolish enough to let one of your own men cut you open. You do not deserve such an esteemed and highly ranked officer to tend you."

Elizabeth felt wounded on the young surgeon's behalf, but he did not seem at all upset by the words of the man before him. To the contrary a faint smile crossed his features.

"I am seeking a Captain Peters," Elizabeth ventured. "Captain Jonathan Peters?"

"It must be quite an ailment you have, my lady," the seated man remarked.

"He is over there," the other added, pointing to the man who still sat playing cards at the table.

Elizabeth thanked him and walked the few steps over to the desk. He did not stop playing cards, although she was certain that he knew she was there, for she stood scarcely two feet from him. Unsure how to respond to such a snub, she coughed slightly.

"Subtlety is wasted here," he said without facing her. "What do you want?"

"Are you the physician, sir?"

"Captain, if you do not mind." He turned to look at her now and Elizabeth took a faltering step back from him. "You do not know how the army works, do you? I am a captain and this tent is my company. You walk in here and you are answerable to me."

"Very well," she whispered, doubting that she really wanted the help of the man before her. "Only, I have been suffering from an affliction-"

"You should be in Kitson's queue. Kitson!" he shouted loudly so that all the inhabitants of the tent turned to look at her, except for the man on the stretcher. "This is one of yours."

"Pardon, sir," Elizabeth whispered. "But I was directed to you for a cure to my headaches."

Captain Peters, who had turned to address his lieutenant, now turned back to her and threw the cards onto the table. "Only headaches? No nausea? Diarrhea? Bleeding from any orifice?" He rose from the chair as she shook her head. "That foolish man had his arm cut open," he shouted, pointing across to the man Elizabeth had met moments earlier. "Those five all have pox," he pointed to the row of men awaiting Lieutenant Kitson's attention. "And that one has pleurisy," he finished, pointing to the man on the stretcher. "They are all real ailments. Headaches are not."

Elizabeth felt her cheeks burn as the man continued, weighed down by his candid speaking and embarrassed by the spectacle he made of her. Her head was spinning and her eyes brimmed as she nodded quickly and left the tent with what little scrap of dignity Peters had left her, but the moment she stepped through the flap, she rushed to the side of the tent and collapsed in a fit of tears.

She did not know how long she sat there weeping, for she was a prisoner to the slow passage of time, before she turned as a shadow fell over her. The young man she had seen being tended in the tent stood before her, and she looked into his round-cheeked face to find a gentle smile and a deep sympathy within his eyes. They were strikingly blue, she realised, making his fair features seem all the more pale.

"You must not mind the surgeon, my lady," he began. "He has been in the army so long that he has forgotten his decorum and propriety."

"You are speaking very kind words, sir," she whispered in reply. "But I do believe it is I who is out of place and wrong here, not the surgeon."

"Come," he continued gently, making no effort to confirm or decry her statement. "My new friend is too shy to tell you, but he wants to help." He waited until Elizabeth took his outstretched hand before he continued talking. "He may not be a doctor yet, but he has assured me he has all his training and has only to pass his examination."

He pulled her gently to her feet and guided her to the front of the tent once more. There, pacing three steps backward and forward by the tent flap, was the young surgeon who had directed her towards Captain Peters in the tent. He ceased his pacing as he saw the other man lead Elizabeth over to him, and he bowed his head toward her. Despite this formal gesture he remained towering over her, for he had an alarming height. Elizabeth released the hand of her guide and smiled across at him.

"Thank you," she whispered, and watched as he only smiled and walked away, rubbing his hand over his newly-bandaged right arm. She turned expectantly to the young surgeon and looked up into his dark eyes. "Your friend said that you wished to talk to me."

"Indeed, though you must forgive me, ma'am, I do not know who you are."

"My name is Elizabeth Tenterchilt. My husband is a captain here, and I foolishly decided to follow him."

"I am told that this is no place for a lady," he conceded. He waited a second, looking down nervously at the woman before him who continued to stare expectantly at him. "Forgive me, once again, Mrs Tenterchilt. My name is Fotherby." He watched as a smile caught her lips, amused by the nervous nature of the man before her who had seemed so capable in the tent. The tear stains on her cheeks recalled him to what he wished to say. "You must forgive Captain Peters, ma'am. He is an old man who does not deal so well with people anymore. By the time he is ready to work with another human being they are so often unable to answer back." He quickly apologised as Elizabeth's face paled. "But he is not a bad man, just unsociable."

"Is it quite proper that you talk of your leader in such a way?" Elizabeth asked, unsure.

"I trust that after the disservice he did you, you would not report me to him," Fotherby responded, the curious smile catching his features once more, as it had done in the tent. "But come, you sought a cure to your headaches, did you not?"

"Yes," she whispered, and despite her age being greater than his, she felt like a child as she continued. "I have always suffered from them, but here they seem far worse. I do not know if it is the sunlight or perhaps," she stopped and shook her head quickly.

"The stress?" Fotherby ventured and she nodded slightly. "And you lose sight with this?" he asked, pulling a small tin from one of his pockets.

"Sometimes," Elizabeth replied, feeling afraid suddenly. She was surprised as he simply nodded and handed the snuff box to her.

"Take this," he announced, with a certainty that settled her mind instantly. "You need only a pinch of it."

"Snuff?"

"No," he said quickly, falling over himself to apologise for suggesting such a thing to a lady. "It is ground tanacetum parthenium. Feverfew. But they have not created boxes for these medicines yet, so I just use snuff boxes."

"Fotherby!" Peters shouted from inside the tent. "The army does not pay for you to dawdle."

"I have to go," Fotherby began. "But please tell me if it works."

"You do not know that it works?" Elizabeth asked, looking doubtfully at the box.

"Mostly it does," Fotherby said, with great encouragement.

"Do I just eat it?"

"If you can bear to. Or put it in boiling water as you would with tea."

"Fotherby, you useless idler!" Peters roared.

Fotherby offered Elizabeth, who had jumped at this angry interruption, the quickest of smiles before he bowed and ducked back into the tent. Elizabeth looked down thoughtfully at the small snuff box and ran her thumb over the tin lid peering down at the letters that were engraved there. She began walking back through the tents, some built of rifles and blankets, others complete canvas structures, but she scarcely noticed.

"Henry Fotherby, Surgeon, 1788," she read aloud.

# Chapter Three

*A Man Beyond Saving*

The evening was closing in around the camp, when Elizabeth stepped over to the large tent where she knew the officers of the regiment, including her husband, would be. She smiled across at one of the guards, who bowed his head as he pulled back the tent flap, and stepped in. The conversation stopped immediately as she ducked into the room and all eyes turned to face her so that she wished to turn away from the gathered crowd and walk once more into the early evening but, gripping the small box in her hand, she walked forward. Her husband rose to his feet and walked over to her, taking her free hand.

"I heard you were unwell, my dear."

"That is true," she said clearly, as Josiah guided her over to where Captain and Mrs Pottinger sat.

"I believe the whole army heard you were unwell, Mrs Tenterchilt," Elias announced, pulling a chair out for Elizabeth. "And our French opponents too, I should not wonder."

"Indeed," Elizabeth whispered, her face paling until her gaze rested on Anne, who had a hidden look of amusement on her face. "But the surgeon was good enough to give me something to ease my headache.

Though, in truth, I have not yet taken it. He warned me that it might perhaps be better taken in tea." Anne frowned slightly while Elizabeth looked at the gathered faces staring back at her, each man in the tent wishing to know what scandal surrounded the events they had been discussing shortly before she had arrived. "I thank you for your concern, gentlemen," she continued, looking at all the faces in turn. "But I assure you I am quite well."

"I am so glad that you are, my dear," Josiah said, taking his wife's hand and kissing it. "I was concerned to learn of what had happened."

"Clearly you had not heard the full account, Captain Tenterchilt," she replied, smiling across at her husband. "Thank you, Mrs Pottinger, for suggesting that I visit the surgeon."

"I am glad that you have resolved your ailment," Anne said, with a smile that might have curdled milk.

Elizabeth remained silent throughout the meal, feeling that she had gained the upper hand over this woman who, for a reason she could not understand, had taken a dislike to her. For the remainder of the evening, Elizabeth stayed sweeter than she had ever known she could be. She took a pinch of the feverfew that Fotherby had prescribed and, while she felt a strange giddiness take her, the crippling headache that she had endured periodically since they arrived at Valenciennes abated.

Over the next few weeks she took the ground feverfew if ever she felt one of her headaches beginning and, without fail, she could see its benefits almost instantly. She continued in every way she could to support Josiah whenever her support was needed, and remained amicable with Elias and Anne Pottinger, feeling that it was doing right by her husband to be so.

July had taken a strong hold on the entire camp, the summer sun streamed down and increasingly the men spent their time outside the tents and free from the trenches. Sun like this was a rare thing to so many of them and they were keen to seize the chance to enjoy it. But Henry Fotherby was not in a position to enjoy the warmth of the sunshine. Instead he was confined to the baking temperatures of the tent, whilst Captain Peters oversaw every case he treated. It felt in the least irksome to him that the doctor treated him as little more than a boy and insisted that he worked long hours, whilst Peters sat at the desk playing cards or drinking from the flask that Fotherby never saw him fill but that never seemed to empty. But Fotherby was a quiet, patient man, and he saw this as training him for whatever he might be expected to face when he became captain of his own battlefield hospital.

Becoming an army surgeon was something that had shocked his father initially for, as the only son and indeed the only child of a modest estate, Henry was to inherit the wealth of his father. However, the young Fotherby had little love for big rooms and empty halls, feeling that he had a chance to offer something more to the world than a private library of over nine hundred books and a wealth accumulated from the labours of toiling men. For as long as he could remember he had known that his mother had died so soon after he had been born, and his father had repeatedly told him that the presence of a medical man might have enabled her to live longer. Since then, Fotherby had committed his life to one of medicine, attending lectures, reading papers and assisting in any way that he could to learn more that might save lives. He had realised early on in this calling that the army had a great need for advancing medicine and also offered him the chance to leave the damp, dark rooms of Wanderford Hall, his father's house.

His greatest regret, he reminisced as he perched on the edge of a chair, scrubbing the sweat from his brow with the back of his sleeve, was that he had rushed his exam, passing only the very first step on the road to being a surgeon. His father, though proud of the commitment his son had made, insisted that the young man funded his own way through his chosen career, as he had done himself. This meant that Fotherby, as soon as his two guineas were made, took his initial exam and enlisted to journey out to the orient. India had been his first campaign, but he had seen very little of war for a typhoon had delayed their vessel, rerouting them to Calcutta, hundreds of miles from Mysore where the war was fought.

Now, he gave half a smile at the vague recollection of the man who came into the tent. He held his hand up as the newcomer was about to speak.

"Wait. I am sure I know you, and I recall faces so rarely." The man before him folded his arms across his chest and smiled slightly. "One of your men had enough of you," Fotherby announced with certainty. "He took his bayonet to your arm."

"Almost," the other man replied. "And I am impressed by your memory."

"What is it that you need, sir?"

"It is a somewhat delicate matter, Fotherby."

"How do you know my name when I am certain I never spoke it to you? And I do not know your name."

"It is Portland, sir, and I know your name because I make it my business to know all men I deal with. But, Fotherby, I am coming to you on behalf of someone else."

"The man who sliced your arm open?" Fotherby said softly, whilst Portland's eyes widened somewhat.

"Yes. How did you know?"

"That wound on your arm was not at all deep. Any man who slipped would have applied a greater pressure and the wound would have been deeper because of it. Similarly, if you had fought this man the wound would have better resembled a stab mark, narrower and deeper."

"You really are observant, sir. Why did you not qualify?"

"I hope to yet," Fotherby replied, with a certain air of pride.

"I am sure you shall," Portland concurred and smiled slightly. "Are you busy here?"

"Too busy to leave," Fotherby whispered. "But too idle to be engaged."

"Then perhaps you can in the least advise me." He carried another chair over to where Fotherby was seated and sat facing him. "Three times now I have been called out because Cullington has tried to strike people with his weapon."

"Cullington is the man who cut you?"

"Indeed. But he is not conscious of it. He commits all these crimes in his sleep and has little or no control over his actions. But I am not sure I can contain this secret any longer. He is becoming a danger to the entire company."

"Can you not just take the weapon away from him before he falls asleep?"

"If we take his gun from him he does not sleep." Portland sighed and leaned forward on the chair so that he was staring into Fotherby's face. "I do not know what to do."

"Send him home," Fotherby replied flatly.

"I cannot do that," Portland began, shaking his head while he sat back on his chair. "He should be returned home in disgrace and what if he has a family he must support?"

"But how much better that would be than if he was killed here for attacking another soldier. Lieutenant Portland, there is nothing short of sedation that will free this man from whatever nightmares stalk him. And then he would be unfit for duty."

"Send him home?" Portland repeated doubtfully. "I am not sure that I have the authority to do that."

"Then send your captain this way and I will tell him the same thing."

"My captain would not accept such an answer. He would have Cullington shot for desertion. No, I shall have to find another way to deal with this, but thank you for your time, Fotherby. If it were my company I would have taken your advice." Portland rose to his feet and Fotherby felt obliged to do the same. "You are a good man, Fotherby. I hope to see you again."

"Wait," Fotherby muttered as Portland turned toward the tent flap. "I do not finish here until Peters decides my day is done, but if you come back this evening I shall try and help your man."

Portland smiled and nodded before he stepped out of the tent.

"Making plans?" Peters asked as he turned to Fotherby.

"Only for once I am finished here."

"Good. Our job knows no hours does it, my boy?" the older man sighed as he turned back to his cards once more. "Men are as plagued in the moonlight as they are in the sun. More so, sometimes."

"Sir," Fotherby ventured, hoping that this pensive mood in which he had found the captain might be used to his advantage. "I hope to return and take my examination soon."

"Pull up a chair, my boy," Peters said softly, and Fotherby felt uncertain suddenly. The surgeon was so rarely this accommodating and he tried to understand what the cause of this benevolence may be. "You may well overtake Kitson and myself when you take this exam. I should be sorry to see you leave."

"Sir," Fotherby whispered, "I am not going to be given the post of captain straight away even if I do pass the exam."

"There is no doubt in my mind. But you have not yet dealt with the horrors of battle. I foresee that this siege may yet result in further bloodshed and your true test as a surgeon will come in that, not in the exam."

"I am prepared to do my duty to try and save all those who need my help."

"But that is exactly the issue," Peters began. "You will not be able to save them all. Some will arrive who require little tending, others who, through the care and diligence which you administer, can be saved. But there will be still more who you will only have the option to leave to their wounds as they bleed out. Are you prepared for such carnage?"

Fotherby set his face and nodded, understanding through the man's words the cold and detached nature that he had chosen to adopt. To have to make such choices over the lives and deaths of men who you had come to know must have been too much for the old man to deal with.

"Sir, I knew what I was enlisting to the very day I enlisted. I only want to ensure that my capabilities are not compromised by my rank. I am the only man beyond sixteen years of age who is employed here without a rank to accompany his name. Even the men who tend the horses, or those who stand beside the men who stand behind the guns, they have a better rank than I, for they do have a rank."

"I am in no doubt that you will pass your exam, Fotherby," Peters replied, ignoring the embittered tone of the younger man's last statement. "But there is something more I must mention to you. If you truly wish, as you claim, to obtain a rank high within the British army, remember that the army swears an allegiance to the crown. The crown accepts the parliament's decisions on affairs of state, which means that you must too."

"I do not understand, sir," Fotherby began. "Have I ever given you cause to believe that I was a rebel?"

"Not yourself, my boy, but watch the company you keep."

"I do not keep company," protested Fotherby. "My hours here are too great to keep company."

"Lieutenant Portland is as close to a rebel as the army will permit, and I will not see you ruin your chances of a future in His Majesty's army because you are tainted by association." He took a drink from his flask once more while Fotherby tried to imagine the crime of which Lieutenant Portland was guilty, for he had seemed only concerned with his men's best interests.

Peters had clearly finished this conversation, for he wafted his hand in a dismissive fashion so that Fotherby rose to his feet and left the older man alone. He walked to the tent opening and stood looking out over the lazy comings and goings in the camp beyond, but seeing none of what was occurring before him. The last afternoon sun stretched down until it reached the horizon and finally Peters permitted him to leave, with words of caution to the young man once more. Fotherby assured his captain that he would be true to the laws of the army, before he stepped outside, leaving his satchel behind him. He waited, watching the sky darken and the stars begin to shine in the clear midnight blue. He was convinced that Peters had no bed elsewhere but slept in the hospital, for he was always there after Fotherby in the evening and always arrived before him in the morning.

After waiting as the minutes ticked by, Lieutenant Portland finally appeared and smiled across at Fotherby who returned the gesture with uncertainty. He could not escape the words that Peters had shared with him and he hated both Peters for causing doubt in his mind and himself for allowing the older man to do so. Unaware of this personal battle that Fotherby was fighting within himself, Portland placed his hand on the other man's arm.

"I hope you can do something for him, Fotherby. I am close to allowing the men to announce that poor Cullington is possessed."

"No man is possessed," Fotherby remarked. "Only possessed by their own haunting memories and fears."

"And how do you cure a man of such an ailment?"

"We shall find out," Fotherby replied with a smile.

The pair walked on towards the trenches until they arrived at the company that Portland belonged to. There were only four tents here, but several make shift tents built of guns and blankets that each housed between two and four men. It was around one of these that a number of men were gathered, and Portland sighed heavily as he pointed towards it.

"That is Cullington's tent."

He rushed forward, leaving Fotherby to follow. The men parted before him and he stepped into the tent, ducking out of view. Fotherby quickly moved forward and tried to get to the tent, but the men had closed in once more and he wasted precious moments trying to reach the young lieutenant.

"Fotherby," he heard Portland's voice call, and in a second the way parted through the men and Fotherby stepped forward.

He had to enter on his hands and knees, for the humble dwelling would not allow for the tall man to even kneel up inside. Portland had one hand on the musket that the man gripped tightly in both hands, pushing him back, whilst Cullington struggled against the superior force Portland applied to the rifle. The man's eyes were wide open, but his gaze took in nothing of his surroundings. Instead he seemed trapped within a memory of another time, or perhaps a fear of a time that had yet to come. His brow was drenched, and his palms were covered in sweat that gave them cause to slip on the musket so that the first thing Fotherby did was prise Cullington's fingers away as they slipped dangerously close to the trigger.

"He is like this every night?" Fotherby asked, wondering how best to proceed.

"Most nights," Portland panted, belying the apparent ease with which he forced the man back.

"Portland!" a voice bellowed from outside the tent, causing both the conscious men to face the opening. "What is the meaning of this commotion?"

"Do what you can, Fotherby," Portland said quickly, crawling out of the tent.

Fotherby frowned and stumbled to the ground as Cullington's musket butt struck his back, recalling him to the task in hand. Without thinking he snatched the man's wrist and pulled his hand behind his back, causing him to drop the musket to the ground.

"Cullington," Fotherby said firmly, and at once the man tried to stand to attention. But the low tent would not permit him to. "Enough, Cullington. What do you hope to achieve?"

It was a vain hope that the man would respond to such a question and indeed he did not make a reply. However, he seemed to relax somewhat and Fotherby breathed a sigh of relief as he helped the man back down to the ground. He waited until he had fallen into a regular pattern of sleep before he shook him awake.

"Cullington, have you a family waiting in England?"

Cullington rubbed his eyes as he sat up and looked across, confused by the sight of the man before him who addressed him with familiarity but who he did not recognise. "I have a mother," he whispered.

"Where does she live? Where are you from?"

"Was I dreaming again?" he asked anxiously. "Did I injure anyone?"

"Yes, but no you did not." Fotherby rubbed his shoulder blade where the musket had struck him before he added, "At least nothing that will not soon recover."

"I do not mean to," Cullington began, but Fotherby shook his head.

"You have a life worth defending, Cullington, that is all. Have you been to war before?"

"Yes, sir."

Fotherby felt his breath catch as the man addressed him as sir, and could not bring himself to correct him. "And do you trust the other men of your company?"

"Yes, sir."

"Then why do you need to hold your musket to fall asleep?"

The man remained silent and studied his hands thoughtfully. Fotherby remained silent too, waiting for him to answer, but with Portland's reappearance at the edge of the tent both of them turned.

"I am sorry, sir," Cullington said quickly, stepping out into the night.

"The good surgeon wants me to return you to England," Portland began as the man stood before him. "The captain wants you to answer to the court. What am I to do with you?"

Fotherby sat inside, staring forward but seeing nothing. Instead he listened to Lieutenant Portland talking to the unfortunate man and wondered once more what Captain Peters had meant about him.

"I do not mean to do these things," Cullington replied.

"I do not want you to cause harm to anyone, myself included. But I cannot bring myself to return you to England with the disgrace of being dismissed."

Fotherby appeared from the makeshift tent and rose to his immense height, looking down at the two men. "He is better placed in England. Not all men were born to be soldiers."

"But-"

"Fotherby," Portland began, interrupting Cullington's protest. "Is there not something you can give this man to help him sleep?"

"Captain Peters will personally cut my hands off if I take anything from his store. And I do not have that kind of medicine."

Portland only nodded and patted Fotherby's arm. He appreciated and understood the position that the young apprentice surgeon was placed in, and yet could not accept that the only solution was to return Cullington home in disgrace. His thoughtful despondency was matched only by Fotherby's overwhelming guilt at his failure to do anything for the soldier he had just met. So desperate was he that, upon passing the hospital tent, he walked in with the intention of relieving the medical store to sedate the poor man. But Peters was still there, flicking the playing cards onto the table. Feeling at once guilty for considering stealing from the store, it occurred to Fotherby that perhaps the dislike Peters had of Portland stemmed from his ability to persuade men of his cause.

"What do you want, Fotherby?" Peters demanded, without turning around.

"Nothing, sir. Though," he faltered, unsure about discussing the man he had just encountered, but equally unsure that he could find sound medical advice from anyone other than his superior officer. "There is a man. He is plagued by nightmares and reacts to the events of his subconscious."

Peters turned to face him and frowned. "One of Lieutenant Portland's men? I told you, my boy, stay clear of him."

"But Cullington, sir. Surely we should help him, no matter who his officer is."

"Send him home."

"That was what I said," Fotherby whispered, and backed up his words with a despondent sigh. "But he would be sent home in disgrace."

"This is the army, Fotherby. We are not a charity."

Fotherby, for the first time he could remember, concluded the conversation with the captain and walked out of the hospital. This night played often through the young apprentice surgeon's mind as the days approached the scorching end of July. He felt torn between his duty to the army and the compassion that he felt towards his fellow man, for Portland had in the least been right in that Cullington would be disgraced should he be sent home. But above all, he considered repeatedly what Lieutenant Portland had done that placed him as a rebel who, from the manner in which Peters had spoken of him, sat almost outside the law.

Diligently he continued his work as the weeks passed, seeing nothing of Portland. He endeavoured to push the case of the unfortunate Cullington from his mind but his work in the hospital, though long in hours and plentiful in patients, was monotonous. He continually felt his mind drift back to him. Finally, when he felt that he could no longer bear the neglect he had shown, he found his distraction.

Fotherby was sitting on the grass outside the hospital tent, his head lowered to avoid the glaring brilliance of the late afternoon sun, when he realised that he was no longer alone. Turning as the newcomer crouched down beside him he smiled nervously across at her, feeling his cheeks redden at being caught in such a contemplative state.

"Mrs Tenterchilt," he whispered quickly. "I am sorry you find me so poorly presented." He rose to his feet as she did the same, and now he towered over her.

"It is I who am sorry to intrude on your thoughts, Doctor."

"I am not a doctor yet, Mrs Tenterchilt," he muttered.

"But I have come to thank you and to return the snuff box which proves your statement incorrect." Here she handed the small tin over to him, highlighting the inscription on the lid. "It says you are a surgeon, and have been some five years."

"An overzealous gift from an over proud uncle, I am afraid."

"Whatever the reason," Elizabeth said softly. "I wished to thank you, for the herb worked wonderfully, and now I am scarcely troubled by the headaches at all."

"I am pleased, Mrs Tenterchilt."

Elizabeth witnessed a burden of sorrow upon the shoulders of the young man that she had not noticed the month before. The war seemed to have tired him and his eyes were almost as dark as the disarrayed hair upon his head. She tried to find words that might give a comfort to him, for his sadness seemed beyond him, but she could think of nothing that might relieve him.

"You must forgive me, Mrs Tenterchilt," he continued, realising the concerned thoughts that were passing through her head. "I am weary, that is all."

"Have a care, Doctor Fotherby. We need skilled gentlemen like yourself to be alert and awake, at all hours."

Fotherby smiled across at her and bowed his head as she placed her hand on his arm, before walking away without offering a further word. This exchange, though brief, offered him a respite from his concerns over Cullington. That a lady, who had no connection to him, should offer him pity when he should be helping others made him realise that he had allowed a little too much of his raw emotions to surface. However, his lament at having too much time to think was about to become a wishful dream as the following day dawned.

## Chapter Four

*Modern Medicine At The Fall Of Valenciennes*

The overwhelming heat of the summer sun had been beating down on the British troops, many of whom had abandoned their jackets and, as the stalemate of siege warfare stretched on, had resorted to drilling with their collars open and without their hats. This, of course, depended greatly on their officer and whether or not they were being observed by a senior ranked officer. In all, each of the men, though pleased to be escaping the blood and death of battle, were becoming tired of waiting. As this continued, conversations were shared in hushed voices over the Austrians' intentions in delaying the siege, for no man could understand why they had not built upon the victory at Famars.

"They have more in common with the French than they have with us," Elias Pottinger remarked as the pair walked through the camp. "Weeks, it has taken to dig those tunnels."

"Weeks in the baking sunlight," Josiah agreed. "Though I imagine it is cooler underground."

"We will be in there soon. Thank God, for my men cannot wait much longer. There is a madness that seems to be seeping through the ranks."

"Perhaps it is as well," Josiah muttered. "I do not like the thought of Elizabeth being so close to battle."

"How is Mrs Tenterchilt?" Elias asked after a second.

"Well. She has seemed in much higher spirits since Anne suggested she visited the surgeon. It was good of her."

"Indeed," Elias responded awkwardly. "Mrs Pottinger thinks of many things we men are incapable of seeing."

"Your dear wife is a woman to put us all to shame." Josiah gave a slight laugh before he continued. "But I did not imagine Peters would be someone who was so ready to help."

"Nor did I," Elias conceded. He knew, of course, that his wife had sought only to belittle and make a fool of Mrs Tenterchilt. When Anne had married him ten years earlier she had been the finest and most advantageous catch a young lieutenant might have made. As the daughter of a general, she was familiar with the workings of the army and was of a class many degrees higher than her husband. And how Elias Pottinger had enjoyed holding this over Josiah and the other officers. Elias had unbounded respect for Josiah Tenterchilt as a soldier, but he could not forgive him for falling in love with a lady of such high degree and having that lady love him back. He had enlisted alongside Josiah, but the man seemed to outshine him in all that they achieved. The knowledge that Captain Tenterchilt's aspirations and military leadership were appreciated by Mrs Pottinger and her father, far more than his own, caused a great pit of jealousy within him.

"Tonight should decide the battle," Josiah replied, ignorant of the thoughts which ran through his friend's head. "They have reached the walls, I understand."

"Good, for my men need to fight."

"Mine too," Josiah agreed. "There is only so much that ranks can achieve without an enemy in range."

"Worsened, surely, by having them in our sights." Elias smiled across at Josiah and reminded himself that this man was his friend. "My lieutenants are always arguing, too."

"Indeed, the wish to progress burns a fire in the hearts of rivalling men."

Elias forced a smile as he considered how Josiah's words echoed his own feelings. "It is not that. They argue repeatedly over politics."

"You should not stand for such a thing, Captain Pottinger. You and I never questioned the politics of the army."

"Battle will drive it out of them," Elias said firmly. "Their problem is that they are too well classed for too low a rank. One is the second son of the Duke of Everton and the other has just inherited the title of Lord Barrington."

"How do such esteemed gentlemen come to sit on so low a rank?" Josiah asked in confusion. "My three lieutenants are either sons of soldiers or, in the case of the third, the son of a clergyman, would you believe?"

"The duke's son is only here because he almost caused a scandal for his father. He has more children than the king has courtiers and he is only at the age of nineteen. And Lord Barrington has more righteousness than is good for any man. He is a pious fool who expects everyone to agree with him all the time."

"It sounds like there is little wonder they argue," Josiah chuckled. "How is it that, when these men lead our country, we are the ones with more sense?"

Elias laughed slightly and shrugged. The two men continued talking for a time on other matters, happy just to share a conversation with a friend. The sun began to fall from her elevated position in the summer sky, and they parted to assemble their men for what was finally going to be the assault on Valenciennes. There was an unnatural hush on the camp and the only voices that could be heard were in whispers, hissing through the onset of the summer evening.

Hosts of stars were becoming visible as the ranks of the British Army began to form within sight of the town walls. Captains Tenterchilt and Pottinger were both there with their companies and a third company under the command of Captain Forrester also presented there. The plan was a simple one. The tunnel beneath the walls of the town were to be packed, and indeed were currently being packed, full of gunpowder. The moment that the hornwork fell, these three companies were to lead the rest of the regiment into the city, and the siege would finally come to its end. This form of warfare had been in existence over hundreds of years and, whilst this meant that it was perfected by the attacking forces, it also meant that the French would be foolish not to expect such an end.

All the same, anxious cries filled the night as debris plummeted from the great height it had reached when the barrels were ignited. One individual who remained silent, though the raised hand to her face suggested she was far from calm, was Elizabeth Tenterchilt. She watched numbly as the stars were concealed behind the billows of dust that bulged into the air and she listened with a horrified sickness as piercing screams and commanding voices stabbed through the night. She tried to block them from her head, certain that if one should be her husband's she should recognise it and she could not imagine what she should do if he failed to return.

"There are no sounds in the world like it," Anne Pottinger announced as she walked to stand beside the other woman. Her face seemed pale in the starlight and her eyes sparkled despite the strong tone with which she spoke.

"It is awful," Elizabeth whispered. "Truly terrible."

"But will it not be so much better to have an end to this incessant waiting?"

"I thought it would. But I fancy I can hear each plaintive cry of a grieving mother with every shot that each gun has fired." She turned to Anne and shook her head slightly. "Do you not worry for Captain Pottinger?"

"Indeed I do," the other woman confided after a pause. "But war is in men's hearts. They are incomplete without it. I content myself to know that, should Captain Pottinger fall, he shall have fallen for the cause he loves."

"I cannot reconcile myself with that," Elizabeth whispered. "I should die alongside dear Captain Tenterchilt before accepting that there was a cause worth him giving his life. I shall return to my tent, I believe," she muttered as she clenched her hand to her stomach as a new wave of artillery fire echoed through the night to her. "I cannot abide this waiting."

Anne looked at her in both confusion and amusement, but she did not care. Each gunshot made her jump, and every time that the night sky lit up with burning gunpowder she instinctively screwed her eyes closed. At first she sat alone in the tent that she occupied with her husband, but anxiety encircled her and the quiet of the canvas room began to drive her to distraction. She felt unbearably tired but could not bring herself to sleep. At last she left the tent and began to walk mindlessly through the camp. Everything was very quiet at first, but the nearer she walked to the trenches that had been dug, the greater noises began to reach her. And what nauseating sounds they were. Men were shouting, crying and screaming. Not the penetrating screams of frightened children or the commanding shouts of orders, but the desperate pleading of men who wanted to be free from torturous agonies. There were words of anger, of hurt, but most distressing of all was the sound of fear in each of the voices. She realised then that she had strayed towards the hospital tent and she cast her mind back to her visit to that tent earlier in the summer and the words that the young surgeon had spoken to her regarding the men who were unable to speak, but these men seemed more than able to talk, though far from able to converse.

Feeling sickened to the point of fainting, she rushed from this part of the camp and walked as fast as she could in any direction that her feet would take her. She did not know what time it was, nor how long this attack had lasted, but the gunfire had stopped. The faint glow of the impending dawn could be seen in the base of the eastern sky and Elizabeth stood and watched with an unequalled anxiety as the ranks of men began returning to the tents. She tried to understand from the soldiers what had happened during the battle and came to the conclusion that the Duke of York had accepted the garrison's parley and was, even now, engaged in talks with the French regarding the terms of their surrender.

Far from the neat array of troops that had marched out many hours before in silence, the men were returning in groups, many laughing and calling to one another. After the horrific sounds of the hospital tent, these happy conversations caused an unfailing smile to catch her lips. All of the men who saw her, standing like a beacon in her pale dress before the sunrise, lowered their heads to her. Some even knuckled their foreheads in a courteous salute. She smiled warmly at them all but, as the multitudes of red coated men passed her, she felt her smile slip. There had been no sign of her husband, nor Captain Pottinger, and as further men passed her with still no trace of either man she felt the same anxious nausea seize her once more.

She walked further into the camp, returning to her tent, trying to persuade herself that Captain Tenterchilt would be there waiting for her. But there was no sign of him and she found herself walking once more towards the hospital tent. She stood outside at a distance so that she saw the men carrying, assisting, or even dragging their comrades in, and once more the terrible sound of pleading men reached her ears. Perhaps her husband was one of them, but she could not bring herself to step any closer to the tent.

How long she stood there, waiting for the courage to step over to the tent, she did not know, but now the sun was over the horizon and the churned route to the hospital glistened red. She began to turn from the spectacle before her but heard a faintly familiar voice call out.

"As much as you can carry," it ordered. "We need clean water."

She looked down at the mouth of the tent to see the flap drawn back by the young surgeon as he commanded men, regardless of rank. He did not stop to hear any reply that they made, trusting that they would follow his orders, but turned back to duck once more into the tent. As he saw her, however, he paused, and Elizabeth watched as his brow furrowed. He was covered by a long white apron that was splattered and daubed red with the labours of his evening's work, and there was little wonder for, as the pair exchanged this glance, he ran his hands down the long garment, only adding to the sickening spectacle.

"Fotherby!" she heard Captain Peters boom. "Get back here!"

The young surgeon, never taking his eyes from Elizabeth, smiled weakly across at her and shook his head before he once more entered the tent and left her to puzzle on what such a gesture might have meant. Lifting her hands to her eyes, she tried to dispel the image of the young surgeon covered in the blood of other men, and to understand what would ever compel a young soul to undertake such a profession.

There were fewer men arriving at the tent now, and Elizabeth took a step forward, feeling that she had to know whether her husband was in there. As she moved, however, the two men that Fotherby had sent out returned with a bucket of water in each of their hands, and she pulled back the flap to allow them in. She regretted it at once, for her gaze wandered into the tent before her mind could stop it. What she had mistakenly thought to be the most sickening image of the surgeon covered in blood, now seemed tame as she beheld the carnage underneath the canvas roof. What world did her husband belong to, that he should wish to leave his three beautiful daughters in their elegant house for a place where a man's only hope of survival was for another man to remove his limbs? The sight of Captain Peters with the jagged saw in his hand, the blade dripping red, whilst Lieutenant Kitson held down the man on whom his captain was operating, made Elizabeth's stomach turn and she stumbled backward. Allowing the tent flap to fall closed, and the macabre scene to disappear from view, she rushed away.

"Mrs Tenterchilt?"

Elizabeth stopped as she heard her name, and turned to face Anne Pottinger. The look of amusement had died from the other woman's face and she took Elizabeth's arms gently.

"My dear Mrs Tenterchilt," she said softly. "What has happened? For your dress is hemmed in blood and your face is drained of colour."

"I cannot find Josiah," Elizabeth whispered, before she recalled herself and met the other woman's gaze. "Captain Tenterchilt has not returned."

"Nor has Captain Pottinger," Anne replied more softly than Elizabeth would ever have expected. "I am sure their companies were simply requested to remain during the negotiations. Do not despair so readily."

Elizabeth nodded as Anne released her arms and she tried to calm her racing mind. "It is quite ordinary for some companies to return sooner than others. You will discover that."

The two ladies walked towards the tents that they shared with their husbands. Before they reached them however, they were stopped by a young officer who rushed over to them, standing before them and bowing his head slightly.

"What is it, Lieutenant?" Anne asked, not recognising the dark features of the man before her but acknowledging the badge on his epaulet to find his rank.

"Captain Pottinger, my lady-"

"What of him?" Anne interrupted, anger masking her fear and Elizabeth placed a reassuring hand upon the other woman's shoulder while she lifted her other hand to her own mouth. "Speak, boy," Anne demanded.

"He asked that you should find him," the young lieutenant finished. "He is in the hospital."

"Is he wounded?"

"Not badly, Mrs Pottinger," he said as the two women hurriedly walked in the direction they had just come from.

As they reached the hospital tent Elizabeth slowed down and tried to block the remembrance of what she had seen in there. She stood still at a short distance from the tent and watched as Anne pulled back the flap. But before either she or her young guide could enter, Captain Pottinger walked out of the tent. He looked exhausted, his shoulders were hunched and dark skin circled his eyes, but relief covered his features as he snatched his wife's hand, drawing it to his lips and kissing it. His own hands were red with blood, Elizabeth noticed, but Anne did not seem to care.

Despite her mistrust of this woman, she felt pleased beyond measure that Captain Pottinger was safe and she took a step forward to the couple at the same moment as a second man left the tent. She felt a recognition flit through her mind as he appeared, his blue eyes regarding her with concern for a moment before he bowed formally to her and, drawing out a handkerchief from his coat pocket, rubbed the blood from his hands.

"Sorted, Barrington?" the young lieutenant asked at the other man's appearance.

"Almost," came the whispered reply. Despite addressing the man his eyes never faltered from the woman before him. "Mrs Tenterchilt?" he continued, and Elizabeth nodded, feeling all the colour drain from her cheeks as Barrington's round face paled too. "I did not know your name when last we met."

"I recall you had been injured, sir," she replied. "I trust you are not badly wounded now."

"Thank you, I am well. And shall be happy to escort you inside if you wish."

"Escort me inside?" Elizabeth felt her throat dry and she looked across at Captain Pottinger as Barrington's gaze travelled towards him. "Whatever for?"

"Oh," Barrington muttered. "Lieutenant Sutton and Captain Pottinger have not spoken to you?"

"No, indeed, you clumsy fool," Sutton remarked cuttingly. "I was sent to fetch the captain's wife, only, and that is what I did. Captain Pottinger has only just stepped out of the tent."

"You are not wounded," Elizabeth said, holding her hand out before her to both block Barrington and have his support, for at once she felt faint as she considered what all of this might mean. "Then whose blood was on your hands?"

"My dear," Anne began, stepping over to the other woman. "It would seem that Captain Tenterchilt has been wounded."

"What?" Elizabeth muttered, and she felt tears spring to her eyes as she placed her hand upon Lord Barrington's chest, feeling that she needed the support. "Is he dead?"

"No, my dear," the other woman continued. "He is in the tent. That is why the lieutenant has offered to take you inside."

"Was it his blood?" she whispered, turning her wide eyes to Barrington once more.

"Yes," he replied. "I carried your husband back on Captain Pottinger's command."

"Thank you," Elizabeth sobbed. "And thank you Captain Pottinger," she added as she turned to the man who stood beside Anne. "What happened to him?"

"Let me take you to see him, Mrs Tenterchilt," Barrington said softly, and pulled back the tent flap before guiding her in.

She had accepted the invitation almost without thinking and felt an awful realisation as she looked around her at the macabre scene. The terrible sounds reached her ears once more and she clung to Barrington as though she were a child. He seemed to think little of this but allowed her to lean against him and sheltered her gaze as they walked past the rows of men. Elizabeth did not look at any of the wounded soldiers, some of whom sat, some of whom were lying down upon the ground, until at last Barrington stopped and walked to stand in front of her so that he could talk to her without looking around.

"Captain Tenterchilt is here," he said softly.

"Does he know I am?"

"Not yet," Barrington said gently. "It is his leg that is wounded. He was shot by the French before they surrendered."

"I must see him," she announced, more to herself than Barrington, who now stepped back and pointed to one of the bodies that lay on the floor, before standing behind her.

It was a strange feeling to Elizabeth to see her husband, who had been a pillar of strength and support throughout their years of marriage, lying upon the ground, unconscious. Forgetting all propriety, she leaned against Lord Barrington's chest, burying her head in his coat to try and escape the image before her. His manners never failed him as he took her hands in his own and stepped back to look down into her face. But it was Elizabeth who spoke first.

"I knew," she sobbed, glancing over her shoulder at her husband. "I knew that he would fall in this war."

"Mrs Tenterchilt, your husband is not dead. Some words of comfort may help him."

"I have none to offer," she whispered, turning her tear streaked face once more to the man before her. "For I unwittingly saw earlier how such wounds were treated."

"Elizabeth?"

She looked down at her husband whose eyes remained closed but whose hand was reached towards her. His hand was pale, as though all the blood that soaked his right leg had absorbed the hue from all around it. She knelt down and took his hand and his eyes opened slightly, but the gaze was too much for her to bear, and she dropped his hand, rushing away from him. Barrington watched her go and frowned slightly as she fled from the tent and out into the camp. He turned back to Captain Tenterchilt, wondering what would drive a man to bring his wife into the theatre of war when she was too fragile and delicate to withstand its horrors.

Elizabeth continued to run, but stopped as she heard her name being called out. Anne Pottinger walked over to her, a curious expression on her face.

"Is Captain Tenterchilt dead, my dear?" she demanded.

"Almost," Elizabeth wept, burying her head in her hands. "I must go home. I must return."

"Why have you fled from him?" Anne said, pulling Elizabeth's hands from her face. "If you travel to war it is your duty to tend and nurse your husband. You must go back this moment."

Elizabeth stared at her before she nodded and allowed Anne to guide her back to the hospital tent. Captain Pottinger was talking to his two lieutenants a short distance away from the tent but all three of them watched as the two women walked to the tent flap. Anne pulled it aside and looked in. She did not seem concerned by the scene before her but as Elizabeth's gaze fell upon her husband, who was now lying on the table in the centre of the tent, and the three surgeons who stood arguing over him, it became too much for her. Turning once more she rushed away, but had only covered a short distance before she collapsed in a faint upon the ground.

It had been with a curious interest that Fotherby had watched Lord Barrington leave the tent, and it was a curiosity for which he was extremely grateful, for the bloodshed that he had witnessed required a diversion for his own sanity. Captain Peters had been right that this was the test of any surgeon, far more than the college exam. But Fotherby felt that he was conducting matters rather well and could not believe that either Peters or Kitson could have doubted his commitment and abilities.

The appearance of Mrs Tenterchilt had confused him, however, and as he watched her flee, followed shortly by Barrington, he considered for the first time the man that his friend had brought in. Whilst Peters washed the life blood from his hands and Kitson carefully stitched the bleeding wound of another officer, Fotherby moved over to Captain Tenterchilt. He had only one wound to his right leg, which he clutched with his right hand whenever he was conscious enough to do so. Kneeling down beside him, Fotherby prised the captain's fingers from the wound, only to find that the man mustered enough strength to lash out at the surgeon. Fotherby snatched his wrist before Josiah could strike him.

"Who are you?" the captain demanded.

"I am the person who is trying to keep you alive, sir." It would not have mattered what answer Fotherby had offered for Captain Tenterchilt sat forward and clutched both his hands about his right thigh and fought against the tears that burnt his eyes, blind and deaf to all else around him. "Captain Peters," Fotherby shouted, as he eased the man back down to the ground.

"What?" Peters demanded. He stepped over to where his young apprentice was knelt down and just nodded. "Kitson, help Fotherby lift this one."

Between the two men, they easily lifted Captain Tenterchilt over to the table in the centre of the tent, while Peters washed away the blood, and pointed down to it when he was ready. Fotherby stood at one side of the table while Kitson and Peters stood at the other, the latter having walked over to his campaign desk to pick up one of the scalpels that rested there. It was with a certain numbness that Fotherby pushed the patient's shoulders down, trying to ensure that Captain Tenterchilt did not move. As he watched Kitson tearing open the fabric round the wound, he considered Josiah Tenterchilt's wife and how she had fled from him. What a fragile creature she was and, as he turned to look at the other men who had been operated on in the early hours of the morning, he began to question the blade that his captain held in his hand.

"Wait," he whispered, reaching across to snatch at Peters' hand and catching himself on the scalpel. "This does not need to be done."

"Fotherby," Peters began, with voice frayed with anger. "You wanted me to help this man. Do not hold me back now, boy."

"But if you cut the shot out you will almost certainly sever his artery. That will kill him."

"Then he shall have to lose his leg," Kitson remarked.

Fotherby looked down at his hand and the blood that trickled from his fingers swelling out through the fine slice that the scalpel had caused. "John Harper," he muttered as his eyes met with Peters. "He taught that you did not need to cut a man open for a shot wound."

"Fotherby," Peters said, a softer tone trying to combat the anger he felt. "He was talking about wounds that barely penetrated. This shot is so far into his leg it might be on the femur."

"He'll die," Fotherby whispered desperately.

"Do you know this man?" Peters shouted angrily across. "This is your challenge, Fotherby. If you fail in this then the army will not have you back no matter how many exams you take."

The weight of the man's words fell heavily on his shoulders as Captain Peters thrust the scalpel towards him. He bit his lower lip thoughtfully as he accepted the instrument from his captain's outstretched hand. Not daring to look at Kitson, he stepped over to the campaign desk and exchanged the scalpel for a thin pair of long-handled forceps and tried to stop his hands from shaking. He knew he was doing the right thing. Whatever Peters and Kitson thought, this was a new battlefield procedure, successfully practised during the American war.

Kitson stepped away from the table, his hands raised in a surrendering gesture, before he returned to tend some of the other wounded men. Peters nodded slowly towards Fotherby before he took Captain Tenterchilt's shoulders and tried to hold him still, but he awoke and tried to free himself of the man who stood over him.

With a strength that surprised Fotherby, Peters pushed him back down with one hand and, snatching the leather strap of Captain Tenterchilt's sword belt, he pushed it into the man's mouth.

"Get on with it, Fotherby."

Fotherby tried to ignore the twitches the man before him made. He applied a tourniquet and, pinning Captain Tenterchilt's leg still beneath him, stretched the wound open far enough to allow the forceps into the man's tissue. If he felt that at any point he was losing his control he considered all that weighed upon his success and, selfishly, he realised that it was not solely this man's life, nor the happiness of his wife whose heartrending distress he had witnessed earlier, that was at stake. It was a proof that he could go on to achieve that goal he had dreamt of as a surgeon. As he delve further into the man's leg, Captain Tenterchilt movements became more and more desperate, so that Fotherby almost lost control of the instrument in his hand, before at last he felt the ends of the forceps close about the shot. Pulling it back as gently as he could, tried to steady his shaking hand. The ball slipped o once before Fotherby pulled it out from the captai leg. Captain Tenterchilt lay still, his eyes were clo. and his body no longer tried to resist the crude surg For a moment Fotherby thought that he had died bu

he poured a sprinkling of wine into the man's wound, the captain forced himself out of the hold that Peters had on him and tried to reach his leg. Fotherby stumbled away from such a gesture but Peters snatched the captain to him and, holding his arm about Captain Tenterchilt's throat, spoke calmly to his apprentice.

"Are you to stitch the wound, Fotherby?"

Fotherby nodded quickly and tried to steady his nerves and his hands to thread the circular needle before he proceeded to apply surprisingly neat stitches to the wound. He felt quietly proud of himself as he stood back to admire his work. But as his gaze turned to the pained face of the man he had just operated on, spitting out the leather belt which was now peppered with tooth marks, he felt his resolve shatter and the needle slipped from his fingers as he fumbled with the knife to sever the thick thread.

Peters released his hold on Captain Tenterchilt before beckoning Kitson over to help the wounded man onto one of the beds. Captain Jonathan Peters walked around the side of the table to stand before the man who, though half his age, towered over him. Fotherby lifted his bloody hand to his face before he spoke.

"He should have the wound opened and cleaned in two days," he mumbled. "That is what Harper says."

"You are the surgeon here, my boy," Peters said softly. "Not Mr Harper. That was a spectacle. You had absolute command, Fotherby."

"Then why am I shaking so much?"

"Because you have done a great thing. Now," Peters continued, returning once more to his gruff voice, "there are plenty of other wounded men. Relieve Kitson."

"Yes sir," Fotherby replied quickly, scrubbing his hands down the blood-covered apron once more.

## Chapter Five

*Resignation and Acquisition*

The French surrendered that day and, to mixed responses, the Duke of York granted them permission to leave the garrison and return to Paris. According to the articles of war, this would prevent those who surrendered from rejoining the war, but opinion was divided regarding whether the French would abide by these rules. Captain Tenterchilt knew nothing of these developments until two days later when, having remained in the hospital, he had his wound reopened and redressed by the young surgeon.

"Captain Peters speaks very highly of you," Josiah remarked as Fotherby placed a fine lint over the newly-stitched wound, using the man's belt to hold the dressing in place.

"I doubt that, sir."

"He said you saved my leg, perhaps my life. Coming from a fellow captain, I can imagine no higher praise." He looked down at the wound before looking across at another man in the tent who no longer had two legs, only one and a stump. "Why did you not save him?"

"He has been saved, sir," Fotherby replied. "He might have bled out if his leg had not been amputated."

"He had the same wound as I. Why did you not save him?" the captain repeated.

"I did not see him being operated on. And I know the gentleman who brought you in and, pardon sir, your wife too."

"Elizabeth?" Josiah whispered. "How do you come to know my wife, sir?"

"She came seeking medical advice, perhaps a month since."

"Oh my good man," Captain Tenterchilt announced, snatching Fotherby's hand and shaking it firmly. "It was you."

Fotherby was confused by this statement but allowed the man to congratulate him, feeling elated in the praise that he offered. Captain Tenterchilt smiled slightly, following the thoughts of the young man, before he swung his legs to the ground and grimaced at the pain it caused.

"You cannot walk," Fotherby said firmly. "That shot may well have fractured your femur. If you walk on it, you will do irreparable damage."

"Then find me a crutch," Captain Tenterchilt said flatly. "For I intend to leave this tent and go in search of my duty and my wife."

"With respect, sir, I fear your days in this campaign may well have come to an end. And if you apply weight to that leg you may still have to lose it." Fotherby sighed and forcefully returned his patient's legs to the stretcher once more. "We are all moving west to the coast, but you will have to return to England, sir. You can offer nothing more to this campaign."

"Then you condemn me and my family to poverty."

"No, sir," Fotherby began, but it occurred to him that this was precisely what he was telling the captain.

"If I cannot fight, I cannot work. I have no hope of providing for my family."

"Sir, in the least you shall be pensioned out of the army."

"Do not seek to pacify me," snapped the captain.

Fotherby only nodded and rose to his immense height before he walked away. The hospital, in those two days, had almost returned to normal. The blood, which had created a churned and slippery floor, had dried and arid soil was once more their carpet. While six of the beds were taken by wounded men, many of the others had already returned to their posts, begun the long journey home, or perished and were buried in graves that had once been the siege trenches.

Lieutenant Kitson sat at a desk, rolling a shilling over the back of his fingers and occasionally reaching to a wooden beaker to quench his thirst. Captain Peters once more had his back to the world as he sat at his campaign desk. All the instruments of their trade were safely packed within the leather-covered wooden box that rested before him as he flicked the cards in his hands onto different piles. He, too, continued to drink from his unending flask and Fotherby gave a despondent sigh as he observed his superiors.

It was not that he believed he was any better than the two men but he had hoped that, after the bloody conclusion to the siege, he would be permitted a leave to return to England and take his exam. Instead he was to travel west with the army once more, and his hope of qualifying became more and more remote. He tried to remind himself that he was in a better position than Captain Tenterchilt and, for the first time in several days, he considered that poor fellow Cullington and wondered what fate he had been left to endure. Captain Tenterchilt would in the least return home a hero of Valenciennes and with his honour intact.

"Sir," Fotherby whispered as he stood behind Peters. "Might I be granted some minutes to go and fetch the captain's poor wife?"

"For what purpose?" Peters replied, without turning to face his apprentice.

"For the purpose of compassion, sir. Captain Tenterchilt is proud and noble and has just discovered news that is beyond disappointing to him. Is it so wrong that he should wish to share his burden with his wife?"

"Our business is not in compassion, Fotherby. What breed of man brings his wife to such a place as this?"

"With respect, sir," Fotherby replied in the same irritated manner as he had spoken these words only moments earlier to Captain Tenterchilt. "I am not married and so could not comment. Are you married, sir?"

"No."

"Then perhaps neither of us should pass comment."

"Watch your words, Fotherby," Peters scolded, turning to the man beside him. "Even your friend, Portland, has not brought his wife to war."

"Sorry, sir," Fotherby muttered. "What is it that you so strongly object to about Lieutenant Portland, sir?"

"He is a man of blinkered ideals, Fotherby, and his ideals are not those of the army, therefore they are not ideals that he should hold having enlisted in the army."

"But surely a man's beliefs are his own and no man should seek to change them?"

"Do not be so naive, my boy," Peters commented, but despite his harsh words his tone was surprisingly patient. "Do you not think I know that you judge me each time that I drink from my flask or that I do not judge you when you refuse an offered drink?" Fotherby remained silent but considered the truth of what the man said. Realising that his words had hit their intended mark, Peters continued. "Go then. Find Captain Tenterchilt's wife. There is little for us to do here but wait to join the rest of the forces in moving forward."

Fotherby watched as the older man drew out his flask and drank deeply from it. Peters offered it to his young apprentice with a wry smile, but Fotherby simply shook his head, knowing that his captain had once more proved his point. Without another word, Fotherby turned away and walked out of the tent and into the evening sunshine of the day beyond. The skies of northern France were filled with pinks and oranges with no blue to be seen and Fotherby smiled to himself as he beheld them. Finding beauty in the world had become a necessity after seeing the cruel butchery that man could do to man. When, at times, the horrors of his job became too much for him to bear, he would consider the beauty of nature and the love that one man could carry for another.

He did not know where he might find Mrs Tenterchilt but wandered through what remained of the camp until, at last, he found her seated upon a low stool at the opening to a tent. Her gaze wandered over a great distance, but took in none of the beauty around her. She was gazing over time and looking back into history with an unbearable sorrow. Fotherby walked over to her and bowed his head slightly.

"Mrs Tenterchilt?"

"Doctor Fotherby," she said, her throat struggling to form each word. "I did not see you there."

"Your husband asked that he might see you, Mrs Tenterchilt. I have come to escort you."

"My husband?" she whispered. "I cannot see him. I cannot bear to see him, Doctor. The image of the hospital on that awful day is still ingrained within my memory and I need to be rid of it."

"I do not believe that you would even notice your husband's wound, Mrs Tenterchilt. But he has some news to share with you, I believe."

"You are clearly privy to this news, Doctor. Why can you not tell me?"

"It is not my place to, Mrs Tenterchilt. Please come." He reached his hand down to her and watched as she considered taking it before she accepted and allowed him to help her to her feet.

"You are journeying west, I believe."

"Indeed," Fotherby replied. "We are to face the French once more, but on the coast this time."

"When will you leave?"

"When I am commanded to by my captain. But, in truth, I am hopeful to return to England as soon as I can so that I can take my examinations."

"You must seek us out when you come to London, Doctor," Elizabeth whispered after a time. "Your aid to me was so gratefully received, and I am certain that I have you to thank for my husband's survival."

"You pay me too much honour, Mrs Tenterchilt. For certain Captain Peters is due the praise and your husband's will to live was beyond admirable."

"He wanted to come to this place," Elizabeth whispered as she stepped over to the hospital. "I cannot understand why he left his home and beautiful children to end in this blood-soaked butcher's tent."

Fotherby frowned at her words, feeling stung by her inadvertent condemnation of his job. But he tried to remind himself that she was lamenting something that had meant so much to her. She allowed him to pull back the tent flap and she walked in before he ducked in behind her. Lieutenant Kitson spared her a quick smile before returning to packing the wagon, and Elizabeth looked across at Captain Peters, who did not turn to face them. Instead, he pointed over to the stretcher where Captain Josiah Tenterchilt sat, leaning forward with both hands about the wound on his leg.

"What are you doing?" Fotherby demanded, hysteria in his voice.

"Elizabeth," Captain Tenterchilt began, ignoring the young apprentice.

"Captain Tenterchilt," she replied, her voice little more than a whisper, but she rushed over to his side. "I was so afraid."

"Whatever for, my dear?" the captain asked as he lifted her hand to his mouth and kissed it. Neither of them paid any heed to Fotherby, who was on the opposite side of the captain, reapplying the belt about the dressing.

"I thought you would die," she whispered, gripping his hand tightly. "And the image of the bloodshed and the barbaric cruelty, that the poor surgeons are left to remedy, shall never leave me. I do believe I shall be haunted by it until I die."

"This is the gentleman to whom I owe my life."

Elizabeth watched as her husband turned his appreciative gaze to Fotherby, who shook his head quickly. "No, sir. It was your will to live that enabled you to do so. But if you continue to attempt to stand or pick at the dressing you may not remain alive."

"You cannot walk?" Elizabeth whispered, turning from her husband's face to the surgeon and then back again. "Will you walk again?"

"Of course I will," Captain Tenterchilt replied as Fotherby rose to his feet.

"As long as you are careful in your recovery," Fotherby cautioned. "I can see no reason why you should not."

As Fotherby turned from them, Captain Tenterchilt looked across at the man he had earlier observed before he continued to talk to his wife. "My dear, it is that young man to whom I owe my very life. But I pray he is wrong about his assessment of what has happened."

"Why?" Elizabeth whispered, her face paling as she watched her husband. "He told me that you had news to share with me. What is it? What has happened?"

"My dear Elizabeth." He lifted his hand to her white face and ran his thumb down her cheek in a gesture so openly affectionate that she felt a terrible fear seize her regarding what he might say. "I have been a poor husband to you, have I not?"

"Most certainly not, Captain Tenterchilt."

"But you should have married a lord like Barrington or Sutton. Instead, you married a poor soldier who was born in ignominy and obscurity. And I have not given you the life you should have had."

"You are frightening me, Josiah," she replied, and indeed her tone suggested the truth of her words for her voice shook as she spoke. "You said that the young doctor saved your life. Is it not true?"

"No, indeed. I am inclined to believe his assessment of my injury. But he has assured me that I am no longer of use to this campaign and has advised me to take my pension and continue life without a profession."

"Captain Tenterchilt," Elizabeth began, relief evident in each word. "We shall always be well provided for. You need have no concern with regard to that. Nor should you worry over your role as my husband, for I have met no man I would rather marry. But we have three wonderful daughters, and a beautiful home. You need not trouble yourself with fleeing from them any longer."

"Fleeing from them?" he demanded, trying to recall his temper but feeling his frustration deepen. "I have sought only to defend them and provide for them. Is that not a man's role? And now I have failed in that."

Elizabeth did not offer him any further words. Indeed, she could find none to say, for his despair at being cast off from the army engulfed him beyond reason. If he chose to define his role within her family in such a way, there was little she could do to convince him otherwise.

The following day saw the departure of Captain Tenterchilt's company and he felt despondent isolation strike him as he regarded it. There was a supply run heading north to Holland once more, and Captain and Mrs Tenterchilt were to join them and gain passage home that way. Captain Tenterchilt barely spoke on the voyage, leaving Elizabeth to her own thoughts, which were predominantly filled with trying to avoid the sickness that had engulfed her on her first sea voyage. Fotherby had instructed Captain Tenterchilt to seek out a physician in London who might remove the second stitches with which he had sealed the wound, and had advised him against putting any weight upon the leg until he had sought out medical advice. To Elizabeth he had given more feverfew and suggested that, on the return trip, she should watch the horizon, to avoid the nauseous dizziness that boat travel might cause. This, she had discovered, worked well and the trepidation she felt before she sailed faded as the journey continued and she reached England in far higher spirits than she had arrived in Holland six months previously.

Upon their arrival at Chanter's House they found it empty, but for the servants who had remained for the long summer. It was of little surprise, for the family always stayed at the large estate house to the north of London during the summer months. It felt strange to Elizabeth to return to an empty house, covered through with dust sheets and with all the shutters closed. She stepped in and at once felt like a trespasser. Whatever thoughts passed through her husband's head as he looked about him, repositioning the crutch in his right hand, he did not speak. But his eyes were weary and there was a resignation to him that saddened Elizabeth even more than the empty house.

"I had hoped our young ladies might be here," she whispered.

"It is as well they are not, my dear," the captain replied. "I intend to be rid of this ridiculous stick before I see them."

"My dear, dear Captain Tenterchilt," Elizabeth said softly, turning to face him. "They would have cared far less than you or I whether you had returned with a stick or with no legs at all, for all they will care for is that their father is returned."

A dark cloud had fallen over Captain Tenterchilt, however, and as the days passed he was increasingly to be found in the spacious Drawing Room with an array of glasses and different bottles as he sought an escape from the pain, both in his wounded leg and in his sorrowful mind. When, three days after their return, he finally consented to accept his wife's request that he should find a physician, he left in the morning and did not return until the sun had sunk from the sky, so that poor Elizabeth was beside herself with worry. She could find no solace in her house and her headaches returned once more to plague her.

"Where have you been?" she exclaimed as Captain Tenterchilt stepped through the Drawing Room door. "I was so afraid that the physician had failed or-"

"There was nothing to fail in," he interrupted. "That young surgeon did a fine job. Or so I am told."

"Then why do you still have your crutch?"

"Because he was right about that, too," Captain Tenterchilt replied, throwing the object down on the floor in anger. But, whether as a result of the wound or lack of use, his right leg buckled beneath him and he collapsed to the floor. Elizabeth stepped over quickly and helped him into a chair while he clutched his right hand to the wound and Elizabeth poured out a glass of claret that she placed into his left.

"Where have you been all day?" she whispered, kneeling by his side and holding his right hand. "You cannot have been there all day."

"No," he whispered, leaning across and kissing her cheek. "I visited Horse Guards and resigned my position. He was right about that too. I am not even forty and I am retired. I have failed you, my dear. No, do not argue," he continued as she opened her mouth to speak. "What are we to do now?"

"I shall write to my father. He will find you a position."

"Your father could not find a suitable placing for me, my dear, even if he respected me enough to try."

"Will you permit me now to request our daughters return?" Elizabeth asked softly. "I want them home."

Captain Tenterchilt nodded after a moment. He was beyond caring who should now see him, for his position could no longer be something to take a pride in. He wished so desperately that the attack on Valenciennes had ended a different way. If he had not joined Captain Pottinger's men then he would not have been under fire. If the young surgeon had not attempted to save his leg, then he should not have to endure the constant pain he was suffering now. And, though the pain was acute, it was his pride that suffered the most. To be viewed as a victim and with pitying eyes as he had travelled through London was almost too much for him to bear.

"Thank you, my dear," Elizabeth said, a smile covering her face, which caused the corners of his own mouth to rise. "They shall lift your spirits, I know it."

"I am certain they shall."

The pair remained for a time before Elizabeth announced her intention to withdraw to bed. The captain watched as his wife left, returning his crutch to him before she went. With a great despondency he studied it, trying to imagine what he had thought his return to London might have felt like, and lamenting his premature retirement. He had not found entry to the army easy. To the contrary, he had worked tirelessly to save enough money to buy a commission, living without so that he could afford it. At sixteen he had enlisted as a Lieutenant and, at twenty-one, he had obtained his promotion to captaincy. Apart from the moment that he fell in love, his thoughts had been of the army since then. And he loved Elizabeth so greatly that he prayed it would be enough to see him through this time.

He clutched at his leg as he tried to rise, but found the pain too great and, collapsing once more into the chair, he watched numbly as the glass dropped to the floor and split in two, the remnants of the claret seeping into the carpet. He peered over at it, watching with a curious fascination at how the liquid bled into the fabric, and with this macabre thought he found sleep claiming him, unable to climb the stairs that would take him to his wife and bed.

Despite the return of his three daughters at the onset of September, a dark cloud hung over Chanter's House. Shortly before the arrival of Rupert and Camilla Jenkyns, the unhappy news that Elizabeth's father had died reached the Tenterchilts, and Elizabeth was beside herself with grief. Her brother was travelling from the

West Indies to visit her and his newly-acquired lands, but it was December when he arrived and, during that time, Elizabeth witnessed the depths to which her family could sink. Following her decision to dress in black, Arabella followed suit and Elizabeth felt the guilt of Arabella's unhappiness weigh heavily on her shoulders. The young girl had not been so unhappy in the knowledge of her grandfather's death until she had witnessed the heartbreak it wrought upon her mother. Imogen, who had anticipated for so long her opportunity to partake in the family as an equal member, would often take herself away to the library where she would trace the heavy type of the voluminous books until her eyes ached. Only Catherine appeared unaffected by the circumstances, although she was greatly disappointed to learn that she could no longer sit upon her father's knee. She would, instead, sit by his feet stroking Gulliver and demanding to hear how bravely her father had defended Britain.

But as winter moved closer, the former captain was so rarely to be seen. Increasingly he remained away from the house until midnight, and Elizabeth was left to console her daughters in his absence once more. She was anxious for Imogen more than ever, for the young child seemed to observe all the disagreements and all the tension that rested over the house but communicated nothing to anyone. On one evening late in November, when the house was asleep with all the children now in their own rooms, Imogen stepped out at the sound of her father's voice. She shuffled along the gallery to look down on the open hall below as her mother walked through and stood before him. Mr Tenterchilt leaned heavily on the cane that he had begun using instead of the crutch and fluttered a handful of papers at his wife.

"More of your friends promoted?" Elizabeth demanded.

"No," came the giddy reply. "Something has finally come from my pension, my dear."

"Your pension or my inheritance? How can you continue to gamble your days away when you should be here? Can you not find a more reliable income? There are jobs that do not require mobility."

"Do not tell me what I can spend my money on," Mr Tenterchilt snapped, throwing the papers at his wife's feet.

"But it is not just your money. If you have so little regard for me and my money, then in the least consider your daughters. Each one of them will be in need of an education and a dowry when they are old enough."

"Did I not just tell you that I have won? And not just money. Estate, my love. A house in Scotland."

"I am pleased for you, Josiah, for you believe this is the most you have achieved in your life." Elizabeth turned from her husband and began ascending the stairs but stopped as her angry gaze rested on Imogen whose wide eyes watched the scene before her.

"I could not sleep, Mama," the child began. "I heard Papa come home and I was worried he was hurt once more."

"My dear Imogen, your father made scarcely a sound when he was wounded and always makes much more noise when he is drunk." Reaching the top of the stairs she placed her hand on the young girl's shoulder and guided her back to her room. Imogen glanced down at the lonely figure of her father before bidding her mother goodnight once more.

This conversation was never mentioned again and indeed the image began to fade from Imogen's mind in the excitement of the oncoming festive season. The arrival of their uncle made Christmas come even sooner and the girls were excited beyond measure to meet their cousin, Julian, who was a little older than Arabella. Upon the executors of their grandfather's will being gathered together, the family lawyer was called upon and wheels were set in motion that would allow probate to be granted. Business being completed in the spacious hall of Chanter's House left few surprises in the will, with Elizabeth's brother inheriting almost everything, though some property in Yorkshire was left to Rupert Jenkyns and Elizabeth was bequeathed a sum of one thousand pounds.

Mr Tenterchilt did not attend either this informal meeting in his own house, nor the granting of probate in the court. Instead, he continued to journey into the city most days, carding and gambling with anyone he could find of equal status, for he had not yet lost all his pride. News of how he had acquired the Scottish lodge from a gentleman by the name of Mr Kildare had left few men willing to sit at the table with him, however, each anxious that his string of good luck might rob them of their own property.

"I begrudge you nothing," Mr Kildare laughed as he sat opposite Mr Tenterchilt. "Any man's luck may change, and that house has been unvisited these past ten years."

"All the same," Mr Tenterchilt continued. "I lament that you and I seem unable to find gentlemen to sit with."

"It is the festive season only, sir," Kildare laughed, looking down at the cards which sat in his hand before throwing coins into the centre of the table. "When gentlemen's wives request their constant attention."

This statement, meant as little more than a passing remark, gave Mr Tenterchilt cause to reflect on his situation. Mr Kildare was a bachelor and as such made scorn at such an idea, but as Mr Tenterchilt walked out, no richer and yet no poorer on the evening's conquests, his thoughts were all for his wife. It was true that, since returning to England, he had scarcely considered her. It was true, too, that she had suffered terrible loss in the death of the father she had adored. It had been a shock to all of the Jenkyns family when she had consented to marry Mr Tenterchilt, for she had ignored her father's wishes, though not disobeyed his command. Josiah Tenterchilt did not belong to the class of Elizabeth Jenkyns, being the son of a farmer certainly did not rank level to being the daughter of a parliamentarian.

He leaned heavily on the cane while he clutched his right thigh. The damp night air caused his leg to seize and he grimaced against the numbing chill that gripped it, before he coaxed himself to continue through the streets. Of course he had known when he enlisted in the army that he might pay his service in blood, even with his life, but having escaped it for almost two decades he had begun to believe that he would escape injury for his whole career. He had wished to maintain his position in the army until old age retired him. To gain promotion after promotion and become the husband that Elizabeth deserved. To add to this shame, he had heard recently from his friend, Elias Pottinger, who continued to defend his country's interests, telling him that he had received a promotion to the rank of major. As Mr Tenterchilt stopped at the high iron railings of his beautiful home, he sighed heavily. This wound, that had rendered him useless to the army and worthless in society, had been inflicted solely because he had gone to Pottinger's aid.

For countless minutes he stood outside the house, simply staring at it. When, some minutes later, he witnessed a gentleman leaving by coach he felt curiosity overcome his self-pity and he walked awkwardly into the house.

"My dear," Elizabeth began at once. "I am so pleased that you have returned at this opportune moment, for Uncle Rupert is trying to convince me that dear Papa's estate is close to the coast. Yet I know it to be close to Malton," she continued, as she guided him into a room where Rupert, Camilla and Elizabeth's brother, Thomas, sat. "I do not believe Malton is by the coast, yet I do recall Papa taking us to Scarborough on occasions."

"Malton is not by the coast, my dear," he replied at once, looking across at the other occupants of the room to ensure that they all heeded his words. "It lies perhaps halfway between Scarborough and York."

"That is a shame," Camilla remarked casually, not seeming to care that her brother-in-law had died to sacrifice this estate. "I would so love to be by the sea."

"She is a cruel neighbour, Aunt," Thomas remarked. "In Antigua we overlook the waters and she so often takes as much as she gives. More so sometimes."

Elizabeth poured a glass of sherry for her husband as he assumed his seat by the fire before she came to sit beside him. Taking his hand in her own, she smiled across at him with a pride he felt was ill aimed.

"It must seem strange to you to be home once more, Josiah," Thomas continued. "Have you found a new occupation to fill your time?"

"Indeed," he replied. "I have acquired a taste for cards while I continue to seek the profession of a crippled gentleman."

"You must sell this terrible, cold house, and you and Elizabeth must travel out to Antigua. A gentleman who runs a sugarcane plantation has no need of his legs, for indeed we are well cared for every hour of every day. The cane pays for our lives and the slaves work for the cane."

"There are some in England who deem such a thing questionable in the least," Mr Tenterchilt replied.

"And do you?"

"I am no abolitionist, sir, but I must admit to the presence of a black slave in this house unsettling me."

"Ah, but Justice is a servant and not a slave. You need not fear the scandal of him making a bid for freedom from your property. He is paid handsomely, for his wife and children live indoors."

"Does he receive a wage?" Elizabeth asked.

"Lord no, sister. If he had money to spend in the market I suspect he should not survive the journey back to the estate for the savages would beat him to death as a traitor."

"How terrible that they cannot celebrate the rising of one of their own."

"Antigua would not suit us, you see," Mr Tenterchilt remarked, kissing his wife's hand.

"I rather like Justice," Rupert remarked. "He is a well-educated man for a negro."

"I believe they have the same capacity to learn as their pale cousins," Thomas conceded. "Though they choose instead to work."

"I do not believe they choose it," Mr Tenterchilt muttered. In truth he found the abolitionist movement aggressive in their outlooks, which they claimed were for the good of humanity but which threatened to rip apart decent society far more than the bloody events of the French Revolution. Yet, in part, he sympathised with them. While men could never be equal to one another, there were such horrendous stories coming from the West Indies that, in spite of all the war and death he had witnessed, he could barely consider that there might be truth to these reports.

Elizabeth's family spent the festive season in Chanter's House with the Tenterchilts. The long table finally had the chance to accommodate a number closer to the one it had been designed for. Rupert's son Timothy, Julian, Arabella and Imogen all sat clustered together discussing the planned entertainments while Catherine sat beside her father and opposite her mother, quite happily ignoring everyone else in the room, except for Gulliver, who sat at her feet and gratefully received any scraps that fell.

It was a very different Christmas to the one they had shared at the end of the year before when the future had been viewed with fear and uncertainty. Indeed, as Elizabeth looked around her family who sat together at her table she felt that whatever the next year promised it could surely not be as dark as the year they had all endured. Mr Tenterchilt regarded the scene with a very different sentiment. He knew that he would struggle in the next year to find a position that could support his beloved wife and his dear daughters in the life to which they had become accustomed. And this burden rested heavily on his shoulders as he regarded the people sitting at the table, feeling judged by some and duty-bound to the others.

## Chapter Six

*Who We Truly Are*

In contrast to the festivities and worries of the family at Chanter's House, Christmas on the continent was a desperately lonely affair. Despite the lack of appeal that Wanderford Hall held for Fotherby, when Christmas arrived in Flanders, unannounced and unmarked, he felt a pang for the simple celebrations of home. Although Wanderford Hall was never decked for Christmas, the strictly adhered to fast of Advent made the feast of Christmas only more exciting. Fotherby's father had heard the preacher John Wesley on many occasions throughout his youth and it was to this man's words that Fotherby owed his own religiously regimented upbringing. His uncle, of course, would heed none of this puritanical approach and, when he had arrived at Wanderford Hall when Fotherby had been ten years old, he introduced his nephew to the concept of a church beyond what his father had taught him. But the young Fotherby found that the method and rule of Wesley's teaching suited him rather well.

While he wrapped a thick woollen blanket about his shoulders and gazed out over the dusting of snow, he considered how desolate this place was but how true to the Christmas story it felt. Lieutenant Kitson had been granted leave to return home to England over the festive period, for there had been a lull in the war over the past two months. Though he felt great shame to admit it, even to himself, Fotherby was jealous that his comrade had secured passage home for the festive season when he had not.

"Merry Christmas, sir," Fotherby whispered begrudgingly, shivering as he shuffled further into the tent.

"Merry, Fotherby?" Peters replied as he turned on his chair. "I did not know you approved of merriment. Is it not a sin according to your teaching?"

Fotherby ignored the man's remarks and sat down on one of the three-legged stools, leaning forward and pulling the blanket over his head. Peters' constant comments about his religious views did not generally bother him but, as he struggled to keep the winter at bay whilst the miserable seconds of Christmas Day passed him by, he felt his usually limitless patience approaching the end of its tether. In his innocence, he had never considered what a desperate time Christmas was without the comforts of a warm fire and strong walls to shut out the bitter cold. The only other Christmas he had spent away from Wanderford Hall had been two years ago when he had been in the scorching heat of the Indian subcontinent.

A boy stepped into the tent and Fotherby looked up long enough to recognise him as a messenger, before resting his head back down on the table. It would most certainly not be a message for him and, indeed, the boy stepped over to Peters. Peters took the letter from his outstretched hand and, in a most uncustomary manner, he smiled across at the boy and handed him a shilling.

"Thank you, sir," the boy replied, shock evident in his voice.

"Careful whose shilling you accept, boy," Peters said, and laughed as the youngster stared down doubtfully at the coin. "They will have you fight and die to accept your next one."

"King's shilling is spent so quickly in the ranks, but I shall see that this one is saved. Merry Christmas, sir."

"Merry Christmas."

He smiled as the boy rushed from the tent, looking down at the gift he had just been given as though it were a guinea rather than a shilling. Peters looked down at the letter in his hand and sighed heavily before he glanced across at Fotherby whose placid eyes were studying him. The smile slid from his face as he saw the younger man watching him.

"You have not received a letter in some time, Fotherby," Peters remarked, the usual cutting tone returning once more to his voice. "Have you no one back home who would send you any form of Christmas correspondence?"

"Indeed I have," Fotherby replied, never taking his eyes from the man but still clutching the blanket about his head. "But as the only living relatives I have are men I would not expect to hear anything from them. Had I a sister or mother, I should be disappointed to receive nothing, but gentlemen make poor correspondents."

"Have you a brother?"

"No," Fotherby whispered, feeling suddenly uncomfortable in this discussion about his family. "I have my father and my uncle, only."

"Then you inherit."

Fotherby knew by his captain's tone that this had not been a question, but he nodded. "Yes, sir. But I am ill-suited to being a landowner. I wanted," he paused and shook his head quickly.

Peters rose from his chair and walked to the tent flap where he stood staring out over the sunset, apparently ignoring the comment that his apprentice had left unfinished. Tipping his head back, he drank heavily from the flask, while he still held the letter in the other hand. A solitary streak of purplish blue marked where the sun had rested only minutes earlier and, in the eastern sky, the darkness of night was creeping in. Somewhere further in the camp, men were singing carols, laughing and shouting out to one another. Fotherby sat up straight and observed this behaviour with curiosity, for Peters had never shown such a pensive side before. The captain eventually turned back and carried his chair to sit before Fotherby.

"What did you want?" Peters asked bluntly.

"Sorry, sir?"

"You said "I wanted", but you did not say what you wanted."

"You would view me as very ungrateful, sir." Fotherby glanced at the captain's face which stared back expectantly at him. "I wanted something more, sir. I wanted to do something with my life that would mean more to people than how many acres I ruled or how many men worked for me." Fotherby lowered his head and muttered, "Why did you become a surgeon, sir?"

"I had two brothers. One inherited and one became an officer in the army. I should have become a clergyman, but I am certain it will come as no surprise to you that I found I was ill-suited to such a vocation. I had no such noble intentions as you have."

"They are not noble, sir. I am rather afraid they were at best naive. I do not seem to be achieving anything here."

"It can feel that way, my boy," Peters began as he rose to his feet. "But to those men whose lives we preserve, and to their wives, mothers, fathers and children, we are saviours. Merry Christmas, Fotherby," he added as he handed Fotherby the letter before carrying his chair back to the desk where he sat down and picked up the cards once more.

Fotherby looked down at the letter that had only "Captain Jonathan Peters" by way of an address, but Fotherby felt his breath catch as he turned the envelope and saw the seal of the Royal College of Surgeons imprinted in the wax. Glancing across at Peters, who was still tossing the cards into piles on the desk, Fotherby opened the seal and read on in interest, muttering the words under his breath.

"Further to your request, a place shall be made available upon Henry Fotherby Esquire's arrival in London that he might perform the examination for the army surgeons' diploma. The account being settled and the five guineas received, Mr Fotherby shall not be required to provide any form of proof, or payment."

Following this, the letter was signed off by the head of the college. Fotherby read through the brief epistle so many times that he could have recited it, before he rose to his feet and stepped over to his captain.

"Are they to accept you?" Peters' began gruffly, not turning to face him.

"I believe so, sir."

"Then when Kitson returns in the new year, you shall be free to journey back to England."

"Thank you, sir," Fotherby whispered, with so much heartfelt sincerity that Peters turned to face him. "And thank you for settling the account. I can pay you back."

"I did not do it that you might pay for it yourself, boy." Peters' tone was irritated. "You may never have received a gift before, but this is what it feels like, Fotherby."

"But why?"

"Back in Valenciennes I saw my successor, when you commanded Kitson and myself with what to do, to save a man who in the least should have lost his leg and would almost certainly have bled out on the table. And, Fotherby, you viewed him as a person. You saved him for all the right reasons."

"This is the greatest gift I have received, sir. I only hope that I shall not let you down or betray your faith in me."

"You will not," Peters replied, turning from the young man once more and dismissively waving his hand to signal that the conversation had ended.

The revelation that he should soon be able to fulfil his calling gave Fotherby cause for great comfort and, as the new year approached, he forgot completely about how dreary Christmas had seemed. He walked through the camp and completed the duties he had with a light step and bright eyes. When Lieutenant Kitson returned to the camp in the first week of February, Fotherby could scarcely contain his excitement but gathered up his few possessions and addressed his captain with thanks once more.

"Winter makes a poor season for soldiers," Peters commented. "I expect you shall return to find us still camped here with little or no battle missed."

"I shall go at once to the College," Fotherby promised. "And I shall return as soon as the exam has been taken."

"No, Fotherby," Peters replied firmly, while Kitson stood a short distance away observing the pair without wishing to be caught listening. "You must pay a visit to your father and uncle. It has been over a year since you saw them and, though not a man amongst the three of you would or indeed should admit it, I am certain you have been missed. But, my boy, if you are not back by the first day of May I shall expect you to return me those five guineas."

"Thank you, sir," Fotherby laughed. "I shall be sure to return in the spring."

Without another word Fotherby left and walked with great purpose through the makeshift tents and on towards the town. They were camped close to Ostend and it was from here that Fotherby was hoping to secure his passage back to England. The high roofs of the buildings were coming into view when Fotherby turned at the sound of his name.

"Mr Fotherby? It can only be you, for there cannot be another man in King George's army who has such height."

Fotherby turned to find himself facing Lieutenant Portland, who was sitting on the back of a tall horse. The man swung down from the saddle and pulled the horse as he ran the few paces over to the young surgeon.

"Where are you going to, my friend?"

"Ostend," Fotherby replied, his eyes narrowing as he looked across at Portland. "Then I am going home for a time."

"Whatever for?"

"To take my exam, sir."

"Then they are to let you be a surgeon after all," Portland laughed, and Fotherby felt the corners of his mouth turn up in a smile at the sound. By contrast, Portland's face became serious and he placed his free hand on Fotherby's shoulder. "Have I given you offence, sir?"

"Offence?" Fotherby whispered and shook his head. "But I thought I had come to know you."

"I hope you view me as a friend, Fotherby, for I can think of nothing that I have done to merit such indifference."

"Is your name Portland or is it Barrington?" Fotherby asked bluntly. "I have to confess to being pleased that I could remember one name, but I have heard you being addressed by another. Who are you truthfully, sir?"

Portland sighed heavily and turned back to his horse, running his hand down its long nose. "Alas, I am both men now."

Scarcely hearing the words that the other man spoke, Fotherby felt guilt at once for raising such a question. He noticed for the first time how stern in sorrow the other man looked, as though he had been laden with a great burden. Without wanting to hear the answer to his own question, Fotherby asked, "What do you mean?"

"I am Portland, as I have been since I was born. But last June saw the death of my father and, in his will, he handed me the name Barrington and the title lord."

"I am sorry," Fotherby whispered and reached forward to place his hand on the other man's back. "I should not have been so cruel in my thoughtless words, sir. I am sorry to hear of your father's death."

"As was I," Portland replied. "But I hope this has resolved any misunderstanding between us, for you are a good man, Fotherby, and I should not like to lose your regard."

"I am an impertinent dolt, sir, but thank you for your kind words."

Portland turned to him and smiled before he remarked, "And yet they want you for a surgeon. Come, let me walk with you into Ostend, for I have new recruits to gather there." Fotherby nodded quickly and the pair walked on towards the town, Portland still leading his horse. They talked contentedly, each happy to have company as they walked on.

"Captain Peters told me you were married," Fotherby said at last, as they approached the docks.

"Indeed?" Portland questioned, a wry smile on his features. "Then I would wager there have been other words spoken of me, and of my dear wife too, no doubt."

"He praised you on not allowing her to travel with us. We were talking of poor Mrs Tenterchilt at the time, I believe. How long ago it seems now."

"My dear Rosanna would not last long here. She did not consent to marry me because I was in the army. In fact, I enlisted after I married her."

"Did she not object to you enlisting and leaving her?"

"If she had done, Fotherby, I should not have done it. She commands me first and foremost, and the king commands second to her. You do not seem as surprised as I would have expected."

"Peters told me you did not have the respect for the laws that the army upholds," Fotherby replied, shrugging his shoulders. "But all I have seen suggested that he was incorrect, until now."

"You must meet her one day, Fotherby. Then you will understand. It is her eyes that command, for they are as hypnotic as the brightest stars in the darkest night. She could tell me anything and I would do it, I know."

"Then I am not sure I wish to meet her," Fotherby laughed.

"But come," Portland said, stirring himself awake from the dreamy state which thoughts of his wife placed on him. "Before we part, tell me what became of poor Captain Tenterchilt, for he came to the aid of our company."

"He heeded my advice and returned home. I do not know beyond that. What became of that sorry man in your company? The one who nearly severed your artery?"

"This story grows further and further from the truth each time you talk of it," Portland laughed. "I saw the wisdom of your advice and I sent him back to England."

"I hope he was not disgraced," Fotherby muttered as he looked up at the tall timber structures of the transport ships. "No man can help his fears."

"He was not disgraced, and he was a strong fit man. I am sure he will have found a position." Portland swung up into the saddle of his horse and smiled down at his friend, who was still only a little lower than him. "Here we part, Fotherby. Good luck in your exam, and Godspeed in your journey."

"Thank you," Fotherby whispered, before he frowned and muttered. "I thought the newly-promoted Major Pottinger had gone to the West Indies."

"And so he has," Portland replied with a smile. "But I am no longer in his company, for I am the newly-promoted Captain Portland and have been given charge of Captain Tenterchilt's former company. Besides, I was deemed unfit to journey to the Indies."

"Unfit? How so? What affliction have you that caused this redistribution?"

"An affliction of the heart," Portland replied, placing his hand over his chest. Without meaning any offence, but without checking his actions, Fotherby laughed at the man before him. Portland did not seem to object to this behaviour but smiled down. "Wait until you are married, Fotherby. Then you will understand."

"I? No one would marry an army surgeon. Captain Peters is proof of that."

"Yet Lieutenant Kitson proves your theory wrong. I will wager you ten pounds that, by the time I see you next, you will have changed your mind. Good luck, sir."

Fotherby watched as his friend turned his horse and drove it forward from the docks. This parting, though abrupt and unceremonious, was harder to bear than his parting from the camp, for he felt that he had offended the other man. He tried once more to understand Captain Peters' harsh criticism of Portland, in light of the Lord Barrington's patience and acceptance of Fotherby's impertinence. Perhaps it was that Portland venerated his wife before the king? Or that he deemed himself above certain directions and orders? But still Fotherby could not believe Peters' comments were justified.

These concerns, however, faded as he boarded the ship that was to take him once more to England and, as the white chalk cliffs of Dover came closer, he felt a giddiness seize him. He remained in Dover for the night before taking a coach to London the following day. London was enjoying the celebrations of victory that were being sold but, to Fotherby, who had seen firsthand the failures of the British army, it all seemed false and sickening. All the same, as he found himself standing before the doors of the Royal College of Surgeons, he felt a well of self-confidence paint a foolish smile on his face but, as he opened the doors and stepped into the hall nervousness overtook him. He walked over to a small room whose door was propped open and knocked lightly.

"Enter!"

Fotherby stepped in and looked at the man who had permitted him entry. He had his back turned and was rummaging through pages in a large set of drawers. He was small and it seemed to Fotherby that he ran a great risk of falling into one of the voluminous drawers himself. This thought caused him to smile slightly and his anxiety subsided a little although, as the small man turned and frowned across at him, he quickly became serious once more.

"What have you seen that has given you such great amusement, sir?"

"I beg pardon, sir. I am unsure where I should proceed, but I have come about taking an exam."

"I am afraid you are two days too late," the man replied, with an air of indifference. "Next exam is on 20th February then again on 6th March. First and third Thursdays each month. If you have a genuine interest in joining the Surgeons' Hall you should have known that."

"I have been in Flanders, sir," Fotherby announced, feeling stung by the man's implication that he was unfit to qualify for failing to know when the exam would be. "Am I to register now?"

"The day before," the small man said briefly. "At least then the surgeons know how many candidates might attend. You might leave your name and never reappear here."

"For five guineas, sir, I would be wherever I claimed to be." Fotherby took his leave of the gentleman and walked out of the office and, indeed, the college.

He had been here before, of course, when in haste he had rushed through his previous exam. He did not recall the nerves that he was experiencing now, and nor did he recall the disappointment at the rudeness of the members of the college. He felt as though he had no place there and, for the first time in many years, he questioned his calling to such a profession. Peters, who was gruff to the point of rudeness, had never succeeded in causing such doubt in him. He walked on through the city, lost in his own dismal thoughts and, in mirror of this, the clouds above opened and spilt down rain.

He remained in London for the night, having to board in a tavern for, despite his time with the army in both India and Flanders, he had no rank amongst them and so could not stay in the army barracks around the city. The draughty room still seemed like luxury after his year in a tent but, all the same, he was pleased beyond measure to be able to climb onto the mail coach the next morning and begin his journey home to Wanderford Hall. He watched as towns passed by until the coach reached its destination of Peterborough, and Fotherby alighted before awaiting a second coach that would take him northwest and into Derbyshire. Occasionally, as he sat waiting, he considered the anticipation that had been cruelly pushed from him by the attitude of the man at the college, but when he found himself considering this he firmly rebuked himself. Self-pity was not a virtue, but a vice of too much self-importance and time.

Night had fallen as he journeyed on toward Manchester, alighting in the dark at a crossroads a short distance from Buxton. The mist that so often clung to the Pennines had blanketed the hilltop so that, despite the darkness, the grey shroud seemed to give out a peculiar pale glow. He did not mind the fog, indeed he had grown up with it, and it was as much a part of his home as the ordered gardens or the cold damp rooms. For a time, he stood, trying to choose which of the five roads he should take, for he had lost all sense of direction. He peered up at the signpost and smiled to himself as he recognised the wooden arrow that pointed home. Without any further delay, Fotherby walked purposefully down one of the roads. It was not a long walk, perhaps three miles from the hilltop crossroads to the drive that led up to Wanderford Hall, but when he arrived it was to find the house enveloped in darkness. One light, muffled behind a thick curtain, shone from the window of his uncle's room, but otherwise the house was as dark as the rest of the surroundings. As he had walked downhill from the crossroads, the mist had abated, and here only occasional tendrils reached their fingers down to the earth.

Fotherby wrapped his long coat about him and stepped up to the door, but as he was about to knock he drew back his hand. He had no wish to awaken the inhabitants and, having been away for fourteen months, one more night could make little difference. All the same, it was a ten-minute walk to the village, even longer in the dark, so he walked around the side of the house to the modest stables at the back. There was a complete darkness here, and he ran his hand along the curved doors of the stalls trying to steady his steps. He walked on until he reached the Tack Room at the end of the corridor, and here he snatched one of the horse blankets and wrapped it around him as he sat down against the wall. It was warm, perhaps warmer than inside the Hall for the beasts gave out such heat with their long slumbering breaths.

There was little wonder, then, that Fotherby fell asleep almost at once. His dreams took him half a world away, recalling with enchanting accuracy the beauties of the orient, and he became so absorbed in the sights and smells of the dream that it was a great shock when he felt someone strike his leg and at once was returned to the cold, misty landscape of the English shire.

"What are you doing here?" demanded an angry voice. "I shall have you arrested for trespassing."

Fotherby pulled the blanket from him and stifled a yawn as he narrowed his eyes to try and see who had awoken him. His gaze took in a man of perhaps fifty years, as portly as a gentleman might be before being described as fat. He had a round head, the top of which was completely bald and reflected the grey half-light of the Derbyshire morning. The only hair he did have appeared as two tufts about his ears, which only seemed to make his head rounder.

"Good God, Henry," the man exclaimed as he recognised the figure before him. "Why are you sleeping out here?"

"Good day, Uncle," Fotherby began.

"Why are you here? Why are you hiding? Have you deserted?"

"I cannot desert, Uncle," he replied, rising to his feet. "I have no rank to desert from. I arrived so late last night that I did not wish to awaken the entire house. I was not hiding."

"Then you are here on leave?"

"Indeed. I have been given permission to be here, you need have no concerns on that."

"Then come, Henry. Let us go and find your father and share this great news." He began walking from the stable and, snatching his small case of belongings, Fotherby followed him. "You must stop growing, young man," his uncle continued. "Did they put you on the rack in the army?"

"I have not grown. And I am not in the army yet, Uncle."

"I am certain you are far taller than me now than when you left. Perhaps I am shrinking."

"You may well be, Uncle. There is a school of thought that, at a certain age,-"

"Enough, Henry," the other man interrupted. "I do not need you to make me feel any older. Tobias!" the older man shouted as he pushed open the heavy door and stepped into the house.

Fotherby took a moment to soak in the nostalgia that finally caught him as he surveyed his home. Wanderford Hall was an ancient building of stone, lined internally with brightly polished wooden panels. The floor was made of thick wooden boards that had been reclaimed from the destruction of the Catholic church in the village some two hundred years earlier. The entrance hall was overlooked by an enormous painting of the Battle of Bosworth Field, in which his ancestor had fought. Its very presence stood contrary to his father's puritanical beliefs, but he had been unwilling to paint over it and lose a part of his heritage. The wooden staircase radiated with the shine of beeswax, and it was this smell that Fotherby inhaled as he closed his eyes, transported over the two decades of his life here.

"Toby!" his uncle shouted once more. "Come see what I found when I was preparing for my morning ride."

"Must you shout everything, Paul?"

Fotherby turned to a door that opened beneath the colossal painting at the sound of his father's long-suffering voice. He watched as a man, as slender in build as his uncle was portly, shuffled out from the doorway. He was dressed as Fotherby always remembered him, with a long black tailcoat over his unadorned white shirt and tight trousers. He moved awkwardly and Fotherby felt a concerned frown cross his face for a moment. But as his father's gaze rested on him, a smile spread across the old man's features and the years of age that had been placed on his shoulders faded away.

Fotherby stepped over to his father and looked down at him, bowing formally as he knew he should. But his father reached open his arms and wrapped them about his son, uncaring of the correct practice.

"Oh, my boy," he began, laughter in his voice, "I did not expect to see you. Why did you not tell me you were to return?"

"I did not know for certain when I would return. By the time I did, I was on my way home myself. There seemed little sense to write."

"Paul, you must delay your visit to the mills. Tonight we shall celebrate Henry's return."

"It is a good thing you did not return a month later, Henry," his uncle laughed. "The fatted calf could not be eaten during Lent, even for you."

"There is nothing prodigal about Henry," his father chided. "He is as selfless a man as you shall ever know. Not a trait he learnt from his uncle, I must say."

"Deride me as you wish, Tobias. It is my selfishness that pays for your living here. Of course I shall stay for Henry's feast. I shall travel north in the morning."

Fotherby watched as his uncle walked out before he turned back to his father, who just shook his head.

"As you see, Henry, your uncle's approach to life is unaltered in your absence."

"But you, Father," Fotherby began. "How are you? You seem weary."

"I am as well as I have been in many years. The better for having you home once more." He ushered his son into the library and, at once, the cloying smell of mould and damp struck Fotherby. "But how did you find the time to leave? I hear that the war consumes much of our army's time."

"I cannot tell you, Father, for I know you will disapprove."

"Henry," his father began in a warning tone, "what did you do to be sent home?"

"No," Fotherby replied gently, "it is not that. I know that you so wanted me to fund myself, and to build my own career, but I am back in England to take my exam and Captain Peters paid for it."

Fotherby felt a frown cross his features as his father began to laugh, before he sat down and pointed to another chair, indicating that his son should sit. "But why should this man do such a thing?"

"Because," Fotherby began, but felt certain that his father's question was meant to be rhetorical, "he felt I conducted myself well at Valenciennes."

"Oh my dear, dear boy. Do you not see, then, that you did pay for it? It is your reward for such diligence in your work. You earned it."

Fotherby spent the day refamiliarising himself once more with the rooms and scenes of Wanderford Hall. At the top of the wooden staircase a large window stared down over the back of the property, across the courtyard where the stables and the walled garden were, and over the parkland to where the hilly terrain set a stunning backdrop to the grounds. This was his most beloved view in all the world. It was true that the front of the house held a more gentle and beautiful view, over the knot gardens and past the opulent fountain in the centre of the drive, which his uncle had commissioned in memory of his sister-in-law. But Fotherby loved the industry of this back view, and the unkempt wildness of the landscape.

For a time, he stood there thinking over all that he had experienced since he had last been here fourteen months earlier. How many men he had seen die, how many he had tried to save and how many he had lost. And, once more, he questioned the course that he had laid down before himself. Was he always to be more haunted by his failures rather than able to celebrate his successes? His mind wandered to Cullington as he gazed out, the man he had neither failed nor helped, and he found a comfort in the stalemate of this case. He was pleased to have resolved his mistrust over Lord Barrington's identity, too, although he still felt remorse for the manner in which he had discovered the truth of the matter. His thoughts then moved to Peters and his objection and disapproval of Portland and, once more, he pondered his captain's dislike of the man.

Finally, he left the window and stepped along the creaking wooden floorboards until he came to his own room. Placing his hand against the door he pushed it open and took a moment to take in the view. It was exactly as he had left it two Christmases ago. From the pile of books beside the bed head, arranged in a spiral as he always did, to the tailcoat that hung from the front of the tallboy. The only difference was that the bed had been stripped, and clean and pressed bedding sat at the foot of the mattress.

When the tall clock at the end of the landing chimed eight o'clock, Fotherby walked down the stairs and into the Dining Room. To recover from his journey and the night he had spent in the stables, he had bathed and shaved before brushing and clubbing his hair, and had changed into knee britches, a plain cotton shirt and a black frock coat. In all, the gentleman who descended the stairs cut a very different figure to the weary soul who had ascended them some hours earlier.

He entered to find his father and uncle sitting at opposite ends of the table, staring across at one another as though they were enemies rather than brothers, and a place was set for him down the centre of one side. He sat down and took a moment to just take in the comfort of being home. His father watched him with heavily hooded eyes that showed great pride and love, whilst his uncle gave a slight laugh.

"What have you been doing all day, Henry? I had hoped you might take a ride through the grounds with me. Perhaps go into Buxton and visit The Sun Inn tomorrow? I can think of many people who would have been pleased to see you."

"I have been washing fourteen months of blood and war from me," Fotherby muttered. "And I am not marrying Widow Gardener, no matter how many times you try to make me."

"Poor girl," his uncle continued. "Only seventeen when her husband drowned, less than a year after her wedding. And she only has one sister left. She has taken a shine to you, Henry my boy. She would be very happy to see you, I know it."

"Not nearly as happy as you would be to have her father in the family," Fotherby replied. "I shall not marry into a family that makes money from something I decry."

"My dear boy," his father interjected, "do not allow your uncle to bully you."

"Tobias," his uncle replied before Fotherby had a chance to speak. "The boy spent all day grooming himself. He must have someone he has done that for."

"Cleanliness is next to godliness," Fotherby replied. "Is that not so, Father? I had no intention to appear at this table without being properly presentable. And the daughter of a brewery owner is not the person at whose feet I hope to lay my heart."

"Good lord, boy," his uncle laughed. "You are speaking like a woman. Take a good look at who you are talking to. Your father, whose health is failing, and I, who am so old I am shrinking, will not be here at Wanderford forever. You cannot afford to think of love like some young girl or common farmhand, Henry. You must think of alliances."

"Enough, Paul," Tobias demanded. "This is meant to be a celebration and you are turning it into a trial. Henry shall not marry anyone he deems morally unfit to join this household. And, for my part, I am proud of that decision."

"John Wesley should be proud of the early grave he has prepared for you," his brother retorted sharply.

Fotherby only sat staring at the plate before him and the food that rested upon it, for his appetite had gone.

Both his father and his uncle continued eating, but he could not reconcile with his uncle's words. Without raising his head, he glanced sideward at his father and considered what his uncle had said concerning his health. It was true that Fotherby had dealt with so much death during the past year, in some of the most horrendous ways, but the thought of his father's death was something he could scarcely bring himself to think upon.

The two brothers began talking once more as though nothing were amiss, and neither of them mentioned the conversation that had begun the meal. Fotherby reluctantly ate the food before him but tasted none of it as he listened to them. His uncle was outlining his plan to journey north to visit one of the mills that he owned, but hoped to return within the month. Paul Fotherby had made so much money in his career overseas that, when he had returned to the British shores he did not known where to put that money. Subsequently, after drinking the local alehouses dry, he had been advised to invest in the wool mills a little way to the north. This he had done and his investment had grown so much that he had secured the purchase of further mills across the county of Yorkshire. While he visited regularly, for he had no love of the house he had handed to his younger brother before Fotherby was born, he employed two foremen at each mill to oversee the running of them. When Fotherby had asked his uncle why he wanted two, he had replied,

"If they argue amongst themselves over power, they will not take it to their heads to argue with me."

Now, the older man looked across at Fotherby and smiled. "Why do you not join me, Henry? You have not been to the mills since you were a boy."

"You should find me dull company, Uncle. And I am certain that I should disappoint you while we were there."

Despite his uncle's lack of respect for the strict lives of the other two men, when he left the following morning, Fotherby felt that a part of Wanderford Hall had become lost too. He spent the next month with his father, reluctant to return to London as he continually questioned his vocation, unsure that Captain Peters had been right in the belief he had placed in him. It was approaching the end of March when his father, seated in a high-backed armchair and watching his son, who continued to read through the books and pamphlets of medical writings that he had collected over the years, opened a conversation on this matter.

"Why are you here, Henry?"

Fotherby looked up from the book he held and turned a confused expression toward his father. "What do you mean? I am here to take my exam."

"Then why are you still in Wanderford? Do not misunderstand me, my boy, I have loved having you home, but in your free time you sit reading medical journals and reviewing texts and diagrams by esteemed physicians. Why are you not taking the exam you were sent back for?"

"I am not sure I am fit to be a surgeon, sir," Fotherby muttered miserably, and he felt his failings only intensify as he had to repeat his words so that his father might hear them. "What if Uncle Paul is right? Perhaps I should be building an alliance and our family's future here."

"Your uncle is not a bad man, Henry. But the one word that so rarely describes him is 'right'. Do not let him dictate to you. I do not want to think that he will continue to dominate life here when I am gone. You have wished and studied all your life for this exam. You owe it to yourself, and all those people whose lives you will save, to see this through. Do you not wish to be a surgeon anymore?"

"No, I do," Fotherby replied with haste. "But I do not wish to leave you when you are ailing, and I do not wish to be a poor son to you. Nor can I reconcile with the self-importance of the attitude I encountered at the college."

"You would never be a poor son, Henry. You have not the cruelty in you to make you such. And though I may be ailing, I have no intention to depart this world so soon. I have many years of life left, and I wish to see you a surgeon before I even consider leaving. As far as the college is concerned you must consider this: Captain Peters, the surgeon who knows your strengths perhaps better than you do, has asked and paid for you to take this test. It is his opinion you should hold in high regard, no one else's."

Giving a faint smile, Fotherby nodded as he considered the wisdom of reason that his father had laid down before him. It made sense, of course, but the younger man scarcely knew what to do with such a heavily-weighted compliment. He rose to his feet and excused himself to retire for the night, but lay awake for many hours staring at the ceiling as he thought over his father's words. In the morning, he had found once more his resolve to continue with his vocation. After spending March in Wanderford Hall with his father and uncle, he announced his intention to return to London on the 31st March so that he may take his exam and journey once more to the continent and rejoin the army.

Making his farewells to his uncle and his father brought a sense of loss to Fotherby. His uncle had given him the address of the house he boarded in when he visited London and insisted that his nephew should stay there.

"I am proud of you, Henry," he confided in an uncustomary moment of affection whilst he accompanied Fotherby to the crossroads to meet the stagecoach. "You must be in no doubt of that. Had my life been different I should have wanted my son to have been just as you are."

These words provided the only comfort and companionship on his journey, but Fotherby found he needed nothing else. It took him two days to journey south to the capital and, the moment he arrived, he visited the college to register for the exam the following day. The man he spoke to was a different clerk and seemed to have little interest in Fotherby, until he discovered his name, at which point the clerk looked him up and down and nodded thoughtfully.

"Be here by ten o'clock in the morning."

There were no pleasantries nor other words spoken and Fotherby left feeling as confused, though not as disheartened, as he had the last time. Now, for the hour was late, Fotherby began seeking the house for which his uncle had given him the address. It took him into the night until, at last, he stood before a house on a quiet street and stared from the house to the paper and back again. When his uncle had spoken of boarding in a house, Fotherby had expected a tavern, or perhaps a hotel. Instead he stared in disbelief at the white stone double-fronted building with the flight of steps ascending. Uncertainly, he walked up and knocked on the door.

It was opened and a wash of light flooded out. A footman, clad in a smart red coat and a large lace collar, stood back to allow Fotherby in, before standing silently in front of him, waiting for the young man to state his business. He wore a grey wig upon his head, emphasising the colour of his skin, which was as black as any man Fotherby had ever seen.

"Pardon my late arrival," Fotherby began. "I was directed here by my uncle, Paul Fotherby."

"Wait here please, sir," the man replied in a heavy accent, before he walked from Fotherby and through a white painted door.

Inside the house everything was as white and shining as it had appeared on the outside. The room he had entered was large, with many doors opening from it, and a flight of marble stairs climbed directly in front of him. At the foot of the stairs on either side of the lowest step stood two marble figures, a man and a woman. They too were a pristine white.

"Sir Manfred will see you now," the footman announced, taking Fotherby's greatcoat and hat.

"*Sir*?" Fotherby whispered, feeling only more uncertain of the house he had entered. The servant was too well trained to venture a comment and instead bowed his head in affirmation before showing Fotherby into the room he had just entered a moment earlier.

This room was different again, lined with paintings and tapestries of foreign lands depicting wealthy white men and their hosts of black workers. A great fire was burning on the hearth and before it sat two people, a man and a woman. The man beckoned Fotherby to stand before him and reluctantly, feeling like a child who was about to be chided, Fotherby did as he was directed.

"I am truly sorry, sir. When my uncle told me he boarded at this address I had expected a hotel."

"Then you do not approve of my house?"

"No, sir, it is not that. Only I feel as though I have intruded into your home."

"Have no concern on that matter, Henry. Your uncle is welcome whenever he has need of the accommodation. I am happy to extend that welcome to you."

"Thank you, sir," Fotherby gasped. "But, forgive me, how do you know my name?"

"Your uncle talks of you often. I feel I know you well already. Now turn, my boy, and meet my daughter, Persephone."

Fotherby turned and bowed formally to the young woman who smiled up at him while she cooled herself with a fan made of feathers.

"Forgive my shabby attire, my lady. I did not anticipate such illustrious company."

"Dear Uncle Paul was quite right about your manners, Henry," she laughed. "And your height too. I do believe you might be as tall as Honest Jackson. Take a seat, please, so that your height is not so alarming." She pointed to an empty armchair beside her own. Fotherby sat down on the edge, reluctant to relax.

"Is my uncle really your uncle?" he asked, for he had never been sure of what his uncle had achieved when he was overseas.

"No," she laughed and Fotherby felt confused by how amusing she seemed to find this notion. "But Uncle Paul has spent so much time with us that I grew up believing he was my father's brother."

"But how did you come to know him?"

"Your uncle and I were in business together," Sir Manfred announced. "In the Caribbean. See here," he lifted a cane that rested by his side and pointed to one of the paintings. "That was our home in Saint Vincent."

"What business were you in, sir?"

"We were merchants. But Paul wished to return to England to help your father. There were so many other people in our profession by then that we agreed to carry our riches back once more to our homeland."

"I see by your household staff that money was not the only thing you returned with."

"Negroes work far more diligently than white men. I trust them much more with my house."

"Why? Surely there are both white men and black who are both good and bad."

"Ah, but I own them."

"In Saint Vincent, perhaps," Fotherby remarked. "In Britain the black man is as free as the white."

"But should they run, they would be found with great ease."

Fotherby considered this in silence and tried to imagine what it would be to live in a place that was so alien that you would always stand out there. Persephone smiled slightly as he pondered this.

"Uncle Paul tells us you are in the army, Henry Fotherby."

"He is perhaps premature with that statement. I am in London to take my exam and, should I pass, I have been assured my place in the ranks of the army. Lieutenant, in fact."

"Then I wish you the best of luck in your exam," Persephone's voice rang, "though from the things I have heard, there can be no doubt that you will pass."

Fotherby spent the evening feeling conspicuous in the praise that she and her father rained down on him, unsure why his uncle had paid him so many compliments and knowing that many of them were unfounded. But if he tried to refute them Sir Manfred simply announced that modesty was so self-deprecating that it was almost a sin. He learnt more of his uncle in those few hours than in over ten years of living with him, and he felt confused by how Persephone's and Sir Manfred's accounts of him altered so greatly from what Fotherby knew of his uncle.

He was shown to a room and he sat down on the bed wondering, for perhaps the first occasion in his life, the situation of the black men and women throughout the British colonies. He could not imagine the turmoil that these men faced, simply for appearing different. His father had brought him up to believe in an equality of men but had adhered to the belief that the social classes were imperative to maintaining that equality. But Fotherby, having witnessed the images in the room downstairs, began to feel uncomfortable in the white men's domination of them. What a world his uncle must have experienced. To have witnessed the horrendous trade in men, women and even children as though they were little more than cattle. There was little wonder his uncle had become such a cantankerous and opinionated man, for being a European in these places must have enabled him to always have his own way.

He pulled off the buckled shoes that he wore and removed his jacket, hanging it over the back of the chair at the desk in front of the window. His belongings were already in the room, all that he could fit into the shoulder bag that he had brought, and the leather satchel holding all the material he was least sure about for tomorrow's exam. But any hope he had of revising had gone for, as he pulled the black ribbon from his hair, he felt overwhelmingly tired. He lay back on the bed and felt his eyes fall closed.

He rose early the following morning, anxiously reviewing in his head all the questions that he might have in his exam as he returned the ribbon to his hair and placed the short wig over the top. Sir Manfred was a perfect host, ensuring everything was ready for Fotherby before he departed for the college and even offering him the use of his carriage, which Fotherby politely declined.

"Good luck today, Henry," Persephone began as she handed him the satchel which he had left on one of the chairs. "Uncle Paul is so very proud of you."

"Thank you," he whispered, feeling a little uncomfortable by how readily the woman before him used his name.

"I am so glad that you came to stay with us," she continued. "I have heard of little else in Uncle Paul's visits but your virtues."

He smiled across at her briefly before he walked out of the house and down the steps. Today was the day that he had both yearned for and feared over three months since Captain Peters had handed him the envelope. Continuing through the city streets, he stepped through the heavy doors of the college as the clock on the wall showed the hour as half past nine. He was not the first person to have arrived, indeed a further eight people stood in the hall and, although he politely greeted them, he did not share a conversation with any of them. As the clock struck ten a short man descended the stairs and addressed the gathered men, who numbered perhaps forty.

The order for the day was this: each candidate was to answer a series of questions presented by the clerk. These were designed to ensure that the candidate was ready to be put forward for the surgeons' questions.

Each man was called in the order he had arrived which placed Fotherby ninth. This part Fotherby found surprisingly easy, and he quietly praised himself in the knowledge that he could have answered these questions a decade ago. He was shown into another hall where all eight of the preceding candidates were seated. By this time, midday was already upon them, but it was not until the clerk had finished all his interviews that the next stage of the exam commenced. It was six o'clock when, at last, the first group of eight candidates were called to take their exams. Fotherby was famished. He had not considered the length of time that this exam might take. Indeed, he had compared it in his mind to the first test he had taken which had concluded in the morning. There was a decanter on a low table in the corner and Fotherby watched as the other gentlemen in the room continued to refill their glasses, becoming more and more vocal as they tried to hide their nerves. Despite failing to consider the possibility of having no food, he recalled that he had brought a flask and, while the other men became merry, he drank silently from it and watched over the room, waiting for his own name to be called.

The ante room was becoming louder and louder as the night wore on, and the noise combined with the hunger that had seized him made Fotherby feel unbearably tired. There must have been another door from the exam room, for no one reappeared after their exams and, as time stretched and Fotherby realised he had been at the college for a full twelve hours, he felt his eyes drift closed. He could not have been asleep for more than a minute when the door to the examination room opened and the final candidates were called in, leaving him alone in the room. Fotherby rose to his feet and walked into the centre of the room, looking at the chairs that lined the walls. All were empty now. He tried to understand why he had found himself alone when all the other candidates had entered the hall. Had he slept through his name being called? Had the volume in the room caused him not to hear his name? He walked back to the seat in the corner and pulled the wig from his head before he rubbed his hand over his eyes.

The room was in absolute silence now but for the slow, steady pendulum of the clock that continued to show his time passing, and he leaned forward studying the wig that he held in his hand and feeling more foolish than he ever had before. The clock showed almost ten when, at last, the door to the hall opened and the clerk walked in. Fotherby, without standing or even straightening in the chair, looked across at him and watched as the man's thin face became confused.

"Pardon, sir," Fotherby began. "But I am at a loss."

"So it would seem," the clerk replied in a neutral tone. "Were you not called?"

Fotherby returned the wig before shaking his head. "No," he whispered, reiterating his gesture.

"What is your name?"

"Fotherby, sir. Henry Fotherby."

"Wait here, Mr Fotherby," the clerk instructed before he returned to the hall and Fotherby was left alone again.

Anxious lest he should once more fall into the hands of sleep, he rose and began pacing the floor of the hall, counting the eight strides he took before turning, and the eight strides in his return. Whilst he paced he tried to clear his head of the disappointment he felt at how the day had run, and instead tried to focus on all the questions to which he had so long studied the answers.

"It takes me ten strides," a voice announced from the doorway to the hall. "But then you must be half again as tall as I. It is ten strides in width and twenty-two in length."

Fotherby, who at the man's voice had turned to face him, beheld someone much shorter than himself. He was portly, and the waistcoat that he wore scarcely held closed, with the buttons straining in their buttonholes. He wore a similar wig on his head to the one that Fotherby wore but the face beneath was round and the blue eyes that stared back at him as he took in all these features were filled with interest, as though Fotherby was a puzzle he wanted to solve.

"I had not tried the length, sir," Fotherby whispered.

"With a gait like yours I would wager it would take you less than twenty," the man laughed and he pointed to the chairs. "Have a seat, Mr Fotherby." Fotherby did as he said and watched as he came and sat beside him. "I was expecting you two months ago."

"I am sorry, sir, I think you must have mistaken me for someone else."

"I have heard words in your favour that I never thought to receive."

"But I do not know you, sir," Fotherby faltered.

"My name is Doctor Oliver Yardley." He looked across at Fotherby and smiled. "I graduated from Oxford at the same time as Doctor Jonathan Peters, your captain."

"Ah," Fotherby whispered.

"He sent a letter informing me that you were travelling to London. So I had expected you two months ago when the letter arrived."

"I have been in Derbyshire, sir. Visiting my father and revising for today."

"Then your resolve in medicine is as strong as it has ever been?"

"Yes, sir. I confess that I have questioned myself repeatedly on my suitability for this employment, but I know I can be of the greatest service in this way. And I want, more than anything, to assist people."

"Captain Peters is a man who is beyond sparing with his compliments. That he has poured so many on you speaks to me far clearer than any exam. He tells me that you are forward thinking in your approach and used Mr Harper's practises in the war. Why?"

"Valenciennes was a long time ago," Fotherby muttered.

"A surgeon has need of a strong memory, Mr Fotherby. And modesty is not a virtue we can afford."

"Captain Tenterchilt had been shot in the leg. To cut out the shot would have severed his femoral artery. By that time, even amputation would not have saved his life and he would have bled to death."

"But Mr Harper deduced this would work only for wounds that were comparatively shallow. This does not sound like one such wound."

"No, sir," Fotherby muttered, trying to recall the steady hand with which he had removed the shot. "It rested on the femur, and so the captain was forced to commence walking with a crutch for, having fractured the bone it had to be allowed time to reform."

"Do you know how many lives have been lost by young men trying to build upon Harper's finds? How many young surgeons have killed men to prove that they can implement his findings on such wounds?"

"With respect, sir," Fotherby replied calmly, "when the alternative is death it is a good time to put the case for living to the test."

"You did a fine job, Mr Fotherby. There is little I can test you on that Peters will not have told you already. I understand that your captain is a difficult man to work with and harder still to impress, but you have done both. He wants you as his lieutenant, Mr Fotherby, and I am inclined to grant him this request."

"Truthfully, sir?" came the whispered reply, and Fotherby realised he was holding his breath anticipating the words that the man was about to speak.

"From Peters' accounts and your calm and methodical reasoning, I have no doubt that you were born to be a surgeon, Lieutenant Fotherby. No other breed of man could withstand such time with our mutual friend."

"*Lieutenant* Fotherby?"

"Indeed," Yardley offered his hand to the young man who took it and they shook hands. "There is paperwork, of course, where shall I have it sent?"

"I am staying in Mayfair, sir. At the house of Sir Manfred Chester. But I am to return to the continent imminently."

"Mayfair?" Yardley laughed. "With knights for friends and a house in Mayfair it is a wonder you have any desire to become a battlefield surgeon. I shall have the paperwork delivered to Horse Guards in the morning."

His spirits were too high to suppress, and any tiredness he had experienced before this interview had faded away. As they both rose, Fotherby towering over Doctor Yardley, the younger man collected his satchel and thanked the surgeon once more before walking out into the city. For a time he was content to walk towards the west end of London and the wealth of Mayfair with no real concern for finding Sir Manfred's house but, as he passed closed shops that smelt already of the next day's produce, he recalled the hours that had separated him from the last meal he had eaten.

When he finally reached the house the hour was so late that almost the entire street was cloaked in darkness, but for the flickering glow of lamps through the glass of door panels in Sir Manfred's lobby. Fotherby walked up the steps and knocked on the door, so lightly that he doubted anyone would hear it, for he did not wish to awaken anyone in the house. He need not have concerned himself for his hand had barely left the heavy knocker than the door was opened by a footman. Fotherby pulled off his hat and shrugged out of his coat before handing them to the other man.

"Thank you, sir," Fotherby began as the servant took them. "I must beg your pardon once more for the late hour."

"You need beg nothing from me, sir," the footman replied, shock in his voice.

Fotherby felt an irrepressible smile cross his features. "No, indeed I do, for it has been you who has been forced to open the door so late for two nights now. I am inexcusable, and I apologise for it."

"I trust your outing was a success, sir?"

"Indeed. But I should have thought with far more planning, for I have not eaten since I left this morning."

"I shall have the kitchen staff prepare something at once, sir."

"Thank you," Fotherby replied and turned as Persephone appeared at the door to the room where he had first met her last night.

"Good lord, Henry," she began with a laugh, "you do not have to talk to them, you know. Come and tell Father and me how you fared today." She beckoned him into the room and showed him to the same chair he had occupied the previous night. "It was a success, was it not? I can tell by your eyes."

"Indeed," Fotherby whispered. The smile on his face had slipped somewhat as he considered the words that he had shared with the footman and how dismissive Persephone had been of him. "I have been accepted into Surgeons' Hall and intend to leave at once to rejoin the army in the low countries. But I cannot thank you enough, Sir Manfred, for allowing me to intrude so into your house."

"My dear boy," Sir Manfred replied, "your uncle and I were business partners and are great friends still. There is no imposition to be had from the nephew he loves so much."

Fotherby continued to talk with the Chesters until the footman entered and announced that there was food prepared for the young surgeon, and that it had been readied in the study, theorising that the Dining Room might be too great for one man to eat alone. Politely excusing himself from Sir Manfred's and Persephone's company, Fotherby followed the footman through to the study and, recalling Persephone's words and anxious in case he should cause trouble for the servant, he did not engage the man in conversation. He was waited on by another black man clad in the house livery of a double-breasted red coat, making him look like he was in the army. This man did not make any attempt at speaking until he offered Fotherby the wine.

"Thank you, but no."

"You do not want a drink, sir? Would you rather it was served to you by someone else?"

"No. To both your questions. It is not that. I do not partake of alcohol, that is all."

"Forgive me, sir," the servant replied. "Forgive my impertinence."

"There is nothing to forgive," Fotherby replied gently, trying to understand the peculiar sorrow that this man had awakened in him with his few words. "But if you could find me something else to drink I should be most grateful."

The servant bowed his head before disappearing to complete the task.

Fotherby lay awake that night, staring at the ceiling and considering all that had happened during the day. He still felt a pride that he was sure he should not have in himself regarding his exam, but it was dampened by the confusion he felt surrounding the Chesters' attitude to their servants. The most confusing thing for him, as he counted the knots in the wooden plank that supported the curtain of the four poster bed, was that both Sir Manfred and Persephone were such openhearted and generous people, that he could not understand why they would run a house full of servants for whom they could not even spare a word.

When he awoke the following morning it was to the sound of birdsong which seemed so alien in the city that he became confused by where he was. It took him some time to recall the events of the day before, but he felt a great smile cross his face as he remembered, with the same pride, how he had finally obtained the goal he had so long been striving for. He rose and washed before he walked down the stairs and into the Dining Room where Persephone and her father were already eating. Both welcomed him as he took a seat at the place which had been set for him and, as each began to congratulate him, he felt his cheeks burn under the weight of such praise.

"I feel I have used you so poorly," Fotherby apologised, as he finished eating and took a sip of tea from the fine china teacup. "I arrived unannounced and so late, and now I leave without spending the time you clearly deserve to get to know you."

"Dear Henry," Persephone's radiant voice chimed, "you shall always be welcome here, as is your uncle."

"Thank you, Miss Chester," Fotherby replied, feeling once more the social uncertainty about how casually she used his name.

He departed from the house in the midmorning, Persephone kissing his cheek before he went, but having to stand two steps above him to reach. She seemed to care little for the propriety that society demanded but stood at the door and watched as the young surgeon walked down the street. For his own part, Fotherby was quietly pleased to be leaving the house behind, as the inhabitants confused him so greatly. Recalling Doctor Yardley's words he walked towards the imposing building that was the centre of the British Army to collect and resolve any issues surrounding the paperwork from the exam.

He was vacating the magnificent building when he heard someone calling his name and turned to see a man who at once seemed familiar, but before he could recall where he knew him from the man limped over to him, assisted by a thin cane, and bowed his head slightly.

"Mr Fotherby, sir, I trust you are in good health."

"Indeed," Fotherby replied, trying to bring to mind whom this man was.

"But why are you here in England? Should you not be in Flanders?"

"I am to return at once," Fotherby assured him before he remembered the face that smiled across at him. "Captain Tenterchilt," he continued, feeling pleased with himself. "How is your leg?"

"The better for your care, sir. In existence because of you," he muttered before he added, "but I am no longer a captain."

Fotherby felt awkward as he recalled that he had been the one who had suggested Mr Tenterchilt resign his commission. "But then why are you here?"

"That, I have left to discover. I received a letter this morning requesting my attendance." He looked slightly concerned, Fotherby noticed, but abruptly laughed. "Come, you must visit our house while you are in London."

"Thank you, sir, but I intend to be aboard a boat to Flanders in the morning. Captain Peters will not tolerate my delay any longer, I believe."

"Then assure me that you shall seek us out when you are next in the capital. I have not yet had a chance to repay the debt I owe you. I am a proud man, Fotherby. I will not rest content until I have returned the good deed."

"But, sir," Fotherby announced. "You have done a great deal for me, as I have obtained my qualification this very week owing to your successful recovery. I could look for nothing further from you."

"Congratulations," Mr Tenterchilt said warmly, swapping the cane to his other hand so that he could shake Fotherby's hand. "But I still cannot rest happy with such repayment that costs me nothing."

"Then when I am next in London I shall seek you out. Good day, Mr Tenterchilt." Fotherby and the former captain bowed formally to one another with wishes for the other's health, before Fotherby continued on his journey.

Via Dover and Ostend, Fotherby journeyed back toward where he had expected to find his regiment, but the war which had rested over winter was once again underway so it took the young surgeon a further two weeks to negotiate his way towards his comrades. Having no horse, he had to walk or borrow lifts on carts, through Ghent and along the river through Tournai until he reached York's men on 30th April as they marched on to Willems.

At the rear of the column marched the women who followed their men to war, and it was past these women that Fotherby hurried. The light step in his movement was all but gone now for he was exhausted beyond measure after so many days of walking and the past three nights when he had been unable to find an inn at which to sleep. If he found himself feeling sorry for himself, or his thoughts drifting back to the comforts of his own bed in Wanderford Hall, he would remind himself that he had now attained what he had spent the last fifteen years dreaming of.

He was consoling himself with one such thought as his feet throbbed and his head spun, when someone fell against him. The regiment were marching through low lying scrub and it was over one of the protruding hummocks of grass that this lady had stumbled. She looked up at him through large blue eyes and clapped her hand to her mouth before she whispered repeatedly,

"I am so sorry, sir."

Fotherby waited until she was once more settled on her feet before he continued to walk on, his long strides leaving her behind so quickly that, as he glanced over his shoulder, he found that he had almost lost sight of her. Without understanding why, he halved his pace and watched as the women moved past him until the young woman he had encountered a few minutes earlier was walking by his side.

"You embarrass me, sir," she began as he walked alongside her.

"I did not seek to," he answered defensively. "I wished only to check that you were well."

"Then thank you for your care, sir, I am very well. Only I am so terribly tired, that I hope we shall shortly be halting for the night."

Fotherby nodded as he looked down at her and smiled. "Soon, I am sure."

This brief exchange of words played through Fotherby's head as he looked down at the small purse he held in his hand as he continued at his usual pace once more. Being a gentleman and unwilling to refuse a wager once accepted, he had kept aside the ten pounds he had bet Portland and the five guineas he had promised Peters should he be late in returning. He had, until this moment, felt certain of retaining all of it. It took him until the column halted for the night before he caught up with Captain Peters and, while the gentleman stood back, waiting for some of the men to assemble a small tent for him to sleep in, Fotherby walked over to him.

"Captain Peters?" he began.

"I was starting to think that you had abandoned your post for good," Peters replied, never turning to face him. "I see you took full advantage of your leave."

"I am sorry it took so long, sir. I have been trying to reach the regiment these past two weeks."

"And was your leave worthwhile?" Peters asked neutrally.

"I believe so, sir."

"Good. But then why are you not in uniform?" he demanded, looking across at him. "Men will not accept you as a lieutenant if you do not look like one."

"Sir, I had to leave the moment I had received confirmation. I only just arrived in time as it was."

"It does not matter, Lieutenant Fotherby," Peters announced and turned back to the tent that had now been erected. "We are journeying to combat and uniforms will, once more, be of little importance to us. All the same, Fotherby, make sure that you purchase yourself a uniform when you are next back in England."

"Yes, sir." Fotherby turned and began walking away but stopped as Peters began talking once more.

"You conducted yourself well, I heard. I knew you would not let me down."

Fotherby smiled as Peters wafted him away in his customary gesture to signal the end of the conversation before he stepped into his tent.

Fotherby slept in the open by choice that night, enjoying watching the clouds that drifted past the stars and trying to recall all the lines of all the constellations and the pictures they were meant to represent. He did not sleep for some time, despite the tiredness that he felt, but was grateful to rest his legs which throbbed with the past two weeks of walking. He watched as each star seemed to spin before his eyes and sleep washed over him. His last waking thought was of his friend Portland and the wager he knew he had lost.

In the morning the troops once again prepared to march on but, before Fotherby could join Kitson and Peters, his conscience ensured that he should settle the debt he now felt he owed Captain Portland. He walked through the regiment, searching for Lord Barrington's company before, at last, he found him.

"Mr Fotherby," Portland began with a smile that was so weary that Fotherby frowned. "Tell me, are you still Mr Fotherby?"

"No, my lord, I am not. I am now Lieutenant."

"Then congratulations are in order, Lieutenant Fotherby. You should have told me as soon as you returned to the ranks, we might have raised a toast to your success."

"What of your own successes, sir? For you seem far wearier than when I last met you at Ostend."

"You need have no concerns for me, my dear Fotherby. I am simply adjusting to my new captaincy and finding that it does not suit me." Portland sighed and took the bridle of his horse as a man approached, guiding it. "I have been forced to try and conduct my duties of lordship from here as well as leading this company, for my brother is too young to manage affairs alone and..." He stopped as Fotherby stared across at him with uncertainty. "Forgive me, Lieutenant Fotherby. I should not burden you with my own concerns. Tell me how England fairs."

"Well, my lord. But I did not come to discuss England with you nor, heaven forbid, gloat over my success. I came to give you what is rightfully yours. My father would be ashamed if he knew I had accepted such a bet, but this is yours." He handed Portland the purse with the ten pounds in and watched as the other man's face lit up in a smile.

"And who is she, Fotherby? Who has cost you so dear in heart?"

Fotherby did not reply but smiled, feeling his cheeks burn as he walked away from Lord Barrington. Indeed he had no answer to give, for he did not know her name. But the woman he had encountered so briefly yesterday had foolishly filled his dreams last night and, with a naivety that would have alarmed his uncle, he had resolved to seek her out and learn more about her.

## Chapter Seven

*An Unlikely Promotion*

The former Captain Tenterchilt had endured a Christmas and New Year with his wife's family, feeling like an outclassed relation in his own home. It had not been of Mrs Tenterchilt's making, indeed he had never had any cause to question the loyalty of his wife for, while in private she deplored his new pastime, she would never speak ill of her husband in front of anyone, even her brother. The only soul she might ever have discussed such concerns with was her maid, who was too experienced to let a word leave her mouth if it had been told to her in confidence. There was little wonder though that, when Rupert Jenkyns departed almost a year to the day after he had arrived, and Timothy Jenkyns left a week later, Mr Tenterchilt had been relieved beyond measure. This was noted by Mrs Tenterchilt, who felt responsible for her husband's unhappiness. Their time became their own once more as spring began to overturn winter.

Their only house guests now were the young Pottingers, Roger and Rose. Major Pottinger, their father, had fallen sick in the West Indies and Mrs Pottinger had travelled to the Caribbean with her father to visit her husband. Mr Tenterchilt was pleased to have a son in the house and tried to encourage Roger to read maps, practice swordplay and plot strategies. He bought the young boy books on military topics and even entrusted a pistol to him, but Roger Pottinger had no interest in war and was content, for the most part, to read other books and entertain Gulliver, who Catherine had adopted as her own. Mr Tenterchilt all but despaired of Roger but, when he mentioned such disappointment to his wife, Mrs Tenterchilt replied flatly,

"With his father a major and his grandfather a general, there is little wonder the poor boy seeks a way to distance himself from such bloodshed. Besides," she added with a tone of dislike that was not often present in his wife, "if Anne Pottinger were my mother, I should do whatever I could to disobey her."

Roger's sister, Rose, was a perfect companion to Arabella for they were almost exactly the same age as one another. They sat and discussed all topics that young ladies might discuss, from the forming of their handwriting to their hopes of marriage in the future. Approaching their tenth birthdays, each girl had high hopes of the lives that lay before them and their dreams were unbounded.

April of 1794 had brought the arrival of a letter to the former captain, and it was in reply to the enclosed command that Mr Tenterchilt was attending Horse

Guards. This had been when he encountered the young surgeon to whom he knew he owed his very life, but for whom he had a certain amount of envy when they discussed his new post as lieutenant. All the same, Mr Tenterchilt wished Fotherby all the very best before he walked towards the heavy doors of the British Army's headquarters.

Upon entering the building he presented the letter to the clerk who sat at the desk and invited Mr Tenterchilt to take a seat but otherwise did not address him. It made little difference to Tenterchilt, who only gazed around, feeling that this was where he knew he should be. Presently, a man walked down the stairs and looked across at him before he spoke.

"Josiah Tenterchilt?"

"Indeed, sir."

"Follow me."

No further explanation was given and the man began ascending the stairs once more. He waited at the top of the stairs for the former captain to catch up before he continued along the gallery and corridor to a large office. Still without talking, he indicated to a chair before taking his own seat at the other side of the desk.

"I understand you were wounded in Flanders, sir," the man said quickly. He seemed to be in a great hurry, not having even announced his rank and name.

"That is true, sir," Mr Tenterchilt conceded, uncertain what the man was trying to say by his statement. "I resigned my commission only on the surgeon's orders."

"I am pleased to hear that. I hope, therefore, that your loyalty to the army is as strong as it ever was. Indeed I heard that it was in defence of another company that you received your wound."

"That is true, also."

"Yes," the man began thoughtfully, and he leaned forward on the desk, watching Josiah Tenterchilt, with his chin on his clasped hands. "There is a situation that has developed in Flanders since you returned to England, one that has taken one of our officers to the front. I will not trouble you with the details of it yet. But we have found ourselves in need of an officer to liaise with our gentleman in Flanders, and it must be someone who knows the terrain." He sat back on his chair. "Your name was put forward to us, Mr Tenterchilt."

"Sir, I would be honoured to take this commission. But it is only right that I must tell you, my mobility is poor. I cannot travel to such places as I once did and nor do I feel that I am a fit person to command men in battle, for I should hinder them as I tried to lead them."

"These things are of little concern, Mr Tenterchilt. You shall be based here in Horse Guards, have only the smallest chance of a journey abroad, and be placed in charge of a household infantry company in name only."

"Then, sir, I accept, with more grateful thanks than I can show."

"But, sir, only the clerks work on a captain's wages here, for the most part at any rate. You shall, therefore, be appointed to the rank of major in your new position. You are to report to General Dover on Monday, he shall give you further details of your post. In the meantime, find yourself a uniform befitting of Horse Guards. Here is the name of my tailor." He handed a card over the desk and Mr Tenterchilt rose to his feet and took it from his outstretched hand.

"Might I be permitted to ask to whom I owe this position?"

"You are permitted to ask, major, but I am not permitted to say." He rose to his feet and offered a wry smile as he saw the look in Mr Tenterchilt's face when he addressed him by his new rank. "Good day, Major Tenterchilt."

"Good day, sir."

Josiah realised, as he closed the door, that he had no notion of whom he had just spoken to, but as he stepped down the stairs and out into the spring day he realised that he did not care. He walked down the street, leaning only occasionally on the cane he carried. Still, as he walked on through London towards the address that was written on the card which had been handed to him, he considered who his mysterious and modest benefactor might be. The only man he could imagine it to be was Elias Pottinger, but he was in the West Indies and had been for some time.

The hour was late when he stepped from a cab and walked up to the doors of Chanter's House. He stepped in and was met at once by Gulliver who threaded between the cane and the major's side. He leaned down and ruffled the long hair on top of the spaniel's head and looked as Catherine appeared from the door to the Dining Room.

"Mama let us eat with her today," she announced as she came and took her father's hand. "Where have you been, Papa?"

"I have some news, my little Cat," he replied quietly as he shrugged out of his coat and allowed the footman to take it.

"Papa has news," Catherine announced as she guided him in.

Major Tenterchilt looked at the scene before him and smiled broadly. Mrs Tenterchilt sat at the table, which she shared with four children, five when Catherine took her place beside her mother. His smile slipped a little as Gulliver leapt up onto his chair at the head of the table and began eating from the plate before him. Roger and Rose both stood at his arrival, but none of his daughters rose.

"I am sorry," Mrs Tenterchilt began, blushing slightly. "We did not expect you to return while we were eating." She picked up the plate that the dog was eating from and set it on the floor. "Down, Gulliver."

Major Tenterchilt was sure that the spaniel followed the food more than her command, but all the same he thanked her before sitting down on the chair. The two Pottingers took this as their invitation to follow his example.

"You must forgive me for being late, my dears," he began. "I had an important task to which I had to attend. I was at the tailor's shop."

"That does sound important," Mrs Tenterchilt agreed, confusion on her face. "What is the occasion?"

"The tailor shop, Mr Tenterchilt?" Roger asked. "I always accompany my father there. It is magic that they turn such flat, lifeless stretches of flax and linen into such garments."

"The occasion, my dears. I have been promoted."

"What?" Mrs Tenterchilt whispered, her eyes glowing. "But you did not have an occupation. How can you be promoted?"

"What is a promotion, Papa?" Catherine asked, disappointed by the outcome of this conversation and wishing that Gulliver had not been usurped in favour of her father, for his news seemed so dull.

"It means that Papa has become more of a gentleman than ever before," Imogen explained. "He has been rewarded with a better rank and a better income."

"Congratulations, Papa," Arabella announced in her silken tones.

"You are a major's daughter now, Arabella," he replied looking down the table to where she sat. "How does that affect your plans for the future?"

"How is this possible?" Mrs Tenterchilt asked, an insuppressible smile on her face. "What happened?"

"I will not tire you with the details now, my dear, for in truth I do not fully know them myself. But I am hungry beyond measure and feel that I have a cause to celebrate."

The change that Mrs Tenterchilt observed within her husband was dramatic and she felt that after nine months of drifting idly through his ludicrous hobby of gambling and sinking into a dark depression, the man she had married had finally returned to her.

"Is it not wonderful that Papa has been returned to the army, Mama?" Arabella asked as her mother stood at the door to her room that evening. "And as a major."

"It is, my little lady. It is where he shall always belong."

"Is that not here, Mama?" Arabella asked, pausing in the action of delivering her hair its fifty strokes. "They cannot expect him to go to war once more, surely."

"Currently, my dear, you know as much as I. I hope that Papa will tell me a little more soon. But it is wonderful, Bella. It is truly wonderful."

She walked out of the room and hurried down the stairs with a renewed skip to each of her steps. Her husband stood in the Drawing Room before the hearth. Both his hands were on the mantle shelf and he was leaning forward staring into the fire so that she became anxious lest his elated mood had slipped.

"Major Tenterchilt?" she whispered as she walked in. "Josiah?"

"My dear," he said, startled from his contemplation. "I was thinking."

"That is a dangerous pastime, Major Tenterchilt. Congratulations, my love. We must celebrate."

"Indeed. Let us host a party, before the departure of our friends to the theatres of war."

"Why do you seem so pensive then, my dear?"

"I was considering the words of the officer I spoke with. He said that I had been put forward for this post, whatever post it may be. But I know no one in Horse Guards."

"But clearly they know you."

"I saw the young surgeon today," Major Tenterchilt said quickly, his voice changing. "Fotherby. He had just qualified, I believe."

"I am pleased. He was a very capable young man and compassionate too. I believe he will go far in his profession. It seemed strange to me though that such a young man could deal so calmly with all that blood and death." She lifted her hand to her face and tried to forget the image that haunted her of the man before her on the table in the hospital tent. Major Tenterchilt must have followed her thoughts for he stepped over to her and tilted her chin so that he could look into her eyes.

"I am safe, my dear. We are both safe."

"Will you go to war, Josiah? Will you be sent once more to such bloodshed?"

"No," he whispered before he leaned forward and kissed her cheek. "It is a job that will scarcely require me to leave London. Have no fear, my beautiful Elizabeth, you shall never again have to face the horrors of war."

Major Tenterchilt returned to the tailor shop the following day, taking young Roger Pottinger, whose eyes, for the first time that Major Tenterchilt had observed, lit up as he watched the tailor work. He was anxious to be at hand and held pins, measures and braiding for the tailor, keen to be of assistance.

"Father has a path readied for Roger," Rose explained to Arabella as the two girls watched Major Tenterchilt and Roger Pottinger return later in the day. "Roger wants to be a tailor, but Father has already secured him a commission in the army the moment he is old enough to take it."

"A tailor is not befitting of a major's son," Arabella agreed.

"Perhaps," Rose whispered. "Would it not be better that a man might choose his profession?"

"I like your brother, Rose. He puts a deeper meaning to the word *gentle*man."

"He has Master Clark, his tutor, to thank for that. But he agrees with Father that the son of an officer should be an officer."

"Papa," Arabella began as her father walked into the black and white marbled hallway. "You look perfect," she said, placing her hand on the bright red coat he was now wearing. He took her small hand and kissed it before he followed her eyes now resting on the young man at his side. She was smiling shamelessly across at him while he lowered his gaze to the floor.

"Are you sure that it is I who look perfect, my dear?" the major laughed. "Come through to the garden. Today is a day too pleasant to be indoors." He watched as Arabella nodded and stood while Roger Pottinger met her gaze and offered his arm which she took graciously. The major walked through the house followed by the young couple who, in turn, were followed by Rose Pottinger. His wife had gone to visit one of her friends, Mrs Darling, to share the news of her husband's new position. Indeed, Mrs Tenterchilt had wasted no time in writing to everyone she knew to impart the news, and to invite many of them to attend a dinner party in Chanter's House to celebrate. This was set for three weeks in the future, at the start of May.

There was no sign of Imogen in the garden, which was little surprise to the major for she so often shut herself in the library, but Catherine was there. The young child made no attempt to turn and face her father. Gulliver sat at her side and watched intently whatever it was she had in her hand. Major Tenterchilt, assuming that it was a stick she held, smiled to himself at this image. The endearing nature of the picture changed, however, as he watched his youngest daughter point the pistol that she held before her and stared down it, lining it up with one of the trees in the garden.

"Cat!" her father called and now she turned, still pointing the gun forward. Rose gasped as she saw the young child, and Arabella let go of Roger's arm to cover her face with both hands, but looked across in surprise as Roger stood protectively in front of her. Major Tenterchilt ignored the three children but rushed down the few steps that divided him from Catherine as fast as his wounded leg would allow and snatched her wrist.

"What is it, Papa?" Catherine began.

"Catherine Christina Tenterchilt, get indoors this minute! I shall talk to you in my study," he bellowed so the young child's eyes brimmed with tears but she nodded quickly, failing to understand what she had done wrong. She rushed past Arabella and the Pottingers and into the house, followed faithfully by Gulliver. Major Tenterchilt looked down at the pistol that he now held in his hand and tried not to consider how differently this misadventure might have concluded. "Master Pottinger," he called without turning to face the boy who, at once, rushed to stand in front of him, "I entrusted this to you."

"Sir, I left it in my room," Roger began to explain, not expecting the man before him to believe his words and preparing for the punishment that would inevitably follow. He was greatly surprised, then, when the major offered him the gun and nodded slightly.

"You are old enough now to carry this. My youngest daughter seems to struggle with the boundaries of privacy. Keep it with you, please."

Roger nodded and took the weapon from the major, watching as the older man awkwardly moved towards the house, stooping to pick up the cane that he had discarded in his haste to reach Catherine.

Major Tenterchilt walked into the house and stepped through to his study. He found Catherine standing before the desk, Gulliver leaning against her, her salty tears falling on the dog's nose so that it continued to lick its muzzle. He walked around and sat at the desk, making him the same height as she was.

"What did I do, Papa?" she asked, her voice trembling.

"How old are you now, Catherine?"

"Almost six."

"Even a boy should not have a gun at your age."

"But Roger does not use that gun, Papa," she pleaded, but stopped as her father struck the desk with his cane.

"That does not give you the right to steal it. People are hung for stealing things from people's houses. You are beginning a long road to the gallows if you continue along this path, and I shall not be there if you do."

"Why did you give Roger a pistol, Papa? It is not fair. Do you love Roger more than you love me?"

"No, my little Cat," he said softly, rising to his feet and moving around to the front of the desk. "But that does not make your theft any more acceptable."

"Papa?" Catherine asked, looking up her father as she leaned against him. "Are you angry that I had the pistol or angry that I took it?"

"Both, Cat. You should never steal. Never. But you might have injured anyone with that gun. What if you had shot Gulliver by mistake?"

"Gulliver is my companion. I would never shoot him." She looked down at the spaniel and giggled as it leapt up and started licking the tears from her cheeks. "I have never shot him."

"Do you mean that this was not the first time you took the pistol?"

Catherine seemed to be weighing up her answer as she looked across at her father, before she smiled and shook her head. "And I can shoot it, Papa," she began. "Last week I managed to shoot one of Mama's plants from ten paces away."

"Your paces may not be considered legal in a duel, my little Cat. But promise me," he continued, leaning down, "do not take the gun again."

She scrubbed her sleeve over her face and nodded before she led Gulliver from the study.

The major did not share this event with his wife, although when Mrs Tenterchilt was bidding goodnight to Arabella that evening, she began to suspect that something had happened while she had been out of the house. Arabella was not brushing her hair as she usually was, she was looking at her own reflection in the glass with an expression that suggested she was surprised to find herself staring back. She did not turn as her mother entered but met her gaze in the glass.

"Mama," she whispered at length. "How old were you when you met Papa?"

"I was seventeen, my little lady. And I was nineteen when I married him."

"How long, after you met him, did it take for you to know that you loved him?"

"A season," she whispered, walking further into the room and closing the door. "We courted all autumn, and at Christmas he asked me to marry him. But then he was called to war overseas and it was another sixteen months before we were married. What is troubling you?"

"I think I might have fallen in love, Mama," Arabella whispered, turning now to face her mother. "But I am not sure I am old enough. I wanted to have London society at my feet and choose from majors, colonels and generals, but I feel like none of them could protect me as Roger did today."

"Protect you, my dear?"

"Cat had stolen his pistol, and he placed himself between me and her."

Mrs Tenterchilt forgot for a moment the point of this story and considered only her youngest daughter. Her face became deathly white and she shook her head quickly. "I wish she were more like you, Bella. Why must she fight and shoot things? Why is Gulliver not calming her?"

"But was it not chivalrous of Roger? Catherine might just as easily have shot him without meaning to."

"Roger is a dear boy, my little lady, and I do believe he loves you greatly, but let us keep this feeling a secret for a time."

"Were you in love with anybody when you were ten, Mama?"

"No, Bella, but I shall not say that you are not. Just do not mention it to Papa. He has high hopes for Roger in the army, as his parents have too. It is best that we keep it to ourselves."

Arabella nodded, feeling no less confused but a little more settled in her mind.

Whatever exchanges of words the parents shared surrounding this incident was concluded without the children knowing. Major Tenterchilt began his post the following week to discover that he was now collecting information sent from Flanders and advising the Duke of York's troops of their best course forward. He was, in essence, a spy. It had become apparent that the cause of the Austrians was becoming lost, and as the year stretched on, they committed less and less to the allied cause, so that by October Major Tenterchilt was receiving dispatches informing him that the Austrians had abandoned the attack force and, furthermore, both the Prussians and the Austrians were negotiating treaties of peace with the French. The fall or retreat of the British army seemed imminent and the major's mood reflected this. By the end of the year he had returned once more to heavy drinking and gambling most nights, sometimes with other officers and sometimes with the gentlemen he had come to know the year before.

Mrs Tenterchilt remained a loving and loyal wife to him, although she was furious to discover that he had bought Cat a gun for her birthday and tried to dissuade the girl from using it. Major Tenterchilt taught her to use the weapon while they were at Chanter's House but, as summer arrived, Mrs Tenterchilt took the children to their estate and was relieved to return Catherine to picking flowers and playing croquet on the vast lawn.

Major Pottinger returned from the West Indies in June, and Arabella was sorry to see her dear friend Rose leave and perhaps a little more upset by Roger's departure. Having fought off the yellow fever that had almost killed him, Pottinger was reposted to Flanders almost immediately, his wife remaining behind this time.

The family returned to Chanter's House at the end of September, and Major Tenterchilt was already absent each day at work and most nights at the gaming tables. It was here, on a cold damp November evening, that Mr Kildare introduced a new gentleman to the gaming table.

"Allow me to introduce Mr Bryn-Portland, gentlemen." All the gentlemen present welcomed the newcomer and introduced themselves one by one.

"What is your profession, sir?" Major Tenterchilt asked at length.

"I am without a profession, major. Currently I am working hard to settle a legal case."

"It is a curious name you have," remarked another gentleman by the name of Grassford.

"Indeed, sir," laughed the newcomer. "Bryn is the name of my maternal grandfather and Portland is the name of my paternal grandfather."

"I hope your business has a successful conclusion, sir," Major Tenterchilt offered, laying his cards down on the table, and watching as Mr Kildare presented a superior hand and collected the contents of the pot.

"And you, Major?" Bryn-Portland asked. "How is it that you have escaped the theatre of war?"

"Escaped?" he muttered the word angrily. "No, sir, I have not escaped. I have a position in Horse Guards, that is all. I was wounded in Valenciennes, fighting the French, and have since been returned to England."

"Valenciennes? I know of that, and the siege."

"Indeed? It was at the siege that I was wounded."

"But my nephew was there. Portland, he calls himself."

"I know no one of that name, sir."

Major Tenterchilt began to feel happier in the gentleman's company after this revelation and they continued to gamble into the night. Mr Kildare watched the gentlemen around the table thoughtfully, no doubt trying not to lose as spectacularly as he had the year before.

## Chapter Eight

*The Return To England*

The nine months that raced past the newly-promoted major dragged painfully for the men on the continent. With the continual failure and desertion of their allies, the British forces were pushed further and further back. Any victory that they claimed only seemed to secure their failure on two more occasions. The troops were exhausted and, as the summer surrendered, it heralded a bitter winter.

The lightheartedness of the spring had fled. There had been battle after battle and the newly-established army surgeon had been forced to accept that there were fewer people who could be saved than were fated to die. The successes of the year before, the qualification in April, all seemed to have frozen away in the bitter onset of winter. The French continued to push the British forces back, for they had been all but abandoned by their allies, and all reports of the Dutch royalists were of failure.

This catastrophic result for the army only reflected Fotherby's own lament that he had failed to locate that lady who had, foolishly, filled his dreams. He could not explain the way that his heart quickened as he recalled the seconds they had met, but neither could he forget it.

Frequently he rebuked himself for easily allowing his thoughts to wander and he wondered if it had been his lack of concentration that had resulted in the high rate of fatalities. Peters, however, continued to support him in a manner that Fotherby was certain he would not if he felt the younger man was neglecting his duties.

"Winters seem to come quicker in a war," Fotherby sighed as he looked about him. Indeed, there had been men he had watched slip into death through the cold alone, for so many were ill-prepared for another winter, and the crushing realisation that they could not defeat the French only made the cold harder to withstand.

"Perhaps we are just becoming old, Fotherby," Portland laughed, breathing warm air onto his frozen hands. "We will be home soon. That is something to celebrate."

"More than fifteen thousand men have been lost. I can see nothing to celebrate."

"Think how many more it would have been without you, Kitson and Peters."

"I am quite sure you put us in the wrong order," Fotherby laughed.

"Perhaps," Portland agreed, smiling across at his friend.

Fotherby returned the gesture but felt unsure suddenly. Peters had never ceased in his criticism of

Portland, failing to ever acknowledge him as Lord Barrington and repeatedly telling Fotherby he should not cross paths with such a rebellious person. But Fotherby could not see it. He tried, as gently as he could, to enquire from Portland why people might suspect him of such social deviance, but the young lord would answer that he could not understand how any soul in Christendom would believe him guilty of such a thing. This answer only puzzled Fotherby further, and he could not bring himself to sever the friendship he had found with this man.

"What will you do when you return home?" Fotherby asked, trying once more to pry into what gave rise to Peters' mistrust of the man.

"First I shall see my wife." Portland smiled across at him. "Then we shall journey on to Cornwall to stay with my family. I wish to see my father's tomb."

"Where does your wife live?"

"In London. But we will return to Cornwall now that the estate is ours." Portland looked across at his friend and sighed. "Where is it that you live, Fotherby? Where the waters are so strong that men grow to such great heights."

"Derbyshire."

"And is your father a giant, too?"

"No," Fotherby laughed. "He is, in height, the same as you."

"And your mother? Is she the height of an Amazon?"

"My father tells me she was."

"I am sorry, Fotherby."

"What for? She died so long ago that I never knew her. Is your mother still alive?"

"To the best of my knowledge," came the thoughtful reply. "She lives in Cornwall still, with my brothers and sisters. You must come to visit us, Fotherby. We have cliffs to rival the hills of Derbyshire."

"The army must finish with us first."

Portland turned to face his friend at this bitter remark and tried to comprehend what fear and resignation might have driven such a statement to be made. "We will be home soon. By the end of next year, mark my words." Seeing Fotherby's downcast expression Portland gave a slight laugh as he continued, "You never did tell me why you lost your bet."

"What bet?"

"The ten pounds you were forced to relinquish in spring. Who was she?"

"I do not know," Fotherby began in a carefree manner that was so forced it fooled neither himself nor his friend. "Although if we had the same wager today it would be you who were ten pounds lighter."

Portland pulled the heavy woollen coat tighter about him and looked over the frozen land. "We will be home soon," he repeated, muttering so quietly that Fotherby was uncertain he had been meant to hear at all.

They parted then, Fotherby trudging back to the hospital and Portland to his lodgings. The army had successfully found houses for the officers or rooms in hotels, but the rank and file were still abandoned to the makeshift tents. These let in the wind, which bit as deep as any bayonet and killed as successfully as shot. Fotherby had resorted to sleeping in the hospital. Peters had a room in one of the buildings nearby but his two lieutenants did not merit such a luxury.

"Where have you been, Fotherby, you idler?" Peters demanded as the younger surgeon walked in.

"What is it, sir?"

"Talking with that renegade, no doubt," he continued, answering his own question. "Three more men with digits falling from their hands and feet, and you spend your time negotiating the downfall of parliament and decrying the king. Remember who funds you, Fotherby." He drank heavily from his flask before offering it to his lieutenant who graciously declined.

"Sir," Fotherby whispered, "all I discuss with Captain Portland are the same topics that I would discuss with any gentleman, and I assure you he speaks well of both the king and the Prime Minister."

"Yes, I can see he would."

"I do not understand what rebellion you believe he is capable of."

Peters turned to him at this remark and rose to his feet. For a time he did not say anything but simply looked at his lieutenant critically so that, despite towering over the captain, Fotherby felt no taller than a child. Peters drank once more from the flask, never taking his gaze from the man before him.

"Talk to your friend of his father."

"His father is dead, sir. And is it fair to condemn a man for the deeds of his father?"

"It is not his father's deeds I condemn, it is his principles. Your father handed his principles to you, did he not?"

"Yes, sir."

"You inherited this ridiculous notion that you should abstain from alcohol, but in doing so you injure only yourself. His father caused turmoil to the very fabric of society. His principles, and those now of the new Lord Barrington, stand counter to others of the House of Lords and better resemble the views of a peasant. I tell you, Fotherby, for I wish you to prosper in your future. Pitt offends the Lords with some of his disestablishment ideas and it would not surprise me at all to learn that your young friend shared the Prime Minister's lesser ideals."

Fotherby took in each of his captain's words and tried to understand what gave the man before him permission to talk so of the Prime Minister when he so strongly objected to the attitude of Captain Portland. But Lieutenant Fotherby was a patient and thoughtful man and maintained his own counsel. He watched as Peters snatched his coat tightly about him and walked out of the tent.

The cold air outside the tent battered the canvas, and Fotherby sat for a time, pulling two woollen blankets about him as he tried once more to comprehend the resentment that his officer had towards his friend. These thoughts confused him into his sleepless night and through the days beyond. Christmas came and went with no comfort or celebration, as the French continued to push the British forces so far back that they were almost in the ocean. Gradually the forces of King George, now totally abandoned by the Austrians and the Prussians, were shipped back to England during the first three months of 1795. It was at the end of January when Fotherby next encountered his friend.

There had been a week of snow, failing to settle yet churning the muddy ground so that the entrance to the hospital tent was brown and slippery. The hospital had been used increasingly by any of the men who could contrive a reason to visit, for it was the warmest place in the camp. Captain Portland skidded into the tent and pulled the tent flap closed. Some forty men were crammed inside, giving a feverish warmth to Portland as he stepped in. Peters looked across at his entrance with a poorly disguised expression of distaste. If Captain Portland was at all upset or even noticed Peters' disdain, he did not show it but, having looked about him and failed to find his friend, he smiled briefly across at the surgeon.

"Portland," Peters shouted across and, as the younger man turned, he beckoned him forward.

"Sir?" Portland asked uncertainly.

"I wish to talk with you. Have you time?"

Portland nodded, but it did not matter for Peters had turned from him and was walking back to his campaign desk. He ignored the other man until he pulled out the chair and pointed at it, waiting for Portland to sit down, and Peters leaned back on the desk to study him.

"What is it, sir?" Portland asked after a time, feeling conspicuous in the man's study of him. "I assure you I did not come here to seek your attention. I am quite well."

"I know why you came."

"Then, what is it, sir?"

"You must follow your course as you see fit, Captain Portland."

Portland bowed his head in an agreement but did not offer any words.

"But your views are your own, sir, and you would do well to ensure that they stay so." Peters folded his arms across his chest and stared vehemently at the man before him who pursed his lips in an expression of defiance. "I knew your father, you know? And your uncle."

"No, sir," Portland whispered. "I did not know."

"It was wrong, what your grandfather did. It was not his place to dismiss tradition in favour of ridiculous notions."

"Nor is it yours, Captain Peters."

"I respected your father, but it was no surprise that with your grandfather's death your father could not survive long. I was, however, sorry to hear of his death, whatever our disagreements."

"Am I to find some comfort in your words?" Portland demanded. "You did not wish to talk to me so that you could insult both my father and my grandfather, surely? No," he continued, and smiled wryly. "You object to their legacy as it lives on in me. And you object to the fact that your lieutenant has found friendship with me."

Peters silently watched Portland for a time once more, only moving to take a drink from his flask. "I am concerned about Lieutenant Fotherby, it is true. I have endeavoured on too many occasions to reason with him concerning the position that an alliance with you might place him in. But he has a patient counterargument to any issue I raise. I want him to become the captain of this tent when I am forced out of it, but Horse Guards will not allow him any advancement if he is associated with a cause such as yours."

"And Pitt's."

"Do not be a fool, boy," Peters spat back. "You and I both know that Horse Guards is run by the Lords."

"Not all the lords are against us," Portland began. "But you need have no fear with regard to Lieutenant Fotherby, for I came seeking him only to tell him that tomorrow I am to return to England. Perhaps you will make my farewell to him." He rose to his feet and glared into the face of the man who had just insulted three generations of his family. "I have never spoken of my political and personal beliefs to your lieutenant and you may rest your mind in that knowledge. I respect Mr Fotherby far too greatly to try and sway his opinion. That seems a greater compliment than you are willing to afford him."

Such a defamation did not seem to offend or concern Peters, who only watched as Portland exited the tent. By contrast, Portland felt hurt and anger swell within him as he walked out into the flurries of snow. There was a faint beam of sunlight struggling through the snow clouds over the west and it was towards this glimmer of light that he marched.

"Lord Barrington!"

Portland turned at this and smiled across as Fotherby rushed over to him as quickly as the muddy ground would allow.

"You have come from the hospital," he continued, pulling his long woollen coat about him. "You are not unwell, are you?"

"No, Fotherby," Portland replied. "In fact, I was looking for you."

"I am here," came the jovial response.

"I am leaving tomorrow. The company is to journey back to England. But I wanted to repeat my invitation to you. I should not like to lose your friendship, Lieutenant Fotherby. I wish for you to visit Cornwall when you are able."

"Thank you. Though I cannot envisage a time when I will be free of this place, I should very much enjoy visiting you in your home. I am sorry you are leaving,

Lord Barrington. I shall have to fend off Kitson's moods and Peters' drunkenness without respite now."

"I think you have a patron in your captain, Fotherby. And, furthermore, I am convinced you will do better with him in my absence."

Fotherby bowed his head slightly. "You have spoken to him."

"He has talked at me, Fotherby. But I assured him of my respect for you and I am not willing to compromise that by discussing my views of your officer in this way. But promise me, when time allows, you will hunt out Barrington Manor."

"If I am able," Fotherby said softly, "I shall make sure I visit Cornwall."

Portland smiled across at the man before he bowed his head formally, tapped Fotherby's arm and walked away from him without looking back. Fotherby thoughtfully watched him go before he turned and walked back to the hospital. He stepped in and looked at the three dozen men who were crammed inside. Considering the words he had just shared with his friend he looked across at Peters, who was ignoring the rest of the tent as he tossed his cards down on the campaign desk. Wishing he had known the words his officer and his friend had shared, but reluctant to ask, Fotherby took the extra blankets he was carrying to where Kitson stood in the corner of the tent.

Over the following three months, the remnants of the British army were removed from the continent in the crushing knowledge that they had failed to defeat the French. It is true that many had lost sight of why they had been fighting the French, the memory of Louis' beheading two years earlier having faded in the failed war that had followed. The glory and might of the British army had gone and now, as Fotherby looked about him, all he could see was debris and the remains of what had once been a great force. He boarded the ship once more to England alongside Kitson and Peters, feeling that the failure rested on his own shoulders. For the first time he could ever remember he wished he could drown his despair as his captain did. Kitson joined Peters as the pair lamented and drank into the night.

Walking about the boat, Fotherby was lost in his own thoughts. He stepped out onto the deck and watched as Europe faded into the distance. Presently he heard the sound of a light footfall behind him and turned to see a woman rushing across the timbers. She was carrying a large jug and her attention was solely on this as she padded on towards the stairs leading down into the ship's lower decks. But Fotherby felt his breath catch as he recognised the woman he had encountered almost a year ago. His feet seemed reluctant to heed his head as he stepped over to her and pulled his hat from his head.

"Allow me to help you."

"Thank you, sir," she whispered in return as Fotherby took the jug from her hand and guided her down the steps.

"What are you celebrating?"

"My father's officer has been granted a promotion. I believe this makes him a colonel."

"I am glad someone can celebrate tonight," Fotherby muttered.

"But you should be celebrating too, sir. You are going home."

Fotherby was about to turn to her and explain the number of deaths he had witnessed and how worthless it had all been but, as she stepped down from the lowest stair and looked up, the words failed him. He was hunched over to accommodate his great height and she laughed slightly as she took the jug back from him.

"What is your name, sir? For I feel certain that I have seen you before."

"Fotherby, my lady. Lieutenant Fotherby."

"Lady?" she giggled. "No man but my father has ever called me a lady. But I do not recognise your name."

"I encountered you last year, I believe. But I must confess to not knowing your name, either."

"Kitty, sir. My name is Kitty Simmons. And I am afraid I cannot detain you any longer for, if the men do not get this soon, the colonel will not be happy."

"Of course, Miss Simmons."

Fotherby watched as she smiled across at him before stepping further into the boat. The feeling that seized him and caused his breath to catch in his throat made him giddy. He rushed back up the stairs and out into the April night, admiring the view before him now with a fresh enthusiasm. The vanishing continent no longer seemed to mark his failure, but the new stage of his life.

This giddy excitement, alien to a man who was usually so measured, remained with him until the ship reached England. He did not encounter Miss Kitty Simmons again on the short voyage and he repeatedly told himself how foolish he was for building such nonsense from two conversations. However, his head would not accept such common sense.

"You have quite a spring in your step, Fotherby," Kitson remarked as they stepped ashore. "You do not seem so disappointed in losing the war."

"I am pleased to be home, Kitson. I could not help the outcome of the war."

"We will not have peace for long," Peters remarked as he looked across at his two lieutenants. "Before the end of the year we will be back on the continent. Mark my words."

"What are we to do until then, sir?" Fotherby asked, tasting the smile on his lips.

"We report back to the regiment's headquarters, Fotherby," Peters remarked, as though nothing could be more obvious. "That means we travel to London."

Kitson nodded before the three continued out of the quay. Fotherby looked about him in the hopes of seeing Miss Simmons once more, but she was not there. Little by little, as they climbed into the coach which was to take them into the town, he began to realise how foolish his dreamy notions were.

Peters did not wait for the other two men as he stepped into the tavern where they would stay for the night. Tomorrow they would travel to London. Kitson walked after their captain, leaving Fotherby to settle the bill with the coachman. Watching as the coach moved away from the building, he took in his surroundings. They had landed at the docks in the mouth of the Thames. The buildings were tall, dank and depressing and he felt unsure as he peered through the windows of the tavern. Eager to take the air, and not have to reason with Peters and Kitson about his abstinence, he began walking through the streets. They were thin and overshadowed by the rickety buildings which looked as if they had not changed in a hundred years. He became quite lost in the labyrinth of roads and, when he next stopped, the town was cloaked in darkness. The stars he knew would be shining in the sky were hidden by thin cloud and the uneven roofs of the building. He was standing in a road before a dark, large fronted building which had been boarded up. Indeed he was alone in the road, and could see no other soul, nor evidence of one.

He was completely lost, he realised, having no idea where he had walked nor for how long. He circled and took in the desolate emptiness of where he was and wondered what had happened to turn this into such a barren place. The door of the house opposite, having no latch to secure it, clattered against its frame. Except for this, there was near silence in the world. Perhaps the most surprising thing of all was how unafraid he felt, for he just sat down in one of the doorways and considered the journey which had brought him here. Not only the steps he had taken to reach this run-down building, but his journey through the war, his friendship with Lord Barrington, his vocation into the army and the sad figure of his captain to whom he owed so much.

Time passed him by as he sat there, questioning every aspect of his life and his very being. But always the subject he returned to was the bitter feud between Peters and Portland, as he tried to understand the origin of such animosity. Recalling that Peters had mentioned Portland's father, his thoughts turned to his own father and, for the first time he questioned the presence of his uncle at Wanderford Hall. Paul Fotherby was older than his father, and should have inherited, but he had moved out to the West Indies and established himself there before returning when Fotherby had been ten years old. He had never thought to question how unorthodox the issue of his inheritance was, nor why his uncle had returned from such a prosperous life in Saint Vincent where he had worked alongside Sir Manfred Chester. There could be little doubt that he was rich, for he had bought and established several mills across the north of England. And then he thought of the huge differences between his father and his uncle. His father adhered to such a strict code of morals which his uncle seemed entirely lacking and, after enduring the taunting of Peters and Kitson over the past few years, Fotherby could understand why. And so he returned once more to assessing himself and the code by which he endeavoured to live his life.

Rising to his feet, he brushed the dust from his trousers and continued walking through the town. He began to pass more people now, other soldiers who were so drunk that they stumbled, while some lay asleep in the gutters of the road. Fotherby, a man who sought to comprehend the concerns and viewpoints of all men, struggled to understand why men would partake in something which would result in their behaviour becoming little better than that of animals. For the most part he tried to avoid them, but he assisted some as they stumbled and helped others to their feet, unable to relinquish his role as their physician. They were not alone in the streets. Other men who saw an opportunity to alight objects from the soldiers passed through, while women, selling themselves for coin from any man, guided the drunkards away. On one occasion Fotherby encountered a young child who sat begging in a doorway, dividing his time between beseeching alms and hammering on the door, pleading to be admitted.

This was the image that haunted Fotherby as he continued through the streets but, as he ascended the incline of the hill, he stepped into a more prosperous area. Shuttered windows revealed warm lamplight through tiny cracks where the shutters joined. The smell of food drifted up from the basements of some of the houses where kitchen staff were already heating the ovens for the arrival of the day. There were far fewer people here. Indeed, Fotherby only encountered one person as he walked through these streets, and that was a man who crossed the road to avoid the young surgeon. Eventually he realised that the sun was rising and that he was as lost as he had been last night. He leaned against a tall market cross, standing in the centre of a square, and watched as traders began to open their shops or step out into the pale half-light of the early morning to catch prospective buyers. Watching the industry of the world gave him a new drive to move on, but he had scarcely taken three steps before someone snatched his wrist and he turned around to face this intruder to his thoughts.

"There is no mistaking you in a crowd," Peters remarked. "You are fortunate not to have your uniform yet, Fotherby, or I might have had you flogged for treating it as badly as you have these clothes."

Fotherby looked down at himself and noticed for the first time the sorry figure he cut, with mud splashed up his pale trousers and dust plastered to his open jacket and shirt. "Sorry, sir. I became lost."

"I can tell that," Peters remarked curtly, and proceeded to walk away from him. Fotherby followed him as he walked toward the tavern where he was meant to have spent the night. He felt like a child, a feeling that only intensified as Kitson, who stood by the open door of the coach due for London, gave a slight laugh.

"You look like you have spent the night in a pigsty," he remarked while Peters climbed into the coach. His two lieutenants followed him and, at once, the vehicle moved through the streets and onward.

Fotherby found himself trapped in a peculiar daze, for he was weary but unable to succumb to sleep. Kitson offered no words and Peters ignored both men until the coach stopped and he stepped down. Fotherby stumbled down from the coach, keen to stretch his aching legs.

"I shall settle our business at Horse Guards," Peters announced flatly.

"So what are we to do?" Fotherby asked numbly.

"What do you normally do when you are in London?" Peters demanded. "It is not my concern what either of you wish to do when you are not in my command. The army has finished with you for a time."

Fotherby felt at once a confusion of rejection and freedom as Kitson announced his intention to return to Surrey, where his wife and child were waiting. He wasted no time in making his farewells and assuring Peters that he would return to London within the month to discover whether or not the regiment would be redeployed. Fotherby watched as Kitson adjusted the hat resting on his immaculate hair and walked away from them.

"Have you nowhere better to be, Fotherby?" Peters demanded. "While we were at war you dreamed of being in England. Now that we are here you surely cannot wish that you were back."

"I might not make it all the way back to Derbyshire and back in time to discover if we shall be journeying out once more. But I shall stay with my uncle's friend here in London."

Peters sighed as he shook his head. "Your duty to your work is beyond admirable, Fotherby, but you have a duty to your father too."

"What duty?"

"You are to inherit. You have a duty to learn to deal with being a landowner now that you have learnt how to be a surgeon."

"But this is what I have wanted to do. For fifteen years my father has known that I do not want to be tied to Wanderford Hall. No," he continued firmly, "I shall stay in Mayfair until I am given orders to return to war."

"Mayfair?" Peters laughed. "You will be called upon by the very best of society there."

Fotherby frowned slightly at the man's response, for it was so uncharacteristic of him, but Peters continued without noticing this expression.

"I told you once before of the position I have lined up for you, my boy." He was serious once more and his voice became stern. "I have told you, too, that this position is one which many others may question and that your alliances will be used to judge you."

"Sir," Fotherby began but stopped as Peters lifted his hand.

"Shut up, boy, and listen to what I wish to say. If it were my choice I should hand over the hospital tent to you as an inheritance, but it does not work this way in the army. You have an overwhelming patience that at times only frays mine to shreds. You deal skillfully and swiftly with wounded men whilst somehow maintaining a care and compassion that puts Kitson to shame. But above all, you seek the best in everyone. This, Lieutenant, shall be either the making of you or your undeserved downfall."

"I cannot change who I am, sir." Fotherby's tone was one of apology while his face remained resolute.

"Neither should you, for it is each one of your attributes that has given me cause to ask that you consider the role of captaincy when I am forced to leave."

"But you shall not retire soon, sir."

"God in heaven, no! I have no intention to leave until I am dead. But you have witnessed the fragility of life. Not one of us knows when death shall come knocking."

"Good, for I have so much left to learn from you, sir. And I am quite sure that Kitson will never take an order from me."

"You must learn to command, Fotherby, and to accept that you will be both respected and despised. But it is your respect of others that will help you achieve command and it is on that issue I wish to talk to you."

Fotherby felt strangely nervous as his commanding officer continued to address him as an equal. He looked around him as though he expected the other people to be listening to his conversation, but he need not have worried for they were all too busy with their own comings and goings.

"I have tried to dissuade you from forming a friendship with a man who I consider will jeopardise your success, for my work shall be my only legacy in this world and I wish to see it secured in you, not left to wither in the lack of commitment and care I see in Kitson."

"Lord Barrington?"

"Lord Barrington, indeed. But, before he left, he spoke words to me that I had chosen to ignore, and those words were regarding you. I have a selfish interest in your position and it has left me blinded to other things. So I would like you to go here before you return home to Derbyshire." He handed a card to Fotherby who looked down at the address on it. "I knew the former Lord Barrington. I want you to know that, were you not in the service of the king, I could not have found you a better friend than Captain Portland. It is only your future career that I believe he threatens. For he has a respect for your manners and values that more than equal my own."

Fotherby was left speechless but nodded his head, unsure how to take such a compliment. He turned the card in his hand and studied it, reluctant to meet Peters' gaze.

"So, go home for a time, Fotherby. For you may rest assured that I shall summon you as soon as we are ordered once more to war. There is no one I would sooner work alongside."

Peters offered no further words but walked away from his young lieutenant, who watched him go with a confusion beyond words but a pride he felt certain was greatly misplaced.

## Chapter Nine

*Persephone and Rosanna*


Fotherby wasted little time as Peters left him, but began walking in the direction of Mayfair. After arriving at the house of Sir Manfred Chester so late on the last two occasions he had been a house guest, he was determined to arrive at a civilised time. He reached the white fronted house in the late afternoon and paused at the steps, uncertain that he should presume to simply arrive there. He walked across the road, rebuking himself for his lack of etiquette. He still carried the card that Peters had given him and he wondered at what the address was. It was somewhere in Westminster, and he was on the point of returning into the city when he turned at the sound of his name.

"Henry! You have come back to us. You must come in at once."

"Miss Chester," Fotherby began, once more feeling awkward about the young woman's familiarity. He pulled his hat from his head and bowed slightly. "I was unsure that I should simply appear on your doorstep."

She took his hand and guided him back across the road. "But of course you should, Henry. You have only just missed your uncle by three days. When did you arrive in London?"

"Only today, Miss Chester. Scarcely four hours ago."

"Papa will be so pleased to see you," she continued as she shut the door behind them. She pointed across at one of the black servants and turned to Fotherby. "Was that bag all you brought with you, Henry? Did you have no other belongings with you in Europe?"

"The army provides all the shelter I need. I do not need to carry blankets or pots like the rank and file."

The servant took the bag from Fotherby's outstretched hand and paused in surprise as the young surgeon thanked him, before he carried it through the door at the back of the entrance hall. Persephone laughed as she guided Henry through to the Drawing Room.

"Father has gone into Town, so there will be only you and I for supper. You must be starved. I heard reports that our army were not prepared for such an extended stay on the continent."

"It is true that I am hungry, Miss Chester."

"Then we shall eat at once." She walked over to pull the bell cord and a servant stepped into the room within seconds. "We shall eat now, Manny," she continued, addressing the young man who had just entered. Without pausing to allow Fotherby any argument, she walked through to the Dining Room, guiding him by the wrist.

"I am not ready to eat," Fotherby protested.

"Father is not here to object to your presentation, Henry, and certainly I do not care."

Fotherby took the seat that was pulled back for him after waiting for Persephone to be seated. She looked critically across at her servant as she regarded the drink in her crystal glass.

"I shall have you flogged," she began, pushing the glass from her. "What is this?"

"Elderflower cordial, my lady," Manny replied.

"Where is the wine?" she demanded.

"Pardon, my lady," came the timid response while Manny glanced sideward at Fotherby. "I believed you would wish to drink what your guest was drinking."

"But why have you not served him wine?"

"For I remember the gentleman from his last visit. He does not drink wine."

"Henry," Persephone began, her cheeks reddening as Fotherby knew his own were, "is this true?"

"It is true," he replied. "Thank you for remembering, Manny."

"It is my duty, sir."

Persephone, clearly disconcerted by this conversation, dismissed her servant. "Why do you not drink wine?"

"I like to maintain a clear head at all times, and I do not believe I can gain anything by drinking it. But I do not want to stop you."

"While you do not? I would not do that, Henry."

"I am quite used to my fellow officers continuing to drink while I do not."

"Uncle Paul does not abstain," she whispered.

"No, but my father does. And while I respect my uncle, I admire my father for his adherence to his moral code."

Persephone smiled across at him. She reached to one side and picked up a feather fan behind which she hid her face. The food was brought out after several minutes, and with its arrival the silence in the room was broken.

"Uncle Paul was well," Persephone's elegant voice chimed.

"That is good to hear," Fotherby replied, relieved to be leaving behind the earlier topic of conversation. "What does my uncle do when he stays here?"

"For the most part he and Father remember days spent overseas. Sometimes they visit Father's club, but both of them love playing cards, so Father's friends often come here. In truth, I find it rather dull when they play cards for I am so often left by myself. But Uncle Paul will also spend several evenings just sitting and talking with Father and me. And then, he talks about you."

"I do not wish to know what he says of me," Fotherby laughed. "I think at times I distress him with my attitude."

"Not at all, Henry. You, he holds in the most elevated place in his esteem. He loves you like a son, not a nephew."

They continued to talk while they ate, but Fotherby was pleased to be able to have a chance to wash and make himself presentable before Sir Manfred Chester returned to the house. His host was surprisingly pleased to have him under his roof once more and Fotherby was confused by the embrace that the older man offered him.

"Have you any other children, Sir Manfred?" Fotherby asked as they sat around the hearth that night.

"No. Persephone has been my only child. She will inherit everything."

Fotherby felt his eyes widen at this remark, unsure that wealth was something he should so openly discuss. He could find no words to offer in reply to this and so sought for a way to change the subject, feeling the weight of Persephone's gaze on him.

"I was told to attend an address in Westminster. Do you know this place, sir?" He presented the card to Sir Manfred and watched as the older man frowned.

"Who told you to go here?"

"My captain suggested that I should visit. What is this place?"

"It is a clubhouse," Sir Manfred replied. "If I might be as honest with you as I am with your uncle, it is not a place I would expect you to visit."

Fotherby took the card back and looked down at it, wondering what Peters had suggested to him. He felt that he had disappointed his host and, although Sir Manfred did not mention it again, he could not escape the feeling of guilt.

This remained with him as he retired for the night. He placed the card on the desk and sat looking at it as though it were alive and an animal he did not trust. He turned as there was a knock at the door and he stepped over to open it. Manny looked across at him and gave a brief smile as he lifted a jug.

"I have brought you some water, sir."

"Thank you, Manny." Fotherby stood back to allow him in. Manny walked in and set the jug down on the washstand before he bowed his head and turned to leave. "Do you know that address, Manny?"

"Sir?" the servant began. Fotherby handed him the card and Manny shook his head. "I cannot read, sir. Are you truly Mr Fotherby's nephew, sir?"

"Truly. Is it so difficult to believe?"

"You are not like him, sir. That is all." Manny smiled across as Fotherby felt his brow furrow. "Is there anything more I can get for you, sir?"

"No. Thank you, Manny."

Fotherby watched as the young servant left the room and he considered this brief conversation into the night while he penned a letter to his father. He rocked the blotter over the paper and read back its contents.

"My dear father, yesterday I returned safely to England and, while I must remain in London for a short time to conclude business and settle some affairs, Captain Peters has been gracious enough to allow me time to return home. Our campaign on the continent concluded unsuccessfully, though I feel that I have acquitted myself adequately. I am staying at the house of Uncle Paul's friend, Sir Manfred Chester. While I am hugely grateful for the welcome and generosity that has been shown to me, I find I am greatly confused by the running of this house and look forward to returning once more to the simple comforts of Wanderford Hall. I hope to return before the end of May. Your loving son, Henry."

The following morning Fotherby rose early, washed in cold water and sought for something that would make him look more presentable than the state in which he had arrived the previous afternoon. He was more than a little surprised to find that a suit of clothes was laid ready on the chair and a frock coat hung from the wardrobe door. They were his own, he realised, washed and pressed since his arrival and carrying a pleasing smell of lavender. After dressing and securing his hair, which had been left rather unkempt in the past year, he walked down the stairs and was met by Manny.

"I am afraid I overslept," Fotherby began, but Manny only smiled and shook his head.

"No, sir. You are the first of the gentle folk to rise." He straightened Fotherby's collar and brushed down the coat before he continued. "Is there anything I can get for you, sir?"

"Directions, Manny. I am returning to Westminster, but what is the best way to get there?"

"I shall have the carriage readied. Will you take breakfast first?"

"I will take coffee if it is offered," Fotherby replied, smiling across. "But I do not want the carriage. My feet will carry me far more safely. My uncle trusts horses, but I am afraid I find them a little too unpredictable."

Manny returned the smile before he went to fulfil Fotherby's wish, returning with a silver tray bearing a silver coffee pot with a china cup and saucer.

"You must go left out the house, sir. Then there is a broad road to the right that will carry you to the river. From there you cannot miss the palace of Westminster."

"Thank you, Manny. Have you been to Westminster?"

"On a few occasions, sir," came the reply, uncertainty in his low voice as he tried to unravel the meaning in the man's words. "But I have little time of my own and only visit when Sir Manfred has cause for me to do so."

Manny walked out and Fotherby drank the coffee in silence, rising to his feet to survey the paintings and trophies which lined the room. There was a strange, sad mystery that grew in him with each image he beheld. He wondered over the lives that were portrayed here, captured in the oil and canvas which illuminated the scorching sun and the endless blue sea.

"I miss that view the most."

Fotherby turned to face Persephone, who stood in the doorway.

"It looks like a beautiful place, if perhaps not such a beautiful situation."

"Oh, but it was, Henry. Before we were chased from it. Saint Domingue and Saint Vincent are magical islands. I wish more than anything that I could return there. Almost anything," she corrected, hiding her face behind the large feather fan. "Will you walk with me through the park today?"

"Miss Chester," he began, "I should love to escort you, but I have a duty first to fulfil. Might we not postpone such a walk until tomorrow?"

"Of course, Henry. But I shall not forget."

"Nor I, Miss Chester. I assure you."

Fotherby set the coffee cup once more upon the tray and excused himself. He followed Manny's directions and found that he reached Westminster palace before noon and now he looked down at the address on the card and considered how best to find it. He walked through the streets, taking circles and becoming so lost that he had to continue returning to the palace before he would begin walking in a different direction. He continued this measured routine until the bells sounded two o'clock when, at last, he located the street he had been encouraged to find. The clubhouse was halfway along the road, guarded by two men who both wore short white wigs and long navy blue jackets. They stood at the top of four steps, by a wide open door. A second door remained closed. Three carriages were lined up along the road, each with a driver wearing a different uniform, so none were cabs.

Fotherby looked at the card in his hand and matched the name to that on the brass plaque beside the entrance, unsure what this place was and why Peters would direct him here when it had offended his host. Fotherby was so clearly outclassed. He stood, for countless minutes, while the two footmen continued to watch him. Eventually two men walked out of the club. They were both strangers to him. They shared brief words with the doormen before they looked across at Fotherby and frowned slightly. Then they boarded one of the carriages and the driver moved on.

Unsure how to take such a slight, Fotherby walked away from the club, turning the card in his hands and counting the number of rails that he passed. He did everything he could think of to avoid solving the riddle of why he had been sent to this place. From the corner of his eye he could see more men leaving and the two remaining carriages were moved forward. He kept his face lowered, reluctant to exchange a glance with the drivers or the men who had stepped into the coaches, but he looked up as the first carriage was halted a little in front of him.

"I cannot believe it," a voice announced as the inhabitant of the carriage leapt down without waiting for the assistance of the driver or the footman. "Lieutenant Fotherby? Whatever are you doing here?"

In his mind, Fotherby had tried to understand what this place was that his captain had pointed him to. He had considered whether it was a military venue, or perhaps it was linked with his ambition in surgery. The one possibility he could never have guessed was the one that presented him with the face before him.

"Lord Barrington," Fotherby whispered, smiling in a confused manner, "I do not understand."

"You do not understand, Fotherby?" Portland laughed. "I do not understand. Surely it cannot be coincidence that has found you outside my club."

"No it is not. But it is far more confusing, sir, for it was Captain Peters who directed me here. Though he gave me no indication as to why."

"That is confusing. But now that you are here, Fotherby, you must come and meet my wife." He guided Fotherby to the carriage and waited until the surgeon had taken a seat before he stepped into it. The carriage moved forward once more. "When Brotherton, the club doorman, told us of a suspicious character, I must admit you were the last person who came to my mind."

"I must have seemed suspicious when I consider it. And, indeed, the two gentlemen who left before you did not seem happy with my being there."

"The taller of the two, he is not a man to make an enemy of," Portland laughed. "That was our Prime Minister."

Fotherby felt his brow furrow at this revelation but remained silent for a time before he asked, "What do you do in your club?"

"Regrettably, we talk." A swift change came over his friend as he looked out of the window. "We talk. For there is little more we can do. It is frustrating beyond measure."

"You are involved in the work of the Prime Minister?"

"It is not his work. It is his hopes." Portland turned to his friend and offered half a smile. "I will let my wife explain it, Fotherby, for she is far more eloquent than I. I become angry about it, she does not. But come, tell me, when did you return to England?"

"Two days ago. Peters seems sure that we will be called out once more, but he has told me I should return to Derbyshire."

"He will see you succeed, Fotherby. He wants to create the best future for you."

"I feel I have to ask you," Fotherby muttered and Portland smiled slightly as Fotherby frowned, "Peters told me that he could not find me a better friend than you. Why, then, does he dislike what you discuss with your friends?"

"He said that?" Portland muttered.

"He said that, since I worked for the king, I should not associate myself with your cause. But that there was no friend truer than you."

"When you meet Rosanna, she will answer your questions."

"Did you return to Cornwall?"

"Yes, I returned but we have a great cause here in the city that requires my presence." Portland smiled across at Fotherby as the carriage stopped. "Come and meet my wife."

Fotherby watched as Portland stepped out of the carriage before he followed him and looked at the house before him. They were on a quiet street, standing before a small house with a large semicircular porch, and it was to this that Portland guided him. The door was opened by a man who wore a long red coat and stepped back to allow the two men admittance.

"Thank you, Chilvers," Portland began, pulling the wig from his head and tapping the servant's shoulder. Chilvers was an old man with white, wispy hair and a thin face, who smiled across at his master. "Where is Rosie? I have someone I would like her to meet."

"Lady Barrington is in the Parlour, I believe, sir. But she is in a lesson."

"Then before I interrupt her I shall introduce you to my esteemed friend." Portland indicated to Fotherby who stepped forward tentatively. "Chilvers, this is Lieutenant Henry Fotherby, a great friend who helped me survive the last two years. Fotherby, this is Chilvers, the poor soul who is left to correct all my mistakes."

"An honour to meet you, Lieutenant," Chilvers began, as Fotherby bowed his head slightly.

"Fotherby," Portland laughed, "you must come and sit for a time, you look exhausted. Chilvers, arrange a drink for Fotherby, please. I shall be unpopular, I know, but I must go and fetch my wife." Portland guided Fotherby, who followed silently, into a large study and at once the sound of music filled the air. Someone was playing a lively tune on a pianoforte in the room beyond and Fotherby felt a smile cross his face. It stopped abruptly as a discordant note sounded, jarring the performance.

"It is hopeless," he heard a woman's voice announce as Portland opened the door.

Chilvers invited Fotherby to take a seat in a leather armchair by the empty fireplace.

"What can I get you to drink, Lieutenant?"

"Whatever is convenient, Mr Chilvers, please."

Chilvers disappeared, leaving Fotherby alone in the room. It was unlike any room he had ever seen before. There was a large tapestry over the fireplace that portrayed two unicorns bowing before a tree, and around the edge were winged cherubs and creatures that had surely come from imagination. It was not the only image to line the walls - there were many paintings of men and women who Fotherby assumed were ancestors of Lord Barrington - but it was by far the most striking. The desk was immaculately ordered. There were no books left on it as in his father's study, and all the papers were neatly arranged into three piles, unlike his uncle's desk which was cluttered and full. A bronze inkwell with two pens rested at the back, close to where he sat.

Fotherby could hear a conversation taking place in the Parlour and he suddenly felt conspicuous. He rose to his feet and walked to the window that overlooked the quiet road where gentlemen and ladies promenaded, each with the smiles and expressions of people who had no cares in the world. There were the same type of houses on the other side of the street and Fotherby found himself contemplating the people who lived there, wondering at the lives they led and the comfort they lived in. Such thoughts led him back to considering the army and the war they had failed to win. He wondered, too, why his captain was so certain they would be returning to war, and considered what Peters had sought to protect him from in his friendship with Portland. Eager to escape such thoughts he began counting the rods in the railing before the house, and was still doing this when Portland re-entered the room.

"My dear Fotherby," he laughed. "Has Chilvers not found you a drink yet?"

Fotherby turned and smiled across at him but shook his head.

"Poor Chilvers," Portland muttered. "He has worked here for almost five decades. He forgets so many things, but I cannot find it in my heart to dismiss him. Ah," Portland added as he turned back to the Parlour and then to Fotherby once more. "Fotherby, allow me to introduce my wife, Lady Barrington. Rosanna, this is Lieutenant Henry Fotherby."

To his immediate shame, Fotherby had decided in his head what Portland's wife should look like. He had imagined her to be beautiful beyond any other living soul and to be perhaps his own age and of a delicate build. In truth, all these things were accurate, except that she was perhaps a little younger. An enormous smile filled her face as she entered.

"You must forgive me, Lieutenant Fotherby. I have struggled with Mr Mozart's sonata for so long, I was adamant that I should conquer it today."

"I have arrived unannounced and unexpected, Lady Barrington. It is I who should ask forgiveness of you." He took in her looks now as he bowed his head, for she was in no way the wife he had expected his friend to have, yet at once Peters' objections became clear. She had jet black hair that was fastened up in a thick red ribbon. Her eyes were exactly as Portland had described them, for they were like two stars in the midnight of her black face. She wore a pair of beautiful pearl earrings that only made her perfect smile more radiant. All the while that he took this in, she watched his gaze, trying to gauge what he was thinking.

"I am not what you expected, Lieutenant Fotherby. I can see that in your face."

"Perhaps not," Portland whispered in a tone that could have given the two words a hundred meanings.

"I confess," Fotherby began as he stepped forward, taking her hand and bowing so low to kiss it. "My prejudices did not anticipate such a revelation. But all the same I am as spellbound as your husband by the image before me."

Lady Barrington laughed as she looked across at her husband. "Lieutenant Fotherby, you are all the things Philip said you were. I am very pleased to have you as a guest."

"Thank you, Lady Barrington. But tell me, do you prefer Mr Mozart's work to that of Mr Haydn? For I find Haydn far more to my liking."

"But I love Haydn!" she replied happily. "Indeed, last year I attended a concert he gave here in London. Only I find Mozart's music so much harder to play that I am determined to conquer it."

Portland watched as the two of them talked happily together. He felt unsure whenever he introduced his wife to anyone, but never ashamed, for he worried always how she would be received. But his friend had proved himself a true gentleman, as Portland had been so sure he would.

"I must excuse myself, gentlemen," Lady Barrington announced after a time. "For I was told that Chilvers would be bringing a drink and I believe I must discover what has happened to him."

She walked out of the room, her beautiful dress hiding her feet so that she appeared to glide. Portland watched her go with a smile before he turned back to Fotherby, who was studying him thoughtfully. Trying to ignore this, Portland indicated to one of the chairs and waited until Fotherby sat before he took another.

"I am not a medical dilemma, Fotherby," he laughed. "You need not stare at me so! Tell me, what do you think of my beautiful wife?"

"I think she is everything you said she was. But I cannot help but wonder why you did not tell me all she was. Why, when this is what Peters most certainly meant, did you not tell me?"

"I do not want you to lose your sponsor in Captain Peters, Fotherby. But when he sent you to the club I realised that you would not lose him. I did not want you to become embroiled in our political battle when you did not fully appreciate what was being fought for."

"Where did you meet Lady Barrington?" Fotherby asked softly, wishing to turn the conversation from his captain.

"My grandfather had land in Saint-Domingue, for he married the daughter of a French colonist. He travelled out there over twenty years ago, to oversee the work that was being done, and found Rosanna's mother. She was trying to rid herself of the child she carried, for she could not bear the thought that her daughter would be raised in the most vile form of slavery. You are a medical man, Fotherby, you can imagine the scene perhaps better than I." Portland lowered his gaze from his friend, whose face was set firm. "My grandfather returned to England with her, but she died on the boat journey here. But not before Rosanna was born. Grandfather brought her into our house as a sister to Cassandra and me. He was not well met in this. My uncle would not tolerate it, having a black child in the house. So my grandfather passed the inheritance on to my father, who was a younger brother. Father dropped the name Bryn-Portland in favour of simply Portland, for our Welsh family were still slave owners. And that, dear Fotherby, is what Captain Peters objected to."

Portland lifted his eyes once more to his friend as he concluded his telling of the bitter tale. Fotherby returned his gaze with a look that spoke of utter turmoil and, indeed, that was what he was feeling. It seemed wrong to him that any human should seek to enslave another, that a mother could be so desperate to spare her child this hopeless life she should seek to kill it, and so despicable that anyone could condone it. Yet Captain Peters was not a bad man. He had supported Fotherby to such a great extent, funding his exam, allowing him the time to return home, and restoring to health any men who he could help, irrespective of rank or status.

"That is what we discuss at our club, Fotherby. The injustice of it all. And imagine," Portland continued, a rueful smile on his face. "Imagine, Fotherby, loving a woman so much, and she loving you in return, but her not marrying you for fear of bringing you disgrace. Four times I had to beg Rosie to marry me, for she did not wish to bring shame to me. Shame simply because she was born black and I white. That is not what God wanted of us, Fotherby, I know it."

"What changed her mind on the fourth occasion?"

"My father," Portland laughed. "He told Rosie that any son who failed to secure his heart's affairs could never secure the affairs of the Manor. He said he would disinherit me. To this day I am not sure if he meant it, or simply wanted to bring us together."

"You come from a very interesting family, Lord Barrington." Fotherby smiled across at him. "But I do believe you have a war worth fighting."

"The more I learn of you, Fotherby, the better I like you. That is a rare thing to find in a man. But if we are to be friends, please do not address me as Lord Barrington. Call me Portland."

"And what should I call Lady Barrington?"

"Rosanna," she announced as she walked into the room. "That is the name my mother gave me. I have no doubt that Philip has already told you about her."

"That is true," Fotherby said softly. "But I cannot bring myself to address you with such vulgar familiarity. You are far higher in society than I."

"You are a dear man, Lieutenant," she whispered. "Call me Mrs Portland if you must, but I would rather you called me Rosanna."

Lady Barrington had returned with Chilvers, who was carrying a tray with a teapot and three small bowls. The old man began filling the bowls from the teapot and Fotherby felt his brow furrow in confusion, but all the same he took the bowl that was offered and thanked him. Portland smiled across at his friend who looked doubtfully at the bowl while Lady Barrington tutted disapprovingly at her husband.

"In China," she began to explain, "tea is sometimes drunk from bowls like this."

"Have you been to China?" Fotherby asked.

"No," she replied softly. "But Grandfather travelled everywhere."

Fotherby lifted the bowl to his lips and sipped the tea. For the rest of the day Fotherby remained in the home of his good friend and did not depart until the sun was casting long shadows outside. Now, he rose to his feet and graciously thanked his hosts before promising to return and visit them once more. He would have happily walked back into Mayfair, but Portland was insistent that Fotherby should take the carriage and so it was readied for the journey while Fotherby bade goodnight to them both.

"You must come and see us soon, Lieutenant Fotherby," Lady Barrington announced. "I owe you so much for protecting Philip when you were both in Flanders."

"I did nothing to protect him, Mrs Portland. Indeed, he assisted me. But you may rely upon my returning, for I have thoroughly enjoyed today and the company of you both."

"You are a rare gentleman, Lieutenant Henry Fotherby," she replied, leaning against her husband who wrapped his arm about her shoulders.

Fotherby thanked Chilvers for handing him his hat, before he stepped out into the sunset. The carriage journey lasted longer than he expected and, by the time he arrived outside Sir Manfred's house, the sunlight had vanished from the sky and night was upon him. He stepped quickly up to the front door and it was opened at once by one of the black servants.

"You are a busy gentleman, Lieutenant Fotherby," Sir Manfred remarked that evening as he sat drinking a glass of claret. "You vanish so early in the morning and we do not see you again until the sun has set."

"Forgive me," Fotherby replied. "I had to see a dear friend. I assured him I would seek him out when I returned to England."

"But you are taking me walking tomorrow, are you not, Henry?" Persephone's voice rang.

"Indeed, Miss Chester. I could not forget that, though you may have to lead me to a suitable place, for I know London as little as Paris."

"Of course I shall, Henry," she laughed, while her father pursed his lips to keep from doing the same.

Fotherby's misgivings concerning his hosts deepened as he lay in bed the following morning, trying to find the courage to rise and journey out. Miss Persephone Chester was certainly beautiful. She was rich and capable of holding a conversation on almost any topic. But Fotherby could not reconcile himself with the constant questioning he had about her social beliefs. It was strange that Peters had warned him about Portland on account of him marrying a black woman when Fotherby felt far less comfortable in a house full of black servants.

He looked across at the door as there was a light knock upon it. For a time he was content to ignore it and pretend that he had not heard, but it sounded again only louder than the first.

"Yes?" he called out gingerly, and the door was opened quietly by Manny.

"Miss Chester is downstairs. Waiting, sir."

"Of course," Fotherby whispered, hoping that she had forgotten.

Manny smiled slightly, perhaps more than he was permitted to, at this response, but remained silent as he helped Fotherby dress. Finally, as he brushed down the frock coat that the young surgeon wore, Fotherby broke the silence.

"Were you born here, Manny?"

"Here in Mayfair?" he asked back before he shook his head and continued. "No, sir, I was born on the ocean."

"On your way to England?"

"No, sir," the black man replied once more, his voice becoming uncomfortable. "Between Africa and the Americas."

"I met a black lady yesterday," Fotherby mused, uncertain that he should push this topic with the young man, who was clearly becoming unsettled. But he felt he had to know the answers to his questions and neither the Chesters nor the Portlands could provide them. "She, too, was born on a boat journey, but the journey to England."

"A lady?" Manny asked, his voice calming. "You mean a servant, surely?"

"No. She is the wife of my dear friend, Lord Barrington. And she is a Lady by all standards of the word."

"Then her owner was better to her than mine shall ever be."

"You are not slaves here."

"In all but name, Lieutenant Fotherby. Your friend sounds like a good man to marry a black wife."

"Good?" Fotherby choked on the word before he shook his head. "In love. But he is certainly not a man to compromise for social constraints. Lady Barrington was raised as a sister to him, and they fell in love."

"You are a strange man, Lieutenant Fotherby. I have never met a man like you, nor your friend. To most I am a possession, a tool to assist."

"But, Manny, you are a human being. As Lady Barrington is and as I am."

"Do you seek to ensnare me?" Manny asked angrily. But it was fear that drove his anger, not maliciousness. "Since you are so interested I can detail for you my worth in ten seconds, Lieutenant Fotherby. I was born in the cramped squalor of a slave ship hull. When Sir Manfred could not sell me for what he deemed was my worth, I returned with him as his own servant to England. My apologies, sir. I believe I have taken too much of your time."

Fotherby's gaze never altered, although he could feel the dizziness that accompanied the determination to withhold tears. Manny walked out of the room without looking back at Fotherby, who lowered his head, feeling overwhelming guilt at pressing the young servant on the topic. After several minutes he walked from the room and forced a smile as he saw Persephone waiting at the foot of the stairs between the two huge marble statues.

"I had almost despaired of you, Henry," she began, her musical voice making each word beautiful.

"I had not forgotten, Miss Chester. How could I?"

"My dear Henry, your manners are so impeccable that I knew you would not."

Having taken so long to appear downstairs, Fotherby did not wish to take longer by breakfasting but offered her his arm and smiled down as she accepted it. They walked out of the house and into the radiance of the spring morning. Silence accompanied them for a time before Persephone spoke.

"Uncle Paul talks continuously. Yet you are as quiet a man as I have ever met."

"Perhaps it is because my uncle talks so much that I remain so quiet," Fotherby replied with a smile. "My uncle and my father are as different as brothers can be, and I am far more like my father."

"Did you inherit nothing from your mother?"

"I do not know. I never knew her. But my father has told me on occasions that I am like her in some ways."

"I imagine it is your eyes, Henry," she continued, turning to study him as they walked towards a wrought iron fence. She waited until he opened a gate and she stepped through. "Your eyes are nothing like Uncle Paul's eyes."

"I believe my uncle's looks changed greatly while he was in the West Indies."

"Where have you travelled to, Henry?"

"India," Fotherby whispered in reply. "Flanders. That is all."

"Is India as beautiful as the West Indies?"

"I have never been to the West Indies. But I loved India. It was open and rich. I would return once more if I could."

"But then why do you not go? You are a gentleman of money and property. You should easily afford to go."

"No. I have a duty, and a duty I love, to help and serve the men of my regiment."

"I confess," she replied, shaking her head as she considered his words. "I do not understand why you chose to work when you will be rich beyond measure upon your inheritance."

"Miss Chester," Fotherby began, "far be it from me to contradict a lady, but I feel I must correct you. Whatever my uncle has told you, Wanderford Hall is a small country estate and I shall never be as rich as you seem to believe."

"Perhaps your house is small, Henry, but Uncle Paul owns seven mills in the north and still has lands in Saint Vincent. You shall be very well provided for." She stared up at him and lifted her gloved hand to her mouth. "You did not know you were to inherit your uncle's wealth?"

"No, I had not thought of it. Nor did I know that he has lands in the West Indies."

"One day you must journey there, for it will rival India in your affections. It is so beautiful."

"I think I have heard enough of Saint Vincent and Saint Domingue without ever wishing to visit. I could not bear to witness the scenes that have been described to me."

"You have spoken to Manny, then," she said with a disapproving tone. "I have warned Father about the impact of keeping such a hot-tempered man. He has no place talking to you."

"It was not him," Fotherby began, trying to defend the man from whom he had demanded an answer. "I met a lady yesterday, Lady Barrington, and her mother was a slave in Saint Domingue."

"A black lady?" Persephone's tone made her words sound as though the very idea disgusted her. "And she is the wife of your friend?"

"Indeed." Fotherby forced himself to remember that etiquette dictated he should continue to hold this lady's arm whilst every principle in him wished to distance himself from her with each comment she made.

"I hope you have not hopes of winning such a lady, Henry. It is quite wrong and contradicts the very nature of our society."

"So my captain tells me. But Lady Barrington is not the lady who holds my affection." He felt his cheeks redden as he spoke and Persephone smiled gently across at him.

"You need not blush, Henry," she whispered, her tone soft. "Gentlemen may fall in love, you know. And those who fall deepest should speak more of it."

"You are very gracious, Miss Chester, but I feel that every word I utter or every move I make, I somehow offend society more and more."

Both of them fell silent for a time. They were not alone in this park, and each couple they encountered would politely greet the other until both of them felt a little foolish with such strutting and Fotherby escorted Persephone to one of the benches. When she was seated he rested beside her and the two talked happily. They discussed trivial issues such as the weather and Fotherby explained about many of the plants which were growing in the gardens there.

Despite his misgivings about Miss Persephone Chester, Fotherby was forced to admit to himself that he began to enjoy her company. And as the day wore on and they returned once more to the house, Fotherby was sorry their conversation was over.

"I have enjoyed this morning, Henry," Persephone began as she stepped into the house.

"As have I, Miss Chester. Thank you."

"Someone left this for you, sir," Manny began as he stepped over to the two of them and offered a silver platter to Fotherby.

"Thank you," Fotherby whispered as he picked up the letter that rested on it.

"Don't thank him, Henry," Persephone laughed. "He is doing his job, only."

Any affection that Fotherby had felt during their outing faded away as he watched Manny bow before walking away. Persephone called after him, ordering that dinner should be readied soon, before she walked through to the Drawing Room. He looked at the letter in his hand and stared at the writing, for he did not recognise it and he wondered who could have known to find him here. Still standing in the entrance hall, he opened the letter and read through it.

"Lieutenant Fotherby, I understand that you have returned once more from your duties overseas. I should like to invite you to Horse Guards tomorrow at midday, for there are matters I wish to discuss with you. I shall expect you. Regards, Major Josiah Tenterchilt."

This brief epistle, from a man he scarcely knew, and in such a formal tone, gave Fotherby a great cause for concern. As the day continued he forgot his confusion about, and distaste of, the question of slavery and the freedom of men, and considered only the baffling nature of the note he had received.

The remainder of the day passed by in this manner and he retired early to bed. However he spent several minutes pacing the floor of the room, and read the letter so many times that the four lines were etched in his memory. He felt that, with the clipped manner of address, the major was accusing him, and Fotherby considered all that had happened with regard to Major Tenterchilt. As he stood in the centre of his room, having shed his coat and shirt, he wondered at how the gentleman, as crippled as Mr Tenterchilt had been, could not only have returned to the army, but furthermore have been given a promotion.

Fotherby marched to the door as a knock sounded and he stood back to allow Manny into the room. The black man kept his face lowered as he shuffled in and waited until Fotherby closed the door before he offered an explanation.

"I wished to apologise to you, sir."

"Whatever for?" Fotherby began. "It is I who should apologise to you for pressing you on such a distressing topic."

"I believed that Miss Chester wished you to catch me out in my behaviour. But I see that you have not told her of our conversation earlier. I misjudged you, sir. And I am sorry for it."

"All is forgiven, Manny. Though, did you see the man who delivered this letter?" Fotherby lifted the paper that he still carried.

"No, sir. I am your servant in this house. Another deals with the door while you are here."

"It is a tightly run ship, this house, is it not?"

"It is a cruelly run house, sir. And I find myself wishing to know your friend to learn what help he can give to us."

"My friend?"

"The man who married where his heart lay, irrespective of colour."

"Ah," Fotherby said, a proud smile crossing his face. "He is a great man."

Manny, having made his apology, excused himself from the room and Fotherby got ready for bed. Sleep was a long time coming, but when it did arrive he slept deeply, without dreams.

It was still dark outside when he was awoken. He could not be sure what the time was, nor for how long he had slept, but something had pulled him from his slumber. There was a knock on the door to his room, impatient and loud, and he realised that it was the first knock that had awoken him. Rising to his feet and rubbing his eyes sleepily, he stepped over to the door, pulling it open. Almost instantly he pushed the door closed once more, so that it was only slightly open, as he recognised Persephone.

"What can I help you with, Miss Chester?" he whispered, his cheeks blooming as he peered around the door.

"I came to see you, dear Henry," her voice rang, not caring who in the house she would awaken with the beautiful sound. "And you need not be so bashful. In Saint Vincent the slaves often work without shirtsleeves and some work naked."

"How can I help you, Miss Chester?"

"What must I do for you to call me Persephone?" She fanned herself with the great feathers of her fan, looking critically at the form of the young surgeon who sought for any way possible to persuade her to leave. Placing her free hand on the door, she pushed against it. "When we are married you must call me Persephone."

"Married?" Fotherby repeated.

"But of course. Both Father and Uncle Paul have spoken on little else for the past three years. We are to be married, Henry."

"But I don't know you and you know nothing of me."

"You mean you knew nothing of this?" Persephone demanded. "All this time I believed you were being well-mannered but in fact it was only that you were ignorant."

Fotherby was unsure that he should feel as relieved as he did by such a statement and, for a moment, he wanted to contradict her. But as she turned on her heel and walked away, fluttering her fan in angry rejection, he gratefully closed the door and pressed himself against it.

He rose early the next morning and began packing his few belongings into the bag he had carried from the continent. By the time he had made his way downstairs both Sir Manfred and Persephone were sitting at the table. Persephone glared at him as he entered and, trying to ignore this reception, he turned to Sir Manfred.

"Thank you for your kind hospitality, sir, but I intend to return to Derbyshire once I have responded to the invitation I received yesterday."

"Of course you are free to leave as you wish, Lieutenant Fotherby." Sir Manfred glanced at his daughter who fanned herself furiously as she watched the young surgeon. "And you shall leave with our blessing, will he not, Persephone?"

Persephone made no answer but rose to her feet and left the room. The two men ate in silence and Fotherby rose as soon as he had finished.

"Do not think badly of my daughter, Lieutenant. She has become accustomed to being unchallenged, but she must learn to take criticism before she can be married."

"But not to me, sir. I have a respect for many aspects of your daughter, but that is where my affection ends."

"Thank you for your candour, Lieutenant."

Fotherby was unsure whether the older man was truly thankful, but he smiled across and left the room before he collected his bag and rushed down the white marble stairs once more. Manny stood at the bottom and smiled across.

"We shall miss you here, Lieutenant Fotherby. Perhaps when your uncle visits us, you might join him?"

"In truth, Manny," Fotherby sighed. "I do not expect to be made welcome here again, and I know there are some words of a less amicable nature that I must share with my uncle."

"We shall welcome you, sir. For what it is worth, we below stairs shall welcome you."

"It is worth a great deal, Manny."

"We have something for you, sir. A gift to thank you for your kind treatment." Manny pulled a small cotton pouch from his pocket and offered it to Fotherby. "It is quinine, sir, that I believe you call Jesuits' Bark."

Fotherby blinked in surprise at the young man, for quinine was sold at such a high price that these servants might just as well have handed him a crown. "Thank you, Manny. Thank you so much." Manny smiled as he opened the door and Fotherby stepped out into London.

# Chapter Ten
## *The Bravest Heart*

Fotherby walked through London, watching as the carriages passed him by, amazed by the tireless yet mindless business that the capital bred. Indeed, he sought for anything to distract him from the imminent meeting, for he was concerned by what message awaited him when he reached Horse Guards. He arrived twenty minutes early and simply stared at the impressive and imposing building from the road at the front. When the church towers rang out midday he prepared to face Major Tenterchilt and whatever topic he wished to discuss. He was not surprised, therefore, to find the major walking purposefully toward him as he stepped into the building. Major Tenterchilt's eyes narrowed as he regarded the young man before him but, recalling the correct etiquette, he bowed slightly. Fotherby felt compelled to do the same before he whispered,

"What is it that you wished to talk to me about, sir?"

"I?" the major demanded, his tone as angry as his face. "I did not wish to talk to you of anything."

"I do not understand," Fotherby muttered, producing the letter he had received yesterday. "You clearly stated that you wished to discuss some matters with me."

The other man snatched the paper and looked at it thoughtfully. "This is not my hand, Lieutenant Fotherby as, I suspect, this is not yours." He produced a letter in the same hand and handed it to the surgeon.

"Major Tenterchilt," Fotherby muttered aloud as he read the letter, "Having returned from our failed war in Flanders there are matters I must discuss with you. I, therefore, request that you meet me midday tomorrow at Horse Guards. Regards, Lieutenant Fotherby." He shook his head quickly. "I assure you, sir, I never sent this letter. It is neither my hand nor my style."

"Someone is playing us for fools, Lieutenant," Tenterchilt replied. "Though what they can hope to achieve, I cannot say. But come," the major went on, his voice softening in the discovery that the man before him was as innocent as himself, "our time need not be wasted. I am finished here for the day and Mrs Tenterchilt could not be happier than if you should grace us with your presence. You must return with me to Chanter's House."

"Nothing would give me greater pleasure than to see Mrs Tenterchilt, but I was to quit London the moment our meeting had ended and return to Derbyshire, for I have left my lodgings."

"Quit London? My good man, have you not scarcely arrived? You must stay with Mrs Tenterchilt and myself for a time."

Major Tenterchilt would not be swayed and, after collecting his cane, he guided Fotherby into his carriage and the two journeyed on to the major's townhouse. Fotherby stepped out on the drive and blinked in surprise, for Chanter's House could easily have swallowed both Portland's and Sir Manfred's houses together. Major Tenterchilt did not seem to notice this but stepped through the door, which was opened by a footman to whom he handed his hat and gloves.

"My dear!" Major Tenterchilt called out. "You will not believe who I discovered at the doors of Horse Guards."

As he spoke Fotherby looked up at the gallery before him to see Mrs Tenterchilt appear. She looked down and at once a smile caught her features as she stepped down the polished wooden stairs and stood beside her husband to address the younger man.

"Lieutenant Fotherby," she began warmly, "you sought us out after all. I am so glad to welcome you into our house."

"Thank you, Mrs Tenterchilt, but it is I who am pleased beyond measure to have been invited. Though I am unsure who concocted such a plan that gave me a sleepless night, I am greatly pleased with its outcome."

To Fotherby's embarrassment, the Tenterchilts refused to accept that he wished to leave London, and that evening found him sitting at a long table with Major and Mrs Tenterchilt.

"I am so glad that you have visited us at last, Lieutenant." Mrs Tenterchilt sat opposite him and smiled across. "It is the least we can offer you for the great service that you wrought for dear Major Tenterchilt. I am sorry that our daughters are not here to make your acquaintance. They are visiting their cousins in Yorkshire."

"I am sorry to miss them," Fotherby replied politely. "I must congratulate you though, Major, on your return to the army."

"You sound as surprised as I, Lieutenant," the major laughed. "Indeed, I still have not discovered who my benefactor was, for I was put forward for my new post by someone. It does not compare to raising arms, but I am able once more to hold my head high. And I can remain with Mrs Tenterchilt, too."

Fotherby smiled slightly before he continued. "Your company are in safe hands, sir. I know the gentleman who was promoted into the position, for when Colonel

Pottinger was transferred to the West Indies, Captain Portland was not deemed a wise man to send."

"Portland?" Major Tenterchilt whispered. "I believed Lord Barrington had inherited the company."

"Indeed. But Lord Barrington's name is Portland."

"I am pleased that the company is well led," Mrs Tenterchilt replied, seeing a frown cross her husband's face and not wishing to offend their guest.

"I know of this man." This was all that the major would say on the matter and Fotherby began to feel that he had once more offended his host in his admiration of Lord Barrington. Mrs Tenterchilt, by contrast, was very happy to discuss Fotherby's friend and rained almost as much grateful praise upon Portland as she did on Fotherby.

"He is the gentleman who carried Major Tenterchilt back," she whispered at length, her face paling as she recalled that day. "Why, Lieutenant Fotherby," she continued, trying to turn her mind to something else. "You have not touched the claret. Is it not to your liking?"

Fotherby looked at the glass before him and shook his head slightly, feeling that he only enhanced the Tenterchilts' disappointment in him as he explained his abstinence. He was shown to his room by one of the servants later in the evening and he stared out of the enormous window, down over the lawn to the lights beyond. He sat on the wide window ledge watching the view with little admiration. Was the issue of Portland's black wife really enough to create such animosity within the country? He walked beside the greatest men and carried a title that should have granted him almost anything he desired. Why then did so many hate him? He recalled his uncle's words about Fotherby's duty to marry and marry well, and questioned once more that ladies might place their hearts where they chose whilst gentlemen had always to carry duty before love. And now his thoughts turned to Miss Kitty Simmons, and he wondered if she was somewhere out amongst the lights, and a faint smile caught his features. Her nervous laugh had seemed like music to his ears and the clear eyes in her pale face had enticed him, capturing his heart and his soul.

She was the last thing he considered before sleep claimed him, and the first as he awoke in the morning. This peculiar daze that she had placed on him lingered as he washed and dressed, and he was only awoken from it when he heard a noise outside his door. He pulled it open and watched as the dog that had been lying down rose to its feet and gave a drawn out yawn while it stretched and padded past him and into the room.

"You must excuse Gulliver," Mrs Tenterchilt said softly as she stepped along the corridor. "He is so used to having the whole house to run in. But he is not normally so calm around strangers. Do you keep dogs in Derbyshire, Lieutenant?"

"My uncle does. But they stay in the kennels."

"I think the children and I are the only ones who are pleased to have Gulliver in the house. The major wanted him in a kennel, but he is the only thing that calms Catherine, our youngest daughter."

They walked down the stairs as they talked, discussing Mrs Tenterchilt's family and Fotherby's family and house in Derbyshire. As their conversation continued, Fotherby came to better understand his hosts. Major Tenterchilt's commitment to the army was second to none and the return to this cause, though it confused Mrs Tenterchilt, had given a renewed pride to both Major and Mrs Tenterchilt.

"But, truthfully," Mrs Tenterchilt continued at the end of breakfast, "my husband owes his very life to you, Lieutenant. It is not a debt that can be forgotten."

"I did my duty by him, Mrs Tenterchilt. I joined the army solely for that purpose. It was unthinkable that he should die when I could save him. And it was the decision that saw me qualify, so you have repaid any debt that you believe was owed."

"What shall you do today, Lieutenant? Have you work in London?"

"No, Mrs Tenterchilt. Indeed, when I met the major I had a resolve to return to Derbyshire at once. But I am grateful to you both for allowing me to stay."

"What sort of people would we be if we did not? No, I am so happy to welcome you to Chanter's House."

"Then perhaps I shall seek out Lord Barrington."

"But you must invite him here, too. And Lady Barrington. Come," she continued, becoming as giddy and eager as a child, "On Saturday next will shall dine together here."

"But Major Tenterchilt may not approve."

"Nonsense, Lieutenant. He may rule his army from Horse Guards, but I shall never relinquish the rule of my home."

Despite Fotherby's attempts to change Mrs Tenterchilt's mind, her resolve was strong. Therefore, when he reached the neat white fronted house two hours after this conversation, it was as a messenger with a written invitation from Mrs Tenterchilt on behalf of her husband who, Fotherby was quite certain, would not approve if he had known. He knocked on the door timidly and glanced up and down the street, which was absolutely silent, before he turned from the door and walked back down the road unsure where he was heading to or why.

"Why, Lieutenant Fotherby," announced a voice just in front of him. "Have you come to visit Lord Barrington?"

Fotherby lifted his downcast gaze to meet the beautiful, strong gaze of Lady Barrington who was walking alongside another, much younger lady. "I came with an invitation, Lady Barrington. But I do not wish to interrupt you. May I escort you both?"

"Indeed you may," she replied, taking his left arm and Fotherby felt slightly uncomfortable as he offered his right to the other woman. "You seem unsure, Lieutenant. Allow me to introduce Delphina Portland, Lord Barrington's youngest sister."

"Good day, Lieutenant Fotherby," the young woman said politely before she laughed and leaned forward to talk to her sister-in-law. "You were right about his height, Rosie. I feel like a child once more."

"Indeed," she replied, smiling up at him briefly before she turned back to the young woman. "It is a pity that Mr Fotherby is a surgeon, for I believe he would look mighty strong at the head of a column."

Delphina laughed, squeezing his arm slightly. "We mean no offence, Lieutenant. Truly."

"Indeed, Miss Portland," he replied gently, "I assure you, none is taken."

He allowed the ladies to relinquish their hold upon him as they stepped into the house. Delphina surrendered her shawl to Chilvers and Lady Barrington unfastened her own bonnet before she took Fotherby's hand and guided him into the house.

"But I am not Miss Portland," Delphina continued, smiling across at him. "Cassandra, my older sister, is Miss Portland." She thanked Chilvers, kissing him on the cheek.

"Delphi arrived from Cornwall yesterday, Lieutenant," Lady Barrington continued as she guided the pair through the room with the tapestry and into the Music Room beyond.

"But surely you did not travel alone, Miss Delphina?"

"No. I came with my brother Harry."

"Harry?" Fotherby whispered. "There are so many of you."

"His real name is Harris," Lady Barrington began, "but he hates it, so we call him Harry."

"And is he here, too?"

"No. Harry is in the court. He is a close friend of a gentleman there." She turned quickly to Lady

Barrington and smiled slightly. "Might I withdraw, Rosie? I feel so terribly tired."

"Of course, my dear." Lady Barrington stepped over to her and the two spoke in whispers that Fotherby tried hard not to hear.

"You must excuse me, Lieutenant."

"It has been a pleasure to meet you, Miss Delphina."

She smiled across at him and both he and Lady Barrington watched as she left the room, closing the door so quietly as she left that it scarcely interrupted their silence.

"Delphi is a dear, sweet child," Lady Barrington announced at last as she turned back to him and smiled. "So very different from Harry. He dropped her here last night and at once left to find his friend."

"She seems very fragile to be travelling such a distance."

"Indeed," she replied as she offered him a chair. "But, come, tell me what brought you to our house. For though I am so pleased to see you, I do not believe you are the sort of gentleman who does anything without purpose."

"I came with an invitation for you and Lord Barrington."

"That is most kind," she whispered, surprise clear in her tone. "Who might this invitation be from?"

"Major and Mrs Tenterchilt. It is an invitation for dinner on Saturday next." He produced the invitation and handed it to her. "But if Miss Delphina is here still then I am certain another time can be arranged."

"That is a worry for dear Philip," she sighed as she lifted her gaze to his own. "We none of us know how long Delphina will be here."

"Is it consumption?" Fotherby asked and was met with an expression of absolute heartbreak, while Lady Barrington nodded slowly.

"You knew, then? And yet you were not worried to let her take your arm?"

Fotherby shook his head slightly. "I chose a path that will take me to all manner of ailments, and I hope to help those afflicted, not flee from them."

"You are a rare man indeed, Lieutenant Fotherby." She reached over and took his hand. "I see why Philip found such friendship with you."

For the following two days Fotherby divided his time between the Portlands and the Tenterchilts, enjoying the company of both in their different ways. With the major he discussed war and the likelihood of journeying once more abroad. With Mrs Tenterchilt he discussed botany, for she was greatly proud of her hothouse and the species she grew in it. With Lord and Lady Barrington he would talk on many topics, allowing them to choose the subjects, for he could not shake the feeling that etiquette of social standing and structure placed his friend far above himself. While with Delphina he would sit and read.

"You are always so lost in your books, Lieutenant," her quiet voice remarked one morning. "Would you read to me?"

"You would not find it interesting, Miss Delphina. I am quite sure that it is a terribly dull topic for any young lady."

"Will you read me something that is not dull, Lieutenant Fotherby? I have, for so many years, dreamt of finding anyone who would sit by me and read and talk to me. Only my family have ever endured my company until now."

"It is no endurance," Fotherby said softly as he closed the book he had been reading. "It is a pleasure to sit with you, but I am dreary company and a terrible speaker."

"I am twelve years old, Lieutenant. I know very well how toilsome I am."

"Twelve? Wait until you are sixteen, Miss Delphina, then gentlemen will queue to tell you how wrong you are."

"I shall be gone by that time."

The blunt calmness of these few words in a brief statement caused him to frown with the sorrowful weight of such an acceptance. Delphina seemed to think nothing of it but returned her gaze to the painting that she was trying to create. But Fotherby stepped forward and took the brush from the trembling hand that had barely the control to rest it on the canvas, far less form lines.

"What would you like me to read to you, Miss Delphina?"

She turned her face up to look at him and smiled warmly as he sat down beside her. "Will you read me poetry, Lieutenant Fotherby? At home Cassandra and Margaret both read me poetry."

"I have little talent for reading aloud and I am afraid that I will disappoint you. But if poetry is your wish, then of course that is what I shall read. Have you a favourite poet?"

"William Blake. Father met him once, just before he died. He gifted Rosie a copy of his book."

"William Blake?"

"Indeed," she smiled as she pointed to a shelf of books. "He was touched by her story, you see, and was a great admirer of my grandfather for challenging social restraints for poor Rosie."

Fotherby followed her outstretched hand and ran his fingers over the books until they fell on the spine of *Songs of Innocence*, which he carefully removed before he sat beside the young lady once more. She pointed to the pages she wished him to read and he dutifully read the poems to her, soaking in the language but disappointed by how the words sounded as they left his mouth.

"I am not sure I am suited to poetry," he muttered as he closed the book.

"You love the words, Lieutenant Fotherby. You have only to embrace the rhythm. Let me take your hand." She lifted his hand and rested it upon her wrist. "It has a pulse, you see, like any other living thing. You must treat each poem as though it were alive."

Fotherby heard her words but they fell silent on his ears as he felt her erratic pulse beneath his fingertips and he once more recalled the likelihood of her earlier statement. Forcing a smile he placed his arm about her once more and stared at the striking illustrations on the pages as she turned them.

"Why are you not afraid of me, Lieutenant? Mother always tells me that I killed my father."

"Dear Miss Delphina," Fotherby replied, "You did not kill your father any more than you will kill me."

"But he choked on his breath as I do. I should not get so close to people, for fear that the white plague may pass to them. But you do not seem afraid of that. I have been kept secret for many years for this reason alone. I do not want to hinder the work that Philip does, and I know I would."

"I am not afraid of you, Miss Delphina. I have encountered many people with many ailments, but God has not seen fit to call me home yet."

"Do you believe it is really paradise? I would like paradise."

"Yes. That is what I believe."

They both fell silent then, each in the blanket of their own thoughts. Finally, Fotherby realised, Delphina had fallen asleep against him. Her breathing was ragged and she twitched slightly each time she inhaled, her lungs struggling to contain any depth of air. He remained with his arm about her so that, when Lord and Lady Barrington returned later, this was how they found the pair.

"Delphi," Portland began as he knelt down before her. "Delphi, it is evening and time to go to bed."

The girl stirred awkwardly and smiled sleepily across at the face of her eldest brother before she turned her reddening face to Fotherby.

"Forgive me, Lieutenant. I meant no impropriety."

"There is nothing to forgive, Miss Delphina."

She took her brother's outstretched hand and both rose to their feet, him guiding her out of the room. Fotherby studied his hand thoughtfully as he tensed his fingers, trying to coax blood back into them, but smiled across as Lady Barrington took the seat that Delphina had just left.

"Philip has asked Harry to return Delphi to Cornwall once more," she began softly. "She should not be in the polluted city air for any length of time, and now summer is dawning there will be only more to choke upon. But I wanted to thank you, Lieutenant Fotherby, as Philip does too. You have been so good to her these past few days."

"She is a dear child, and the more I learn of Lord Barrington's background, the more I appreciate it. I told him once that he sounded to have an interesting family, but I believe I underestimated you all so wrongly."

"Philip wants you to meet Cassandra," she continued, the light returning once more to her eyes. "He wants you to marry her, but I have told him that you have already given your heart." Fotherby felt his cheeks burning as she spoke and he looked away from her quickly. "So, come my dear Lieutenant Fotherby, for I have need of some happy news. Who is she?"

"I do not think," he began, but stopped as she laughed slightly.

"A woman sees far more than a man in affairs of the heart. Is she a lady of high degree? Or perhaps she is already engaged?"

"Not that I am aware of, I assure you."

"I am teasing you, only, Lieutenant." She smiled as Fotherby swallowed back still more embarrassment.

"She is neither of those things. She is the daughter of a sergeant. A rank my uncle will never allow for me."

"Does he command you so easily?"

"No. Except that he speaks the truth when he declares I have a duty to marry wisely. I have no love of Wanderford Hall, but I have a duty to it and that dictates my place in society."

"As Barrington Manor did Philip's?" She shook her head slightly. "You will be a greater man with the lady you love by your side. She will enhance your attention to duty."

"Simmons," he whispered. "Kitty Simmons is her name. But I have no assurance that she holds me in any regard."

"Love at sight, my dear Lieutenant. How strange that a man of science should find love so poetically."

"It may be only a fancy."

"No. It is a year since you paid that wager to Philip. A fancy does not last a year. Harry has fancies that last scarcely a month."

Fotherby did not visit the house of Lord Barrington the following day. Mrs Tenterchilt had invited him to visit Hampstead and, having neglected his host for the past three days, Fotherby was eager to correct this wrong. If Mrs Tenterchilt was upset by his absence she did not show it. She was only happy to be repaying the great debt she felt she owed him.

As Saturday dawned over Chanter's House, Fotherby felt a certain trepidation as he considered the welcome that Lord and Lady Barrington might receive on entering the house. This, once more, raised a question within him of the equality of men irrespective of colour. He walked down the stairs, still considering this, and stopped as he encountered the major.

"You seem deep in thought, sir," Major Tenterchilt began. "What is troubling you, Lieutenant?"

"Might I talk with you, sir?" Fotherby began. "It is concerning this evening's guests."

"Come into the study, my dear Fotherby."

The softening to the major's voice confused Fotherby, and he felt obliged to follow the request through this alone. He stepped into the book-lined room and took the chair that Major Tenterchilt offered him.

There were two walls of books and the major's desk was piled in the same pandemonium as his uncle's always was. The crutch that he had advised the major to use rested in the corner and, following the surgeon's gaze, it was of this that Major Tenterchilt first spoke.

"I wanted to keep it. It reminds me how close I came to death and how much I owe to those who enabled me to survive."

"You must include in that list Lord Barrington, sir, for it was he who carried you back."

"And so I do. That is why I have not argued with Mrs Tenterchilt's wish to entertain them. That and the fact I am quite certain never to win."

"Sir, Lord Barrington is a true friend to me, and Lady Barrington also. I am anxious that you might view them so, also."

"I have concerns over Lord Barrington, Fotherby. I have encountered a gentleman who knows him very well and has little praise to grant him. However, I shall not discard the debt I owe him in carrying me into your hospital."

"It was Captain Peters' hospital," Fotherby muttered.

"Very well. But I hope that I have the decency and respect for any man to give him a chance to prove himself."

"And, pardon sir, any lady too?"

"So it is Lady Barrington you are less certain of?" Major Tenterchilt nodded slowly. "And any lady, too."

Fotherby noticed that Major Tenterchilt did not press him on the matter, but the two talked on other matters. They discussed the war, the mysterious benefactor of the major in gaining his promotion, and the matter of the newlywed Prince of Wales, to whom Major Tenterchilt raised a toast. Little by little Fotherby became happier with the notion of the dinner that loomed this evening and, when he sat on the window ledge in his room and once more surveyed the distant view of the city of London, he felt more of his uncertainty drain away. He brushed and plaited his hair, and stepped over to the wardrobe to remove the coat which he had placed there almost a week ago. He was surprised to find that his hand rested on the gold gilt brocade of an officer's coat, where it hung on a wooden hanger. Pulling it from the wardrobe he looked down to find his name written on a card that was tacked to the red lining. He felt unsure as he shrugged into the jacket and paused for a moment to admire himself before the glass, feeling both an overwhelming pride and a sinking disappointment at how proud he felt.

"My dear Fotherby," the major announced as the lieutenant reached the bottom of the stairs. "Does it fit?"

"Perfectly, sir, thank you. But I must pay you. This is such fine cloth, it must have cost a fortune."

"Perhaps so, Fotherby, but it was not I who bought it."

"Then who-"

"I only collected it. I understand it was commissioned some time ago by your uncle."

Fotherby bowed his head as he tried to take in this news. He had been so angry with his uncle for trying to mastermind an engagement between Miss Chester and himself, but he recalled now how much his uncle had done for him, and his strange, uncharacteristic words when last he had met him. Major Tenterchilt seemed to follow some of his confused thoughts and smiled slightly.

Both of them turned to the door of the house as there was a knock upon it, and it was opened almost at once by one of the serving staff. Fotherby smiled across as his gaze rested upon Portland, and the major watched thoughtfully as Fotherby stepped forward.

"Major Tenterchilt, please allow me to introduce Lord Barrington."

"Sir," their host began, as he bowed his head slightly. "It is an honour to meet you, and to have the chance to thank you, for my wife and my surgeon both tell me that I owe my very life to you."

"It is my considered opinion, sir, that it is your surgeon to whom you owe your life."

"But where is Lady Barrington?" Fotherby asked.

"To my shame, Fotherby, I must admit to having no idea. She departed in my carriage a little before I left the house. She claimed she was going to find something for this evening and that I was to leave ahead of her. I find that I cannot refuse her command. You know, surely Major, that wives cannot be easily dissuaded from their plans."

"Indeed I do," Major Tenterchilt laughed slightly and gestured that the two younger gentlemen should follow him through to the Drawing Room. As they entered, Mrs Tenterchilt, who had been discussing the menu with her housekeeper, turned to face them and at once her face lit up in a smile.

"Lord Barrington, it is so wonderful to welcome you into our home. But where is your wife? Where is Lady Barrington?"

"She will be arriving shortly, Mrs Tenterchilt, I have no doubt. And please allow me to say how wonderful it is to see you in such good health."

"Thank you, sir," she laughed. "Far better than the last time I saw you, I assure you."

All of them turned as the butler opened the door and announced with a set face the arrival of Lady Barrington and her companion. There was not a soul who remained calm as they looked at the two women. Major Tenterchilt felt his eyebrows raise at the sight of a black woman in his house, while Mrs Tenterchilt's face paled.

"Good God," she whispered.

"Major Tenterchilt," Portland said as though nothing were amiss. "Mrs Tenterchilt, please permit me to introduce my wife, Lady Rosanna Barrington."

"Lady Barrington," the major announced formally as he bowed his head, while his wife forced a smile, bowing her head but remaining silent.

"It is most kind of you to invite us," Lady Barrington began, her tone suggesting that she had not expected any other welcome. "And it is particularly good of you to allow me to bring a companion." Here she motioned to the woman who stood by her side, clad in a pale dress beneath her fair features, so she was as different from Lady Barrington as a woman could be. Fotherby's gaze had never left her since she had entered the room, but now as Mrs Portland stated the name "Miss Kitty Simmons," he quickly looked away.

"You are most welcome, Miss Simmons," the major began, realising that his wife had spoken all the words she could bring herself to.

"We should eat," Mrs Tenterchilt managed after a moment.

As though the movement into a different room had awoken the manners of all present, conversation began to flow freely. Lady Barrington, it would seem, had arranged with Mrs Tenterchilt via a brief correspondence of letters that she might bring a companion, and Fotherby was seated beside Miss Simmons for the meal. Major and Mrs Tenterchilt sat at opposite ends of the table while Lord and Lady Barrington sat opposite the lieutenant.

"Miss Simmons, I did not know that you knew Lord Barrington," Fotherby remarked softly while the others spoke.

"In truth, Lieutenant, I am unsure why I am here, but that I owe a great deal to Captain Portland."

"How so?" Mrs Tenterchilt asked.

"My father was in his company, and my mother died on the eve of the company's departure to Europe. I was set to be left alone without a house, or any means to find one, but he allowed me to follow my father to the continent."

"I found ladies have little place in war," Mrs Tenterchilt whispered, her face becoming ashen.

"You are fortunate indeed, Mrs Tenterchilt," Lady Barrington announced gently, "that your husband can continue in the profession he loves without facing the battlefield once more."

"Indeed. I thank God each day for it." Silence overcame the table for a moment before Mrs Tenterchilt sought a different topic. "Tell me, Lady Barrington, have you children?"

"No." She placed her hand on her husband's and smiled slightly. "One day, I hope. Have you children, Mrs Tenterchilt?"

"Indeed. We have three daughters, although they will not be back until the end of the week. I miss them terribly when they are away."

"Tell us something of yourself, Lady Barrington," Major Tenterchilt commanded. "How did you come to become Lady Barrington?"

"I married Captain Portland, Major."

"But you are surely not English?"

"No, sir, I was born halfway between Saint Domingue and England, so have no birth land. But I walked first on British shores so I claim myself a Briton."

"Lady Barrington and I were raised as brother and sister," Portland explained.

"I know your uncle," Major Tenterchilt said softly, and Fotherby visibly stiffened at such a remark while Mrs Tenterchilt and Miss Simmons looked confused.

"Then you know very little to recommend me to you," Portland laughed.

"Currently, Lord Barrington," the major continued, "I am of the opinion that I have invited the correct Portland under my roof."

"Thank you, sir," Portland responded with such heartfelt appreciation that he could find no further words. Fotherby looked from one man to the other and felt an insuppressible smile cross his face. It only grew as he looked at Miss Kitty Simmons, who sat beside him.

"You seem in very high spirits, Lieutenant Fotherby," she remarked softly.

"Indeed I am, Miss Simmons."

Under the gaze of Lady Barrington and Mrs Tenterchilt, Fotherby and Miss Simmons talked happily on so many topics. And though they were so very different in their birth and social placing, Fotherby discovered that Miss Simmons shared many of his ideals. Her interest in him was as quietly great as his own in her and when, at the end of the meal, they all withdrew to the Drawing Room, he offered his arm to the young lady. She accepted it readily and gave a nervous laugh as she looked up into her eyes.

The evening was complete and, with the exception of Fotherby, the wine had been drunk when there was a firm knock upon the Drawing Room door and the doorman stepped in.

"Pardon, Major Tenterchilt," he began. "There is a gentleman with a message for Lord Barrington and I do not believe he wishes to wait."

"Excuse me, Major," Portland said, before he lifted his wife's gloved hand to his face and kissed it gently. "I must enquire as to this urgent demand on my time."

The gaiety in the room subsided for a moment while Portland left the room and Lady Barrington forced herself to smile. Her hosts invited her to a chair before Major Tenterchilt poured out a glass of wine that he placed in her hand. Silence now throbbed the air, and each anxious face regarded the other with concern. It was Lord Barrington who broke this silence as he rushed into the room.

"I fear I must excuse myself, Major. Please Rosie, if our hosts might be so gracious as to extend their welcome, remain with them."

"Of course," Mrs Tenterchilt said at once, before her husband had time to say anything. "You are most welcome to stay."

Portland snatched Fotherby's wrist and looked across at him pleadingly. "Will you come with me, Lieutenant? Please?"

"You have no need to beg of me, sir. Excuse me, Major Tenterchilt. Ladies." Without considering what he was doing, he leaned down and kissed Kitty's hand before he and Lord Barrington rushed out of the room.

"That sounded bleak," Major Tenterchilt remarked, more to himself than the rest of the room.

"Nonsense," Mrs Tenterchilt stated, but she was clearly as shaken as her husband. "I am certain it is something quite routine."

"Thank you," Lady Barrington whispered. She tried to rid her mind of what might have happened to have pulled her husband and his friend so prematurely from the room and, as she motioned Kitty to join her where she sat at the table, the ladies began talking on frivolous topics such as music, dresses and the fine wine that they were drinking. The evening lasted a further two hours and neither Portland nor Fotherby returned. It was approaching midnight when Lady Barrington and Miss Simmons finally left Chanter's House. Their hosts stood at the door, despite the late hour, and watched as they departed.

"What an evening, my dear," Major Tenterchilt remarked as they stepped back into the house.

"Who would imagine a black woman might become a lady?" she replied. "And she is so sophisticated. I admit I enjoyed every moment of her company. And Miss Simmons. What a timid soul she is. I do believe she and Lieutenant Fotherby are in love almost as much as we were when we met."

"You have an eye for marriage, my dear," he laughed.

"I am pleased for him, it is true. I feel I owe so much to the young surgeon. And I like to think that he will be well cared for and loved. And, my dear Major Tenterchilt," she added as she took his arm and they walked once more into the Drawing Room. "I am certain she does love him. Are we not the proof that love need not follow social constraints?"

He turned to face her, kissing her cheek, but remained silent as he considered all that the evening had taught him. Above all, he wondered what had forced the premature departure of the two gentlemen and what truth there was in the words of Mr Bryn-Portland concerning his nephew.


As soon as Fotherby's gaze had fallen upon Chilvers in the hall at Chanter's House he felt a sickened feeling grip him. This only intensified as Portland remained silent on the journey back to the house. He did not assist Chilvers from the carriage, as was his custom, but rushed into the house. Fotherby helped the old man down from the coach and waited until the servant, who had been as silent on the journey as his master, guided him into the house. Fotherby stopped in the hall to see Portland striking another man across the face. This aggression, which Fotherby had never seen in his friend, caused him to falter.

"How dare you?" the younger man demanded. Chilvers, Fotherby noticed, remained silent as he closed the door. "We are not in Barrington Manor now."

"Chilvers," Portland began without turning, "lock that door and show Harris to a room. Do not let him leave this house."

Fotherby regarded this young man through newly-seeing eyes in the discovery that this was the brother of whom he had heard mention. The man, who could not yet be twenty, rubbed his struck cheek. He had a round face and blue eyes, but here the similarities with his brother ended, for Harris was a slender man, whose clothes hung loosely from his shoulders. The pristine white wig that rested on his head fitted so perfectly that none of his own hair was visible beneath. Straightening the gold coat that he wore, he rested his hand on the hilt of his sword as though he was trying to threaten his brother, but Portland never moved.

"I will not be kept a prisoner here."

"You should be back in Cornwall by now," Portland remarked as he took the key from Chilvers' outstretched hand. "And you have no right to be free to return to the fops that you love so much when you refused to help the sister who loves you so greatly. Now get out of my sight before I consider using the blade you carry."

Fotherby watched on as Portland pushed his brother towards the stairs before he turned his crimson face to the eternally calm features of the lieutenant. He purposefully closed his hand about the key before he snatched Fotherby's wrist.

"Can you help her, Fotherby? Can you help Delphi?"

"Portland," he began gently, "I will do whatever I can for her, but I have never seen a man make a full recovery from consumption."

"God, I will kill him!"

"It is not Harris' fault," Fotherby said softly.

"He should have taken her home. She could have been safely home now. But he could think only of himself."

"Where is Miss Delphina?"

Portland guided him up the stairs and into a high-ceilinged room that had gold filigree patterns on the walls and a rich rug on the wooden floor. The only furniture in the room was a high four-poster bed and a wash stand which had a low chair before it. The curtains were drawn and an angry fire burnt in the grate. While Fotherby took in his surroundings, Portland rushed forward to the bed and looked down at the thin figure there, whimpering in her sleep each time she tried to take a breath.

"Delphi?" he whispered as he reached to take the child's hand.

The sound of his friend's voice awoke Fotherby's senses and he snatched the jug that stood on the washstand and tipped it over the flames on the fire. Steam hissed as it rushed out into the room but the incessant smoking ebbed. Finally he walked over to the window and pulled open the curtains. It was dark outside with few lamps burning in the houses close to them and the stars shone over London, mocking the heartbreak beneath.

"Go and sleep, Portland. There is nothing you can do here."

Fotherby removed the bonnet which Delphina still wore and unfastened and removed her shoes before handing them to her brother and, sitting on the edge of the bed, lifted her frail form to try and ease her breathing.

"Philip?" Delphina asked weakly. "Why am I not home?" She began coughing so violently that her brother discarded the bonnet and shoes and dropped down to his knees beside the bed. Fotherby, without relinquishing his support on the child, snatched the wash basin and watched with a despondent nausea as

Delphina coughed a putrid, bloody substance into it. When she finally ceased choking, he lifted the feather pillows and rested her back against them so that she was able to sit, before he rose to his feet and assisted Portland to do likewise.

"Tell me truthfully, Fotherby. Will she die here?"

"You are asking me to question forces over which I have no power," Fotherby muttered. "I cannot know that any more than she or you. But I promise you I will do my best to help her."

Fotherby sat diligently beside Miss Delphina throughout the night. He heard Lady Barrington return some time later and, by the anxious conversation he could hear taking place, he realised Portland had not taken his advice. Delphina spent much of the night beyond his words until, after coughing weakly once more, she turned her dark eyes up to him and a flicker of recognition passed over them.

"Lieutenant Fotherby," she panted pitifully. "This is not paradise."

"I am afraid we have to face the gates of heaven for a time before we are permitted entry."

She struggled to breathe as she tried to form words, and this struggle was painful also to Fotherby. Taking her trembling hand, which fitted easily within his own, he placed her fingers on his wrist.

"Try to match your breath to my pulse, Miss Delphina. Do not try to breathe too deeply."

The subdued morning light was trickling into the house when a gentle knock sounded on the door and Lady Barrington peered around to find Delphina with her head on Fotherby's chest and the lieutenant with his arm around the child's shoulders. Fotherby smiled across at her arrival, before he lay Delphina gently back on the bed.

"How is she, Lieutenant?"

"Alive," Fotherby replied as he rose to his feet. "I am sorry that I left so abruptly."

"Nonsense, Lieutenant Fotherby. You have saved dear Delphina. I would permit any social injunction to preserve a life. But you look as though you have not slept."

Fotherby only smiled and nodded before he guided Lady Barrington from the room and then shut the door.

"She is a strong-spirited little lady," he whispered.

"But?" Lady Barrington continued, "come Lieutenant Fotherby, be honest with me, I beg you."

"But the inevitable has only been delayed, Lady Barrington. She will not live long here, and I do not anticipate that she will reach sixteen."

Despite hating himself for the words that he spoke, the woman before him did not seem to share his attitude.

Instead she placed her hand on the sleeve of his new coat and smiled up at him, a gesture of such beauty in her dark face.

"But you have given her to us for that short while longer. Thank you. Now," she continued, blinking her eyes a little but otherwise successfully masking her sorrow, "you must wish to wash. Let me show you to a room."

After cleaning his hands and face in a basin of warm water, Fotherby stared at his reflection in the glass over the fireplace of his room. There were soot marks covering the bottom of the mirror and distorting the image there. But it was the bleak acceptance which he hated the most about the man who looked back at him. He walked out of the room, down the stairs and was about to enter the Drawing Room before he paused, his hand hovering over the door handle.

"They are, all three, in there, sir."

Fotherby turned to see Chilvers who had been standing behind him. "I believe they have cause to discuss issues without me there. Has Lord Barrington permitted the door to be opened yet?" Chilvers nodded and Fotherby pulled on the jacket he was carrying. "Then I shall leave quietly, Chilvers. And tell Master Harris to empty and clean the basin in Miss Delphina's room."

He stepped from the house as silently as he could, joining the street and the collection of people walking there and feeling that, in his new uniform, he fitted in well with the other gentlemen. He knew, though, that this was not where he belonged. He returned to Chanter's House without knowing how he got there and knocked gently on the door. He explained to Major and Mrs Tenterchilt the reason that he had been forced to leave, omitting only Harris' role in the affair. He was gratefully surprised by how gently they responded. Mrs Tenterchilt could only raise her hand to her mouth, while the Major set his face hard and whispered,

"She is only a year older than Arabella."

"We must do something to help them, my dear," Mrs Tenterchilt said firmly.

"I rather fear there is little that can be done, Mrs Tenterchilt. I did not tell you that it might distress you, only I wanted you to know that I would not so lightly have abandoned the party last night."

Fotherby remained a further five days with the Tenterchilts before he left for Derbyshire. He visited Lord Barrington to tell him of his departure, but when he arrived Chilvers explained to him that Lord and Lady Barrington had returned to Cornwall with Miss Delphina. Harris, Fotherby noticed, was not mentioned.

"Perhaps you will give them this when they return." Fotherby handed a letter to the butler. "It is an invitation to Wanderford, for I should like them to visit."

"That is very kind of you, sir," Chilvers said softly. "She was much improved when they left. And though Lord Barrington wished you had remained, he understood why you did not."

Fotherby smiled weakly at the butler and returned the bicorne to his head before he left the house and gratefully began the journey home.

## Chapter Eleven

*An Excursion To Buxton*

Wanderford Hall had been in the Fotherby family for over three hundred years, but in that time it had been extended, both in grounds and buildings. On one occasion, some one hundred and fifty years ago, it had been attacked by the Roundheads and the house, that had been granted by the Stanleys after Bosworth, had lost one of the wings to a fire. Now it boasted a stunning front that always caused Fotherby to smile as he beheld it. Shuffling the sling bag that he carried on his shoulder, he stepped down the broad drive, his long legs carrying him quickly to the house.

He did not knock but stepped into the hall. He was met almost at once by one of the servants, who offered him a smile as he took the hat and coat from the young lieutenant, as well as the bag that he carried.

"Your uncle is out riding, sir. And your father is in his library."

Fotherby thanked him and stepped into the library, breathing in the age of the room and trying to remind himself that he belonged there. His father had his back turned to his son and was staring out the window that overlooked the side of the house, his hands on the wooden ledge as though he needed the support. He had not heard his son's arrival. Fotherby stepped over to him and felt a smile cross his lips.

"Father?"

"Henry," came the startled reply. "Oh Henry, my boy, I was beginning to doubt that you would make it back."

"I do hope I shall never be late to any appointment I have set with you, Father."

"I should not mind if it could not be helped, Henry." His father looked critically at him for a moment, as though he had not seen him since he entered the room. "You do not look well, Henry. Are you sick?"

"No," came the whispered reply. "I am only so tired I do not know what I am doing. I shall lie down for a time, I think."

His father only nodded as Fotherby, in a manner completely uncharacteristic of the young man, walked in a daze over to the door. He climbed the stairs and stood at the great window, considering all that had happened in the year since he had last stood there. How different it looked in the radiance of late spring. Colour was everywhere and even the distant hills shone a mysterious blue. Being home felt strange, for it truly ended the chapter of his life which had been written during events on the continent. It was this that had caused a pensiveness in him and, since leaving London yesterday, he had been unable to shake himself out of such thoughts. He walked along the landing until he came to his room, in which he found his belongings. His fatigue was so great that, scarcely had he laid down upon the bed, than sleep overcame him.

He did not dream but, in the safety and comfort of his own room, slept on until there was a knock at the door that startled him so much he sat up quickly, gasping for breath. The door opened slightly and his father walked in.

"It is almost dinner, Henry."

"I shall be down presently, Father. I fell asleep."

"When I received your letter I was concerned about you."

"I know I should have written to you earlier," Fotherby began, but stopped as the old man sat on the chair at the desk and leaned forward to study his son.

"It was not that. I felt you were asking more questions than you could hope to find answers."

"But is that not how life works, Father? In the least it is how my life seems to go."

"Finding answers is not the difficult thing, Henry. We know the answers, we have only to match them to the right question. That is the difficult part."

Fotherby watched as his father rose and leaned forward to kiss his son's forehead before he left the room. Although unsure whether it was the sleep he had gained or this brief conversation, Fotherby felt much more content.

As May gave way to June, the bloodshed and horrors of the battles on the continent began to fade from Fotherby's memory, as did the events during his stay in London. However, he ensured that he wrote to thank Major Tenterchilt for allowing him to stay. This brought to mind the events that had taken place when he stayed with Sir Manfred Chester, and he resolved to talk to his uncle about the plans he had made for his nephew. The only other person he wrote to was Miss Kitty Simmons and, as July shone down on the Derbyshire countryside, this letter yielded a long-desired response, which gave him the determination to confront his uncle in regard to Sir Manfred Chester and, more so, Miss Persephone Chester.

The following morning, knowing that his uncle would be out, Fotherby sought his father's counsel. He was to be found, as always, in his library. The old man lowered the book he was reading and smiled across at his son.

"You have quite a spring in your step this morning, Henry."

"I have a question, Father. Something that books will not tell me, nor parchments. It is about Uncle Paul."

"Do not trouble yourself with him, Henry," his father replied, closing the book and placing it on the arm of the chair. "He is not a bad man, but he is not a good man either."

"How am I to take these words from his own brother?" Fotherby asked, but his mind flashed back to the brief interaction he had witnessed between Portland and Harris.

"As true."

"I met a gentleman in London, to whom he directed me. The man used to work in Saint Vincent with my uncle. What was his career in the West Indies, and why did he not inherit Wanderford Hall?"

"He would have inherited, but he wanted money. While we are viewed as wealthy by those who see this house, it is not so. Wanderford Hall consumes almost as much money as it gathers. And Paul wanted money and all it could buy. So, when he was twenty-five, he announced to our father that he was going to make money in the western trade. I believe he met his friend over there."

"So you inherited Wanderford Hall because he would not accept his duty to it?"

"Yes. I had already trained as a lawyer and I persuaded our father to wait and see whether Paul would return. But his mind was made up and, when he did return to England, he was rich beyond measure and refused to take Wanderford. Almost immediately, he sailed once more out to the Indies. Our father died some years later and I was called to run the estate."

"What made him come back?"

"They were ambushed one night, he and his friends. One of them, a young man, was beaten to death. Paul could not be free of it, so the small company disbanded and they returned once more to England, very wealthy but equally haunted. I offered him Wanderford Hall, by rights being his own, but he would not take it."

Tobias Fotherby watched as his son fell silent and tried to understand and reconcile with all that he had just heard. Certainly it explained the abrupt arrival of his uncle at Wanderford Hall and the displacing of the Chester household, each of whom he was sure would far rather have been in Saint Vincent than London. And it went a little way to explaining why his uncle had tried to establish a marriage between Miss Chester and himself.

Thanking his father, Fotherby left the room and walked to the stables, pacing the corridor between stalls as he awaited his uncle's return. It was the giddy barking of his dogs that first alerted him to his uncle's arrival and Fotherby stepped out of the stable, into the courtyard, and watched as his uncle dismounted.

"Henry!" the old man called across. "I did not know you had wished to go riding. I would have waited for you. Though I do believe you would need one of the farm horses to keep your feet off the ground."

"I was waiting for you," Fotherby replied, stroking one of the hounds that came and sat against him.

"Something serious, then. What is it?"

"I stayed in London at the address you gave me."

"So it is about Miss Chester." There was no question in his uncle's voice but Fotherby felt compelled to answer.

"Yes. And while I appreciate the bitter past you and her father share, I do not appreciate that you make arrangements, to which I am key, without my knowledge. Far less my consent."

"So you waited here to deride me? I did not have you pegged as the skulking type, Henry."

"I am not skulking. I have not spoken of this in the time I have been here to spare my father from this argument. That same reason is why I waited here for you."

"It is not I who shall make this an argument." He led the horse into the stable and called to the groom to tend it before he returned to the courtyard, walking past Fotherby but continuing to talk. "I am sorry you did not like Miss Chester, Henry, but I am not sorry that I tried to establish an engagement."

"But without telling me? Why must everyone seek to marry me to one woman or another?"

His uncle rounded on him and stared up into his face. "Because the only person who does not see the significance of your marriage is yourself. Because you are too busy looking to fall in love like some simpering girl that you, and you alone, fail to see that a good marriage is what will serve you, and more importantly Wanderford, well. It is my own fault," he added, turning away from his nephew. "I should not have supported you and your father, then Tobias would have had to remarry and you would have learned the social duty that is of any gentry."

"I have found the woman I intend to marry, Uncle," Fotherby whispered, his voice growing in confidence as he considered the letter he had received yesterday. "So you may cease trying to wed me to any woman who may be unmarried or widowed at the age of twenty."

"Indeed, Henry? And where does she live?"

"Camden."

"That is precisely what I would have expected."

Fotherby watched as his uncle walked away, followed by the five dogs, each leaping up at him to try and gain his attention. He felt as though he had fought a battle with the man, and he could not be sure which of them could claim the victory.

The following two weeks were filled with a hostile silence from his uncle and the young surgeon found himself wishing to be anywhere but Wanderford Hall. He longed for Captain Peters to order him to the battlefield, for there he might at least be useful, something he felt he was failing at as he sat arranging his desk or flicking through the pages of medical journals, seeing nothing. On occasions he would stand at his window and sketch the view or, if the weather permitted and the clouds did not hang too low, he would leave the confines of the hall and sit in the wooded valley or climb the towering hills and draw whatever he could see. In this he would recall the beauty in the world, trying to remind himself such beauty could still exist in such a bitter time.

His solace came in the exchanging of letters with Miss Simmons, to whom he felt he could be the better side of himself and who continued to write to him in an increasingly regular pattern. He heard nothing from Peters, who he assumed had distanced himself through a disappointment over Fotherby's friendship with Portland. And of Lord Barrington he heard nothing. Nothing, that is, until the middle of July when a letter arrived in a hand that he did not recognise. Furthermore, upon opening it, a delicate scent filled his nose and he felt his brow furrow as he read on, eager to discover the identity of the sender.

"Dear Lieutenant Fotherby," the penmanship announced in a script that flowed in great curls and few straight lines. "It has long preyed upon my mind that there has been a silence to divide myself from you, when in truth we owe you so much. My self-recrimination at allowing two months to pass without correspondence is great and I am truly sorry that it has taken so long. We resided in Cornwall throughout June and returned to find your kind invitation at the start of July. If your invitation still stands, despite such a passage of time, we should be both delighted and honoured to travel into Derbyshire. I am forced to say that Philip is given to dark, subdued moods as the cause that he so passionately upholds continues to fail in parliament. I am therefore eager to turn his mind to something else for a time. Yours in great friendship, Rosanna Portland."

Fotherby did not waste a moment in penning his reply, desperate for the company that they promised and anxious for his friend. Subsequently, in the last week of July, Wanderford Hall was made ready to entertain Lord and Lady Barrington. Fotherby's uncle improved in his temperament, no doubt pleased by the titles that preceded the name of his nephew's friends. His father made arrangements with the staff that all should be readied for their arrival, while Fotherby waited impatiently like a child.

The long shadows of a late summer evening were stretching out when a carriage, pulled by two white and two brown horses, journeyed sedately along the great drive. The hour, approaching nine, was so late that no one in the house was looking for their arrival. Fotherby was sitting opposite his father, both reading, while his uncle sat at a desk a short distance away, a bottle of wine in his hand. All three turned as the door opened and one of the servants walked in, his face ashen so that Fotherby instantly felt himself frown.

"They are here, sir," the servant whispered, addressing Fotherby's father. "Lord and Lady Barrington."

"Then why are you pale, Carter?" Paul Fotherby demanded, rising to his feet and slamming the bottle down. "Show them to the Drawing Room at once and we shall be in presently."

Fotherby glanced across at his father who was studying him thoughtfully as the servant left the room.

"Henry," he began, "what is it about your friends would cause Carter such anxiety?"

"I can think of nothing, Father. Except, perhaps, the hour of their arrival." Fotherby offered no further explanation but rushed into the Drawing Room. Portland, who had helped his wife to a chair, turned at his arrival and smiled across at his friend.

"It is so good of you to invite us, Fotherby," he began, but stopped as Fotherby laughed.

"It is you who have been good to visit. I hope you both enjoy Wanderford Hall."

"I love it already, Lieutenant," Lady Barrington said softly. "The fountain in the drive is stunning, and the rooms are a perfect size."

"Allow me to introduce my father, Mr Tobias Fotherby," he continued as his father stepped into the room. "Father, this is Lord and Lady Barrington."

"It is a great honour to meet you, sir," Portland began, bowing his head. "You must be so very proud of your son."

"Pride is a sin, Lord Barrington," the old man replied. "But I am afraid it is one I am guilty of where Henry is concerned. Lady Barrington," he added, turning to face her. "I do not believe Wanderford has ever housed one of your kin, but you are very welcome as the first."

Neither of the young men seemed sure how to take this welcome but Lady Barrington only smiled and allowed the older man to kiss her gloved hand. All four of them turned as Fotherby's uncle entered the room and he looked across at the gathering. Before Fotherby could say anything, his uncle spoke.

"Words fail me, Henry. For the same reason, I am sure, they failed Carter." Fotherby felt his eyes narrow as he gazed across at his uncle, who continued talking. "Welcome to Wanderford Hall, Lord Barrington. And you also, Lady Barrington."

His uncle sought to avoid talking to him for the rest of the evening, while he talked contentedly to the other three inhabitants in the room. They took a light refreshment, before Fotherby's father invited the guests to retire for the evening, and he and his brother also withdrew to their beds. Fotherby was left alone, staring blankly at the empty hearth as he tried to unravel the cause of his uncle's behaviour. Without a doubt Lady Barrington's colour had come as a surprise to him, but he had talked comfortably with Mrs Portland and had only snubbed his nephew.

After some time asking many silent questions and finding no answers, Fotherby extinguished the lamp that rested on the table and walked through the hall under the heavy gaze of his ancestors, fighting the battle that was to win them Wanderford Hall. Climbing the stairs, he paused to look down over the view that lay before him.

There was not sufficient light to show the full scene, but he stood watching, feeling the shadow across the land only added to his baffled state of mind.

The following morning he rose early and stepped lightly downstairs. Wanderford Hall was silent and his footsteps were the only sound to be heard as he walked purposefully out of the doors of the house and continued until he reached the fountain which Lady Barrington had complimented him on the previous evening. Here he sat, away from everyone, and tried to understand what he had witnessed and the peculiar expression he had seen his uncle adopt. The sun climbed higher in the sky, and he was uncertain how long he had sat there before he heard the sound of gravel behind him.

"Might I join you?" Mrs Portland asked gently. He smiled across at her and nodded, but remained silent as she sat beside him. "This is beautiful, Lieutenant. I love the sound of running water."

"My uncle had it built by an Italian gentleman in memory of my mother."

"What a wonderful remembrance." She turned to face him. "Thank you for renewing your invitation. I am so pleased to be here. We were sorry not to have the chance to thank you for helping Delphi."

"How is she?"

"As well as I have ever seen her. She spoke often of you. You claimed a place in her heart, I think."

"She might be the bravest person I have ever met," Fotherby replied, smiling across. "I am glad that she was improved."

"Do you know who I saw at the start of July? Miss Kitty Simmons. She has become such a lady since I saw her last. And she never ceased smiling. I could not help but ask myself why." She looked across with amusement at the young surgeon. "But now I see."

"Miss Simmons has been kind enough to maintain a correspondence with me."

"Oh Lieutenant," she laughed. "I am so very pleased. Mrs Tenterchilt and I spoke of little but you at that dinner, and she was adamant that you and Miss Simmons would make a perfect couple."

"I am unsure whether I am grateful or affronted."

"You are entitled to a little of both, I think. Shall we return and breakfast?"

She gave him no room to argue but took his offered arm and the pair walked back. Over the next few days, Lord and Lady Barrington became the centre of life at Wanderford Hall. Lady Barrington would amuse herself, wandering through the gardens or joining Fotherby's father in his library, where they would discuss all manner of topics ranging from the

Derbyshire landscape to religion. Lord Barrington would take long rides each morning with Fotherby's uncle, who still maintained a silence where his nephew was concerned. On occasion, Fotherby watched his uncle survey the guests critically, especially Lady Barrington who he continued to study as though she was a puzzle to solve. In the evenings the brothers would retire early and leave the young officers and Lady Barrington alone to discuss anything that took their fancy.

"Does war still rage on the continent?" Fotherby asked. "We hear so little of our nation's affairs here."

"No," Portland replied. "The Prussians made peace with France and poor Pitt has been left with no trust even from some of his closest men. What a costly, bloody mess it all was."

"Yet would we not both return tomorrow if we were summoned?"

"Through duty, not through desire."

"I do not wish to see either of you depart," Lady Barrington said firmly. "I have taken it into my head that neither of you should be exposed to such suffering any longer. Philip, you have your duty to the estate, and Lieutenant, you have a duty to a certain young lady to stay safe."

Portland smiled at his wife. "Poor Fotherby. He will not stand a fighting chance now that you have designs for him, my dear."

"I am weary of proposals," Fotherby muttered. "Should it not be I who makes the proposals?"

Portland only laughed as though the younger man had made a joke. "You are a little too progressive for your uncle, I think, Fotherby."

The conversation turned then, but it was this subject that troubled Fotherby as he lay awake, staring at the ceiling of his room and following the cracking plaster with his eyes. All thoughts of his uncle, however, were soon to be pushed from his mind.

The next day, Fotherby joined Lord and Lady Barrington on a journey into Buxton to experience the delights of this town. It was not a long journey, taking perhaps an hour in the carriage in which the guest had arrived a week earlier. For the duration of their journey they happily discussed many topics, laughing as much as they talked.

Buxton was a town in the making. The Duke of Devon was creating the small village into a town that he hoped would one day rival Bath. The imposing Crescent dominated the town and, while Lord and Lady Barrington stepped out of the carriage and admired the sweeping row of houses, Fotherby felt them intrusive and alien to the village he remembered visiting in his childhood. He glanced across toward the small structure a short distance away and considered how, when he had visited in his youth, St Ann's Well had been the sole building here. Now it was weighed down by the great buildings surrounding it.

"This is charming," Lady Barrington announced as she took her husband's arm, ignoring the faces that turned to look at her. "What is it that has caused you to frown, Lieutenant?"

"It is not how I remember it, that is all." Fotherby guided them across to the road and towards the small shrine where a cluster of people stood. "This is what the duke has built Buxton upon."

"And," Lord Barrington began, "as a man of science, do you believe there is a true benefit to the waters?"

"Drawn from the well or drawn from the pump?" Fotherby asked, uncertain how best to answer the question. "From the pump I must declare it to be no superior to the waters you will find from the well at Wanderford."

"Which turned you into a giant," Portland laughed.

"But people have claimed miracles from here for hundreds of years," his wife continued. "Do you not believe in miracles, Lieutenant?"

"I do," Fotherby muttered, unsure what answer was expected from him. "But I do not pretend to understand why God chooses to grant a miracle to one person and not another."

"It is a shame Delphi could not join us," Portland whispered, more to himself than to the others. "God would not have denied her a miracle."

Fotherby had no answer to his friend's comment, and he did not believe that the gentleman sought one. All three of them turned at the sound of a man's voice close to them.

"There is no amount of holy water can wash her clean," he laughed, gesturing across at Lady Barrington.

Perhaps it was the resignation within Lady Barrington's eyes, or the heartfelt statement that her husband had just made which still echoed in Fotherby's head, but the young surgeon felt so greatly affronted on behalf of his friends that he stepped over to the gentleman.

"What do you mean by your remark?"

The man, who stood a foot shorter than Fotherby, glared up at him while his friends stood talking quietly amongst themselves. "She's blacker than a miner," he continued. "There is nothing that can alter what she is."

Portland took a step forward but stopped as his wife held him back.

"She is a lady, sir," Fotherby retorted. "Far more than you are a gentleman." A ripple of shocked comments spread through the gathered people, not only those with the insulted man, but others who stood close by. "Come," Fotherby said, with a more gentle tone. "In the least you owe Lady Barrington an apology."

"An apology?" came the angry reply. "I owe her nothing."

Portland stepped forward, ignoring his wife's protests. "Who are you?" he demanded angrily. Fotherby placed his hand on his friend's chest, holding him back with surprising strength.

"If you shall not apologise, sir," Fotherby continued with a tone far calmer than he felt. "Then you leave me no alternative but to demand satisfaction for the honour of this lady."

"You foolish boy," one of the other men interjected. "Do you know who you are challenging? This is the Duke of Everton's brother."

"Francis Sutton," Portland said angrily. "I might have known."

While Fotherby's resolve did not waver, he felt puzzlement cross his face at the recognition his friend paid to the man before him. "I have no doubt, sir, I shall see you again soon. Lord Barrington," he continued, never taking his eyes from the man before him. "Please take Mr Sutton's address."

"Lieutenant," Lady Barrington began, taking his hand as he turned from the man he had just challenged. "You do not need to do this. I am used to these comments."

"But that does not make them right, or justifiable." He turned as Portland stepped over and Fotherby offered him a thin smile.

"Perhaps we should go to our lodgings," Portland said quickly. "It is my hope that I can talk you out of this and allow me to defend the honour of my own wife."

They found rooms in The Sun Inn and Lady Barrington sat on the sofa, trying to encourage the two men to do the same, but her husband pressed himself against the door while Fotherby paced the floor, counting the eight strides repeatedly.

"Fotherby, you do not need to do this. Indeed, you should not do this."

"Philip is right, Lieutenant," Lady Barrington added. "We did not travel to Buxton to see you dead."

"You might offer me a little more faith," Fotherby laughed, but the gesture was forced and convinced no one in the room.

"You are not a fighter, Fotherby," Portland continued. "Let me fight this duel. You are someone who heals people, not harms them. You are a surgeon, not a soldier."

"Surgeons make the best duellists," Fotherby answered, ceasing his pacing and thrusting a letter towards his friend. "Now, will you deliver this, or must I go?"

Portland took the letter with great reluctance and looked down at it. "Can I say nothing to persuade you to allow me this fight?"

"No," Fotherby whispered. "That man was deplorable, and I will not allow such insolence to my friends, who are here on my invitation."

Portland stepped out of the room and Fotherby finally sat down on the sofa, dropping his head into his hands. He lifted his gaze as he felt a gentle hand upon his arm and looked across at Lady Barrington.

"Sometimes, not often, but on days like today," she began, "I wonder if it would not have been better if I had been born a slave and died a slave."

"No man or woman should be a slave to another. Portland would be lost without you."

"He would not have my cause to fight. Indeed, he should not have inherited Barrington Manor or any of the worries and cares that it is built upon. And you

- 308 -

should not be in this position now. Fotherby, you have no pistol to fight a duel. And you have peace in your heart, not conflict."

"You are right, but I do not recant any word I said. Nor should you wish for another outcome to the one you have. For you have a right to it."

Portland was gone for almost two hours, but to the poor surgeon it felt like an eternity. The anger that had driven him to speak out against the man was unlike anything he had ever felt before. While he struggled to understand what had caused him to speak in such a manner, he realised it was the knowledge that, if he had not spoken, Portland would have. During his quiet and insular childhood, he had never had a friend who he so admired and wanted to protect as the friend he had found in Lord Barrington.

"Here," Portland began as he pushed the letter that he carried on his arrival toward his friend. "It seems that no amount of talk will appease that most vile man."

"How do you know him?" Fotherby asked as he accepted the letter and looked down at it. It had no address and did not even carry a name.

"His nephew was a lieutenant in the same company as I. He is a despicable man, too. But, Fotherby, Francis Sutton was a colonel in the American war. He has years of experience as a fighter."

"Oh Philip," Lady Barrington interrupted. "Fotherby has not even a pistol. You must stop him from doing this. I do not feel aggrieved," she continued, rising to her feet and gripping Fotherby's sleeve. "Please do not do this."

"See sense, man," Portland agreed. "Let me fight this on your behalf."

"You have not a pistol either," his wife interjected.

"None is needed," Fotherby replied, lifting the letter.

"He has recanted?" Portland asked in disbelief.

"No, he wishes to settle the dispute with the sword." Fotherby smiled across at his friends. "It is a good thing. My aim is poor."

"Can you fence?" Portland began. "He has military training."

"I carry a sword, do I not?" Fotherby retorted, feeling that such constant doubt from his companions was more frightening than the impending duel.

"There is an island in the River Wye," Portland sighed. "That is where he intends to meet you."

"I know. It is all in here." He lifted the letter once more.

"I never thought that Buxton would turn out to be such an eventful place," Portland muttered. "I did not look for such a terrible outcome."

"I have not lost this duel yet. I am going to retire for the night, though I must thank you for so readily accepting the role of second."

"I would happily take the role of principal if you would but let me."

"I invited you to Derbyshire," Fotherby said softly. "I did not invite you to be insulted and have to carry that insult in silence. I am quite sure I am only doing what is morally right."

Portland stepped aside from the door and allowed the lieutenant to leave the room. His wife rushed over to him and clung tightly to him as tears streamed down her cheeks.

"He will be killed, Philip. We must do something."

"I cannot. It would only undermine Lieutenant Fotherby, and I would not do that to him. Nor could I ever admit to Sutton that his behaviour is in any way acceptable."

"I will go to him. I will go to Sutton and beg him to withdraw."

"No, my dear Rosie, he will not accept such a thing."

"But you must do something."

Portland kissed her tear stained face and nodded before he walked out of the room and the inn in search of the residence of Francis Sutton. He gained admittance immediately and tried to recall why he had come.

"I did not expect to see you again so soon," the man before him announced as he rose to his feet. Mr Darlington, a man of an age closer to Portland's late father than himself, was Sutton's second and, while a lawyer by profession, he was a well-known duellist in his own right, settling conflicts on behalf of his clients.

"I have not come here lightly," Portland began but stopped as Darlington lifted his hand.

"He wishes to withdraw, does he?"

"No," Portland replied angrily. "I wish him to withdraw. It is my wife who was insulted. It does not sit well with me that Lieutenant Fotherby will fight the duel that I should be fighting."

"You can save your words, Lord Barrington, for Mr Sutton will not take back his. And nor should he. It is deplorable what you have done in marrying that poor creature. She can never be a lady and you have proved yourself to be no lord in marrying her."

Foolish though it might have been, Portland could not stay his words. "Whatever the outcome of the morning's fight, I will not be satisfied until my wife has heard an apology from the lips of both Sutton and yourself. You are no human being if you believe any of the words that pour from your foul mouth."

Portland turned his back on the man before him and walked out into the onset of night. He had journeyed there to try and appease the man but had succeeded only in angering himself and the opponents. He stepped into the inn and walked up to the room under the burden of his thoughts. His wife rushed to him and, though he clung to her tightly, he could find no words to comfort her. They remained in this sorrowful embrace as the night closed in around them, both too afraid and sad to speak.

## Chapter Twelve

*Answering The Question Of Honour*

The sword Fotherby wore by his side had scarcely left its sheath. He carried it only as a part of the uniform he wore on such occasions as the trip to Buxton had promised to be. That night he had drawn the long thin blade and spent countless minutes studying it, trying to recall all that he had been taught. It served his purpose well that Sutton had chosen the sword, for he was poor with guns, but he could only imagine that Sutton had made this choice knowing himself to be a superior fencer. He could not imagine what his father would make of such an event, but drew some consolation in the knowledge that his uncle would certainly approve of this approach.

He had tried to sleep, but he only achieved snatches of slumber before he awoke, fearful that he should miss his early appointment. He need not have worried, however, for an hour before dawn there was a knock on the door. Fotherby pulled it open and found Portland and Rosanna standing before him. Portland was wearing the tailcoat he had travelled in yesterday, with a lace cuffed shirt beneath, while Lady Barrington wore a light red dress and a black shawl that she had placed over her head like a veil. Neither of them spoke, nor did Fotherby who sheathed the long blade, snatching his jacket before he followed Lord and Lady Barrington.

This silence clung to all three of them as they walked the short distance in ten minutes. There was a gathering at the edge of the river and as Fotherby's gaze counted six gentleman he felt his brow furrow.

"Unless this woman is skilled in surgery, you are feeling mighty confident or mighty foolish," Darlington remarked.

Fotherby stayed silent but watched as Portland's face became set. Before he could say anything, however, his wife placed her hand on his chest. "Let us resolve this matter without any further matters arising."

Despite the large gathering that Sutton had assembled, only six people stepped into the small boat that was to take them the short distance to the island while the three other men were posted about the perimeter to deter the constables if the law should make an appearance. Lord and Lady Barrington accompanied Fotherby, while Mr Darlington and the surgeon, Doctor Shipton, accompanied Sutton. The island was scarcely large enough to make the duel legal but, according to the duelling code, Darlington and Portland marked out the twenty paces, dropping their handkerchiefs to the ground while the surgeon marked the third and Rosanna Portland placed her shawl in the fourth corner. Being deemed the most neutral person present, Shipton commenced the fight, while Portland and Darlington watched on from outside the square, helpless to assist their principals.

Fotherby had a far greater advantage over his opponent for, being tall, he had a further reaching lunge to the man before him. But, while Sutton had not the graceful elegance of the lieutenant, he fought with such aggression that on three occasions he almost forced Fotherby from the square. Mrs Portland stood in the corner where she had placed her shawl and watched through fearful but dry eyes as the fight unfolded before her. Fotherby had never engaged in a duel before, but as the fight continued, he became more and more certain that the man before him had fought many. Sutton continued with a rage that was almost overwhelming, but Fotherby continued to escape the blows which the man repeatedly aimed at his body. The sword had already cut through the loose shirt sleeve the lieutenant wore, but he had failed to draw blood from the young man. According to the conditions which had been decided upon, the pair were to fight until one of them was no longer able and, to this end, Fotherby had been a little more guarded in his style of fencing, interested far more in protecting himself than delivering strikes against his opponent.

The fight moved about the square, both combatants carefully watching the imagined lines that boxed in their honour, for whoever stepped out would forfeit the duel instantly. As they approached the corner where Lady Barrington stood, Fotherby faltered. His footing slipped as his gaze rested upon the woman for whom he was fighting this duel. She lifted her hand to her face as Fotherby stumbled but, as though seeing her gave him more determination, he stepped back and lowered his weapon allowing his opponent to thrust his sword forward before Fotherby swiftly raised his own blade, cutting open the man's arm and causing him to drop his weapon. He pointed his sword at Sutton's chest and stared into his angry eyes, before he glanced at Lady Barrington, who smiled and allowed her eyes to brim with grateful and relieved tears.

"Your apology is accepted," Fotherby said sternly as he lowered his blade. "That wound should not be deep, but as a surgeon, I must advise you to put the doctor you brought to good use and get it stitched at once."

Portland and Darlington exchanged words while Mrs Portland rushed over to her husband and gripped him in a relieved embrace.

"My apologies, Lady Barrington," Darlington muttered, as though the words were the hardest he had ever spoken.

"Your apology, likewise, is accepted," she said softly, only relieved to lean against her husband's side and have her champion restore her honour in the duel. The three of them turned at the sound of metal on metal, to find the combat appeared to have resumed.

"Sir," Doctor Shipton demanded, facing Sutton. "This is entirely out of the code of practice."

"Until one was unable to fight," Sutton said angrily. "Was that not the condition? And, see, I fight still."

"Because your opponent had secured a victory and had the decency to allow you to pick up your sword once more." Shipton stood between the two men. "This is unprecedented, sir."

"Sutton," Darlington began, stepping into the square. "In God's name, man, do not lose any more than pride on this fight. You should not damage your honour. Mr Shipton, would you kindly return with us to The King's Head and tend to Colonel Sutton? Good day, my lady," Darlington said quickly, as he pulled his principal away, collecting his handkerchief as he went.

Shipton also collected his discarded handkerchief and joined the two departing men as they boarded the small rowing boat that returned them to the riverbank. Portland watched as Fotherby looked thoughtfully at his sword before collecting the handkerchief he had thrown to the ground and offered it to the young surgeon to clean the blood from his blade.

"Honour intact," Fotherby laughed slightly as Mrs Portland ran over to him. "What an awful man."

"Thank you, Fotherby," she began, standing on tiptoes to kiss his cheek. "I cannot tell you how greatly I appreciate what you have done for me."

"Nor can I, my dear Fotherby," Portland added.

Fotherby only smiled as he lifted Mrs Portland's shawl and returned it to her before he ushered them down to the boat, which had returned to ferry them the thirty feet to the riverside. Fotherby remained silent as he stepped ashore and followed Lord and Lady Barrington back to The Sun Inn. The silence felt entirely different to the silence that had clung to him as he had journeyed out in the misty half-light, but now he felt too exhausted to say anything. It did not matter, however, for Portland and his wife were happily raining praise upon the surgeon.

"Please carry on," Fotherby said softly as Portland announced their intention to eat. "Only, I am so weary, I hardly slept last night. I think I shall have to lay my head down."

Having excused himself from his guests, Fotherby walked up the stairs and collapsed onto the bed, easing the sliced jacket from his left shoulder, and looked down at the red shirtsleeve beneath. He had been a fool to believe that any man who could speak such poison to a lady would adhere to a code of honour, but he had been determined not to allow Sutton a victory on any grounds. Slowly, he peeled up his cuff and looked at the deep wound thoughtfully with a curious, detached manner that surprised him. He had never received such a wound before, indeed he could not recall ever bleeding this much, but he had a grim determination that seemed to calm him as he witnessed the blood that spilt from the four-inch gash on his forearm.

Portland and his wife took breakfast downstairs before they returned to their room and Lady Barrington changed into a white dress that only seemed to enhance her dark beauty as Portland beheld her. She smiled as she saw his expression.

"Is it possible that I can love you more each day," he began, "when yesterday I gave you all the love I had?"

"I believe it is entirely possible, Philip. For that is how I view you. But you must save a little love as I must, for our dear brothers and sisters, and now Lieutenant Fotherby, too."

"He is the very best of men," Portland agreed. "I wish Harry would behave more like the good surgeon."

They both turned at the sound of a knock on the door and Portland stepped over, pulling it open. He was surprised to find Fotherby leaning on the door frame, and the lieutenant gave a slight smile.

"Forgive me, Portland. I have a request to make of you."

"You look drunk, Fotherby," Portland began. "Did you decide that a duel was a good occasion to break your abstinence?"

"No," Fotherby laughed so weakly that Portland felt a frown cross his face. "I wondered if I could entreat you to find Doctor Shipton."

"Shipton? The surgeon?"

"Yes, the surgeon."

"God, Fotherby," Portland began as he snatched Fotherby's right arm and spun him around to see the blood that trickled down to his hand and watched a moment as the drops fell to the ground. "Of course I will go. Rosie," he called back and, in a moment, his wife stood beside him, "would you stay with Fotherby while I go and find the surgeon?" Lady Barrington's eyes became wide as she looked at Fotherby's arm and she nodded quickly.

"I am well," Fotherby began, trying to dissuade Mrs Portland from remaining with him. "Only, it needs stitching and I have not got my equipment with me."

"It is a good thing," Portland continued as jovially as he could while he helped Fotherby back to his room, sparing only a brief glance for the discarded coat and the bloody sheets, "you warned me when we first met that your needlework was not good."

"Oh Lord, Fotherby," his wife began as she picked up the coat from the ground and looked at the sliced and bloodied sleeve. "Why did you not say anything? Lie down. Philip, go quickly."

"No," Fotherby muttered as he looked thoughtfully at his arm. "I think I am meant to keep it elevated."

Portland left the room, rushing down the stairs and hurrying to find the landlord. After learning where he might find Doctor Shipton and assuring his host that his friend's condition was in no way contagious, he rushed out into the morning light. The sun was already burning through the mist that had clung to the town when last he had ventured out, and he spared a brief glance for the striking greenness of the tall trees and the expansive park a short distance away before he stepped quickly through the crowds of people in search of the address the landlord had given him.

"Philip!"

He stopped as he heard a voice call from across the street and at once a smile caught his features as two ladies hurried across the cobbled road to stand before him.

"Cassandra? Margaret?" he began, unable to fathom why these two ladies were to be found in Buxton. "How did you get here?"

"Rosie told us you were journeying to Derbyshire," the taller of the two explained. "And as Mother is in London, and so is Harry's concern, we decided to come and surprise you."

"You do not seem quite so pleased to see us as I had hoped," the other said softly. "Was it because I called across to you?"

"No," he replied. "I am quite sure there is little you could do that would upset me, Margaret. I am just amazed to find you here. Where are you staying?"

"At The King's Head. It is a little distance from here, but we thought to take in the parkland today."

"I know it," Portland replied, lifting first Margaret's and then Cassandra's hand and kissing them.

"But Philip," Cassandra continued, "you seemed in terrible haste when we interrupted you. It is not Rosie, is it? Is she well?"

"No," he replied, "it is not Rosie. It is my friend with whom we have been staying. He is in need of a surgeon and I was going to find one."

"Good lord," Margaret said softly. "Let us hope we have not detained you so long that any further harm has befallen him. You must continue at once, Philip."

"We are staying at The Sun Inn. There." He pointed to the establishment that was only a little further down the road. "Rosie will be so pleased to see you both."

"Then the moment we have toured the park, we shall seek you at the inn."

Forcing himself to recall what his task had been, he parted from the two ladies and rushed towards the chambers of Doctor Shipton. He stopped before a tall black door and clattered the knocker three times, waiting to be granted admittance. When the door remained closed he pounded his fist upon it, drawing the attention of the passers-by and, eventually, that of the people indoors.

"How may I help you, sir?" asked a straight-faced gentleman as he looked down on Portland.

"Is Doctor Shipton within?"

"Yes, sir. But he was called upon early this morning and has currently retired."

"But he is needed. With great haste, sir, please. For my friend might just bleed out if he is not given attention soon."

"Can a gentleman have no rest?" demanded a voice from further within the room. "Who is it, Stone?" The doctor appeared at the door and a look of recognition passed his features. "Lord Barrington, is it not?"

"Yes sir. And I know you were called prematurely from your bed this morning to settle a matter of honour for my wife, but my friend is wounded and he did not tell me until now. In truth, sir, he has need of you at once if you can come."

Portland was surprised by how little persuasion the doctor needed. He nodded and at once collected a compact carry case before he stepped out of the house and walked alongside his guide. The pair were silent until they reached the inn but their speed was great and, when they stepped into the inn Shipton finally spoke.

"What befell him?"

"I do not know," Portland began. "He was unharmed when the combat ended, yet now he has a gash down his arm with enough blood to fill a pail." He guided the surgeon to his friend's room and opened the door.

Fotherby was seated at the desk, his head resting on his right arm and his eyes closed, while Lady Barrington held the young man's left hand up. They both turned to look at the newcomers' arrival although Fotherby's gaze could scarcely make out more than the fact that two figures stood in the doorway. He narrowed his eyes, trying to focus them, but it was to no avail.

"Thank God you found him, Philip," Mrs Portland began. "For several minutes ago he just drifted out of consciousness and I could gain no sense from him."

"You had the insight to lift the wounded limb," Doctor Shipton replied. "That is good."

"That was not my insight, sir. It was his own. Might I entrust Lieutenant Fotherby into your care, Doctor? For I am afraid I shall only bring him more harm."

The doctor nodded quickly and set the box he carried onto the table, causing Fotherby to jump back to his senses.

"Doctor Shipton, sir," the younger surgeon muttered in a voice that slurred his name.

"Good God in heaven," Shipton began. "I thought it was you." He took Fotherby's left hand from Lady Barrington who stepped back to join her husband. "I knew your father and mother."

"My mother has been dead for twenty-five years."

"Last time I spoke with your father you were planning to join the army, to fight for King and country."

"No," Fotherby replied. "I did not fight. I too am a surgeon now, but I did not bring my own case, for I had not thought to use it."

"Does your father know about this morning's misadventure?"

"No." An urgency gripped Fotherby's voice and he forced his head back so that he could turn a pleading gaze to the doctor. "And you must not tell him, please.

It would kill him." Fotherby turned his to his friends and smiled slightly. "Portland, thank you. I did not think," his voice faded and Shipton caught his head as he lost consciousness.

"Can you help him, Doctor?" Lady Barrington's frightened voice asked. "You must help him."

"I have every intention of helping him, Lady Barrington. Today I witnessed a gentleman fighting a charlatan. I have already stitched the charlatan. I could not in good conscience allow the gentleman to die." He turned his gaze to Portland. "Lift him onto the bed."

Portland did as he was instructed, struggling to move his friend for he was a good deal taller than him. Fotherby awoke the moment Shipton washed down the wound and he watched with a fascination as the surgeon tended him as he had tended so many others himself. Portland excused himself and his wife, and Fotherby looked up at the face of the older surgeon.

"I have never been wounded before. I am always sitting where you are. Never lying here."

"I hope that you will never again find yourself in such a situation. I must admit I was a little surprised at the subject of your duel. Perhaps more so that your uncle had allowed your friend's wife to stay at Wanderford."

"What do you mean?" he asked, watching as Shipton began stitching his arm

- 327 -

"Your uncle had many dealings with black people. Men, women and children. And I do not think they are of a similar nature to those of your friend."

Fotherby only heard the words, he could not acknowledge their meaning, for he watched in a hypnotic fashion as the needle in the man's hand continued to bind together his arm before he placed a lint dressing over the wound and wrapped bandaging around it. By the time Shipton had concluded his work, Fotherby's eyes were closed and Shipton saw himself out of the room. Portland immediately opened the door to his own room and looked across.

"He is asleep," Shipton said softly.

"Thank you, sir. Thank you so very much. What do I owe you?"

"I shall send a bill to Wanderford."

"No, sir," Portland said quickly. "You heard Lieutenant Fotherby's words. He does not wish his father to know. Name the price, sir, and I shall redeem it."

"I shall return in two days to change the dressing. I shall settle the bill with you then."

"Two days? We were to return to Wanderford tomorrow."

"I think your plans will have to be altered, Lord Barrington. It would be a welcome surprise if your friend is walking tomorrow."

Whether it was that Fotherby was stronger than Shipton had believed or that he was determined to prove the surgeon wrong, he ensured that the following evening he rose and dined with Lord and Lady Barrington, though he scarcely ate anything. The reason he had forced himself to rise was as a result of the two other ladies who sat at table with them. It was not entirely the case that he had risen to meet Miss Portland and Miss Webb. In truth, Lady Barrington had been unwilling to leave his bedside and, to his discomfort and embarrassment, Miss Portland had also sat by.

Cassandra Portland was the most beautiful woman Fotherby had ever seen. She had a slight curve to her cheeks and a moist eye that caught the light so she always seemed to be smiling. Indeed, her lips were so frequently turned up in a genuine expression of happiness that she might have nursed him back to health through this alone. Like her brother, she saw no obstacle in Lady Barrington's colour and Miss and Mrs Portland talked to one another as the greatest of friends, as each considered the other to be so.

"What of Miss Delphina?" Fotherby asked softly as those seated around him continued to eat. "With yourselves and your mother absent, who is tending her?"

"Her nurse," Miss Portland replied quickly, before anyone else at the table could speak. "And, of course, David dotes on her."

"David?"

"Our youngest brother," Portland explained.

"There are so many of you. I am a little jealous, if truth be told."

"Have you no brothers or sisters, Lieutenant?" Miss Portland asked.

"None."

"Nor have I," Miss Webb replied. "And nor has Rosanna. That is why we were both blessed to have been welcomed into Barrington Manor."

The shrewd young surgeon felt his eyes narrow as she addressed Lady Barrington in such a way, for he had become accustomed to the members of the family referring to her as Rosie. Indeed, he felt that Miss Webb was a puzzling member of this giant family, and it was on this topic that he spoke to Miss Portland the following morning.

Aside from her perfect looks, Cassandra Portland was eloquent and knowledgeable and, the more Fotherby came to know of her, the more he questioned that she was not already married. At twenty-five years old and with the money that was attached to her, it was a great mystery to him.

"Margaret, that is Miss Webb, was our grandfather's ward. He knew her father, but he was a gentleman who fell far from favour long before Margaret was born."

"And what of her mother?" Fotherby asked thoughtfully.

"She does not know and, truthfully, not one of us does. Excepting perhaps Mother." Miss Portland smiled across at Fotherby. "Philip talked so often of you that I feel I know you already."

"I am certain that he built me into a far greater man than I truly am," Fotherby replied nervously, recalling what Lady Barrington had said about how Portland had wished the pair to marry.

"I do not think so. You fought a duel to defend Rosie's honour and, furthermore, I know you did it to protect Philip."

"How do you know that?"

"Because, were I a gentleman, I should have done exactly the same. Rosie and Philip are my greatest friends, Lieutenant Fotherby. That you were willing to defend them at such a risk to yourself only makes you an even better man than Philip had led me to believe."

"You are frighteningly perceptive, Miss Portland."

She did not say anything more but lifted his right hand and kissed it before she walked from the room.

Doctor Shipton, true to his word, arrived two days after he had stitched Fotherby's arm, impressed by the progress his patient had made. He did, however, demand that Fotherby should stay in Buxton for a further four days so that he could remove the stitches from his arm.

"I am trying to protect your father from the news you do not wish to share with him," Shipton had answered firmly When Fotherby had tried to dissuade him. "However, if you would rather I attended Wanderford Hall in four days' time, I shall do so."

Feeling foolish and guilty in deceiving his father but fearing for the old man's health should he find out, Fotherby had been forced to agree to Shipton's request. And so the small company spent a full week in Buxton during which time Fotherby came to learn more of Miss Portland and Miss Webb, although the latter spent almost all of her time with Portland. Often when they walked out, for the weather was bright and the temperature high, Portland would escort Miss Webb and both Lady Barrington and Miss Portland would walk beside the young surgeon. This did not seem to trouble any of them, but Fotherby felt uncomfortable at how the attention was divided.

August was well underway when they returned to Wanderford Hall. Fotherby had invited Miss Portland and Miss Webb to join them, feeling that it was the right thing to do and that he was not yet ready to say farewell to Cassandra. As they stepped down from the carriage, which had been a little tight for the five of them, Miss Webb took Philip's arm and walked a little way ahead. Lady Barrington followed by herself and Fotherby offered his arm to Miss Portland, who took it happily.

"Does Miss Webb always claim so much of Portland's time?" Fotherby asked, wishing to address the issue that so concerned him.

"Margaret has never forgiven Philip for not marrying her, Lieutenant. But her mother being at best obscure, meant that our mother would not permit such a thought."

"But surely he broke with tradition by marrying Lady Barrington."

"Indeed. But they have a love and understanding of one another that no social stricture could deny. But Margaret has a spell over Philip. I do not understand it, for she is not at all like Rosie, but she enchants him. So much so that what you see before you is so often how our outings run."

They reached the others and Fotherby pushed open the door, before permitting entrance to his guests. His uncle met them almost at once and graciously welcomed them before he turned to face his nephew.

"Well, Henry. I hear you have been busy in Buxton."

"What?" Fotherby whispered. "What do you mean?"

"You went for a few days and stayed four times the length, bringing back with you two charming, but additional, ladies."

Portland looked sideward at his friend's pale face turning more ashen as his father appeared.

"I am glad you are all safely returned. Henry, there is a visitor to see you. He is in my study."

The gaiety of the young party vanished as the two older gentlemen guided the Portlands and Miss Webb into the Drawing Room. As he walked past his son, Fotherby's father took his wrist and looked into his face with such disappointment that the younger man felt tears stab at his eyes. He watched as his friends and family walked through a door at the other side of the hall before he walked to the study door beneath the giant mural of Bosworth Field.

It had to be Doctor Shipton. Who else knew to find him there and could have told his father and uncle of what had happened? For he was certain that they both knew. Perhaps Commander Sutton had found out where he lived and had decided to redress the balance of honour. These thoughts flitted through his head as he pushed open the door and he frowned as his gaze rested upon a gentleman in a military uniform with a powdered wig on his head. With his back turned, this man could have been anyone but, upon hearing the door open, when he spoke Fotherby recognised at once his identity.

"Imagine," he began, without turning to face the young lieutenant. "I am sitting at a table of officers who are questioning my wisdom, my sanity even, when I talk about discarding with military protocol and promoting a boy who has only just qualified over a man with ten years' experience. And as I sit there, mentioning your name," he said firmly, turning now to Fotherby and pointing his finger accusingly, "one of the officers, a veteran of the American wars, informs me that he will never support the rising of someone who only two days earlier insulted the honour of another veteran."

"I believe he insulted his own honour, sir," Fotherby whispered.

"How could you do this? Why do you think that I warned you away from Mr Portland? God knows it was not for his sake but for yours. This is what I knew would happen." Captain Peters glared across at the younger man and continued in a voice that was so quiet that Fotherby could scarcely hear him. "I hold no ill will against Barrington, except that I hold him solely responsible for your current situation. So when I travel to Ceylon at the end of the week, it will be Kitson who accompanies me, not you."

"Yes sir," Fotherby muttered, at a whisper even quieter than the man before him. "I am sorry for the trouble I caused you. And that you felt any embarrassment or shame, I am sorry for that also."

"Why do you do this, Fotherby?" Peters asked, desperation in his voice.

"Do what, sir?"

"Whatever is morally right. For once, will you not think about what might help you?"

"I cannot compromise, sir."

"With reluctance," Peters said walking over to him and pulling back his sleeve to reveal the healing wound on his forearm. "I must admit to having a high regard for your conduct, Lieutenant Fotherby. But when you joined the army, you pledged to compromise everything for King and country. I am sorry that this was a promise you were not able to keep. Good day, Fotherby."

"Good luck, sir," Fotherby muttered and watched as his captain left the room. He walked unsteadily over to the window and stared out over the grounds of the house, his house, but saw nothing. For so many years he had known this to be his vocation, as strongly felt as any priest might. And now, despite the constant work and the support of Captain Peters, he had lost it. With an inordinate amount of self-loathing he realised that he was questioning why he ever chose to fight the duel, and then he felt only greater shame.

When the door opened again it was his father who stepped in and found his son sitting on the floor beneath the window, his hands gripping his head and his eyes closed. Fotherby heard him enter but could not bring himself to lift his gaze to him, full of shame and guilt. Tobias Fotherby offered his hand down and, seeing that his son was making no attempt to take it, he began speaking.

"Henry. You have guests here. You cannot afford to spend your time alone."

"I am so sorry, Father," came the miserable reply. "But I do not feel in any mood to entertain."

"Captain Peters has left."

"Yes. I should have gone with him, but I chose to ignore his warnings and follow what I deemed best. Father, I should never have formed a friendship with Portland. Peters was right. I have broken my promise to the army, and to my commanding officer. And now I do not have a place. Not just in the army, but anywhere."

"I like Lord Barrington. He is eloquent and well read. And I like Lady Barrington, too."

"Did Peters tell you about the duel?"

"Yes. He told me. He arrived yesterday and demanded to see you. And then he told me that you had fought someone over an offence. And, Henry, I cannot tell you how sick I was with worry that you had not returned home."

"I did not want you to know."

"Were you ashamed of your actions?"

"No," Fotherby answered, with resounding strength. "Colonel Francis Sutton is a vile man and had no honour to defend. I could not sit by and do nothing." He rose to his feet now and looked at his father, biting back tears. "What could I have done, Father? What could I have done to have remained a gentleman and retained my place as an army surgeon? Tell me, please, for I can see no compromise."

His father gave him no answer. Indeed, there was no answer. Fotherby struggled through a further week with the presence of Portland and his family but, as he bade them farewell, he only felt more lonely. Portland had tried to insist that they departed shortly after Peters' visit, but Fotherby's uncle and father had requested that the guests stayed a while longer. The sole comfort that Fotherby gained was in his exchanging of letters with Miss Kitty Simmons and, as October claimed its hold on Derbyshire, Fotherby announced to his father his intention to journey down to London. Neither his father nor his uncle tried to dissuade him, each having witnessed the terrible loneliness and neglect that the young man suffered.

## Chapter Thirteen

*Betrayal By A Black Lady*

Since the arrival of Lady Barrington at Chanter's
House, Mrs Tenterchilt had struggled to come to terms
with the two worlds in which she found herself. She had
never given any thought to the lifestyle her brother had
adopted in the West Indies, nor the equality of black and
white men but, having found and enjoyed the
companionship of Lady Barrington, she had spent
several weeks trying to discern the correct moral code.
She had decided to regard black men and women as
equal to white and, to this end, had begun discussing the
matter with her daughters so that they might never find
the integration of black men and women as confusing as
she had done.

"But Uncle Thomas calls them savages," Arabella
pointed out. "And he knows them very well, for he owns
many."

"But he has not met the lords and ladies of these
people," Mrs Tenterchilt began. "He only sees the lower
class."

"I am glad we may view them as fellow men. Mr
Blake, the poet, believes that they are God's children as
we are. Man Friday was as great a hero as Robinson

Crusoe," Imogen replied as she picked up her embroidery.

"I am glad, too," Catherine added. "I enjoyed Justice's company when he visited. He was the strongest man I have ever met."

In the autumn, as the parliament reconvened, Mrs Tenterchilt also wrote to her cousin who had a seat there and beseeched him to offer his support to Pitt's cause. Feeling, therefore, that she had begun to amend her former prejudices, she enjoyed a peaceful Christmas surrounded by those people she loved the most in the world.

Now, however, Christmas seemed a long time ago. March had stormed into London, chasing February with violent winds and heavy rain. Imogen was reading in the corner of the room, leaning over the book as she soaked in each of the words. Arabella was sitting beside her mother, who was demonstrating quilling to her daughter, with Arabella's skillful, light fingers making easy work of the fine papers. Catherine sat at her father's feet and held Gulliver on her knee. They all looked up as Major Tenterchilt rose.

"I have an appointment, my dears, that I am afraid I must keep."

"But Papa," Imogen began. "The weather is terrible. You should not go out in this, It will not do your leg any good."

"Thank you for your concern, dear Imogen. But, with thanks to the skill of Lieutenant Fotherby, my leg scarcely troubles me now."

"When can I accompany you, Papa?" Catherine asked.

"Not to this appointment."

"Your father is going to play his games, Catherine," Mrs Tenterchilt said, failing to conceal her disapproval, or perhaps uncaring that her children should see it. "In much the same way as you play with your toys."

"But Papa has not got toys."

"No. He plays with cards."

"Many gentlemen do it," Imogen said, without lifting her head from the book.

Major Tenterchilt wished good night to all of his children and his wife before he walked out of the room. He collected the cane which he had come to carry more through habit than necessity, and donned his coat before he walked out into the night. The evenings were stretching out now but, by the time he reached the clubhouse, it was dark. He was met there by Colonel Pottinger, who he guided into the building and made introductions on the man's behalf. Grassford, Kildare and Bryn-Portland welcomed the colonel to their table and, as the cards were shuffled and dealt, the conversation sprang to life.

"The major remarked that you were present on the fields of Flanders in the war," Kildare began as he thumbed through his cards.

"Indeed," Pottinger remarked as he lifted a card from the deck.

"Major Tenterchilt furthermore informed us that you had the new Lord Barrington as one of your lieutenants." Bryn-Portland peered over the top of his cards to watch the newcomer's response.

"That is true, sir."

Tenterchilt watched as this exchange unfolded, curious to try and learn more of the confusing figure of Lord Barrington.

"He is my nephew," Bryn-Portland continued.

"He is a righteous man," Pottinger replied cautiously.

"He is a pious man, you mean, sir. I feel that I owe him less as an uncle than I do as a gentleman, so you need not be so politic in your answer."

"Truthfully, sir, I found your nephew to be greatly out of place in my company and I was not in the least disappointed to lose him."

Bryn-Portland smiled slightly before discarding the queen of spades onto the table. "I have no wish for another black woman," he remarked flatly. "They have caused me enough trouble."

The conversation did not linger on Lord Barrington but, as the gamblers met each week, some reference would inevitably be made to the disappointment or dislike that the gentlemen had of him. As May arrived in London the group sat down for what was to be the last evening before Bryn-Portland returned to spend summer in Wales, and Grassford in Norfolk. Pottinger was in a poor mood as he reached the clubhouse and glared across at Major Tenterchilt.

"I have little interest in talk, Josiah," he said firmly. "I feel I have fought a battle today."

"What happened?" the major asked as he pulled open the door. "You have never been a man to struggle with conflict."

"Roger. That boy needed more than a belt to put respect into him."

"Your son is not a boy from whom I would have expected conflict."

"No," Pottinger replied angrily. "For you may gift him a pistol and be a benefactor, but should I try to inspire him to use it he treats me as a malefactor."

The major did not offer a reply but tried to imagine the disappointment he might have faced if he had a son who refused to follow in his footsteps. Pottinger's eyes narrowed as he glanced sideward at his silent friend. It was true that he had fought with his son, and furthermore had come to blows with the young man, over the career he had chosen for him. But had his indignation ended there he may not have found himself in such poor humour. In addition to this he had entertained his father-in-law, and the general had delighted in promoting the virtues of Major Tenterchilt and declaring that the major would never have accepted such disobedience in a son.

"I shall scarcely know what to do with a Wednesday evening after this week," Kildare began as he looked at his cards.

"Three does not seem enough to merit a game," Major Tenterchilt agreed. "Have you a wife to return to, Mr Bryn-Portland? In truth I realised that, aside from the nephew you deplore so much, I know nothing of your family."

"Yes. I have a wife. She lives all year in Wales, for she has no interest in London, and has no wish to encounter those who usurped our titles."

"Lord Barrington was very courteous when he attended Chanter's House," the major replied as he looked down at his hand. "And Lady Barrington, too."

"Lord and Lady Barrington," Bryn-Portland hissed. "They are children playing games, nothing more. And she is a savage."

Pottinger, pleased to have a conversation to carry his thoughts from the events of the day, watched on with an amused smile.

"Are you an abolitionist, Major?" asked Kildare.

"My politics are answerable to the king, sir. But I am given to say once more that Lady Barrington, black or no, presented herself favourably."

"I imagine she did," Bryn-Portland muttered. "She is a Jezebel who has corrupted the very fabric of my family's nobility." He watched, as others did, as Major Tenterchilt collected the contents of the pot.

The evening's conversation turned then but, as the darkness of night closed in around them, a madness seemed to take the impassioned Bryn-Portland and, every time the major collected winnings, he scowled across. Grassford bowed out of the games and watched on, confused by the mistrust and hatred that seemed to have taken hold of the gamers. Kildare also folded out of the game and Pottinger followed closely behind.

"Come now," Bryn-Portland announced as he looked across at Major Tenterchilt. "I have come to the end of my purse strings. What do you say to the carriage that waits outside for me?"

"Very well," Major Tenterchilt replied, watching as the notes of promise piled in the centre of the table.

"In God's name, men," Grassford began. "It is a game. You are not fighting a duel."

"Oh, I believe we are," Bryn-Portland muttered under his breath, but laughed for the benefit of the other men. "My townhouse," he said loudly, tossing another paper into the centre of the table.

"And mine," Tenterchilt replied.

"It must be quite a hand you have, sir."

"Indeed it is," Tenterchilt replied. In truth his cards had only a height of queen but he could recall seeing all the kings placed in the pile of discarded cards, as well as the queen of spades which was the only lady that could top his own hand.

"My estate," Bryn-Portland said, throwing in a final paper.

"And mine," repeated Tenterchilt, drinking heavily from the glass of port beside him.

All the gentlemen turned as there was a crash behind them, where Bryn-Portland's valet was now picking up the shards of smashed glass. The gentlemen turned back to the table as Major Tenterchilt presented his hand of cards and each man present turned expectantly to Bryn-Portland, who placed his cards out one by one. His final card stared up at the gentlemen who witnessed it with disbelief. None more so than Major Tenterchilt as he beheld the queen of spades.

"Won by the black lady," Bryn-Portland laughed as he collected the voluminous pile of winnings. "Perhaps not all black women are bad for my family."

"I saw that card go down," Major Tenterchilt whispered.

"Are you accusing Mr Bryn-Portland of cheating?" Pottinger asked in disbelief.

"No," the stunned major muttered, uncertain of himself suddenly. "Congratulations, sir. I am certain Chanter's House will appeal to your wife and may even coax her into London. Though I must ask that you grant me a week to settle such matters."

"Of course you may have a week. I shall talk at once to my lawyer."

Major Tenterchilt watched with a sickening feeling as Bryn-Portland departed alongside Kildare. Grassford looked thoughtfully over to where the tray had fallen and shook his head.

"I could swear I saw that lady go down," Tenterchilt said once more.

"As I believed I did," Grassford began. "But, with the wine that has been drunk, one game runs very much into another."

"Let me take you home, Josiah," Pottinger said quietly as he looked down on the table and realised that three black queens rested on it. He opened his mouth to highlight this fact but, as he watched the newly-impoverished major grip his head in his hands, he felt a bitter sense of justice. This may have been a man who could influence and guide men, but now he had nothing. His wife's father would surely struggle to find anything favourable in this man. He collected all the cards and helped Major Tenterchilt to his feet, before he and Grassford helped the major into a carriage.

Major Tenterchilt did not speak as he travelled in the Pottingers' carriage to Chanter's House. He struggled out in silence, feeling that the anxiety that weighed heavily on him caused his leg to throb once more and all energy to drain from him. He thanked his friend for the journey and watched as the carriage departed. He stood for so many minutes before the house, guilt and fear pouring down on him. The night was complete about him and the sounds of London were deadened by the blackness as he walked forward and placed his hand on the door to what had been his home. Pushing it open, he beheld with heavy eyes all that he had built for himself and all that he had now lost. When he met Elizabeth Jenkyns fifteen years ago, he could not have imagined that all of this would become his, nor that he could lose it so quickly and foolishly. He allowed the footman to take his coat and hat but retained his cane.

"Where is my wife?"

"She has withdrawn for the night, sir."

Major Tenterchilt nodded and walked into his study and, pulling open the top drawer, he looked down at the pistol that rested there. He lifted it up and studied it with a fascination but set it down quickly as the door opened and his wife walked in.

"Good lord, Josiah! What are you doing with that?"

"Sparing you from terrible news."

"Surely you mean robbing me," she continued, her usual measured approach returning to her tone. "Robbing me of an explanation."

"Robbing you of your inheritance, my dear."

"Major Tenterchilt," she began, pushing the pistol beyond his reach and kneeling down beside where he sat on the chair. "You have claimed all that was mine since that day we met. Do you recall it? Meeting on the roadside. I still wonder what made me talk to you. It was most out of character."

"You would have been better if you had not done."

"What has happened?" she asked fearfully. "For I cannot imagine life without you."

"You were wearing a yellow gown and wide brimmed bonnet," he whispered, smiling sadly across at her. "I was more nervous than I had ever been in my life."

"Thomas was horrified," she replied as she leaned forward and kissed his cheek. "For a lady to talk to a soldier without introduction? It was unheard of. But I knew. I knew even then."

"And you shared all that you had with me, and I have lost it."

"Lost it?" she whispered as she leaned away from him and stared hard at his guilty face. "What have you lost?"

"Our home, my dear. I have lost it all to a man who, I am certain, sat at the table with the sole intention of humiliating me."

"You gambled Chanter's House?" she hissed, rising to her feet. "How could you?"

"And the estate. I had a certainty of winning," he responded as he dropped his head into his hands. "I could not lose."

"And yet you did."

"Every day for the past fifteen years I have thanked God that your carriage wheel splintered. Until now. This night I lament it." He reached across the table and picked up the pistol. "As you can see, my dear, it would have been better if you had left the door unopened and me with this."

Mrs Tenterchilt stared at her husband, willing herself to hate him for taking this house and the land that had been her only gift from the mother she had lost so many years ago. But, as she watched him lift the pistol, she tried to imagine her life without him and she felt an emptiness seize her. She snatched the gun from him and threw it across the room.

"I cannot believe that you have lost the house and estate, and I cannot bear to consider what is to become of us and our daughters. But nor can I bear to face it alone. Do not leave me, Major Tenterchilt, for I do not think I shall survive without you."

Rising to his feet, Major Tenterchilt embraced his wife, trying to find the strength to support her but feeling that, in truth, she was by far the stronger half of the couple. For her own part, she needed her husband and loved him far more than she could admit at this moment.

The following day Mrs Tenterchilt rose early and ensured that she had time to discuss matters with her husband before he departed for Horse Guards. She sat at the dressing table and watched his reflection as he came to stand behind her.

"I shall visit Mr Dermot today," she said flatly. "He will be able to advise us on what is the correct course of action."

"Thank you, my dear." He leaned forward and kissed her hair.

"There is something more, Josiah," she said sternly, turning to face him. "I cannot bear that this might ever be repeated. Therefore, you must make me a promise."

"What is it?"

"I will not tolerate gambling of any kind. For I have lost greatly to it and gained so little. And know this," she added, steeling herself to speak the words that she had tried to contrive through the sleepless hours. "If you should fail in this promise, I shall take our daughters and begin a new life for us, for I shall not have you lose all that is theirs as well as my own."

Major Tenterchilt stared down at her, his face becoming hard and stern.

"I mean it, Josiah," she continued. "I will not compromise my children for a roll of a dice or a turn of a card."

"Very well, my dear," he said, struggling over the concession.

She stood and kissed his cheek before he walked from the room. When the children arose, Mrs Tenterchilt requested a moment of their time from their studies and guided them all out into the garden.

"Now, my dears, we are to begin an adventure. But before we journey away from this place, I would like you to make a picture in your mind of all that is before you, for it could be a long time before we stand here again. What do you see, my little lady?"

"There are flowers on the trees," Arabella answered. "And a house that shall one day be my own."

"And do not forget it," Mrs Tenterchilt whispered, tears forming in her eyes. Arabella longed to question the cause of her mother's tears but did not want to be the cause of them spilling. "And Imogen, what do you see?"

"Five types of trees, and sixty-seven of flowers. I counted them last summer. And beyond is a city that chokes on its industrialisation and is weighed heavy by its glory."

Her mother stared down at her and could only nod, unsure what answer she could give to the child who was scarcely ten years in age but spoke as eloquently as a lady of thirty. "And my dear little Catherine, what do you see?"

"A land that Gulliver and I have conquered. And where we are very happy to live. But I am ready for an adventure, Mama. And Gulliver will be too. Are we going to France?"

"No, not France. I am going to visit Mr Dermot to discover where we shall be staying."

"Your lawyer, Mama?" Arabella asked.

"Yes, my dear. Now, you all have lessons to attend."

She watched as they returned to the house, before she followed and rang for her maid. Penny appeared almost at once and bobbed a curtsy.

"I need to go out, Penny. Into London. Could you have the carriage readied?"

"Of course, ma'am."

"Penny?" she asked. "Would you be sad to leave Chanter's House?"

"No, ma'am. But I should be sad to leave the Tenterchilts."

"Do the servants know what occurred last night?"

"Everyone has a guess to make, especially as the scullery maid lifted the major's pistol that had been cast to the floor. But no one knows for sure, ma'am."

"Thank you, Penny," she replied, not offering an explanation.

The journey into London gave her the time she needed for her tears to fall unchecked. But, as she arrived at the lawyer's chambers, she brushed them away and stepped over to the door, knocked once and entered. She was met by a young man who bowed his head slightly.

"Mrs Tenterchilt," he began, without any prompt while he took her cloak. "My father is upstairs in his office. You came unannounced, I hope nothing is amiss." It was impossible to tell whether the young man had a genuine interest to support his words, for his face never altered and his eyes remained cold in their blue gaze.

"I am sorry to inform you, Cornelius, that things are beyond difficult. Is your father able to receive me at once?"

"I am certain of it," he replied. "And sorry to hear that you find yourself in difficulties. Rest assured that Father will do all he can. I am pleased that you have come," he continued as, having hung her cloak on a hook, he guided her up the stairs to the lawyer's office, "for I wished to thank you in person for your invitation. I was sorry my father and I were unable to attend the party. Since my mother's death he has scarcely left this office."

"I was very sorry to hear of it," Mrs Tenterchilt said softly.

He bowed his head slightly, but offered no reply. Instead, he pushed open a door and stood back to allow Mrs Tenterchilt to enter. "I shall leave you then, Mrs Tenterchilt." He closed the door and walked back down the stairs.

"Good morning, Mrs Tenterchilt," began the old man who sat at a wide desk. He struggled to push himself to his feet, but stopped as she began talking.

"Please, Mr Dermot, do not rise on my behalf. For I am here to inform you that I am bankrupt and have nothing to suggest I am worthy of any such gesture."

"That I cannot believe," he said calmly as he continued to rise. "To me you shall always be Sir Timothy's daughter and worthy of the highest degree of respect."

"Thank you," she whispered, feeling tears tug at her eyes by this simple remark and gesture of loyalty. She blinked them away as she recalled her purpose in being here. "I must speak bluntly to you, sir. My husband has lost all our money and, furthermore, all of our land and property. I am therefore at a loss and must entreat you for any advice that you may have on such a sorry position."

"What of the major's position? Will he retain his wage?"

"To my knowledge he is discussing that fact as we speak. But we are homeless, Mr Dermot, or shall be by Wednesday. Where am I to live?"

"Can you not entreat your uncle to house you? Or your brother?"

"I have no way to explain this to you, sir, but despite my husband's actions in losing both Chanter's House and the estate, I do not wish to be parted from him. Both my uncle and my brother have sought for my separation from my husband for many years and would accept only myself and my daughters. I want my family to remain together."

She was pleased to find that the man made no effort to dissuade her but instead nodded and sat back on his chair. He rubbed his chin as he tried to resolve the matter before, at last, he sat forward and raised his finger as though to emphasise the words that accompanied it.

"But you still have land, Mrs Tenterchilt."

"How so?"

"Cast your mind back to three Christmases ago. You entrusted to me a document that your husband had acquired. They were the deeds of a house in Scotland."

"I recall," she muttered. "But Scotland, Mr Dermot? That is so far away."

"You might try and sell it," he suggested.

"I do not wish my husband to have any more access to money, Mr Dermot. He has never learnt its importance, being born without it, and the temptation to spend instead of invest is too great for him."

"Then," he paused and leaned forward, "there is the possibility that your name alone might appear on the deeds."

"That my husband shall not own the house?"

"Indeed. Would the major consider such a thing?"

"I am certain he shall. And I want it to pass to my daughters after me. I shall not have my brother or my cousin claim it. My poor Arabella has already lost her inheritance once."

"Then I shall have Cornelius draw up the papers and, with your permission, I shall attend Chanter's House tomorrow to witness them signed."

Major Tenterchilt did not initially wish to accept this arrangement but, realising that his alternative was for his wife to return to her family without him, and acknowledging this was of his own doing, he consented. He felt his eyes narrow as he watched the frail man sign the paper as a witness but knew that the only person in the room he truly did not trust was himself. As the lawyer folded the paper, the major began talking.

"What is to happen now, sir?"

"You shall journey with all haste to Scotland, Major. I do not believe that your wife wishes to witness Chanter's House's new inhabitants arriving. And that I understand."

"Thank you," Mrs Tenterchilt said, as the old man kissed her hand. "I cannot thank you enough for your care and diligence in our case."

"It is an honour, as it always has been, my lady."

He turned and walked out of the study, handing the paper to his son, who had stood behind him all this time. Now the young man began collecting up the bundle of papers and, bowing his head formally, stepped out of the room. He stopped as he heard a voice from behind him.

"What is happening Mr Dermot?"

"Miss Tenterchilt," he began, as he looked at the young lady who stared back critically at him. "It is not I who should be the one to tell you."

"Mama is worried. Should I be worried too?"

"No, Miss Tenterchilt, you will have no need to worry. I am certain of that."

Arabella watched as he walked out of the house, and turned to Imogen who was standing at the top of the stairs.

"I cannot tell you why, Bella," Imogen began as she climbed down the stairs, carefully gripping the banister.

"But now he has said that, I feel only more inclined to worry."

Arabella placed her arm about her sister's shoulders and kissed her forehead. "Mama has always trusted Mr Dermot, Imogen. I am certain we shall have nothing to fear."

## Chapter Fourteen
*The Poetic Judgement And Justice*

Obscurity was a preferred state of existence for Lieutenant Fotherby, never more so than in the realisation that a matter of honour had ranked higher than merit. He had not visited the Chesters, the Tenterchilts nor the Portlands at the end of the year, but had spent his Sundays escorting Miss Kitty Simmons on strolls through the city parks. On weekdays he journeyed out to Greenwich to help in the hospital there. He was paid poorly for this but, for the most part, he wished only to lose himself in the work he was able to do. The hospital also provided him with a place to sleep and food so that every penny he made was saved to enable him to return once more to Derbyshire.

He spent Christmas at Wanderford Hall with his father and uncle. His uncle's disagreement with him had faded now, seeing that the young man needed a time to recover from the sore disappointment he had suffered. During the first three months of the year Fotherby remained in Wanderford, travelling to Buxton often to offer any assistance he could to Doctor Shipton, who he came to regard as a mentor. Shipton never made demands on his time and would ask no questions of the young surgeon, but ensured that a day did not pass without telling Fotherby how greatly he appreciated his help. As March came to an end, however, Fotherby wished once more to return to the capital.

"I shall miss your help and your company, Fotherby," Doctor Shipton began as they made their farewells. "Be sure, when you do return, to visit me. But I have one further request to make of you."

"What is it?" Fotherby stood by the large black door and pulled it open. "If it is in my power I shall see it done."

"I would like you to consider this. Wanderford Hall is your duty as well as your home."

"You sound like my uncle," Fotherby laughed.

"But if you should take the final exam at the college you might follow your vocation from here. There is little call for an army surgeon and there has been little cause for one here since I was a child, but there is a great need for physicians. You have all the knowledge and more than you would need. I shall not be here forever, Fotherby, and there is only one other physician in Buxton, and he is a drunken fool. Think on it."

Fotherby assured him that he would and, indeed, it was this that filled his thoughts as he journeyed south to London the following day. He stood for several minutes outside the doors of the college and questioned repeatedly why his feet had led him there before he walked on through the city. He arrived at Lord and Lady Barrington's house as the April evening was just taking hold and was relieved to see a light burning through one of the windows. Stepping up to the door he knocked lightly and waited until Chilvers opened it.

"Lieutenant Fotherby," he said warmly.

"Good evening, Chilvers," Fotherby responded in a tone to match. "Are Lord and Lady Barrington at home?"

"No, Lieutenant. They are attending a concert this evening."

"Thank you, Chilvers. I shall leave you in peace, then."

"You can wait."

"No. I am quite sure they shall be tired when they return and will have no wish for company."

"Shall I tell them you called?"

"No, Chilvers, but thank you." Fotherby turned from him but stopped as he collided with someone. "Pardon, sir."

"Mr Harris, sir," Chilvers said quickly, as the newcomer ignored Fotherby and rushed into the house.

"Mr Portland," Fotherby said quickly, looking at the blood that poured from the man's nose.

"I need no help from you," Harris replied angrily, trying to stop the blood from spilling onto his pale pink coat as he pressed a handkerchief to his face. "Chilvers, have the floor cleaned."

Fotherby was about to leave but stepped forward as Harris reached out to Chilvers and lost consciousness. The old man had not the strength to hold him and Fotherby lifted him easily while Chilvers invited him into the study, his face becoming anxious as Harris began to choke.

"Fetch me a basin please, Chilvers," Fotherby said calmly and, as soon as the old man had returned, he pushed Harris' head over the bowl, which he rested on the younger man's knee. He sat beside Portland's brother until he regained consciousness and begrudgingly offered his thanks to the surgeon. Chilvers collected the basin and Fotherby rose to his feet as Harris retired quickly to his room.

Feeling uncertain with regard to what had just happened, Fotherby walked to the door and was about to excuse himself from the house when the front door swung open and Lord and Lady Barrington entered. They were laughing with one another and took a moment to recognise that they were not alone.

"Good God!" Portland exclaimed as his gaze rested on the surgeon. "What has happened?"

"Lieutenant Fotherby," Lady Barrington began at the same moment. "Are you hurt?"

Fotherby looked down at himself and realised that Harris' blood was splashed down his coat and shirt. He smiled slightly as he shook his head. "This is Master Harris' blood."

"What?" Portland asked. "Where is he?"

"He withdrew for the night."

"Chilvers," Portland continued as the old man entered, followed by a maid carrying a mop and pail. "Please make sense of this for me. What has happened to my brother? And by what stroke of God's blessing was Lieutenant Fotherby on hand to deal with it?"

"The surgeon came seeking you and Lady Barrington, sir. And Master Harris, I believe, had an altercation with a gentleman."

"How is he?"

"Aside from his nose, sir," Chilvers replied, "I would say only his pride is wounded."

At this statement Portland relaxed at once and held his wife to him. "What fortune that you were here, Fotherby. But please tell me, to what do we owe this long-awaited visit?"

"I wished only to apologise, though I am eight months late, for my behaviour at Wanderford following Captain Peters' visit."

"Captain Peters is a man capable of bringing on anger or pensiveness in any man, Fotherby, I shall not hold that against you. And when I learnt of the manner of his visit, I understood more."

"Truthfully, Fotherby, you shall never need to apologise to me," Lady Barrington added. "But you must have supper with us, and you may change into one of Philip's shirts while your own is washed."

"I intend to be in Greenwich in the morning," he began. "I was working there in the hospital last autumn and I feel I must go where I can do good."

"But you can do good here, Lieutenant."

Fotherby reluctantly accepted the offer, and stayed that evening with the Portlands. The following morning he rose to find his own clothes washed and pressed, for which he was greatly pleased, as his friend was as different to him in build as he could imagine. He walked quickly down the stairs but stopped as he was met by Chilvers, who ushered him into the Dining Room, where the two brothers sat across the table from one another.

"Thank you, Chilvers," Portland began as he smiled at his friend. "I did not want you disappearing as you did last time."

"Lieutenant Fotherby," the young man across the table began. "I do not believe we have ever properly met, but I do believe I owe you both thanks and an apology. Perhaps more than one."

Fotherby smiled across as he viewed Harris Portland for the first time as the man he truly was. He had not powdered his face, nor did he have the pristine white wig over his shaved head. His nose was swollen after whatever had befallen him last night but, aside from this, he bore no mark of the altercation.

"I accept both, thank you."

"Harry and I were talking of returning to Cornwall for a time," Portland continued as Fotherby took the seat that Chilvers pulled out for him. "I should like to return the courtesy that you showed Rosie and me, and invite you to Barrington Manor. Will you come with us?"

Fotherby looked from Portland to his brother and back again before he asked, "When will you be leaving?"

"Almost immediately," Harris replied. "I have reasons to leave town and Philip has not been home since October."

"Then I shall leave you at once," Fotherby began. "You must have matters to resolve here before you go."

"Fotherby," Portland said gently. "We want you to come too. Will you?"

"Delphi talks of no one but you," Harris persisted. "And I am quite certain that Cassandra will wish to see you once more."

Fotherby smiled slightly and nodded. "Thank you. Yes, I should be most happy to accept your invitation. I have never been to Cornwall before."

Harris had spoken the truth about the swift manner of their departure for, the following day, Lord and Lady Barrington left their townhouse, accompanied by Harris and Fotherby. The carriage journeyed on with little conversation. Harris had not returned to wearing his pale jacket and wig, but wore a loose-fitting lace shirt and long trousers, no longer looking like a court dandy but a country gentleman. He divided his time between sleep and gazing out of the window and clearly did not wish to speak. Lady Barrington seemed elated to be returning to Cornwall and had an irrepressible smile on her face while, by contrast, her husband watched his younger brother through concerned eyes. Fotherby witnessed all of this but remained silent.

They spent a night in Bath before their journey turned south and they travelled into Cornwall. The smell of the sea was the first thing that struck Fotherby as he stepped out of the carriage and stretched to his full height. The second was the imposing building before which they had stopped. The western sky, that was blood red in the sunset, silhouetted the colossal four storey building. The drive was not as long as Wanderford Hall, and the house did not have the parkland surrounding it which Fotherby's home could boast, but it was an ancient structure with almost as many windows in it as stones.

"What do you think of Barrington Manor, Fotherby?" Portland asked as he ushered his friend, his brother, and his wife indoors.

Fotherby did not answer at first, perhaps because he was overwhelmed by it or perhaps because the carriage journey had left him terribly weary. However, as he stepped into the hall and admired the sweeping staircase which led onto galleries on all four sides of the room, he smiled and whispered,

"It has an unequalled charm."

"Lord Barrington," a footman began. "Your mother is in the Drawing Room."

Portland waited as Fotherby relinquished his hat, before he guided him to one of the doors and opened it wide. Fotherby found himself smiling at once at the sound of someone reading poetry, Shakespeare he thought, but she stopped abruptly as they noticed the door opening and the four travellers stepped in.

"Philip!" the reader exclaimed, casting aside her book and leaping to her feet. Lieutenant Fotherby hung back as Cassandra greeted each of her brothers with warm embraces and kissed Lady Barrington's cheek with equal affection.

"Oh, my boys," a thin voice added, and he watched as a tall woman rose to her feet and held open her arms. "Lord Barrington, you have finally returned to me. Your father never spent a Christmas in London, you know. And my dear Harris, what of the corridors of power?"

"I am rather afraid I have been forced to flee them for a time, Mother," the young man explained as he stepped into her open arms and embraced her tightly.

"No, my dear boy. Your brother will see you safe, have no fear on that account." She turned to Lady Barrington and continued. "And Rosie, my beautiful dark princess. I miss you so much when you leave. You must ensure that Philip stays here, where his seat and his home are."

"I do try, Mother," Mrs Portland replied, "but Philip is determined to see his law passed in parliament. But see," she continued, pointing back to Fotherby who still stood in the doorway. "We have brought a guest. Please allow me to present Lieutenant Henry Fotherby. Lieutenant, this is our dear mother."

Fotherby, uncertain how to continue from such an introduction, bowed his head slightly and smiled across at the older lady whose face turned pale as she clutched Harris' arm.

"It is him," she whispered. "Harris, do you see it?"

Fotherby frowned as Harris tried to help his mother to a chair, but she pushed him back and rushed forward to Fotherby and stood staring at his features as though she were trying to identify a peculiar breed of animal. Portland sighed and nodded to Cassandra who took her mother's shoulders to guide her away from the confused surgeon.

"You must join us for supper," the older woman continued, addressing Fotherby now. "And sit by me."

Fotherby did not speak but took a chair beside Cassandra and watched and listened as the conversation turned. The dowager never took her eyes from him for more than a second and, when supper was finally served, she sat Fotherby to her right-hand side and studied him once more.

"Was it awful?" she asked, interrupting Cassandra.

"Was what awful, my lady?" Fotherby replied.

"Your death. Was it awful?"

Fotherby stared, confused by the woman before him. Portland placed the spoon he held into the dish before him, dropping his head into his hands, while Harris looked away. Cassandra, with a patience that only a daughter can carry, spoke to her mother.

"This is Lieutenant Fotherby, Mother. See how young he is. He is younger than Philip, so he cannot be Father."

"Nonsense, Cassandra. Do not seek to correct me. I can see in his eyes that it is your father."

"Pardon," Fotherby said softly. "But I believe you have mistaken me."

She only laughed, as though he had made the mistake, but throughout the entire meal she continued to talk to him about exploits she had shared with her late husband as though she expected him to know them. Fotherby politely corrected her on all occasions, but her mind was made up and no amount of talking could deter her from her ideas. The six of them dined alone and it was only at the end of super that Lady Barrington asked,

"Where is Margaret?"

"She is in her confinement," Cassandra whispered, and Fotherby felt at once relieved that something could detract from him.

"Confinement?" Portland repeated.

"Indeed, Philip, and I think you should talk with her as soon as you are able."

"Where is she?"

"In the Groundman's Cottage. It is out of courtesy in case her claims are true."

"What claims?" Lady Barrington asked.

"Those are claims that she is better presenting."

Cassandra would say nothing more on the matter and she quickly began talking to her younger brother who she sat beside.

"Where are your two youngest children?" Fotherby asked, now eager to turn the conversation away from Miss Webb.

"Delphina told me, Lieutenant Fotherby," the dowager replied. "She told me that no one had ever shown her such kindness since her father was alive."

"And is Miss Delphina well?" he persevered.

"I do not know. You are the surgeon, not I."

"Mother," Portland began sternly. "Fotherby is my guest here. Show him some kindness."

"I shall take you to see Delphi after supper if she is awake," Lady Barrington said softly.

Fotherby thanked her but did not try and venture a conversation after this. Instead he offered answers as polite but brief as he could manage whenever he was asked a question, or sat regarding the peculiar family he had joined. Harris smiled across at him as though he could follow the lieutenant's thoughts, but ventured no words. When supper finally ended the hour was late, but Lady Barrington insisted on taking Fotherby to visit Delphina. The moment they left the Dining Room she turned to face him, standing before him and blocking his path.

"Do you see now, Fotherby? Do you see why Philip did not wish to return home?"

"She is in grief," Fotherby muttered. "That is all that ails her."

"She should be locked away," she replied bitterly. "Her grief has caused such hurt. She set Harry on this doomed road, she ignores poor little Delphi through spite, and she has ended any hope Cassandra has to marry."

"I think no worse of you or any of your brothers and sisters because of your mother."

She offered him the weakest of smiles and stood on tiptoes to kiss his cheek, before she guided him up the broad stairs, through a door up more stairs until she stood at a white door with painted letters and pictures on. Halfway up were the words "Miss Delphina Sally Portland" while above them were painted a sun and clouds in a blue sky.

"Harry painted it," she began. "When Delphina was four she was so ill she could not leave this room for almost a year. Harry wanted to make it welcoming for her. He was not always what he is now."

She knocked on the door and pushed it open a little. There was a light inside that flickered as the door opened and Fotherby heard the young frail voice that had been such an inspiration to him.

"Rosie," it began, "I did not know you had come home."

"This very evening. But are you well, Delphi? Are you well enough to receive a visitor?"

"What visitor would visit me here?" There was an eagerness to her fragile voice that caused Fotherby to smile. And, as Lady Barrington pulled open the door and stood back so that he might step into the room, Delphina gave an excited cry.

"Lieutenant Fotherby, did you come all the way to Cornwall to visit me?"

"I did, Miss Delphina," he replied as he stepped in. "And do I find you in improved health?"

"Much improved for seeing you, Lieutenant. But I do not wish to speak of myself. Will you sit by me and tell me what is happening outside the walls of Barrington Manor?"

Fotherby moved the low chair from the fireside so that it was beside the bed. He took the pale hand she offered to him. Lady Barrington excused herself and Delphi looked expectantly across at the calm face of the surgeon.

"I was sorry you disappeared in London."

"I did not think I had a place in the discussions which were to follow. And I knew that you were improved."

"With thanks to you, Lieutenant. I never had a chance to thank you. And I was waiting for a chance."

"Waiting, Miss Delphina?"

"Lieutenant Fotherby, I have spent almost a year in this room. I watched the summer sunsets from this window, the winter storms over the sea. But, with the exceptions of the times when David has opened the window for me, I have heard only the sounds of this room." She placed her free hand over his wrist and closed her eyes as she listened to his pulse. "My nurse told Mother I should not leave my room, and would not again. But now I have thanked you, my conscience is clear and I am ready to stand before God."

Fotherby placed his other hand over her own and smiled across at her. "You had no need to concern yourself over such a thing. But I am pleased that you did, for it has given me a chance to express my admiration for you." He waited as she opened her eyes and looked across with confusion. "I have witnessed so many people approaching the same journey as you, but never have I witnessed anyone facing it as bravely as you. You have been a true inspiration to me, Miss Delphina."

"It is not a fear I have, Lieutenant. It is a sadness. For I shall miss my brothers and sisters so greatly and know that I should not hope to see them for a long time."

"I believe time will not matter in eternity." Fotherby lifted her hands and kissed them both. "But the hour is late, Miss Delphina. I shall leave you to sleep."

"I cannot sleep, Lieutenant. Each time I lie back I cannot breathe. Will you stay by me?"

Fotherby nodded, feeling he was unable to deny anything to the young woman who was approaching so prematurely the conclusion of her earthly life. He lifted the feather pillows behind her, watching as she sat back, allowing her to leave her bony fingers on his wrist as she used his steady pulse as a lullaby. When in this way she had fallen asleep, he placed her hand on the bed and left the room.

He recalled, as he silently closed the painted door, that he was in a house he did not know and that the hour was so late that sleep had claimed the house as well as the inhabitants. He tried to recall where Lady Barrington had guided him and he was able to trace his steps down to the hall once more. There was still a light visible beneath the Drawing Room door and, knocking quietly, he pushed it open. He was surprised to hear the sound of sobbing and was about to close the door once more, but stopped as he heard Cassandra's voice.

"Philip?"

"No, Miss Portland. I am sorry to intrude on your thoughts."

"Forgive me, Lieutenant. You must find us poor hosts. Mother accusing you of being her husband, I weeping in the shadows, and little Delphi balanced between life and death."

"It has never been in me to judge, Miss Portland. But on the contrary, I find you a most accommodating household. I am only sorry for the grief, fear and tears that I have found. If there were anything I could do to amend such things, I should gladly try."

"I believe you would, Lieutenant, but I am rather afraid we can only wait for Mother to tear the walls of Barrington Manor down around us and little Delphi to slip into eternity." She rose and walked over to him. "But come, you must have ventured here for a purpose. What can I help you with?"

"I was looking to be directed to a room."

"Of course. I shall show you to your room." She did not speak but took his hand and guided him up the stairs and along the gallery until she arrived at a door which opened onto a room at the front of the house. "It is not as neat as Wanderford Hall, I am afraid. But should you need anything you have only to ring for the servants." She pointed to the pleated cord that hung down by the fireside. "Goodnight, Lieutenant Fotherby."

"Thank you. Goodnight, Miss Portland." He paused and whispered, "these shadows linger over us only because there is light somewhere."

"The shadows are cast before me as though I have left the light behind. I cannot see through it anymore." Cassandra offered no more words but walked out of the room.

The following morning was met with a glorious light that streamed through the window of Fotherby's room. He had not drawn the curtains the previous night so that, the moment the sun topped the leafing trees, it awoke him. The house was in a different mood that morning. The dowager talked freely with Fotherby, making no reference to the confusion in his identity that had dominated conversation last night and had given him cause to secure the latch on his door. Philip was at the table talking with Harris, while Cassandra and Rosanna laughed happily. It was as though all the bitterness and sorrow of last night had melted in the sunshine.

"I shall go and visit Margaret today," Lady Barrington announced and at once Cassandra's smile faltered.

"But today I wished to go riding with you. Can you not spare me a day before you call on Margaret?"

"Of course. Philip, will you go and call on her? I do not like to think that she is left alone."

"Take Lieutenant Fotherby with you," Cassandra began. "And Harris, why do you not accompany them?"

"You are making me nervous, Cassandra," Portland laughed. "Have I something to fear from Margaret?"

Cassandra shook her head and laughed slightly but, later in the morning as the ladies prepared to go riding and the gentlemen to visit the shamed ward, she took Fotherby's arm and slowed her pace so that the other three walked on ahead.

"I do not know what to believe from Margaret, Lieutenant. But I should like to know the truth of the matter and cannot trust Philip to find it. He is spellbound where she is concerned and, whatever the truth, this might prove to be the cruelest enchantment."

"I shall always protect your brother, Miss Portland. I hold him in the highest esteem."

She parted from him as they reached the stable. The groom appeared, leading two horses out into the small courtyard, each saddled for a lady. However it was not the horses that caught Fotherby's attention but the groom himself, for he was certain he knew the man.

"Thank you, Cullington," Cassandra said, as she accepted the reins from him.

Portland grinned across at Fotherby and the two followed Harris through the grounds towards the cottage which Miss Margaret Webb now occupied.

"I feel certain I know that man," Fotherby muttered, glancing over his shoulder as though he expected to be able to see the groom, though they had walked some distance along a track.

"And so you do. Do you recall when I first came into the hospital tent?"

"Yes," Fotherby began. "He was the man plagued by nightmares."

"I could not send him away in disgrace," Portland continued. "So I found him a job here, to tend the horses. Which ensured I was no longer attacked by him."

They stopped at a small house with two tall chimneys, and Harris walked to the door and knocked. It was opened by a maid who wore a long apron over her black dress and remained silent as she admitted them, but she could not hide the look of contempt upon her face. Perhaps Harris and Portland did not care, or perhaps they did not notice, but they walked in without sparing her a word.

"Margaret," Harris began as his eyes rested on the woman who sat by the fireside, "who has left you in this predicament?"

"Philip," Margaret said softly, ignoring the younger brother, "is it not a wonderful thing?"

"I see very little which is wonderful in your situation, Margaret," Portland replied. "But I shall see justice done by you."

"Justice?" she repeated. "Do not be so foolish. You are already married."

Fotherby felt his brow furrow as he glanced across at Portland who shook his head. Harris only lowered his head into his hands and waited for the force of her words to strike his elder brother.

"What do you mean?" Portland whispered, his throat dry and his words hoarse.

"I have only lain with one man, Philip, and that man is standing before me. Do you not recall when we were in Derbyshire? The dear surgeon mourned his lost commission and Rosanna was with Cassandra."

"Margaret, you are mad," Portland continued. "I am no more the father of your child than is Harris or Fotherby."

"So you are going to deny it?" Margaret demanded.

"Enough," Harris said firmly, taking the woman's shoulders and gently encouraging her to be seated once more. "Philip would not do such a thing. He would not do anything to hurt Rosie."

"But she cannot give him a child," Miss Webb continued. "I shall give my child to you, Philip, as you wanted. A son for you and Rosanna. You know as well as I that she will never give you a child, for they can only breed with their own kind." She looked at each of the two brothers. "You cannot deny it, Philip. You told me you longed for a child."

"I did," Portland whispered. "I do not deny that I said such a thing, but I will never substantiate your claim, for it is madness."

He did not say anything more but turned from the room and stepped out of the house. Fotherby followed him, anxious about his friend, but Harris remained in the cottage.

"Leave me be, Fotherby," Portland said angrily.

"I promised Cassandra," Fotherby began, his long strides easily matching those of his friend. "I promised her that I would find the truth of this matter."

"So Cassandra believes I am the father," Portland spat.

"She believes that you do not see clearly where your grandfather's ward is concerned."

"I love my wife," Portland said firmly, detaching each word with great purpose. "But it is true that she seems unable to conceive."

"Could you be the father of Miss Webb's child?"

Portland faltered and studied his hands for a time before he shook his head. The delay in his response caused Fotherby's stomach to turn.

"Are you certain?"

"Leave me be, Fotherby," he repeated, and strode away.

Harris walked from the cottage and stepped up to Fotherby, folding his arms.

"Margaret swears it is true, Lieutenant."

"And your brother swears it is not. I do not know what to believe, for Cassandra tells me that Miss Webb has beguiled Lord Barrington, and it is true that the two of them spent no shortage of time in one another's company at Wanderford."

"Margaret has always followed Philip. She was furious when he married Rosie. But she has captured Philip's sense and, throughout their childhood, she could persuade him of anything." Harris looked down at his feet, unwilling to meet the surgeon's gaze, but Fotherby felt that the behaviour of the two brothers spoke far more than their words.

The claim that Miss Webb had made cast a shadow over the house. Portland denied it but each time that the subject was discussed he seemed too distracted to give a believable answer. Harris would spend more and more time at the cottage, and Fotherby could not understand why. Cassandra begged Fotherby to find the truth of the matter, but he could not give her the answer he knew she longed to hear. Their mother viewed all the happenings in the house with a heavy heart. She would demand Fotherby walked through the grounds with her, and her initial confusion over his identity returned so that the young surgeon awoke on the Sunday, after almost a week at Barrington Manor, determined to leave.

He collected his belongings and opened the door onto the gallery to find a commotion on the opposite side. Not wishing to intrude, for there were three servants talking to members of the family, but having to get past them to walk downstairs, he walked sedately forward.

"She will not come," Cassandra was saying to one of the three servants.

"Cassandra," her mother's voice called from inside the room. "I shall not have you go to her. I shall not let you."

"Enough, Mother," Cassandra said firmly. "You will not stop me."

"You will leave this house if you disobey me."

"This is no longer your house," she snapped back, but stopped as one of the servants cleared their throat to indicate the presence of the surgeon. Cassandra opened her mouth to speak to him but, before she could, Lady Barrington rushed onto the gallery and seized his hand.

"Are you well?" he whispered, as tears streaked down her cheeks. Since the revelation of her husband's affair with Miss Webb, of which Fotherby still questioned the truth, she had not spoken with the surgeon nor any of the family, but confined herself to her room.

"I am, Lieutenant. It is Delphi."

Without waiting to hear any more, Fotherby dropped his bags and rushed after Lady Barrington. They came to the painted door that stood open, and Lady Barrington rushed in while Fotherby looked inside feeling like an intruder. Harris stood close to the door, a handkerchief over his nose and mouth but tears brimming in his eyes, while Lady Barrington ran to her husband, forgetting in her grief the bitterness that threatened to divide the couple. Delphina rested on the bed, struggling to breathe as she tried to talk. Fotherby stepped over to the bedside and helped the young lady sit so that her head rested on his chest.

"You are never afraid of me," she struggled, taking several seconds over each word.

"No," Fotherby answered calmly, holding her tightly to him while her two brothers and sister-in-law stood back and watched on.

"Do you think there will be poetry in heaven?"

"I am certain of it, Miss Delphina." He took her thin hand and kissed her forehead as her eyes fell closed and her breathing became shallower.

"Delphi?" Portland whispered, stepping forward as though he had only just come to his senses. Cassandra rushed into the room and stopped abruptly beside Harris as she witnessed the scene before her.

Fotherby felt strangely calm as he rested the body of the child back onto the bed and stood aside, allowing her family to come to the bedside and mourn. Portland knelt beside the bed and clutched her lifeless hand, his eyes full but his cheeks dry. His wife wept as she stood behind him, her hand on his shoulder. Harris remained by the door for a moment before he turned and walked out of the room, while Cassandra stepped to the end of the bed and stared on in disbelief.

"I was too late," she whispered, turning to Fotherby to weep. "I should have come at once."

"I am certain she bears you no ill will over such a matter," he said softly, feeling awkward as she stepped over to him and wept onto his chest. He remained still, unsure what etiquette dictated in such a situation but being content to place his hand upon her back in a comforting gesture.

After several minutes, Portland rose to his feet and, clinging to his wife, left the room. Cassandra, after begging that Fotherby forgive her impropriety, left the room too, though she was in such a daze that he was not sure she knew the words she spoke nor the actions she made. Stepping over to the window, Fotherby opened it wide and took in a deep breath of the April air. The sun was hidden behind white clouds that threatened no rain but moved with great speed as the wind whipped them. Keen to empty his thoughts of the events of the morning he began counting the leaves on the branches that stretched up the great height of the window.

"Is she dead?"

Fotherby turned at the sound of someone other than himself in the room and looked to find a youth standing in the doorway. He had a thin face beneath perfectly presented hair and wore a frock coat which hung open about his shirt. There was an expression of guilt on his face and Fotherby frowned slightly.

"Yes. She died a short time ago."

"And I was not here," came the bitter reply, and now Fotherby realised why he had appeared guilty. "I was not permitted to be." Not wishing to intrude on this boy's thoughts, Fotherby excused himself and began leaving the room before the child continued speaking. "Mother blamed her. She blamed Delphi for Father's death. But I suspect it was only that she blames herself and cannot bear the guilt."

"You are David, then," Fotherby began, realisation dawning on him.

"Indeed," he replied, turning back to Fotherby and smiling. "And I know who you are, for both Philip and Delphi love you so greatly and admire you above all other men. You are Lieutenant Henry Fotherby."

He nodded and walked out of the room, leaving the youngest member of this confusing family to grieve over his sister.

Miss Delphina Portland was buried three days later, her body laid beside her father's in the ornate mausoleum that stood in the local churchyard. All the family were present, alongside many of the people from the three villages surrounding Barrington Manor. Even her mother attended the funeral, dressed in a long black dress with a veil over her face. Lady Barrington, escorted by her husband, sat outside the elaborate building and watched as the sexton closed the colossal doors that divided the living from the dead.

"She saw the best in everyone," she whispered, as she rose to her feet. "Do you suppose we can be like that?"

"I tried," Portland responded, as he took his wife's face in his hands and kissed her forehead. "But it did not work well for me."

Fotherby, who had escorted Cassandra to the mausoleum, walked a step behind them and tried not to hear the words they spoke. But Cassandra had no interest in talking and so their words came clearly to him.

"I need to ask you, Philip. I need to know. I had never thought to question you on anything and I have tried not to do so. But I need to know."

"Do not ask me, Rosie. I do not want you to ever do anything against your wishes. I have been faithful to you since we were married. I have never deserted my promise to you, even when lands and seas have divided us."

"I believe you, Lord Barrington," she whispered and leaned her head against his arm as they walked on toward the carriage that waited to take them once more to Barrington Manor.

Fotherby walked Cassandra to the carriage and watched as she, Harris and their mother climbed into the carriage before Portland helped his wife in and turned to the boy who had brought up the rear of the sad procession.

"Go home, David. I shall walk with Fotherby."

"You should go with Rosie," came the measured reply. "Send the carriage back."

Fotherby nodded quickly and watched as Lord Barrington climbed into the carriage and the five Portlands began their return to the house.

"Are you always this quiet, Lieutenant?"

"When I have cause to think."

"I am sorry your stay at Barrington Manor has been so bleak. They say there is a madness to this corner of the world. I am sure that you are in agreement with that statement now."

"I am not sure that I believe geography can have such an effect."

"Indeed? But we are penned in by moor and sea. There is a little too much space to think. He pointed to a figure who stood in the corner of the graveyard. "But you are considering that woman."

"I want to believe your brother," Fotherby said softly as he regarded Miss Webb, who had struggled out, despite her condition, to pay respects to Delphina Portland.

"Margaret will never forgive Philip for marrying Rosie. She will stop at nothing to come closer to him."

"How do you see so much?"

"Boredom," David laughed. "I was divided from my brothers and eldest sister by a daughter who consumed all of my parents' time and interest. I begrudge them nothing, but I barely know them. My education has been paramount and convenient to the other members of the family. So I see what happens in the house, but have no one to discuss it with."

"Do you believe him?" Fotherby was uncertain why he felt he could trust the opinion of the young man beside him more than the truths of his eldest brother.

"Believe Philip? Entirely. I hope to follow him. His example means more to me than my father's or anyone else's. Mother wants me to follow some career in London, but after seeing the path she has set Harry on, I am not inclined to take her advice. I want to join the army."

"But everyone else says Miss Webb could convince him to do anything with a word."

"And convince him of anything. That is how I know he is innocent. For she cannot convince him of this."

There was a curious logic to his words that Fotherby had to respect. He smiled down at David before he began walking towards Miss Webb. Seeing him approach, she waited for him to reach her, watching his every step and ignoring the observant gaze of the youngest Portland, who witnessed all this in silence.

"Lieutenant Fotherby," she began. "Have you come as Harris does every day to beg me to reconsider my words?"

"Not at all. I think you are foolish for venturing out so close to the end of your pregnancy, but I understand why you did."

"She did not deserve this. That child suffered more in her brief years than anyone should in a lifetime."

"If you believe that, Miss Webb, why are you causing suffering to others? Can you claim to respect Miss Delphina's courage and yet condemn and ruin the lives of those she loved?"

"I should have married Philip," she began in a bitter tone. "He always came to me when he wished to share knowledge or information, yet he proposed to a savage. At least she knew she should not marry him. Three times she turned him down but he would not accept her decency or respect her understanding that she was so far beneath him. Did you know that he begged her to marry him?"

"I knew."

"So, while you were lamenting your failure through supporting Rosanna, and she and Cassandra laughed and talked over such nonsense, I saw an opportunity to take that which should have been mine. I make no apologies for my love of Philip, though he constantly tries to battle his love for me."

Fotherby looked down at her, trying to hide his disgust. "You do not love him. You want to own him."

"You do not believe him, do you?" She laughed. "So, you see, I already own him. Harry has offered to claim the child is his own and marry me. Are you to offer the same? Perhaps you who all adore Lord Barrington so greatly would even try and blame the boy," she continued, gesturing to where David stood a short distance away. Turning back to Fotherby, her face became stern. "He should never have married her when he loved me. I shock you, Lieutenant, but you chose to come and address me. Did you not expect me to be embittered to have been left to my fate?"

She walked away from him awkwardly and Fotherby watched her go, confused by the hatred that so clearly dominated her. This brief conversation plagued him and he lay awake on many nights trying to understand the guilt apportioned to each of the parties in the conundrum. One great relief to him was that Lord and Lady Barrington were once more displaying their love and admiration of one another. Indeed, as they took turns in the sunlit garden or travelled into the nearby villages together, they seemed to love each other even more than ever before. The arrival of May also saw the birth of Miss Webb's son whom, much to the distress of the family, she named Philip. She continued living in the cottage, for none were entirely sure that they were not related to the infant, excepting Harris and David, whose loyalty to their elder brother knew neither sense nor boundary. Fotherby saw little of David, who had spoken truthfully concerning the education that his mother had laid before him and, as they sat down to dinner on a Sunday towards the end of May, Harris sighed heavily.

"I intend to leave for London soon," Harris began, drawing the attention of everyone present.

"You do not mean to leave me, Harry," his mother began. "Cassandra is such poor company and Lord and Lady Barrington have much to celebrate between themselves."

Cassandra stared down at her plate but remained silent.

"You cannot go back yet, Harry," Portland began. "It is not even two months since your altercation. Give these men time to forget your argument before you travel back. Wait until autumn."

"I am weary of Cornwall," Harris petulantly answered, and scrubbed his hand over his unshaved hair. "Summer here is so sleepy."

"I suspect that this summer shall not be," Portland began as he kissed his wife. "For we have news."

Cassandra lifted her head slightly and looked at Lady Barrington, who smiled broadly at the gathered family. The dowager lifted her hands to her face and gasped.

"Oh, Lady Barrington. Have I guessed correctly?" She leaned forward, across Harris, and took Lady Barrington's outstretched hand. "Is there to be a child in Barrington Manor, Rosanna?"

"Yes, Mother," came the ecstatic reply and at once the seated people around the table clamoured over one another to offer their congratulations.

While this news was well received by the Portlands, Fotherby felt that it was time he departed and gave the family time to celebrate themselves. The following day, Portland had the carriage readied to commence the lieutenant's journey and he accompanied his friend to the crossroads at a distance of nine miles where Fotherby was to join the stagecoach. Portland would have taken him further, but Fotherby declined his offer.

"In the least you must stay at our house, Fotherby. Chilvers will be so pleased to see you, and you must share with him our news."

"Thank you. I shall happily bear the news of Lady Barrington's condition, though I fear his heart may have been broken to hear of Miss Delphina."

## Chapter Fifteen

*The Confession Of The Guilty*

Fotherby bade his friend farewell and journeyed on to the capital. He reached London the following day and went immediately to Lord Barrington's house to share his news, which was received as he had expected. Despite the offer of board, which Chilvers repeated, Fotherby declined and found lodgings closer to those of the person who had occupied his every thought.

"I have missed you, Henry," Kitty began, as she leaned on his arm while they walked through the streets. "It might only have been half a year, but it has seemed like an eternity. Is Cornwall as enchanting as Lady Barrington described?"

"I am afraid it is. There are tricks there that I can only put down to magic."

Kitty's face paled as she took in his words. "But all was well there, was it not?"

"Yes," Fotherby lied as he smiled down at her. He wished so strongly to protect the young lady from all the bitterness that he had discovered in the West Country.

"Good," she continued, her gentle smile returning to her face, giving him cause to copy her example. He guided her toward a large square and helped her sit on one of the benches. "You have been so very quiet,

Henry," she began as he perched on the edge of the seat beside her. "I am beginning to suspect that you have something that weighs heavily on your heart."

"I have," he replied. "But more because I am afraid than sad."

"Afraid? I did not know you were ever afraid, Lieutenant."

"I am afraid of what you might say, Miss Simmons." Tucking his hand into the breast pocket of his coat he took out a small velvet pouch.

"I do hope I shall never let you down, Lieutenant Fotherby," she whispered as she stared excitedly at the object he held.

"Nor I you, Miss Simmons. But I am a poor man at present." He tipped the contents of the pouch onto his palm and smiled across at her. "But when I have a little more money, would you consider me?"

"Dear Henry. It is you, and you alone, who have lifted me to the position of a lady. I do not care for money." She watched as he put the ring into her cupped hand before he lifted her other hand and kissed it. "This is beautiful."

"It was my mother's gimmel ring, but there is not a soul upon whom I would more happily bestow it. Will you marry me, Miss Simmons? I have prospects. One day I hope to become a captain and I shall inherit."

"How long must we wait to marry?" she asked, following the clasped hands on the ring and prising them apart to reveal an enamelled heart.

"I wish to have enough money to give you all you deserve, Kitty. And I have some saved."

"I want to be married by twenty-five, Henry. For after that society no longer considers a lady suitable for marriage."

"I have time, then?" He smiled down at her as she nodded.

"Four years, Henry."

Feeling elated by this brief conversation, Fotherby at once wrote to his father to share the news. He visited Sergeant Simmons to gain his blessing on the marriage and felt that, as summer overtook spring, there was little that could happen to deter his spirits. As July drew to a close, he prepared to travel to Cornwall once more, for he had assured his friend he would return to assist as needed with the birth of his child, who Lady Barrington expected at the start of September. But he left with a new security, as though having settled his heart he could face any hardship with ease.

He arrived at the same crossroads where, some months earlier, he had made his farewell to Portland on the penultimate day of the month. The sun had not yet set and he began walking in the direction of Barrington

Manor, with no notion of reaching it in the light but no wish to stay at any of the taverns he passed as he walked onward. Grateful only to have a chance to walk after the long coach ride, he continued towards the dazzling setting sun. He reached the road which ran along the cliff top and turned south. The sun had faded entirely when he reached Barrington Manor and he walked through the enormous gates and on up the driveway. There were lights in some of the rooms but, dismayed by the hour of his arrival, Fotherby walked to the servant's entrance at the side of the house. He was admitted at once and, having been recognised, ushered towards the main body of the manor.

"I do not wish to arrive so late," he protested, but it was in vain.

Having been shown to the Drawing Room door, he felt obliged to enter. He knocked gingerly and walked in. There was no one inside and, while a lamp burnt on the table, there was little to suggest that anyone had been there recently. Taking a seat with great relief, for his feet throbbed after such a long walk, he tried to remain awake. As he found his thoughts drifting he would rise and pace the floor, counting his immense strides. He was doing this when the door opened and he spun around to face his friend.

"Fotherby," Portland began. "I did not believe you should make it in time."

"I would not have stayed in London for the King himself. How is Lady Barrington?"

"Tired, but radiant," Portland said, an irrepressible smile. "She will be so pleased you are here, Fotherby. I think she has missed you. But come," he continued, offering Fotherby a glass of cordial. "Something has happened to you."

"Am I so transparent?"

"Perhaps I have just come to know you a little better. What has given such colour to your cheeks?"

Fotherby felt like a foolish child as he lifted his hands to his face to conceal his embarrassment. Portland only laughed and invited his friend to sit opposite him.

"What of life here?" Fotherby continued. "I recall many bitter events in the start of the year. I trust, in three months absence, matters have resolved in Barrington Manor."

"Harry wishes to go to London. He hates the summer here. But I am reluctant to allow him, for affairs such as his are long-lasting in their bitterness. Mother is distracted with Rosie, for which Cassandra is pleased as it is giving her a chance to engage in topics she had forsaken for the past three years. And David," Portland paused and frowned slightly. "He may well outstrip us all with his endeavours. But each Sunday he spends sitting outside the mausoleum."

"And the other inhabitants of the Manor?"

"You mean Miss Webb, surely, for you cannot hide your thoughts. She is in the cottage still. Rosie has sought to make peace with her but she will hear none of it."

"Is she still as adamant in her claim?"

"She still claims it but with far less vigour. While I, Fotherby, will repeat my innocence to you."

Fotherby did not question him any further, but the two friends continued to talk contently into the morning hours. It did not matter what they discussed, only that they were pleased to have the opportunity to talk without the constraint or consideration of anyone else.

Over the next week, Fotherby felt that his months in London had been little more than a dream, for he felt he had never been away from this place. Lady Barrington was as perfect as Portland had painted her and, while she was pleased to see Fotherby, she had confined herself almost entirely to her room, appearing only for dinner or supper. Fotherby would go walking out with Cassandra most days, while Harris had taken to visiting the taverns in the nearby villages in a hope to drown his boredom.

The following Sunday awoke with a peculiar mist that rolled up from the sea, easily climbing the cliffs that formed a part of the Barrington estate. The sun was visible as a circle in the sky, but its effects on the world below were scarce. Lady Barrington had walked down the stairs to oversee the rest of the family departing for church, but for Harris who had failed to return home the previous night. The service lasted so long that it was almost midday when at last the family departed from their box pew, the other inhabitants allowing their nobility to leave first. Fotherby felt uncomfortable as he walked past the villagers and was pleased to climb into the carriage beyond the lychgate. Cassandra and her mother had already entered, and Portland paused as he watched his youngest brother disappear into the mist towards where his father and sister lay.

"What do you think to our new clergyman, Lieutenant Fotherby?" the dowager asked as the carriage moved forward. "Or are you void of an opinion as a man of science?"

"I assure you, ma'am," Fotherby replied softly. "My science has never seen cause to rival my faith. I found him to be well read and certainly with many interesting and valuable lessons."

"But?" she added, as the surgeon finished abruptly.

"But he has an unfortunate voice to preach."

"You can easily replace unfortunate for dull or tiresome, Fotherby," Portland laughed. "You are amongst friends here."

The members of the carriage laughed as Fotherby's cheeks burnt, before silence surrounded them. It was not a long journey to the house and, when they arrived back, Portland stepped out and assisted first his mother and then his sister from the carriage before waiting as Fotherby climbed down. The four of them then entered the hall, which was filled with light after the dull grey of the mist outside.

"Rosie!" Portland called and, upon receiving no reply, he rushed up the stairs to his wife while the two ladies surrendered their shawls and bonnets to the servants.

"Harry?" his mother questioned as he stepped out of the Drawing Room. "You look dreadful. Where have you been?"

"Thank you, Mother," came the mirthless laugh. "I was at The Lion, and I think I slept there, for I awoke to find the landlord splashing water in my face."

"Why do you do this?" Cassandra demanded.

"Enough," the older woman said firmly. "Harry has a right to follow whatever pastimes he wishes."

"Even when he drags our family through the mire?"

"Do not question me, Cassandra," her mother snapped.

Cassandra did not venture any further words but moved over to the stairs, beginning to climb them. She stopped as Portland rushed towards her, a paper in his hand. But it was the expression on his face that caused the four other people to turn to him.

"Fotherby," he began as he reached the bottom of the stairs. "Come with me, I beg you."

"What is it?" Harris asked.

"Why are you such a soak?" Portland demanded. "I cannot trust you to help me now."

He snatched Fotherby's sleeve and pulled him towards the door, but as he pulled it open, Portland discarded the paper and, releasing Fotherby's arm, ran out to meet Cullington. The groom walked laboriously towards the house as he carried Lady Barrington in his arms and Fotherby watched as Portland easily lifted his wife from him and rushed back to the house. His mother had begun ordering the servants to make ready a fire in the room. Cassandra opened the door while Harris looked intently at the surgeon.

"You must help her, Fotherby. You must help them both."

Fotherby looked up the stairs to the room where Lady Barrington had been taken before he picked up the paper that Portland had dropped and, tucking it into his pocket without reading it, he ran up the stairs, taking them two at a time. Without waiting to be admitted, he stepped into the room and walked at once to the open window and pulled it closed. The fire that had been laid in the grate was lit now and Cassandra was already removing Lady Barrington's sodden gown. Portland sat on the bed clutching his wife to him and repeatedly muttering her name.

"Do something, Lieutenant Fotherby," his mother began. "Please do something."

Feeling the weight of the entire room, indeed the entire house, bearing down on him, Fotherby stepped over to the bedside.

"Support the child while I turn her on her front," he began softly, but Portland would not relinquish the hold he had on his wife.

"Philip," Cassandra began, prising her brother from her sister-in-law. "Do as Fotherby says."

Realising that Portland was not listening to either Cassandra or him, Fotherby snatched Lady Barrington from her husband's arms and turned her onto her front, striking the back of her chest so that, at once, she began coughing out water. Portland lifted his fearful gaze to the surgeon as Fotherby began propping up the pillows on the bed.

"She needs to be out of these clothes at once," he continued. "Get her dry and warm, and keep her on her side." Cassandra nodded to each of his orders. "She may have inhaled more water, so keep a movement to her chest." He walked backward to the door and left the room to find Portland's mother waiting outside.

"I knew you should do it, Lieutenant Fotherby."

"I am afraid it still might not be enough," Fotherby confided. "But I pray to God it is."

He sat down on the floor and watched as she walked to her second son, who waited in the hall below. Fotherby did not know how long he sat there before the door was pulled open and Cassandra stepped out. He pushed himself to his feet, but she barely noticed him as she called over the balustrade.

"Harry! Harry, go for the midwife at once."

Harris Portland did not need a second time of asking, but rushed out of the house. Fotherby looked down at Cassandra who now gripped his hands in her own.

"Will you take Philip? He should not be in there."

"And take him from his wife? I think that is precisely where he should be."

"He has lost his senses, Lieutenant. I am afraid for him almost as much as I am for Rosie."

They waited almost an hour before the midwife arrived and she immediately insisted Portland left the room. Fotherby had to guide him from Lady Barrington's side, for he was unable to move. As Fotherby closed the door Portland walked down the stairs, ignoring all the other people in the house, and into the Dining Room where he sat alone at the long table with only the bottle and glass for company. David Portland returned to find the house in anxious waiting, unable to find from anyone what had happened, for only his eldest brother seemed to know and he had drunk himself into a terrible state.

When the sun had left the misty sky, Cassandra finally stepped from Rosanna's room and looked down at Fotherby, who sat on the floor beside the door. He struggled to his feet feeling unbearably tired.

"Lieutenant," she began but, unable to find any other words, she lowered her head and her shoulders shook. Fotherby rubbed his eyes.

"How is Lady Barrington, Miss Portland?"

"Feverish, exhausted, and desperately unhappy."

"And the baby?"

"She did not survive her birth."

They turned as the midwife walked out of the room and looked at the two of them, apologising as though the bleak outcome was her own fault. Cassandra, recalling her duty, led the midwife to the hall below, where she instructed one of the servants to arrange the carriage for her return. Fotherby stepped down the stairs, and stopped a short distance from the gathered family who remained in a stunned silence, each lost in their own thoughts.

"Will you tell him, Lieutenant?" Cassandra began at last.

Fotherby stared at her and willed himself to refuse her, but he could not. Cassandra's perfect eyes, only more beautiful as they wept, pleaded with him to do this, and he realised that he could not say no to such a request. He nodded and stepped forward, feeling the gaze of everyone on him as he knocked on the door to the Dining Room and entered. Portland was seated, as he had been for hours, drinking wine. He had abandoned the glass, which was pushed into the centre of the table, and was drinking from the bottle.

"Portland?" Fotherby began softly.

"There is only one reason you would be here, Fotherby," came the reply, as he set the bottle down on the table. "Is Lady Barrington dead? Has Miss Webb succeeded?"

"Miss Webb?" Fotherby muttered.

"She wrote a letter," Portland went on, drinking once more from the bottle. Fotherby pulled out the paper that he had forgotten about and offered it to his friend. "That is it. Have you read it?"

"No. It is not my business to read it. And I beg you to forget Miss Webb for a time. You are needed to be strong, Lord Barrington. Lady Barrington needs you to be strong."

"Rosie is alive?"

"Yes. And she needs you, Portland."

"And our child?"

"Was born asleep," Fotherby whispered.

Portland rose to his feet and stepped over to the surgeon. "You are wise not to drink alcohol, Fotherby. It takes nothing away and deadens no grief."

He stumbled to the door, and would have fallen but Fotherby snatched his arm and pulled open the door. He helped him up the stairs, past the gazes of the family and the servants who peered from doorways or across the gallery. Ignoring them all, Portland reached for the handle to the room he knew his wife would be in. The image inside the room of the mother clutching her dead child, tears dropping onto its lifeless form, stabbed Fotherby's heart and he shut the door quickly as Portland walked towards his wife.

Feeling the need to be away from the house, Fotherby walked out into the night and watched as the carriage returned. For the first time since Lady Barrington had taken ill, he recalled the man who had carried her up to the house and he walked to the stables.

There was a warm glow to the building after the darkness outside and he looked about him. The horses stared back, all manner of horses. The carriage horses were being stabled a little further down the corridor, but it was not Cullington who was tending them. Concerned suddenly, Fotherby turned as he heard someone say his name.

"Lieutenant Fotherby, sir?"

"Cullington," Fotherby replied. "I wanted to know you were well, and to thank you in the part you played in today's tragic events."

"To thank me?" the man whispered. "You should not thank me, Lieutenant, and no amount of cures can heal what I suffer from."

Fotherby followed him as he turned and walked back to the Tack Room. "What do you mean?"

"I heard Lord Barrington's daughter was dead." Cullington made no attempt to turn and face the man he addressed but sat down beside a collection of empty bottles that almost rivalled Portland's, although these were beer bottles. He offered one to the surgeon, who declined. "I lost my son, too."

"I did not know you were married, Cullington."

"I am not." He turned now to face the other man. "I fell under the charm of a lady who claimed she loved me. God forgive me, I meant no harm. I did not know what she meant to do. Lord Barrington saved me, Lieutenant Fotherby. He gave me a position and supported me. And in return I allowed his wife to nearly drown and his daughter to die. I did not know what she meant to do," he repeated.

"You were the father of Miss Webb's child," Fotherby announced with certainty.

"I would have married her, Lieutenant. She is a bewitching woman. But when she asked me to deliver a letter to the house I did not know what she intended to do. She drowned my son, Lieutenant. And, as Lady Barrington sought to save him, she became trapped beneath the water."

"So you walked in to save her."

Cullington nodded. "How I have repaid the graciousness of Lord Barrington! I have been a fool and have lost everything."

"But you saved Lady Barrington," Fotherby said softly. "She might have died alongside her child if you had not saved her. Though it may not be easy or pleasant, you owe it to Lord Barrington to tell him the truth."

"I shall tell him," Cullington said after a moment. "I shall tell him for I can bear it in silence no longer. When he has concluded his mourning, I shall tell him."

Fotherby left the room, that smelt more like a brewery than a stable, and walked back to the house. He did not stop at any of the rooms but walked to his own and closed the door. Sleep was a luxury that Fotherby could not seem to enjoy. Every time he drifted into slumber he was awoken by the terrible image of Lady Barrington clutching her stillborn child. The night seemed unending, and he was already up and dressed as there was a knock on the door to his room. He did not give the early hour any thought, nor who it could be that arrived at his door at such a time, but he was still surprised to find David standing before him.

"Good morning, Lieutenant," he began, in little more than a whisper. "I need your help."

Fotherby frowned as the young man walked away and only looked back once as he stepped quietly across the landing, checking that Fotherby was following. To the surgeon's surprise, David led him down the stairs and out into the morning. There was no mist now, but a breeze that pushed from the west, striking the two of them as they walked around the side of the building.

"I was going to take Goliath out," David began. "He is always already saddled by sunrise. Goliath is my horse."

"That hardly seems a matter for a surgeon," Fotherby replied as they entered the stable.

"On that I would agree with you. But come and see what I found when I went to collect Goliath's tack."

Fotherby followed David into the Tack Room and sighed as he surveyed the image before him. Cullington was hanging from a blanket belt that he had secured to one of the nails in the rafters. His eyes were open, but his hand was cold as Fotherby reached up to take it.

"Poor man," Fotherby muttered.

"Why did he do it?"

Fotherby did not answer him. In truth, although he knew the reasons Cullington had for such an action, he could not understand why any man should wish to take their own life. David seemed remarkably stoical for such a young man and helped Fotherby lower the corpse to the ground, sliding closed the unseeing eyes.

"I liked him," David announced, shaking his head. "He told me tales of the army."

Feeling that he was in some way responsible for Cullington's death, after the man had confessed the night before, Fotherby shared all he knew with Portland later in the day. Lady Barrington had requested a quiet burial for their daughter, whom she had called Maria after the dowager, and the family prepared for this in great solemnity. Portland had informed the law of what had happened and ordered that he wanted Miss

Margaret Webb found and tried, for the woman had disappeared after the events at the lake.

Lady Barrington announced her intention to leave for London some time later and Portland, who could not deny her anything, consented, offering to return Harris to the capital city. Fotherby parted from them and journeyed north to Derbyshire, but not before he had shared a quiet conversation with the grieving mother.

"I hope you will not feel that we blame you at all, Lieutenant Fotherby," Lady Barrington had begun as they sat in the quiet of one of the gardens. "I want you to know that there is no man I hold in a higher regard than you."

"You have no need to place such words and regard at my feet, Lady Barrington. I seem to have been unable to end this terrible hardship your family has suffered since I first arrived. I assure you, I blame myself enough."

"That is what I was afraid of. But I hope that you will see the truth and the sense in my words. You gave a dignity to Delphi in her death, and you fought for my honour and my life. Such things will never be forgotten. If I should not see you for a time, I wish you to know that I will never cease to recall all you have done for my family. And I know now that Philip shall be well cared for when he and you are called once more to war."

Three hours later, the fractured family departed from one another. As the tall walls of Barrington Manor faded into the sea mist, Fotherby felt relieved beyond measure to return to his home, where little changed and heartbreak and suffering were events of the distant past.

## Chapter Sixteen

*Strawberries and Whisky*

The arrival of Major and Mrs Tenterchilt in Scotland eleven months ago had found their new home in a state of disrepair. Petrovia Lodge had been built forty years earlier as the English strengthened their hold on the Scottish landscape. It had not been built to provide a permanent residence but to signify a controlling power of the people who had lived in the nearby village. It had almost as many rooms as Chanter's House, but the rooms were small and dark and, after being accustomed to spending their time in the country at the estate house, the lodge was very small indeed.

Arabella was dismayed to find her new room and spent much of her first month staring through tears at her belongings in the dismal grey surroundings. For three nights she had woken the household screaming as mice and rats scurried through the room, so that eventually she had to consent to admitting Gulliver to rid the room of vermin. As summer overtook the glen, however, she began to admire the stark beauty of the landscape but, in her heart, she longed more and more for the excitements of London.

Mrs Tenterchilt was surprised to find that the person who settled most successfully in Petrovia was Imogen, who would now divide her time between the books they had brought and gazing out of the windows. On one occasion, Mrs Tenterchilt watched her second daughter walk out onto the grass before the house and turn a full circle before she arranged a blanket on the ground and sat down to sketch the view before her. Gulliver settled beside her, and Mrs Tenterchilt found herself trying to view the scenery as her daughter saw it, but she could only see a vast stretch of emptiness as barren hills climbed out of the thin stream at the foot of their grass.

Catherine loved her new environment for a very different reason. Having been forced from London, her father was confined so often to the house, and this allowed the youngest daughter far more opportunity to learn from him. In addition to teaching her to shoot, Major Tenterchilt taught her to fence and, while his wife demonstrated crafts to her two eldest daughters, he would take Catherine down to the river to fish, or teach her to ride her horse as the Hussars rode theirs. She excelled in her role as her father's son and sought to learn as much as she could of the art of war.

Mrs Tenterchilt had shared Arabella's sorrow but, for the benefit of her husband and her children, she endeavoured not to show it. Only when she was with her maid would she speak candidly about her thoughts on the move. The family had retained only two maids, who were now left to run the house alone, although Major Tenterchilt sought a groom from the nearby village to manage their stable.

Major Tenterchilt was true to his wife's wishes in every particular. He had gifted the house to her and, whenever his duty had taken him into towns, he ensured that he did not frequent the clubhouses where dice were shaken and cards dealt. He had been fortunate to retain his position within the army, at least in part, so he continued to correspond with the army and provide intelligence through a series of letters. His pay had been cut, but his unknown benefactor had ensured that Major Tenterchilt retained his rank.

Spring seemed late that year, so that May had arrived before the trees came into leaf. Major Tenterchilt stood at the door to the house, watching down the grass as Imogen and Catherine threw a ball to one another while Gulliver leapt to try and catch it. Arabella was sitting with her mother on a wooden bench that he had constructed for them to enjoy the view. The image before him, soaked in the light of the climbing sun, that lit up the river into a silk ribbon, was perfect, and Josiah felt a great satisfaction as he gazed out.

He looked down at the letter in his hand and smiled slightly. It was an invitation to a ball in Perth, a military event that he had been requested to attend by the gentleman with whom he had been maintaining a correspondence. He did not know his name. Indeed, he knew nothing of him but that he had provided him with important movements of the enemy. On occasions, he had requested things of the major: supplies, pay or arms, but he had never given the major his name or rank. When the major corresponded with him he addressed the letters to J.J. and was left trusting that the army would see it reached the correct gentleman amongst the regiments. They had not failed thus far.

Not having the heart to disturb the scene before him, Major Tenterchilt walked back into his study and began writing a reply. J.J., whoever he might have been, had written to him from Perth, and there was an address of a boarding house to which the major replied.

"My dears," Major Tenterchilt announced that evening as they sat at dinner. "Your mother and I have been invited to Perth for some days. I would like you to behave as well for Penny and Anne as when I am here."

"My dear Major Tenterchilt," his wife replied. "I knew nothing of this."

"To a ball in Perth. Do you mind?"

"I should love to."

"When may I attend a ball, Papa?" Arabella asked as she looked at her parents, unable to conceal her envy.

"When you are sixteen, my little lady," her mother said gently. "I had to wait that long. It is what a lady does."

The conversation turned then but, two days later, when Major and Mrs Tenterchilt prepared to travel south, Arabella walked down to the carriage with her mother and raised an issue which had been on her mind for the past year.

"Mama, will Papa's friend be at the ball?"

"Which friend, little lady?"

"Colonel Pottinger."

"I expect that he will be," her mother replied gently.

"Will his son be there, Mama?"

"He might be, but I do not know that he will be. I expect that they will be older gentlemen. But if he is there, dear Arabella, I shall make sure that I remember you to him."

"Thank you, Mama." Arabella, who was now almost as tall as her mother, kissed her cheek and bade farewell to her parents. She, accompanied by her two sisters and the two maids, waved to the carriage as it drove down the long drive.

Mrs Tenterchilt was beside herself to be able to journey out of the glen, and watched as they passed through the softening landscape. The ball was to be on the first evening of June and, while each man present knew that it was an opportunity to strengthen the army's presence in Scotland, the ladies seemed pleased to have a chance to enjoy the dancing.

The venue of the ball had been decked in greenery and blossom. Long tendrils of ivy and honeysuckle adorned doorways and banisters. Its opulence caused Mrs Tenterchilt to sigh as she stepped into the first room and the major turned to her and smiled.

"Do you suppose there shall be anyone I know here?" she asked as she looked about.

"I would be surprised if Mrs Pottinger were not here, for there is her husband."

"Then I shall have to go and find her," Mrs Tenterchilt said softly.

Her husband watched as she walked through the crowd, then turned to his friend and walked over to him. Colonel Pottinger lifted the glass he held as he approached.

"Major Tenterchilt," he called. "Sir, I did not know I should see you here."

"Indeed, I live quite close now."

"Of course," Major Brentwood said softly. "Pottinger told us of your predicament."

"How do you enjoy Scotland?" Pottinger asked.

"More than I had thought to. And I have been fortunate to secure my position even in this remote corner of the world."

It felt peculiar to Major Tenterchilt to be amongst his comrades once more, but he was pleased to have the opportunity to talk to those who shared his interests and concerns. Of course, the talk was almost entirely of war and, while Major Tenterchilt went from officer to officer, he tried to learn the identity of his correspondent by language, topics or mannerisms. Having arrived at the beginning of the evening he was able to witness each person as he walked into the hall.

It was perhaps an hour after he had arrived, while he stood at the side of the large room, that his wife returned to his side. She had a smile that lit her face and Major Tenterchilt took her hand and kissed it.

"My dear Major Tenterchilt," she began. "You will not believe who is here."

"Then you found Anne Pottinger?"

"Yes," she replied, her smile slipping for a moment. "But look." She beckoned someone toward her.

"Lieutenant Fotherby," the major said warmly. "Two years have passed and I could swear that you have grown two feet taller."

"Two years, indeed," Fotherby replied. "But I see Scotland suits you. Mrs Tenterchilt tells me you have lived here a year now. I went to Chanter's House to seek you and found it empty."

"Indeed," Tenterchilt said softly. "But Scotland is a fine place to build a new home. You must come to Petrovia and see our home, Fotherby."

"Thank you, Major. I should be honoured to attend your house."

"Indeed," Mrs Tenterchilt added. "For you did not meet our daughters when last you visited."

"There is only one man in the King's army has such height," announced a voice from behind Fotherby, causing the young surgeon to turn around. Major Tenterchilt watched with interest, while his wife openly scowled at the newcomer.

"Captain Peters, sir," Fotherby began. "I did not know you were returned from the east."

"At the start of the year. We might have returned sooner had we not been forced to rely on the Navy."

"And Lieutenant Kitson, sir, is he well?"

"Yes, Fotherby," Peters replied thoughtfully. "He is well."

"Is he present tonight?"

"No, he is in Surrey with his family. I am surprised to find you here."

"I would not be had Major Tenterchilt not invited me." Here he indicated to the major, who bowed his head slightly to the army surgeon.

"Then you knew I should find Lieutenant Fotherby here," Mrs Tenterchilt said sternly to her husband.

"I had not heard that he should be present," Major Tenterchilt replied.

"My apologies, sir," Fotherby said. "For I left at once to arrive in time and did not know that a reply was required."

Major Tenterchilt waved aside the young man's protests and watched as the two men before him continued talking. He had not invited the surgeon, although he was pleased, as always, to renew his acquaintance with the man who had saved his life.

"This, then, is your greatest success, Fotherby," Peters continued gesturing to the major. "Sir, did you know that you enabled Fotherby to qualify?"

"Indeed," Tenterchilt replied. "The young man has thanked me often for it."

"Still fighting duels, boy?" Peters continued. "Still in league with political rebels? I imagine that you heard of the unrest in the West Country when the vote was refused."

"I heard of it, sir, but neither Lord Barrington nor myself was involved."

"And making enemies, Fotherby? Have you heard from Commander Sutton?"

"No, sir. My time has been spent almost entirely in Buxton or Greenwich, furthering my vocation."

"Vocation?" Peters laughed. "Yes, I imagine we must be called to it, for we would be mad to choose it. Have you a mind to return to your post?"

"If the army has a mind to offer it."

"When I travelled to the east, I left behind a boy," Peters said sternly, looking up at his lieutenant. "But now I have returned to find a man."

Major Tenterchilt smiled slightly at this, pleased to find that the young surgeon was being given the credit due to him. Fotherby did not seem sure how to take such words but smiled, with no small amount of sorrow, as his cheeks burned to the colour of the jacket that he wore. Overcome by this image of humility and sadness, and certain Captain Peters had spoken all the words he needed to, Mrs Tenterchilt stepped forward.

"Lieutenant Fotherby, I have a mind to take some air. Would you escort me?"

"Your wife seems in much higher spirits than when last I saw her, Major," Peters said, as he watched his lieutenant guide her towards the terrace where a small band of musicians played. "And you a rank higher than last I saw you. I must admit you would not be standing on two legs now if I had not given the boy a chance to prove himself."

"Then I am as indebted to you as I am to Lieutenant Fotherby."

"Tell me, do you fight once more?"

"No, sir. For while I may walk easily, I am not able to do so far, or for long. I should be a hindrance to the army."

"Yet someone found you a post within it." Peters looked levelly across at the man before he added, "It was good of you to invite Lieutenant Fotherby."

"I am not certain that I did," came the muttered reply.

Peters looked at him as though he was mad, before he pointed to the major's glass. "Come, Major, let us find a drink. I tire of Fotherby's virtuosity where alcohol is concerned and would enjoy a drinking companion before I am forced to observe his piety within my tent once more."

Major Tenterchilt thanked the older man and followed him to the long table where the punch rested and, having filled their glasses, the two walked past the dancers until they reached a small table, at which they sat. This apparent gentility from a man who was known, not only in the regiment but to the whole army, as a bitter recluse, confused the major who sat silently. He watched as Peters poured some of the contents of his hip flask into his glass of punch before he offered it to Major Tenterchilt, who graciously accepted.

"Strawberries and whisky," Peters said softly. "Two of the only things the Scots are good for."

"Have you been often in Scotland?"

"No," the surgeon replied flatly. "It is a dismal country and, for all my life, I cannot understand why we fought so hard to keep it."

"I live here."

"I know." Peters turned to watch the dancing for a time, waiting for the major's response but none came. "When you lost your bet."

"Indeed, sir. Are my hardships so well known?"

"When a man loses so heavily you may be sure they are known. Mothers and nursemaids will use you as an example of why gambling is a sin." Peters turned back to the unimpressed major. "And then we get righteous individuals like Fotherby."

"I am sorry to have disappointed you," Major Tenterchilt said sarcastically.

"Your apology is accepted."

Major Tenterchilt felt his temper boiling at the man's response and his presumption to address him in such a manner. Opening his mouth to share his thoughts, he stopped himself as Peters continued.

"I did not nominate you for this job that you should throw it all away on a foolish bet."

"You?" Major Tenterchilt choked on the word. "You nominated me for the job?"

"Indeed. And the rather mysterious man who appointed you was my brother. Do not rebuke yourself for not knowing. He is an elusive gentleman at best. Reclusive, almost."

"I do not know what to say, sir."

"Then do not say anything. Women may fall over themselves in grateful thanks that at times becomes embarrassing. Gentlemen, thankfully, do not have such desires."

"I am grateful. But why did you nominate me, Captain Peters? When there were so many other, far more decorated, officers?"

Peters drank from the glass before him until it was dry, at which point he raised the flask to his lips. "Perhaps," he said at last, "because I could not bear the thought that you would have died under my knife. You were owed your life. That is the noble version."

"And what is the more common, and no doubt honest, version?"

"You owe a great debt to Lieutenant Fotherby," he continued. "He has no one to speak on his behalf within the army, but has great ability and insight as a surgeon.

I wanted to ensure that he should have someone to oversee his promotion when I am gone." Peters sighed and looked at the empty glass, suddenly thoughtful. "I did not know what manner of role should arise, but I beseeched my brother to offer you a position when one did. He owed me more than one favour. But I have heard that, whatever your mysterious role might be, you have excelled in it. For when you were exiled by your misplaced wager it was my brother, not I, who allowed you to keep it." Captain Peters rose to his feet and looked down at the major, in rank above him, yet so much younger. "Enjoy the ball, Major Tenterchilt. I believe I shall retire for the night. I have a long road ahead of me and I mean to be in Edinburgh by midnight."

"Then you are not staying in Perth?"

"No, sir. I would not stay so far north of the border. Strawberries and whisky, Major. But, excepting that, I owe the Scots nothing and trust them with less."

He turned then and walked away. Major Tenterchilt watched him go with great confusion. He could not understand the conflict that sprang within him, unsure whether he was hurt that he had been offered the position through his connections rather than his own merit, but feeling certain that, as Captain Peters had placed faith in him for whatever reason, he had a duty not to abandon such a post. He did not leave the table but stared at the glass in his hand as he pondered such matters.

"Major Tenterchilt," he heard his wife's voice announce. "You seem terribly melancholy. Will you dance?"

Josiah smiled across at his wife, who had returned on the arm of the young surgeon. "No, my dear, my leg will not permit it. But you have my blessing to dance with Lieutenant Fotherby, should he wish to."

"Of course," Fotherby muttered. The major watched the young man, impressed by his ability to inspire his superior and amused that the young surgeon remained ignorant to the existence of such a supportive beneficiary.

When the ball was over, Major Tenterchilt escorted his wife to the boarding house to which he had addressed the letter to Mr J.J. after making their farewells to Lieutenant Fotherby. When his wife, elated by the adventures of the ball, had retired to bed, Major Tenterchilt sought the landlord of the house.

"Sir," the major began. "Have you a gentleman staying whose initials are J.J.?"

"No, sir," came the cautious reply. "But we received a letter addressed to him."

"I know," the major replied. "For I sent that letter and was given this as his address."

"I might have discarded the letter, but the next day it was collected."

"Who collected it?"

"A young girl," the landlord said, embarrassed to admit that he had given it to someone to whom it had not been addressed. "But she asked for it specifically and, furthermore, paid a sixpence to collect it."

The following day, Major and Mrs Tenterchilt returned home. Their daughters were pleased beyond measure to have their parents returned to them. Catherine grumbled about how Anne had forced her to wear a dress, while Arabella was delighted to receive the shawl that her mother had brought her, but was sad that her mother had not had a chance to speak favourably of her to Roger Pottinger, for he had not attended. Imogen thanked her mother for her gift but she was most grateful simply to have her family united once more.

Major Tenterchilt felt that he had been gone three months instead of three days, for his discovery been a momentous journey. He secluded himself in his study for several days until, at last, when midsummer arrived and the days stretched to their full length, he was persuaded by Catherine to abandon his books and take her riding. Still, as summer wore on in his Highland lodge, Major Tenterchilt became more intrigued than ever before to understand his current position and the man with whom he corresponded.

## Chapter Seventeen
*An Unbearable Guilt*

Attending the Perth ball was most uncharacteristic of Lieutenant Fotherby, but Miss Simmons had requested that he should. Fotherby would have liked her to have been by his side, but she had returned to London a week before Major Tenterchilt's invitation had arrived. Her father had escorted her to Derbyshire and the pair had resided in Wanderford Hall for four weeks over April and May. It had been Fotherby's hope that his father might meet and approve of his choice of fiancée and, indeed, Tobias Fotherby found her to be a charming girl, while Sergeant Simmons spent a good deal of time with Fotherby's uncle. Simmons' father had been a gamekeeper, and it was on this topic that the two men happily talked most evenings.

Fotherby returned from the ball some days after the event, and was seated now looking down at a small miniature in his hand.

"She is very pretty," his father remarked. "But then you are a fine painter."

"It is easy with such a subject," Fotherby replied, blushing slightly.

"I am glad that you have found such a lady, Henry. She is gentle and sweet. And I am glad that your uncle did not choose her for you."

"Do you truly love her, Father?"

"She will have much to learn, Henry," his father replied cautiously, rubbing his heavily hooded eyes. "But I am certain she would do anything you ask of her." The old man picked up one of the books that rested by him, before he set it firmly down. "I miss my books," he sighed. "Would you read to me for a time, my boy?"

Fotherby took the book from his father's outstretched hand and began reading it aloud. It seemed strange to him that his father, whom he had rarely seen without a book by his side, was now unable to read as his sight was failing him. In age, he was not so different to Captain Peters, yet despite the frivolous and poor lifestyle Peters had adopted, he did not suffer from such an affliction.

This thought caused Fotherby to lie awake, staring up at the knots in the wood above his bed. He had a great fear, he realised suddenly, that he should lose his father. As though, because his sight had failed him, he was suddenly susceptible to all manner of far more terrible ailments. He spent the following weeks shadowing him, anxious that the old man might need him. His work in

Buxton waned, until he only visited Doctor Shipton rarely and never stayed more than one night.

Returning from Buxton at the start of July, his uncle met him at the doorway and offered him a confusing smile.

"You have a letter, Henry," he began before Fotherby had even reached the house.

"I expect it is from Miss Simmons, Uncle."

"It does not look like her hand." He stood back to allow his nephew in, before he followed him to the small table in the hall where the letter rested.

"It is not her hand," Fotherby muttered, confused by the perfect letters that formed his name. "I shall tell you all you need to know of it, Uncle," he continued, laughing slightly at the other man's behaviour. "Is my father in his study?"

"What should he do in his study, Henry? He is in the Drawing Room."

Fotherby felt his smile slip at his uncle's words, but walked through to the Drawing Room and announced his arrival to his father.

"My dear boy," his father laughed as he rose to welcome his son. "Being unable to read has not made me completely blind."

Fotherby embraced his father before he sat down on one of the chairs and opened the letter with interest.

"To Lieutenant Henry Fotherby," it began. "I am left the sorry task to share with you our tragic news. Our dear sister, Rosanna Portland, died in London on the third day of June. It would appear she was left greatly weakened after childbirth and, upon contracting a fever, was unable to recover. She rests now beside her daughter with the words that she inspired Mr William Blake to write:

*When I from black and he from white cloud free,*
*And round the tent of God like lambs we joy:*
*I'll shade him from the heat till he can bear,*
*To lean in joy upon our father's knee.*
*And then I'll stand and stroke his silver hair,*
*And be like him and he will then love me.*

My dear brother, Philip, suffers terribly through this loss, but continues, in Rosanna's name, to fight for equality between men of black and fair colouring. We have seen nothing of Harry since before Rosanna's death and neither have we heard anything. Mother is greatly distracted by this and so often demands from poor Cassandra answers to all manner of questions. Forgive me for carrying such bitter news, but it is my belief that you should be told. Yours in friendship, David Portland."

All the while that Fotherby read the letter his father watched as his face paled until, as he concluded reading, he turned to face his father and shook his head.

"I have just had terrible news."

"That, I could tell without you speaking a word. What is it, Henry?"

"A dear, dear friend has died. Lady Barrington, who stayed with us two years since."

"I am very sorry, Henry. And very sorry for Lord Barrington, too. I recall," his father began, but stopped and shook his head. "It does not improve with time, but rather becomes bearable."

"Should I visit them, Father? Does it seem I am concerned or would it seem that I sought to interfere?"

"You know them far better than I, my boy. But sometimes a visitor can be a most welcome distraction."

Being unsure about his father's words, Fotherby returned a correspondence with the youngest Portland, whose reply reached him in the middle of July. David Portland requested that he should attend, believing that the arrival of a new but trusted friend could bring a spark of life into the heart of this crumbling family. Therefore, the end of July found the young surgeon, now in his twenty-fifth year, arriving at the imposing structure of Barrington Manor. It seemed angry and dark as the sun set behind it, as though it wanted him there as little as he wished to be there. He felt weary for this grieving family who, in the few years he had known Portland, had lost a father, a sister, a child and a wife.

The cause of his late arrival had been a visit to the churchyard, to that corner where the Portland family tomb rested. Two small holly bushes had been planted at the foot of the steps and, for the first time, he noticed the crest over the doors. It was the same image he had witnessed the first time he had met Lady Barrington, of two unicorns bowing to a tree. But one of them had now been painted black. The day was so still and the air so peaceful that Fotherby had lingered there for over an hour, touched by the tenderness with which these memories were preserved. He had passed many people as his long legs strode up to the manor, but none of them spoke.

He stepped up to the door and knocked quietly, wishing that no one would hear him, but presently the door was opened and, upon being recognised, the surgeon was admitted at once.

"Lieutenant Fotherby," announced a voice in surprisingly high spirits. "I did not know you were travelling to Cornwall."

"You did not?" Fotherby asked as he looked up at Portland, who rushed down the stairs to greet him. "I received a letter from your brother."

"From Harry?" Portland's face grew dark as he muttered his brother's name.

"No. From David."

"That boy," Portland laughed. "No doubt you have heard our bitter news."

"I have. And I and my family were truly sorry of it."

"Thank you, Fotherby." Portland walked towards the Drawing Room and stepped back to allow Fotherby to enter. "Now, you must tell me of yourself. What pastimes have filled the life of Henry Fotherby?"

Fotherby sat opposite his friend, confused by his manners. He had been certain that Portland would be as lost in despair through his wife's death as his youngest brother had claimed. But the man before him laughed, joked, smoked and drank happily, despite the bitterness of the past few years and the late hour of the guest's arrival. The stunned surgeon offered nothing more than answers to questions and bemused smiles as he smoked his pipe and tried not to let his brow furrow.

"I am tiring you, Lieutenant," Portland laughed, as Fotherby tried to conceal a yawn. "Of course you must go to bed. You seem troubled by something."

"I am surprised," Fotherby replied honestly. "I am surprised to find you in such high spirits."

"Whatever can you mean? I have lost my child and my wife in one year, misplaced my brother, and failed to secure the motion in parliament that I live and breathe for. But, see, I am still alive." Fotherby watched as he drew a tiny bottle from his pocket and drank all it contained. "If you cannot sleep, Fotherby, you need some. I have more somewhere, that I was given."

"Is that laudanum?"

"It is," Portland responded, reaching out to the man before him as he stumbled slightly.

"Come," Fotherby said softly, fighting his own tiredness to assist the drugged Lord Barrington up the stairs. He arrived at the door to Portland's room and reached for the handle.

"Stop," Portland demanded, pushing himself to his feet and stepping backward so that Fotherby had to snatch his wrist to keep him from falling over the gallery balustrade. "That is Rosie's room. She might be there. I do not want to see her."

Fotherby, without relinquishing his friend, walked over to the room he had occupied both times he had stayed at Barrington Manor and dragged his friend inside. Portland collapsed on the bed and turned away from his friend, who tried to imagine the enormous pain Portland felt, but could not hide his disgust at the behaviour of the man before him.

"Do not judge me, Fotherby," came the reply to his thoughts. "No assessment you can make will come close to the self-loathing I feel. It is an escape, you see? I feel that nothing can touch me when I take it."

"That is good to know," Fotherby replied firmly as he sat down in the chair before the empty fireplace. "For, when stock allows, it is what I have given men before they lose limbs."

Portland did not respond, but Fotherby watched as his friend fell asleep. Sleeping in the chair may have been uncomfortable, but he was so tired he could have slept anywhere. He was awoken by the smell of food and he stared across at the desk to find a tray of food on it. There was no sign of Portland, the bedding had been straightened, and Fotherby began to think the confusing nature of last night's discussion had been nothing more than a dream.

Having eaten and washed, he descended the stairs to find the house was silent. There was no one in the Dining Room, or the Drawing Room, and even the servants were not to be found. Fotherby began to feel that he was trespassing and the thought that he was unwelcome here returned once more. He returned upstairs, but, as he reached the top he heard voices for the first time, shattering the silence with their words.

"How do you know what I saw?" Mrs Portland demanded. "You do not trust me, and respect me far less."

"That is neither true nor fair, Mother." Cassandra's voice replied, her patience fraying. "But I do not believe that you saw Father walking on the moor, for Father is dead."

"It might have been Harry. Will you go and see if it was Harry?"

"Yes, Mother." Cassandra appeared at one of the doors and looked across in surprise. "Lieutenant Fotherby, I did not know that you were here."

"My apologies, Miss Portland. I was on my way to my room."

"Of course," she said softly, and Fotherby beheld the slightest smile catch her perfect features. "But I meant that I did not know you were at Barrington Manor."

"Your brother wrote to me, sharing your sad news and asking me to visit."

"Philip?"

"No," Fotherby repeated as he had done last night. "David."

"Dear little David. He is quite alone now." She sighed. "I must go, for Mother will be watching out of her window and will not be happy if she does not see me walk out."

"Might I accompany you, Miss Portland?"

"By all means, Lieutenant. I should welcome company." She took his arm and they walked down the stairs and out of the house. "Since Margaret's betrayal and Rosanna's death I have not had any company," she went on as they walked through the gardens. "I have lost Harry to London, and Philip to melancholy, but Mother fills my time, for which I am grateful."

"What of your other brother? And what did you mean he is alone?"

"He lost little Delphi, his dearest friend. Harry has engaged in some terrible foolery that has stolen him from us. And Philip, whom David adores, has become lost through melancholy and laudanum. Mother never had a great deal of time for him."

"But what of you?"

"Mother takes every minute of my time. I check over his work, but I am afraid that he has outstripped me with knowledge and reason. I should not wonder if he were to follow in your footsteps and become a doctor."

"And your mother?"

"Her mind has failed her. Almost every day she sends me out looking for Father, Harry, and Rosie. She swears she has seen them and will not rest until I have gone to search for them. She will be at her window now, watching us."

They walked on through the grounds. The high walled gardens on the south, round the rugged coastline to the West and through the courtyards to the north of the house, past the stables and through the front door at the east once more. They talked of all manner of trivial topics: the trees, birds, sea and land. And, little by little, Cassandra's smile returned to her beautiful face.

"You have reminded me what it is to laugh, Lieutenant. And I am grateful of it."

They stepped indoors once more and she relinquished her hold on his arm with great reluctance before she walked upstairs to her mother's room. Fotherby watched her go with a sad smile.

"Lieutenant Fotherby. I knew you would come."

He turned to face the young gentleman who had invited him to Barrington Manor. Perhaps due to his age and the heartbreak he had witnessed, David Portland was barely recognisable from the child Fotherby had met last year.

"You need not stare so hard at me, Fotherby," he laughed.

"I was recalling when I met you. You were a boy."

"A boy becomes a man very quickly when circumstances and events demand he should. Have you seen Philip since you arrived?"

Fotherby nodded. "I spoke to him last night."

"Then you see why I needed you to come."

"There is nothing I can do that you cannot."

"He will listen to you. He does not listen to me, for he was an adult when I was born and views me as a child. But I have discovered where he keeps the laudanum and have safely removed it to a place I know he will never go."

"Lady Barrington's room?"

David nodded and smiled slightly. "He talks as though she were only a dream. I think, to him, that is all she is now."

"It does not improve, but it becomes more bearable."

"Those are wise words, Lieutenant."

"They were my father's."

Both of them turned as Portland walked through the door. His eyes were dark in his pale face and he shivered as though it was cold outside, but the sun had shone all morning.

"Philip?" his brother began.

"I am well, David. I had to visit town. I am sorry for my behaviour last night, Fotherby. I believe I was a little out of sorts."

"I understand," Fotherby replied quietly. "We should go out riding, Portland."

"But you hate riding."

Fotherby shrugged his shoulders in a nonchalant manner. In truth he did hate riding, but he was as determined as David to restore Portland to health and break his addiction to the laudanum which gave him peace to sleep each night.

Cassandra had spoken truthfully about her mother, who would not join her two sons and guest at the dining table, but insisted that Cassandra looked for her father and brother at her window and through the grounds of the Manor. Trying to tempt his friend from his reliance on the opiate took time, but David never tired of the challenge and would follow Fotherby's direction and advice. Fotherby would walk out most mornings with Cassandra as she sought her dead father to appease her mother, and would ride, fence or shoot with her two brothers in the afternoon. Each evening they sat down to dine together and then, at night, Cassandra would sit with Portland and Fotherby and discuss books, music and plays. As September dawned it was to Portland's announcement that he intended to return to London. Concerned by his abrupt decision, and fearing that he was returning there solely to anonymously obtain more of the drug, Fotherby tried to dissuade his friend.

The nights were drawing in, casting a chill over the great house. Autumn had taken a strong hold over the land, the leaves were turning to gold and the air caught in Fotherby's throat as he walked out beside Cassandra.

"I am afraid I cannot persuade your brother to remain any longer. He means to leave tomorrow."

"You cannot be expected to keep him safe from his own foolishness, Lieutenant."

"David intends to travel with him."

"He is devoted entirely to his brother. Philip was a second father to him. I feel I have been robbed by Mother of my brothers. I do not know them anymore."

"The care you give your mother is admirable."

"Admirable but suffocating. I am sure that I can never be free from her."

"You are a beautiful person, Miss Portland," he replied softly, turning to her. "You shall make a wonderful wife for a fortunate gentleman."

Cassandra's eyes brimmed with tears that she was unable to keep from spilling as she forgot propriety and clutched him to her. Fotherby was unsure how to respond to such a gesture, but placed his arm around her, seeing the support she needed.

That evening found Cassandra, Portland and Fotherby seated before the fire in the Drawing Room. Each was silent for a time, lost in their own thoughts, before Cassandra whispered,

"The sea fog is drifting in, Philip. Perhaps you should wait a while before returning to London."

"It makes little difference to the carriage, Cassandra. Besides, I have assured David that he may come to London with me. He has not seen it in years." Portland's hand sank into his pocket before he corrected himself and rubbed his eyes. "I am so weary."

"Perhaps we should go to bed," she ventured. "You have a great journey ahead of you tomorrow."

"It is a strange thing," her brother mumbled. "I expect Rosanna to be waiting for me there. That is why I need to go, to know that she will not be."

"I understand," Cassandra said softly, and all three of them turned as they heard someone clattering down the stairs. The dowager pushed open the door and snatched Cassandra's hand.

"He is out there."

"Mother," Cassandra said angrily. "Our father is dead. I will not go out into the night to look for a ghost. If he walks abroad it is because you have summoned him with your reluctance to let him rest."

"How dare you talk to me in such a manner, girl?" she demanded, striking her daughter across the cheek. Portland stepped forward and gently coaxed his mother away from his sister. "It was Harris. My dear Harry. He is out there with your father."

"Very well," Cassandra replied, rubbing her cheek and glaring across at her mother. "I shall go search. But when I find no one there I shall have you locked away. For it is you who has poisoned this family since Father's death. You willed Delphi to die, and it was you who persuaded us that Margaret might be telling the truth. You have destroyed this family!"

Fotherby, who had stood up at Mrs Portland's arrival, stepped towards Cassandra but she lifted her hand to block his approach before walking out of the door. She slammed the door and they listened as the house door was closed in a similar fashion before Portland let go of his mother.

"He was there, Lord Barrington."

"No, Mother, he was not."

"Do you agree, then, with Cassandra?" the old woman's voice shook as she spoke.

"In part. I do believe that you see Father because you will him to be there." He turned to the surgeon who stood still, his head lowered as he tried not to pry into the conversation that was unfurling before him. "Fotherby, would you help my mother to her room? I have to find something."

"I know what you seek," Fotherby said firmly. "You would be better taking your mother than seeking your poison. I am going to find Miss Portland."

Portland frowned, surprised by the force with which his friend spoke, but Fotherby had no intention of apologising. He struggled to understand the behaviour of either of the two people in the room. How Portland could continue to rely on an opiate, when he had a family who needed him to be strong, Fotherby could not fathom. But he found the behaviour of the dowager appalling. Cassandra had devoted her entire life, both her past and her future, to her mother. She had forsaken any hope of marriage and a family of her own, and her mother still treated her with such contempt.

Walking out into the night, Fotherby took a moment to allow his eyes to accustom to the dark. The sea mist was thin around the house but it acted like a mirror, throwing back the light that seeped from the windows of Barrington Manor. It was not a solid wall but seemed to have openings, like doorways through which he began to walk. Trying to ensure that he kept the house to his right, he walked in a clockwise direction calling out as he went.

"Miss Portland?" his voice almost echoed back at him, and now he realised that he had lost sight of the house and had ventured further into the night than he had intended. But for his words, the only sound he could hear was the sea, indicating that he was now on the west side of the house. Presently he heard another voice. It was Portland, who called out his sister's name somewhere nearer the house, and Fotherby felt relieved to have company in his search.

"Lieutenant Fotherby," came a sobbing response to his calling.

He spun a full circle to try and see Cassandra, but the mist was playing cruel tricks with his vision and fine shards of light stabbed at his eyes.

"I cannot see you, Miss Portland."

"I do not know where I am," she cried. "But the sea is so close."

"Stay where you are, Miss Portland. I shall find you. Just keep talking so that I can follow your voice." He moved in the direction of the frightened voice, treading carefully, for the edge of the steep cliffs were not marked and nor were they visible in the shroud of fog.

"I thought I heard Philip's voice."

"Indeed," he continued, stepping back quickly as the ground vanished before him. "He is looking for you too."

"I wish we were at Wanderford Hall," she wept. "That summer has given me such happy memories during this year."

"I recall it with great fondness, too," Fotherby lied, still threading his way along the cliff top.

"I imagined your uncle to have been a terrible man," she laughed nervously. "But, in spite of his past, he was a gentleman."

"His past?" Fotherby whispered, the words inaudible to the imprisoned woman. He continued a little louder.

"I did not know that you knew my uncle prior to your visit to Derbyshire."

"I did not," came the reply, that at once sounded much relieved. "But I know of Sir Manfred Chester who, Philip told me, worked with your uncle. Oh, Fotherby, I can see you!"

At the elation in her voice Fotherby turned a circle once more to try and locate her, but he realised with terror that he could not see her. "Miss Portland, do not move! I cannot see you! It is only a trick in the mist!"

But before the last word had left his mouth he heard a sickening cry that almost caused his heart to stop. He did not believe he could ever hear a more haunting and horrifying sound than her scream of utmost panic. Even so, it did not compare to the terrible hollowness that welled within him as it abruptly stopped. He collapsed to the ground where he stood, trying to steady his breath, but it caught in his throat and he realised tears fell down his cheeks. Burying his head in his hands he tried to understand what had just happened, tried to will it to be untrue, but there was silence in the air now, except the sound of the waves.

After a time, he rose to his feet and stumbled, tripped, and staggered back to the house. He was unsure where to find it, except that he had to walk away from the sea. He did not know how long he spent trying to find Barrington Manor until it rose sharply before him. He reached it by the stable courtyard to the north and, as he passed the entrance to the Tack Room, he recalled the chill of Cullington's story. A man who had been saved from disgrace by a lord, had unwittingly betrayed his saviour, before guilt led him to take his own life. Fotherby could almost feel and understand that guilt now as he opened the door to the house and pressed himself against it.

"Is she dead?"

Fotherby looked up at the stairs where, halfway down, David Portland stood. He met the young man's gaze.

"Once again," he began, recalling these words that had been shared sixteen months earlier. "Yes."

"I thought I heard her," his voice trembled and he sat down on the stairs, leaning against the banister, trying to hide his face from the man before him.

Fotherby, respecting the efforts of the youngest Portland, walked to the open Dining Room door and beheld an image so horribly familiar from a year previous. Portland sat surrounded by bottles and broken glass from where he had let them fall. His darkened eyes tried to focus on Fotherby as he entered, but he could tell it was his friend by height alone.

"Why do you not join me?" he said, detaching each word as though he thought he could hide how drunk he was.

"No, thank you. I will go out at first light and bring her back," Fotherby promised.

"To join the Portland family in its mighty tomb," came the bitter reply. "There will be more of us there than live in the house now. I wanted you to marry her, you know? I wanted us to be brothers."

"I know." Fotherby's voice became soft as he took the chair next to Portland's. "Lady Barrington told me."

"She saw everything, Fotherby. And I saw nothing but her."

"She was all you described her to be. She knew I had laid my heart before another. But I have thought of you as a brother for so long without being tied by the bonds of marriage."

"I have failed this family. As Lord Barrington I have brought only ruin to my grandfather's house. I am inclined to agree with your captain, I should never have claimed the title nor my father before me."

"Captain Peters sees only your rank and title. He had no knowledge and consideration for who you truly were."

"I long for war now, Fotherby. Is that not terrible? To escape behind rank and run heroic deeds, I scarcely care if I should fall. Just to be free from England and all it has thrown at me."

There was nothing Fotherby could say that would comfort Portland, and he did not believe there was anything that could console the man. He was true to his word and, the following day as the mist cleared, he accompanied a group of men to recover the broken body of Cassandra Portland from the rocks at the foot of the cliff. He closed her beautiful eyes that stared in terror at her fate, and tried to forget her expression, but it remained trapped in his head. Portland wrote a letter to Harris informing him of their news, but received no reply and, when Cassandra was committed to the mausoleum alongside her family, Harris was not in attendance.

Fotherby parted from the family at the beginning of October. He accompanied Portland back to London and assisted him in the hunt for his brother, but no one could be found who knew where Harris Portland was. He encouraged Portland to attend events, to which he also invited Miss Simmons, in the hope that he could inspire a life within the man once more. As a damp December gripped the capital, however, Fotherby took his leave and returned once more to Derbyshire. He had invited Lord Barrington to attend, but Portland announced that

he would return to Cornwall to spend the festive period
with his family.

## Chapter Eighteen

*The Death And Life Of John Johnson*

Wanderford Hall always looked magical in the snow. The drifts that mounded up at the sides of the house grew to almost the height of its young heir, as the westerly wind forced the flakes against the stone walls. Leaving the house had become almost impossible, and Fotherby stared wistfully at the miniature of Miss Simmons, hoping that she would understand the cause of his silence. Indeed, he had written her several letters, but had been forced to add them to the growing pile of papers so that, at the end of February, when the snows began to drain away, he tied eight together and sent them on to his sweetheart.

Miss Simmons had informed him that she had encountered Lord Barrington and his brother, David, on their return to London after Christmas, for which Fotherby was greatly pleased. He had become anxious that his friend might take it into his head to end his life as Cullington had done but, from Kitty's words, his young brother was keeping him occupied. She made no reference to Harris, and Fotherby felt a chill take him as he considered the young man's disappearance.

Fotherby had hoped to visit London in the spring but, during the long winter, his father's health had declined.

He had caught a chill during January and the infection had left him almost completely deaf, so that Fotherby felt he could no longer communicate with him. As April arrived and the garden burst into bloom, he would take his father out walking, encouraging him to take the fresh Pennine air and enjoy the smells of the flowering grounds. His uncle also showed an uncharacteristically caring side, no doubt haunted by this image of his younger brother failing so dramatically. He postponed all planned excursions to his mills and excused himself from all invitations.

One evening in early May, Fotherby was standing on the landing and admiring his beloved view out to the distant hills. His uncle ascended the stairs and stood beside him.

"You are more like me than you care to admit, Henry," he began after a time. "The industry that you need in your life is what drove my own life too. Your father prefers the other view."

"Father can barely see now."

"I received a letter from Sir Manfred Chester today."

"Indeed? And is he well?"

"You are so good at feigning interest," his uncle laughed. "Persephone is to be married."

"Indeed?" Fotherby repeated.

"Yes. And all his wealth goes to her."

"Uncle," Fotherby began, his tone weary, "I have no love for Persephone Chester. You have met the woman I am betrothed to and claimed to like her."

"She was charming, Henry. But charm will not be enough to run this estate."

"It is Father's estate."

"Oh Henry," his uncle said plaintively. "Even you, with your patient optimism, must see that your father's health is precarious. Your wife must be able to run this estate."

"I will run the estate, not Miss Simmons."

"Are you ready?"

His uncle's words struck his chest with their driving force and, for a time, Fotherby only stared across the scene and tried to take in the full weight of the question. There were no words to say in reply, for his heart felt heavy each time he asked himself the same question. His father's health began to improve with the warmer weather and, as June turned to July, Fotherby began to believe that his father, despite being unable to read his books or hear the sounds of the world, still had years of life in him. All the same, when he received a letter in the middle of July, it caused him great concern.

"You seem particularly serious, Henry," his uncle laughed as he walked into the Dining Room, followed by four dogs. "Even by your own pensive standards."

He had wasted no time in introducing his dogs to the house when he realised his brother was unable to prevent him. Indeed, Fotherby's father had taken to eating alone and the young surgeon was becoming only more anxious about him once more.

"I am going to leave Wanderford for a time."

"But I thought you hated Wanderford. Why are you so disappointed?"

"I do not hate it," he protested. "And I am worried about Father."

"How long will you be gone for?" his uncle asked as he took his seat and one of the dogs came to sit next to Fotherby, tilting its head back and staring expectantly at the food on Fotherby's plate. "Where are you going?"

"India."

"But you loved India, Henry. You must be so pleased to be returning."

"But Father is ill."

"I can look after Tobias. You have a life of your own to live, and your father would agree with me. I shall strike you a bargain. Come back safely by the turn of the century and I shall keep your father alive."

"You seem rather confident in your abilities to tend him," Fotherby replied thoughtfully.

"I? Not at all. But since you gave your time to Doctor Shipton, he has been far more diligent in his care toward

Wanderford. But you need to be confident, Henry. If you are not, you will not survive war in such a climate."

"Did you ever travel to India?"

"No," came the short reply, and presently he busied himself with discarding food from his plate to the dogs.

That evening, Fotherby found his father sitting before the fire in his study, staring with unseeing eyes into the flames. It was stiflingly warm in the room, for there would not normally be a fire burning in the month of July. Fotherby walked over to him and knelt down by his side, taking the old man's hand.

"Henry," he whispered, a smile catching his face. "I did not notice you coming in."

"I have to leave," Fotherby began, before recalling that his father could not hear his words. He formed letters on his father's hand, spelling out his destination.

"India?" the old man asked, and watched as his son nodded, the movement visible although the tears running down his cheeks were not. "That is wonderful, Henry. I shall look forward to your return."

Fotherby leaned forward to his father and kissed his cheek, before rising and walking out of the room. His uncle oversaw his departure to London, where he accompanied Peters and Kitson to East India House, for they were to join the East India Company as far as Calcutta before uniting with the ranks of the army.

Kitson made no attempt to conceal his contempt toward the East India Company and explained to Fotherby how they were unwilling to share any supplies with the army without being fully reimbursed.

Indeed, Kitson seemed in remarkably high spirits. Fotherby did not observe the usual scowl upon his face, nor did he suffer at his cutting remarks. On much of the journey, which lasted four months as they travelled around Africa to avoid Napoleon's forces on the Nile, Fotherby was alone. He stared across the endless blue spread of the southern ocean and recalled how young and untroubled he had been when he last made this journey. He looked down at the thin circle of metal that formed one third of his mother's ring and wondered what the keepers of the other two thirds were doing. Miss Simmons had one part and her father had the final third, being the gentleman who was witness to their betrothal. When he had been in London, Fotherby had ensured that he had seen Kitty and had promised that, on his return, he would marry her at once, for there was money to make on campaigns and he suspected his father may no longer be alive when he returned.

"You must take care, Henry," Kitty's soft voice had replied. "You must remember that you are responsible for two hearts, now."

"I will return, Miss Simmons. I promise. And I promise I shall wed you within a month of my landing."

"I feel I should not call you Henry when you continue to call me Miss Simmons."

"I am afraid propriety has taken a hold on me, Miss Simmons, that I seem unable to discard. When we are married you shall no longer be Miss Simmons and I might then address you by your baptismal name."

"I long for it, Henry." She had leaned against him as she spoke. "It has been three years and more since I knew I loved you. I would have married you at once."

"I would not. You deserve a house to live in, Miss Simmons, and the security of a better standing than mine."

"You have made me believe it."

Fotherby awoke from his memories at the sound of his name, and turned to find Peters standing before him. The captain did not smile, nor did he acknowledge that Fotherby had seen him, but stepped over to join his lieutenant and stared over the ocean.

"I was surprised to see you in Perth," the man's gruff voice began, and at once Fotherby felt like a child.

"I was surprised to have been invited." He glanced across at the man beside him. "I was sorry for the shame I brought you. I am not sure I have done anything to merit being accepted back to this position."

"No?" Peters turned to him. "I heard favourable accounts to the contrary. Mr Hardy at Greenwich, Mr Shipton at Buxton, I even heard that you had left a party to attend a sick child."

"Were you spying on me, sir?" Fotherby asked, feeling his cheeks burning.

"Yes. Do not look so surprised, Fotherby. I have no intention of leaving my legacy to any man I deem unworthy, and I had to know you would take care of my work. I heard about what happened to the child, too."

"I do believe she was the bravest soul I have ever met," he whispered, recalling the courage with which Miss Delphina Portland had confronted her illness.

"Did you know that Lord Barrington's company is part of the battalion being transported to India?"

"No, sir," Fotherby replied, unsure whether or not he was pleased. "I have not spoken to Lord Barrington in many months. Not since Miss Portland's funeral."

"I was sorry to learn that, too."

"How did you learn it, sir?"

"That does not matter, boy. But I was sorry."

"I do not believe you came to pass on condolences to a man you neither like nor admire."

"No. There is someone I wished to talk to you about." Captain Peters turned to face Fotherby. "A man I trained alongside, by the name John Johnson."

"That is an interesting name, sir," Fotherby ventured, as his captain fell silent.

"I suspect it was not his name at all. But he died and was buried in America with that carved on the grave marker. Since then, he has served the British army by name, volunteering information to help secure the successes of our campaigns." He studied the man beside him, before he shook his head and sighed. "Do you understand what I am telling you?"

"Not really, sir," Fotherby answered honestly, unsure who John Johnson was and what his death and work had to do with him.

"Just look out for him in India, boy," Peters snapped, before he walked away from Fotherby, drinking from the flask which seemed as much a part of him as his limbs.

The remaining journey was uneventful, indeed Peters seemed determined to ridicule Fotherby whenever possible and he and Kitson would often spend their time laughing and drinking. Feeling now that the situation had not changed since they had been in Flanders, Fotherby found his thoughts always drifting back to Miss Kitty Simmons, and he would spend countless hours gazing at the portrait he had carried out to India with him.

The three surgeons spent a brief time in Calcutta before, in the new year, they joined Colonel Wellesley's forces in Mysore. It was here that Fotherby was reunited once more with Portland. They arrived in the late evening at the beginning of February to find the main force of the British troops already established. Their tent was pitched and Fotherby admired it with a sense of achievement, for Peters and Kitson had both left him to oversee its erection.

"Lieutenant Fotherby! I knew it was you."

"Captain Portland, sir," Fotherby began, taking in the appearance of the man before him. He was no longer pallid with darkened eyes, but tanned by the sunlight, and it was a genuine smile that caught his lips. "I was told you were here."

"Indeed, and grateful of it. But how are you, Fotherby? For I have not heard from you in so long. Although I encountered Miss Simmons in London last spring and she informed me of your understanding."

"I am well. Pleased to be back in India and happy to see you well."

"And your father and uncle?" Portland asked. "Are they well?"

"My uncle is in perfect health. I do believe he has preserved himself through salt and alcohol and shall long outlast me. Father was well when I left."

"I am pleased to hear it." Portland sat down on the ground and sighed. "What a poor generation we make, Fotherby. Trailing on from our fathers with too much conflict and so many different directions."

Fotherby sat beside him and shook his head. "We do not all yearn for conflict, nor seek different directions. I should be proud to follow in my father's footsteps, as I know you also should be."

"You are a rare gentleman. You have a depth and patience that is wasted on the battlefield."

"I am not on the battlefield," Fotherby pointed out, unsure how to accept such a compliment.

Over the following two months, the British troops fought the sickness, poor conditions and boredom, but Wellesley's men did not have the chance to fight their enemies until the spring arrived. The dry season was upon Mysore and the British soldiers were struggling to withstand the heat. Some had fought in the last war here, and remarked upon the ease of this campaign compared with the last, but all were ready for the commencement of combat when they reached Seringapatam in April.

During the month-long siege that readied the army for its final assault on the city, Fotherby had little to do. He was returned to the insignificance of being the third surgeon in an often empty tent. There were always enough people to ensure that he could not leave the scorching tent, yet too few to make his job bearable. He had initially seen Captain Portland each day but, as the siege developed, the young captain was detained and delayed more by his role within the army.

"I am going for a time," Peters announced from where he rose at his campaign desk. "I trust I can leave this tent in your safe keeping, Lieutenants."

"Yes, sir," Kitson began. Of late the scowl had once more returned to his face and Fotherby believed that this had been as a result of a letter he had received during March. Fotherby himself made no answer but, as soon as his captain had departed, loosened the cuffs and collar of his shirt and, sitting down at the desk. picked up a parchment that he began using as a fan.

"Do you suppose this can last much longer?" Fotherby asked as he looked across at his fellow lieutenant.

"The siege? I imagine it will last until the monsoon, then we will all be swept in the river and out to the ocean. But it is tedious. If there were work to do beyond these mundane treatments it would at least give our being here a purpose."

"I heard that you became a father once more," Fotherby ventured.

"A daughter. Another daughter." He sat back and scowled.

"Is that so bad? You have a son, too, do you not?"

"Indeed," Kitson replied, glancing sideward. "And I need not ask you about affairs of the heart for, when last you looked set to usurp me, you had dropped from favour as the result of a duel. To protect a lady's honour, I understand. And I have seen the ring that rests around your neck."

Fotherby ceased fanning himself and lifted his hand to his neck, feeling exposed by Kitson's words.

"She must be quite a lady, Fotherby, for I believed that no one would come between you and your devotion to your work."

"The duel was a matter of honour, but not for Miss Simmons."

"Simmons?"

"Indeed, her father is stationed here as part of the siege."

"Keeping his eye on you no doubt. He almost certainly asked to be placed here for no other reason."

"He did not ask," Fotherby answered innocently. "He is a sergeant and goes where he is sent."

"A sergeant? Not a commissioned officer?"

Both of them turned as a voice boomed from behind them. "Get out of my chair, you idle mope!"

Fotherby jumped to his feet and turned to face Peters as he returned.

"Kitson," Peters snapped, but never took his eyes from Fotherby's face. "There are fresh water supplies being drawn. Go and oversee that at least three barrels make their way here."

Fotherby watched as Kitson hurried out before he turned his gaze back to the irate captain. "I am sorry, sir," he began, bowing his head in acceptance of his guilt. "I meant no offence."

"Get a stool," Peters demanded and Fotherby walked over to where a low three-legged stool sat in the corner of the tent. "Do not sit there, you dolt. I have no intention of shouting across to you."

Fotherby moved the stool over to the desk and set down the paper with which he had been fanning himself. "I did not read it, sir," he muttered.

"Read it now," Peters' gruff voice ordered.

"Sir, it is not my letter."

Peters did not answer him but glowered across. Feeling that he had already exceeded the limited bounds of this man's patience, Fotherby picked up the paper and looked down at it, checking first the names of the sender and recipient.

"I know this man," he faltered as he looked up. "Major Tenterchilt was with me when I met you in Perth."

"I know," Peters said flatly.

"But who is J.J.?"

"John Johnson," Peters stated, as though nothing could be clearer to understand.

"Sir, this letter contains information that we should not be party to. It is the movement of forces, the directions of battles. It is the very blood flow of the army."

"At times I despair of you, Fotherby. You are either entirely blind or ridiculous in your naivety. Sometimes I wonder how you ever became so skilled in your profession."

Fotherby felt overwhelmingly confused as he read through the letter again, and felt only more foolish as he admitted, in a voice little more than a whisper, "I do not understand."

"Of course the lords and princes lead the forces through the lands. But those that power the British army are those that can fade into the shadows. Intelligence is what drives the British army, and those who deliver it must be certain not to be caught. Think, Fotherby, it is time you cease trying to find answers and commence asking questions."

"You are a spy?" Fotherby whispered. "Why?"

Peters stared at the young man, his lips pursing and his eyes narrowing. "I will never be questioned."

"But you just told me to ask questions, sir," Fotherby retorted.

"No, that is why I do it." He sat back now and regarded his young lieutenant. "I will not be caught and, if I were, no one would think to question a surgeon on the plans of the army. But, tomorrow, I am leaving this tent and, while others may dispute this, I am leaving it to you."

"Tomorrow? Sir, what do you mean 'leaving'?"

"May will spark a new wave of attack against Tipu and I do not foresee that the British forces will so lightly be dismissed as they were a week ago."

"But why are you leaving, sir? You assured me your place would be in your tent until you died."

"Do you wish me dead?" Peters demanded, and watched as Fotherby shook his head. "I am travelling north to Hyderabad. I will not tire you with the complications or reasons for such a move, but it must suffice to say that I shall not be returning to Mysore, nor to the British army."

"But, sir," Fotherby began.

"Do not speak like a pathetic schoolboy, Fotherby. It is time that you rose to the challenge you have been set." Peters made no attempt to soften his tone, but his words became kinder. "You have an unparalleled skill in your work, your sickening morals make you unimpeachable, and your adherence to duty is unquestionable. I would not trust this to Kitson, for when his moods take him he is as likely to sell any information for the cost of a drink. So when I, as John Johnson, sent his final letter to the good major, I ensured that Wellesley would promote you over Kitson. Do not let him bully you."

"I am quite certain he shall, sir, and I am equally certain that I would not blame him."

"That is a matter that you must resolve, Fotherby." Peters turned as Kitson stepped into the tent, his face holding a look of puzzlement as he beheld the sorrow on Fotherby's face.

"You have brought a darkness to Lieutenant Fotherby's face, sir. Did you suggest he should not marry Miss Simmons?"

"To the contrary, Lieutenant Kitson," Peters replied, wafting his hand dismissively at Fotherby. "Lieutenant Fotherby's choice of wife is exactly as rebellious as I would expect from such a revolutionary. Did you bring those barrels?"

Fotherby did not listen to any more of the conversation, but folded the letter and tucked it into the pocket of his red coat. He walked out into the onset of evening and tried to understand all that he had just learnt. In his simple folly, he had viewed Captain Peters as an embittered man, driven to drink by failures in his profession and having no one to trust. But, in truth, Peters had simply created a character to disguise the true nature of his role in the British army. Yet now he wished to appoint an unprepared and untutored successor to take on the perilous duty.

The air was still and arid as he breathed deeply, trying to steady his thoughts. Gazing at the city beyond the river, Fotherby considered the job before him. According to Major Tenterchilt's letter to J.J., Tipu Sultan had a preferred method of attack using a form of artillery called rockets, which had been the cause of the British assembling their camp over the river, for they were so far reaching. In addition to this, the major had used details provided from the last conflict to suggest a means of combat. This, Fotherby correctly assumed, Peters had shared with those commanders who occupied the enormous tent on the summit of the hill.

Fotherby did not sleep until the night was complete. He stared up at the stars and found that he was already taking Peters' advice, as more questions, to which he might never know the answers, flooded his head. Tomorrow the deadlock was to be broken, his captain was to depart to whatever fate awaited him in Hyderabad, and Fotherby felt a nervousness at what the coincidence of these two events might mean.

# Chapter Nineteen
*The Storming of Seringapatam*

Captain Peters was not a man comfortable with sentimentality. Therefore, when Fotherby awoke the next morning and walked in a sleepy daze to the hospital tent, it was to find that Captain Peters had already left and his equipment had been removed from the desk. Perhaps most unsettling of all, the cards had also gone. Fotherby stared at the campaign desk with a greater sorrow than he would have believed possible for the man who had so often ridiculed and belittled him, but for whom he had a great respect. There was no sign of Kitson either and, as Fotherby picked up the red coat with the captain's third star already on the epaulets, he tried to anticipate the man's vile mood.

"I hear congratulations are in order," a cheerful voice announced. "Captain Fotherby."

"At a high price," Fotherby replied as he pulled his coat on and offered half a smile to Portland. "How did you know?"

"Lieutenant Kitson is in a rage. I am quite sure the entire British army has heard. And I do not limit that to those in India, either."

"I have not seen him, yet," Fotherby muttered. "Peters told me he would only leave when he died. I felt

I had years before I should have to resolve this, and I might have shaken free of Kitson by then."

"This is one meeting I want to witness. It is high time someone taught him how to control his petulance. He is as bad as Harry."

"Did you find your brother?" Fotherby asked.

"No. He will be out in London or one of the boroughs, chasing women and owning no responsibility. But while I have not heard from him I can only assume he lives. What a poor Lord Barrington he will make."

"You will not die yet."

"But nor will I remarry, so the title shall pass sideward."

Fotherby felt combined sorrow and relief at his words but, before he could say anything in reply, Kitson walked into the tent. His eyes narrowed as he marched up to Fotherby and glared into the younger man's calm features.

"You both planned this, of course," Kitson spat.

"I knew. But I did not plan it, Kitson. He told me he would not leave until he was dead."

"Is it not enough that you have land and wealth? I have a family."

"And you are far from destitute," Fotherby interjected, his placid manners only angering the man before him. "But if it would settle your concern a little more, I will give you the increase in my pay."

"I would take nothing from you." Kitson turned as he noticed Portland for the first time. "Yet, despite handing you his legacy, you still cavort with the man he despised."

"Careful, Lieutenant," Portland began. "Do not let your temper lead you to words you may regret."

"Do you seek to threaten me?"

"I only speak the truth, sir. I had no quarrel with Captain Peters, though you are correct that our politics differed." Portland smiled across at Fotherby. "Now that I have seen this display, I shall leave you in peace, Fotherby. Though, in truth, I do not believe you will have peace for long."

Throughout the day, Kitson worked hard to ignore every word Fotherby spoke. The lieutenant sat at the campaign desk as though he had a right to be there, and watched as Fotherby paced the floor of the tent, waiting anxiously for the first sound of battle that Peters had promised, and praying that he would have the strength to command the tent. Peters had ruled with a ruthlessness which he could never emulate, and Fotherby tried to remind himself of the reasons Peters had named him as his successor. On no fewer than three occasions he rushed to the tent flap upon hearing distant gunfire, but there was no evidence of a fray. He arranged his tools, straightened the linen and counted each of the times he repeated this. He need not have concerned himself, however, for when the wall was breached at dawn the following day, it was with a force that caused the ground to tremble.

Neither Fotherby nor Kitson had achieved much sleep that night, each considering their place in rank of the hospital tent. There was the confusion that Fotherby recalled at once from the Flanders campaign that immediately followed any form of battle, enhanced by the ignition of Nizam's arsenal ahead of the planned time, with no one certain who had ordered that such a thing should be done. Carrying the wounded back to the tent was almost impossible for, although the river was able to be crossed, it was at least four foot in depth. Some who were carried back were drowned, and few were able to be treated. Many of them walked themselves back to the hospital tent and Fotherby was relieved to find that Kitson, despite his bitter disappointment at the events of the day before, did not relinquish his duty to the men.

Perhaps through returning to work, or having to take responsibility for the lives within his own tent, Fotherby was too tired to stand as the sun set. He pulled one of the stools to the tent flap and looked down at the city beyond the river. After the busy nature of the day, the scene seemed remarkably calm, and he felt the waves of sleep wash over him as the river washed over the land.

"Fotherby?"

"Yes?" he whispered, rubbing his eyes.

"Busy day?" Portland ventured as he squatted beside him.

"Very. But I suspect that tomorrow shall be worse."

"No," Portland replied. "Tomorrow we are to do nothing, to lure them to complacency. Then on Saturday we are to storm, at an hour they can least expect."

"That is our plan?" Fotherby asked.

"Indeed. Major General Baird is eager to have justice for the events of the last war and is rallying two columns from the 73rd and the 74th to storm the city."

"And what of you and the rest of the 33rd?"

"Wellesley is heading a third column in case it should be needed. The 33rd will be there."

"I do not know how Captain Peters did it," Fotherby yawned. "I never saw him sleep."

"But you never saw him when he was first a captain. I have no doubt that any battlefield surgeon feels as you do when they first have their own tent."

Fotherby longed to share with his friend the complicated nature of the job that Peters had left him, but knew he should not. Portland, acknowledging how exhausted his friend was, bade him goodnight and walked further into the camp. Sleepily, Fotherby returned to the interior of the tent and watched as, upon his arrival, Kitson strutted out. He sat at the campaign desk and ran his long fingers over the carved lines, some in the design and others caused by its years of use.

He fell asleep then, without pillow or blanket but too weary to care. His dreams were bleak, for they combined the deaths of the three Portland ladies, and this time Miss Kitty Simmons joined them. She was suffering from the same wounds as many of the soldiers who had survived the return to camp, with limbs crushed by the violently thrown masonry that the premature explosion had caused. But he was unable to save her, so that everything he tried only worsened her condition until, at last, she died in his arms.

The following day was one of peace, as Portland had told him it would be. There was no gunfire to be heard, but the troops continued to drill, creating the continued sound of warfare. Fotherby spent his time tending those who had arrived yesterday, while Kitson sat at the desk. He began to realise why Peters had taken to playing cards, for he was unable to leave these wounded men and yet they spent great stretches of time unconscious or without needing his assistance. The custom of the area was to sleep after midday, for the heat was unbearable, and Fotherby found that he followed this example almost unintentionally.

"I did not think you would make it out of the tent," Portland's voice began as Fotherby turned to face him. The evening was drawing in now, the sun sinking low against the horizon and long shadows were cast by the men and tents on the Indian landscape. "I saw Kitson down by one of the fires and realised that he had no intention of bringing you food." He set a wooden plate of rice down before the surgeon. "So I brought you some."

"Thank you." Fotherby stared down at the food and tried to will himself to eat. "I dreamt of your sisters last night," he mumbled. "And Lady Barrington, and Miss Simmons."

"Do you believe they watch down on us, Fotherby?" Portland asked, as he pulled one of the stools to the desk and sat down. "Do you think that they see us more now than when we were in Flanders?"

"I am certain of it."

"Then why do I feel so far away from them?" Portland asked, his voice becoming desperate. "I came to war to be free of my thoughts and the memories, but I have been chased by them."

"You have only to close your eyes," Fotherby said softly. "Your memories should make them close to you."

Portland only smiled sadly, and sought a new topic of conversation. "Have you heard from Miss Simmons since you came to India?"

"Twice. In the new year and then again scarcely a week since. I asked her if she should ever travel out here. Can you imagine a more beautiful place? But she is very settled in London."

"She will teach you to love the city," Portland smiled. "Rosanna taught me to love it for, before we were married, I hated the city as much as you." Portland turned suddenly as though he expected to find someone there. "It is the strangest thing," he added, closing his eyes. "But I believe you were right, Fotherby."

Fotherby watched his friend with great pity as he tried to imagine what it would be to have and lose sisters and a wife. Portland opened his eyes and stared across at his friend.

"Eat up," he continued, suddenly happy and carefree once more. "Tomorrow you are going to need all your strength. But I must go, for I have a matter I must resolve with the colonel."

The newly-promoted Captain Fotherby watched as Portland rose to his feet and departed, before he stared at the plate of rice and dutifully ate, though he tasted none of it.

That evening he sat by the tent flap, smoking his pipe and staring over the camp, which seemed quieter than usual. He had much to consider but felt that an eternity would not be enough time. Lifting his hand to the ring he wore about his neck, he wondered whether Miss Simmons wore her half in a similar way, a thought that caused him to blush and begin coughing on the pipe smoke. These thoughts next turned to consider Portland and the loss of his wife. He considered how he would feel to lose Miss Simmons, trying to imagine the emptiness, and a void opened within him that he did not believe he should ever fill. This thought of loss turned to his father, for Fotherby could not bring himself to hope that his father would be alive on his return to England. His thoughts encompassed his uncle, the rest of the Portland family, Doctor Shipton, and Captain Peters, whose enigmatic departure still puzzled him.

The camp had fallen silent by the time he lay back upon the long grasses that easily bent beneath him. He stared up at the stars and wondered at how different they were to the stars he had learnt in England. This thought was still in his head as sleep claimed him and the next thing he knew was that Kitson stood over him, kicking him in the side.

"I suppose it is a captain's right to sleep as he wishes," he muttered as, upon Fotherby awaking, he walked away.

Fotherby rose to his feet and stared down over the camp. How different it was to the camp it had been last night. It was now very much alive. Young men were hurrying to be ready, while the older men only chided them for their haste. Fotherby picked up his coat, that he had rolled into a pillow, and walked into the tent.

"Kitson," he began in a tone that was surprisingly firm. Lieutenant Kitson turned to face him, startled that such a sound could be made by such a passive man. "I did not ask Peters to promote me. I fully expected to work in your tent when the captain left. And I would have done. I expect you to be gentlemanly enough to reciprocate."

"It is easy for you to say such things, Captain. It was not that way around."

"I suggest that you consider what gave you cause to become a surgeon, Lieutenant Kitson, for if you do not put the running of this tent before your own dislike of me, men will die. And I have no time for a surgeon who would allow that to happen."

Fotherby held the other man's gaze silently as the seconds passed by, before he turned at the sound of someone addressing him. Portland stood there, his uniform complete, but with his collar hanging open.

"You are going to war, then," Fotherby began, stepping over to his friend and leaving the lieutenant to consider his words. "Third column? You look a little well dressed for such a position."

"You cannot lead men when you use your coat as a pillow," Portland teased, placing his hand on Fotherby's arm and laughing slightly. "But I had a purpose in coming here, and one I must relay at speed for the ranks are forming even now."

"What is it?"

"I want to ask something of you, Fotherby. When the conflict of the day is over and we have won, for I am certain we shall, come and find me in the city. Do not sit here in the tent waiting to be called. Come and find me, for I shall be ready to go home."

"We are always the last ones to leave," Fotherby replied, "but I shall come and find you. The moment my duty here is finished."

"Thank you, Fotherby. I have always thought to trust you. Although when I found out about your Mayfair friends and your uncle I admit to being surprised."

"What of my uncle?" Fotherby asked, with a confused smile. He recalled the last words Cassandra had spoken to him regarding her surprise at finding his uncle agreeable.

"You know of his past, do you not?" Portland asked. "When he was in the West Indies?"

"He was a merchant," Fotherby whispered.

"In a way he was, if you can view selling men and women, and children even, as commodities. But you did not know?" Portland asked, seeing the look of confusion and disgust on his friend's face. "God, Fotherby, I am sorry. I did not know that you were unaware."

"He left that life," Fotherby answered loyally.

"I know. And I was impressed by him when we met. The best of us is not the one who does no wrong, but the one who rights the wrongs he has done." Portland smiled across at Fotherby. "You have been a truly great friend to me and all my family, far greater than I deserved. Come and find me, Henry, when today is over."

Fotherby blinked in surprise at the sound of his Christian name but nodded quickly, assuring his friend that he would, before he wished him luck and safety in the day's endeavours.

"Goodbye, Kitson," Portland said, without raising his voice. "I am quite sure you are listening, you need not hide it."

"It is not I who is hiding something, Captain Portland," Kitson replied with a surprising amount of meekness which caused Fotherby to stare at the man.

"Goodbye, Fotherby," Portland said at last. "And thank you again."

Fotherby watched his friend leave, with a feeling similar to how he had felt when Captain Peters had left. He walked to the tent flap and pulled it open to watch as Portland walked down the hill into the camp, never turning back.

"That is the walk of a determined man," Kitson said in an impressed tone. He stood beside Fotherby and barked a humourless laugh. "I have never understood what makes men do it, but then you were right, Fotherby, I chose to be a surgeon to try and help those who did not have sense to protect themselves."

"What do you mean?" Fotherby asked, his voice hoarse.

Kitson only shook his head. They did not talk to one another for a time but, as the sun rose to its peak position and the heat became almost unbearable, the sound of battle reached the hill. The explosions of guns and rockets, the cries of men, the frantic screams of the city dwellers. And each time it became harder and harder to endure in silence until, at length, Kitson shattered the peace of the tent and announced to his captain the arrival of the first casualties.

To begin with the men were those struck by the rockets, many when the tired explosives were almost spent, so their wounds were not too severe. Then men arrived carrying comrades from the first two columns, but it became apparent that the third column had not been needed. Fotherby was in a dazed state. He cut, cleaned, sawed and bandaged without considering anything but the job in hand so that, as the evening drew on and the steady stream of people coming to the tent ceased, he felt as though he was awakening from a dream.

"Get a drink, Kitson," Fotherby muttered, as he washed the blood from his hands in a basin of water. "I think you have deserved it."

"Thank you, sir," Kitson replied. He seemed to think nothing of his response but Fotherby felt his breath catch at this address. "You had better find Captain Portland, sir," he continued. "He wanted to go home."

"Lieutenant Kitson," Fotherby replied with a weak smile, "I am quite sure Portland is capable of making his own way home. The 33rd were not even in the battle."

"Fotherby," Kitson said softly, "his words earlier were not the speech of a third column. Nor that walk the dawdling strut of a surplus soldier. That was the speech and walk of the Forlorn Hope."

"What?" Fotherby demanded, as he stared at his lieutenant and tried to recall all the words that he and Portland had shared. He rushed out without giving Kitson a chance to answer, but sped through the tents, uncertain how he intended to find his friend when he had no notion of where to search. There were few men in the camp now, most having penetrated the town after the battle, in search of Tipu's famed riches. Fotherby stood on the opposite bank of the river and stared across at it. Parts of the city smoked and the gaping breach revealed an open square of debris where buildings had once stood. Hysterical cries of women could be heard, but otherwise the only sound was the movement of the river.

"Hoping to cross, sir?"

Fotherby turned to three soldiers who were sitting around a fire a little further along the riverbank. "I am not sure it is sensible," he muttered in reply.

"Sensible?" the soldier repeated. "No, sir, it is not sensible. But I could help you cross if you had a mind to."

"Did you fight today?" Fotherby asked.

"Yes, sir. Saved the horrors of your tent if not the horrors of battle."

Fotherby was about to question how these men knew him before he looked down at the bloodied apron that he still wore. "Where do I cross?"

Talking to the three soldiers, Fotherby learnt a little of what had happened during the storming of the city. The British had been victorious, as Portland had predicted, in a brief time but at a cost of hundreds of lives. The three soldiers, who were all in the 74th Highland regiment, accompanied Fotherby across the river after finding a boat to take him, each pleased to be on the other side, while Fotherby stepped onto the far shore and stared at the remnants of battle. How much more affected he was by the death and corpses before him than by the dying men in his tent. He stepped over to one of the British soldiers who lay at the opening and turned him over. He was a young man, perhaps not yet twenty, with a hole in his right temple and eyes that stared out, searching forever for that promised glory.

His three guides had left him now, going from corpse to corpse to see if they knew any of them. Fotherby stood and looked down at the carpet of bodies, unsure what he expected to find but certain what he hoped not to. He knelt down beside an Indian soldier, who he moved respectfully aside, before he turned over another one of the British corpses. With each unidentified body a greater hope filled him that Kitson had been wrong in his assessment of Portland's actions until, in the shadow of the enormous wall, he stared down at the face he had prayed he would not find here. Initially he stood, towering over the body, tears burning his eyes, before he knelt down and clapped his hand to his face.

"Are you well, sir?" one of the three soldiers asked. "Is this the man you sought?"

"Yes," Fotherby whispered as he lifted Portland's head. He carried no wound save one, to the left side of his chest. His eyes were not open as many of the dead men, but were lightly closed as though he was asleep. Fotherby placed his hand over the bloodied shirt, which was almost dried now, but there was no heartbeat beneath his flat palm.

"I know this man, sir," the soldier continued. "He was a captain in the 33rd, was he not?"

"He was."

"Led the second Forlorn Hope, sir." The soldier looked on for a moment before he knelt down opposite Fotherby. "Died almost at once, sir."

"Oh God," Fotherby muttered. He lifted the body of his friend and watched as the Scottish soldier also rose. "I told him I would find him. He wanted to go home."

"The journey to Britain, sir, is six months. I do not think the captain will make such a trek."

"But he has a tomb waiting for him in Cornwall. Beside his wife and daughter, and his sisters. I will take him back, though my duty here is far from complete."

"Sir," the other man began, "I intend to return to Britain shortly."

Fotherby stared at the man before him and tried to understand what he was trying to say. "I do not know you."

"My name is Keith, sir. Second Lieutenant of the 74th Highland Regiment."

"When do you intend to leave, Second Lieutenant Keith?"

"Within the week, sir. I have been granted permission by my captain to return to Britain in the first vessel."

Fotherby nodded reluctantly and Keith and the other two men escorted him, and Portland's body, to the other side of the river once more. Portland lay on the bloodied table in the hospital tent as though he were a king lying in state, and Fotherby stood mutely beside him for so many minutes. Kitson had not retired for the evening but continued in his work, watching his melancholy captain in silence. The tent was far from silent, however, although Fotherby scarcely heard the noises. Eventually he stirred from his thoughts and prayers and began, once more, assisting those he could help.

Fotherby spent almost every penny he had to ensure that Second Lieutenant Keith was provided for to return to Britain, and Fotherby also entrusted a letter to the young officer. He had to trust him, for he could not return with the body, being bound by his duty to remain. He looked at the letter and sighed slightly as he read it back.

"David Portland, No words can express my heartfelt regret at the subject which accompanies this letter. This is only enhanced as I must admit to being absent from your dear brother when he fell and from failing to acknowledge the last words he spoke to me. While the gentleman who bears this message to you knows far more of events than I, it is my understanding that Lord Barrington chose to command a band of the Forlorn Hope and fell quickly and perished swiftly. There is little more I can consider to write, for my heart is heavy and my soul distant. I loathe myself for bearing this grievous news and find myself wishing I had done a better job of persuading him from such a foolish notion. Though I am given to say that I believe, through this role, he obtained a reunification with that soul he most longed to accompany. I beseech your forgiveness once more. Yours in friendship, Henry Fotherby."

As he watched his friend embark on what was to be his final journey, Fotherby felt that his heart was so heavy it weighed him to the ground. As May drew to a close, he continued to work diligently and tirelessly so that, when evenings came, he was too tired even to dream. The air became dry and difficult to breathe, hindered more by the number who became ill from drinking river water as they moved northeast toward Calcutta. Clean water was becoming a rare but desperately needed commodity. In such bitter situations, Kitson and Fotherby set aside their disagreements and tried to help those who suffered from the effects of dehydration. But, as June arrived, more and more people were trying to survive on less and less water.

# Chapter Twenty

*An Old Feud With A New Victim*

The horrendous deaths of those who had been poisoned by the river water were a bitter warning to the other members of the regiment. All walked on through the jungles on paths which no longer resembled roads. At different times, often totally without warning, huge temples soared over them, their pinnacles climbing higher than any of the buildings the men had seen before entering the jungle. Here, there were wells and the men would drink thirstily, trying to fill their flasks from the large buckets. The barrels would be filled and the men journeyed on. The commanders hoped that they would reach Calcutta before the monsoon season began, but each man present prayed that the heavens would open and pour down any amount of rain upon them.

"I do not understand why we did not return to the port in the south," Fotherby muttered, as he walked alongside the cart that carried the three barrels they had last filled eight days previously and were now all but empty.

"They have different ideas," Kitson replied. He was sitting on the cart, preferring to ride rather than walk. "I expect that we are to make a show of force."

The beginning of June was very different in the subcontinent to its mild British counterpart. Many of the soldiers were unprepared for such aggressive heat. The officers also shared a lack of vision and, subsequently, the water that should have lasted two weeks was gone in ten days. There was little comfort on the march and almost as little in the evenings, for fires had to be lit to dispel insects from the roadside camp. Only a handful of tents were erected, most men preferring to sleep in the open, although this had its own dangers, and three men had already died from snakebites. Fotherby slept in the back of the cart, staring up at what was visible of the heavens through the huge leaves overhead.

He had come to love India, he realised as he listened to the intense sound of calling insects and watched the razor thin clouds skate across the star-studded sky. He felt calmed by the lullaby of the jungle and slipped into a sleep that was too deep for dreams.

The following day the column moved out once more, with little more than enough water to wet their lips and no hope of finding more. Fotherby and Kitson had to, on occasions, help men onto the cart, for they were unable to journey any further on foot.

That evening, Fotherby and Kitson sat on the back of the stationary cart they had taken as their own. Neither of them spoke for, although they had discarded their feud, they still had little in common and neither trusted the other. Presently, Kitson rose to his feet and looked across towards the rest of the column as it stretched before them.

"Stand up, Fotherby," he said quickly, with a greater animation in his voice than Fotherby had ever heard. "You are taller than I. What is happening?"

Reluctantly, Fotherby rose and turned to look in the direction of the commotion. "I cannot see anything in this light. I would imagine someone is questioning how three tuns of water disappeared so quickly and someone else has not the mind to answer him." He sat down once more but turned to look over the edge of the cart as the irate sound came closer.

"Where are those damned surgeons hiding?" demanded a voice.

"Not hiding, sir," Kitson replied, jumping down from the cart and stepping over to the man who had spoken.

"Trying to take some sleep," Fotherby reiterated as he moved to the edge of the cart and watched as two men walked into view. One of them, clearly the man who had spoken, looked angrily across at Fotherby as though he believed the state of his friend was in some way the fault of the young surgeon. His companion had blood pouring from his nose and mouth and his eyes were glazed, seeing nothing despite being wide open. "What happened?" Fotherby asked, as he and Kitson hoisted the unconscious man onto the cart.

"Insubordination," the other man replied. "That is what happened."

"How did he sustain these injuries?" Fotherby muttered, trying to get the answer he was looking for.

"The peasant struck him in the face with the butt of a musket."

"He is lucky to be a short gentleman," Kitson interjected. "If he had been taller than his assailant, he could easily be dead."

"Get off me," the wounded man began. "Where is that damn sergeant? I'll see him hang for this." He pushed Kitson aside but, as he stepped from the cart, he collapsed to the ground.

"What is it about men that make them so ungrateful of our care?" Kitson asked, as he and Fotherby lifted him once more to the cart.

"Will he survive?" the other man asked. "Our colonel will wish to know."

"He will survive," Fotherby replied calmly.

"Though his future may not be spent in the same manner as his past," Kitson muttered, laughing as though he had made a joke. "He will not have the looks to support it. A gentleman with a broken nose and fractured jaw is far less appealing to a lady."

"How dare you speak so?" demanded the other man. "He is a gentleman."

"Enough," Fotherby said firmly. "Who is your colonel?"

"Pottinger, sir."

"And who are you?"

"Lieutenant Young, sir."

"Then, Lieutenant Young, you may return to Colonel Pottinger and tell him that, although appearing a little different, his officer will be well enough to return almost at once."

"I should not stay, sir?" the other man asked.

"I expect you would not want to, but an extra pair of hands would be gratefully welcomed."

Fotherby's assessment of the matter had been far more accurate than Lieutenant Young had anticipated, for Kitson held the wounded man still while Fotherby cauterised the wound in the man's nose. Young, who had assured the two surgeons that he would steady his comrade's head, became pale at the sight and had to reach back to the side of the cart to steady himself so that Fotherby had to hold the man still himself.

"Lieutenant Young?" Kitson asked, handing his captain a cloth to clean the blood from his hands. "Your friend will be well."

"He is not my friend," came the shaky reply. "He is my captain."

"I understand," Kitson muttered as he glanced at his own captain, who was lifting the wounded man to prop him against the barrels before climbing down and joined the two lieutenants.

"He will be fine," Fotherby pointed over his shoulder. "Will you, Lieutenant?"

"I will," the younger man answered determinedly. "But Simmons will hang for this."

"Simmons?" Fotherby hissed, his face turning as pale as Young's. "Sergeant Simmons did this?"

Kitson looked at Fotherby as he handed back the bloodied cloth and rushed through the camp. All manner of thoughts flashed through Fotherby's head as he rushed through the gathered men until he reached the group of four men that included Sergeant Simmons. He wasted no time in walking up to them where they sat on the floor, huddled around the fire and talking in hushed voices.

"Sergeant Simmons?" Fotherby began, so that the man rose to his feet. "God in heaven, why did you do it?"

"Do what, Henry?" he began, as he moved over to the young captain. "You have blood on your hands, my boy. You are not hurt, are you?"

Fotherby looked down at the dried blood on his hands and shook his head quickly. "This is not my blood, Sergeant Simmons. This is the blood of the man you struck. Why did you do it?"

A dark look passed over the other man's features as he turned away slightly. "I did not mean to, Captain Fotherby. But I felt I no longer had control over my hands."

"But something must have made you do it, sir. What was it?"

"His horse," Simmons whispered in reply, and Fotherby felt his brow crease at the man's cryptic answer. Before he could question the sergeant, however, two men walked forward and stood between them.

"Sergeant Simmons," one began in a detached tone. "You are called to answer to the court martial on the offence of insubordination. Offer your hands."

Simmons looked across at the man who was to become his son-in-law with a desperate expression that Fotherby could not bear to witness, for there was nothing he could do to comfort him. Offering his hands submissively, he called out.

"You have to help me, Captain Fotherby. I did not know what I was doing."

The attention of many of the soldiers had now been gathered and all watched as the man was guided away. Fotherby stumbled back to the cart as though he was drunk, and did not stop for anyone or anything.

"Sir?"

He blinked out of his thoughts as Kitson snatched his wrist.

"Where are you going, Fotherby? If you continue that way you will become lost in the jungle."

"Where has our patient gone?" Fotherby murmured looking into the cart, for there was no sign of him.

"He was not in a rush to stay. Though I have to admit that, upon hearing my name was Kitson and not Fotherby, he was a little more willing."

"What do you mean?" Fotherby asked in confusion.

"That he knew he hated you but had no notion of who you were nor what you looked like, only that you were a surgeon."

"That makes no sense," Fotherby laughed nervously. "I do not believe I have ever met him before."

"He clearly knows you, sir." Kitson offered half a smile before adding caustically, "And he has made his assessment of you. Was I right in my assumption? Was it your own Miss Simmons' relative?"

"You and I have been officers for years," Fotherby mused, ignoring Kitson's questions. "We have been struck by soldiers so many times that I can scarcely recall them all. We have never laid a claim of insubordination. Why should this one stand?"

"You know very well. The men who strike us are not in control of their actions. They are wounded and, as such, will lash out at anyone."

"But this man was sick, too."

"He did not come to us for help," Kitson pointed out with an unimpressed tone.

"This lack of water and disregard to rationing is driving half the men to madness and the rest to organ failure. This man had given leave to his senses, Kitson, as they have when we are stitching and sawing. He cannot hang. He is only guilty through the officers' neglect to correctly ration."

"That sounds a little like insubordination, too. Watch your words, Captain Fotherby."

The following day the regiment continued to march northeast towards Calcutta but, as Fotherby forced himself to remain conscious to keep marching, he began to suspect that they would not reach the city. At midday, the column reached a small village to the grateful cheers of all those in the line, for the village held a temple with a deep well before it. Fotherby was as relieved as the other men, and beseeched the officers to allow him to be responsible for rationing the water so that it might last a time longer. He was granted permission in this and, when they journeyed north two days later, Fotherby kept a close watch on the distribution of the water.

They reached Calcutta at the end of summer, only five days before the monsoon arrived. During the remaining journey, Fotherby had not spoken with Sergeant Simmons, or discovered the identity of the man who despised him so intently. However, upon reaching Calcutta, the court martial appeared to be the first thought in the minds of the officers. Simmons' trial was set for the following Monday and would occur within Fort William, the East India Company's imposing garrison. Now, Fotherby sought Simmons out and found him in one of the cells deep within the fort. The older man rose to meet him and pressed himself against the bars of the door, begging Fotherby to free him.

"I cannot simply release you," Fotherby began, looking about him for where the key might hang. "I need to know what happened so I can speak for you tomorrow."

"I cannot tell you any more, for that is all I recall. He took our water to give to his horse. I could not stand by and watch men die so that an officer may not have to walk. I did not mean to strike him, though. I intended only to speak with him."

"I know well what dehydration may do to the mind, Simmons. I believe you did not mean to."

"I want you to take these, Henry." He handed three letters through the bars. "I never did understand why you chose my daughter, but I do not want you to think badly of her for what her father has done."

"Sir," Fotherby interjected. "You speak as though you were already dead. I do not see how a court martial can condemn you."

"Because you were not born where I was. You have a profession, you have an estate. I have a three roomed house in London that I rent for myself and my daughter, and I cannot read beyond what my job requires. We are different men, Captain Fotherby. You have had the grace to bridge our worlds, but it is you who is unusual in choosing to do so."

Fotherby did not respond but promised to be at the court martial and speak favourably for the man who was being wronged. He walked from the cells and stopped as his gaze rested on the man Simmons had struck. It is true that any favourable looks he might have benefited from were now paled. Kitson's assessment of the crooked nose and his squint jaw had been accurate, but his eyes burnt brightly and vehemently as he looked across at Fotherby.

"Sir," Fotherby called out and walked over to him. "I trust you are in better health than when I last saw you."

"It would seem that way, would it not, Captain Fotherby?"

"I understand that you know me already, sir. But I am at a loss, for I do not know your name."

"My name is Sutton, Captain. I formerly served with that good friend of yours, Portland, before his savage wife caused his premature promotion."

Fotherby stared in surprise at the harsh words of the man before him. "Captain Portland was indeed a great friend, and his wife was a true lady."

"Oh dear," the man replied harshly. "So will you call me out to defend her honour?"

"Sutton," Fotherby whispered, nodding to himself as he recalled where he had heard the name before. "Then you are related to the Colonel?"

"Indeed. He is my uncle. And how I have waited for the moment to redress that foolish event which turned a decorated veteran into a figure of ridicule. I am only sorry that your liberal minded friend is not here to witness it. Though, by all accounts, he did nothing to defend his wife's honour. No doubt ashamed of her in the end."

"How can you say these things? I had a quarrel with your uncle, not you. And whatever battles and animosity existed between you and Portland, your words disgrace only yourself."

"You would have lost that duel."

"But I did not," Fotherby replied calmly, but this only angered Sutton more. "Is this why you are continuing with this case against Sergeant Simmons?"

"This," he snapped in reply, pointing to his jaw. "Is why I am persisting in this case."

"For the sake of your recovery it would have been better if you had not spoken."

"What is Sergeant Simmons to you?" Sutton asked, ignoring the surgeon's double-edged advice.

Fotherby frowned down at the man, confused, for he had been sure that no one would carry such a case forward unless it was through spite. He did not respond to Sutton but walked away from him to the room he shared with Kitson.

Kitson was not there, as Fotherby had been quite sure he would not be, for the lieutenant would certainly be wherever there was alcohol to be found. He looked at the letters Simmons had given him but would not read them, for he promised himself repeatedly that he would help the sergeant be released. Instead, he sat at the desk and penned two letters of his own. The first was to Kitty and, as he wrote it, he set the tiny painting of her on the desk and looked across at it.

"My dear Miss Simmons, Events of a most complicated nature have detained your father and myself in India for a time longer. It is my hope, however, that the war being over I shall return in time to make you my wife before your twenty-fifth birthday. You have never left my thoughts, my dearest Kitty, both in waking and in sleeping, and it has been the thought of you that has carried me through the horrors I have witnessed. You are the beacon I know will safely guide me home. It is with ever deepening sorrow, however, that I must relay to you the death of Lord Barrington. I find I am quite alone in Calcutta and facing trials I had not anticipated, but long for the day that I am carried safely to you, my dear. I do not wish to close this letter, but fear I must. You stay in my thoughts and prayers always and that must suffice until I may return to make you my wife. Your adoring servant, Henry Fotherby."

He hovered his hand over the painting as though he was summoning it to life and closed his eyes as he had told Portland. It was in this way, then, that Kitson found him, as the lieutenant pushed the door open and walked in with a confident swagger.

"I have changed my mind, Fotherby," he announced. "The men of the East India Company are gentlemen indeed."

"You are drunk," Fotherby pointed out.

"So are they. So should we all be after that journey."

"Alcohol only drives a harder thirst."

"Do you never tire of being godly, Fotherby? Do you never wonder why other men find comfort in a bottle?"

"I have never felt the need of such comfort."

"Pious parson," Kitson spat as he collapsed on one of the beds. "Captain Sutton said he had seen you."

"Indeed. I wished to learn why he disliked me so intensely. I believe I have found out."

He received no response from his drunken lieutenant and tucked the painting once more into his coat pocket, drawing out the letter Peters had given him on the eve of his departure. Finally, when he was certain that Kitson had gone to sleep, and had heard his drunken snoring, Fotherby began writing his second letter. It was not the one he knew he should write, but the one that his heart drove him to write.

"To my beloved father and my dear uncle. I trust and pray that this letter finds you in the best of health, and that summer has been more kind to you than the season has been in India. Despite this, I continue to be amazed and impressed by the Indian landscape and all the people I have met within it. I do not know when I shall next return to Wanderford, only that I intend to make it home with great speed. It is my hope that I might return to you by Christmas, but that is dependent on the ships sailing smoothly between Calcutta, where I write this, and England. It is with a sorrow beyond any I have yet known that I must relay the death of Lord Barrington, who fell at Seringapatam. I feel I have lost a brother. Furthermore, I am now truly alone, for Captain Peters has retired. I am, therefore, writing to you as Captain Fotherby, a title I felt certain to find pride in but that, thus far, has brought me only trouble and loss. I long to see you once more and pray each day and night to be reunited safely with you. Your loving son and nephew, Henry."

There was no window in the room, but Fotherby was sure the hour was late enough to go to bed. Kitson's snores kept him awake for much of the night, but he was almost grateful of it for it allowed him time to consider the events that the morning were set to hold. When sleep did take him, it was to a plain of bitter dreams. He was relieved to be awoken by Lieutenant Kitson coughing.

"You are a righteous fool, Fotherby," Kitson muttered as he lay on the bed, staring across at Fotherby who was shrugging into his coat. "But, sickeningly, you have an even worse habit of being right." He clutched his head as he spoke and whimpered like a child.

"I am going to the court martial," Fotherby announced, with no sympathy. "Get yourself plenty to drink, Kitson, it is the best cure for what ails you."

"More drink?" Kitson asked doubtfully, before he continued. "Why do you care so much about this trial? Is it some relative of your sweetheart?"

"It is her father."

Kitson lifted his hand to his forehead before turning from his captain. "Good luck, Fotherby. I hope you get the result you deserve."

Fotherby walked out of the room and through the corridors of the fort. The prospering East India Company demonstrated its wealth with the expansion and decoration of Fort William. Indeed, one of the commanders who had accompanied the army at Seringapatam had returned with great wealth from Tipu's collection. Fotherby spared only seconds to admire them as he hurried on his way.

Sergeant Simmons stood before the panel of officers, silent with respect and fear. Captain Sutton outlined the case against the sergeant and there could be little doubt that the man's injuries were true, for many of the gathered men commented on the appearance of the captain, a matter that only drove him to feel a greater belief in his cause. Witnesses were called, Lieutenant Young and another lieutenant by the name of Hershaw, but none of the rank and file who had been at the event. Indeed, the officers seemed to wish this event to pass quickly and wanted nothing more than to conclude the matter. The court recessed for a time before Colonel Pottinger was called to give references for each of his men.

"I must declare that this event surprised me, sirs," the colonel replied. "It is out of keeping with Sergeant Simmons' usual behaviour."

"Then you have never seen anything in him to suggest such disregard for rank? Is it not true that he is envious in his outlook? We have also heard that he uses his daughter as a means to establish a better position in society."

Fotherby, who was seated at the back of the small room, rose to his feet. This action drew the attention of everyone present, allowing Pottinger time to consider his answer carefully. Fotherby moved forward along the side of the room until he stood alongside Sutton, making every attempt to ignore him.

"It is true that Sergeant Simmons has climbed through the ranks," Pottinger said firmly. "But envy and ambition do not always go hand in hand."

"And what of Captain Sutton, Colonel Pottinger?"

"He is a gentleman, sirs. What more can I say? I trust him enough that, upon our return, my own son will be placed in his company."

"Then, by your assessment of your men, sir, do we believe Captain Sutton or Sergeant Simmons?"

"Captain Sutton, sir," Pottinger replied almost silently. "Though I must reiterate that Sergeant Simmons has been a reliable soldier until this time."

"Thank you, Colonel."

"Sirs," Fotherby said quickly, as Pottinger walked to the side of the room. "Allow me please to speak."

"What is your name?"

"Fotherby, sir. Captain Henry Fotherby." He stepped forward. "I am one of the battalion's surgeons."

"What do you wish to say?"

"Sirs, the case of Sergeant Simmons at first sight seems simple to judge, but the circumstances of the events have not been laid before you in their entirety. Through lack of careful planning, no doubt attributed by utter relief at having drinking water, all the company's water had been used. We were down to our final drops and many of the men were suffering from dehydration. It is my opinion that Sergeant Simmons' lack of control and fit of rage was caused by a momentary madness induced by the lack of water."

"No one else saw fit to strike their officer."

"But Captain Sutton was taking the men's water to give to his horse. Sergeant Simmons was only protecting the safety, indeed the very survival, of the men." Fotherby sighed and collected his thoughts. "Place yourself in their position, sirs. The water is running out, there is only enough for one more cup each, but your captain seizes it from you to water his horse. Can you not see the fear? The desperation? And in a drained and dazed state such as the lack of water created in the men, does it not stand to reason that anger should follow?"

"Do not listen to this man," Sutton began, seeing the look of sympathy on the faces of the men before him. "This is the man Sergeant Simmons' daughter is to marry. He will say anything to see him released."

"I speak the truth only," Fotherby replied firmly. "To my shame, I was more inclined to learn the truth because I knew this man. But it is also true that I treated you as my duty dictated. I am not a man who deals in falsehoods, even where my own interests are concerned."

"Enough," announced one of the men before them. "Neither of you serve your purposes well with such a spectacle."

Fotherby turned as he felt someone take his arm. Colonel Pottinger guided him from the front of the room and walked along the side until they reached the back corner.

"Your adherence to the truth is admirable, Fotherby. Furthermore, I am indebted to you on more counts than you can know. But, Captain, the decision of this court martial was made long before you or I took the stand."

"What do you mean?" Fotherby muttered, feeling the blood drain from his face.

"All cases of insubordination have been treated far more seriously since the ghastly affair in France. I am rather afraid that, where that word is brandished, there are no men found innocent."

Fotherby watched as the colonel left the room, before he shakily walked to take a seat. He watched the scene before him, but could no longer follow the events. Blood pounded in his ears and he could not hear what was being said. People walked past him out of the room, all talking to one another, but he could not make out their words. He did not stir from this state until his eyes met with those of Sergeant Simmons. They were filled with fear and resignation, and spoke of the verdict that his spinning head had allowed him to escape being passed. Fotherby stumbled to his feet but the older man had already been taken from the room to the execution that the sentence carried. Sutton left the room without sparing Fotherby a glance, and the young surgeon was suddenly alone, overlooked by the trophies and riches of the East India Company.

## Chapter Twenty-One
*The Fall Of A Noble Family*

The injustice Fotherby had witnessed did not leave him as the season wore on. The execution of a man, whose only crime was induced by the conditions forced upon him, seemed not only unjust but inescapably cruel. On so many occasions he sat with his pen poised to relate the bitter news to Miss Simmons, but he could not bring himself to. He remained away from people as often as he could, walking through the city of Calcutta, trying to lose himself in its wilderness of buildings. When it was announced in the third week of August that one of the enormous Indiamen was to make a voyage back to England, however, the news created mixed emotions: he was sorry to be leaving India but pleased to be returning to those people who had been left to him.

It was the last day of December before he finally returned to British soil after sixteen months away. The grey, dismal skies of the city of London bore down heavily on him and he shivered against the rain falling lazily from the sky. It was a poor sight after the rich beauties of India. His journey had not been idly spent but there had still been too much time to consider the great difference between the boy he had been when last he sailed home from India, and the man he had become.

He tried to count all the people he had lost since then, but the thought only caused his shoulders to hunch and his eyes to water.

He knew the duty he had to Miss Simmons, to inform her of her father's death, but his feet carried him to Horse Guards without his mind knowing why. He stood there for so many minutes, hours perhaps, becoming gradually more and more wet.

"Lieutenant Fotherby?" began a voice in utter disbelief. "Good God, man, you are soaked to the skin!"

"Major Tenterchilt?" Fotherby began, his voice little more than a whisper. "Why are you not in Scotland?"

"A complicated issue, Lieutenant. Suffice to say, I was requested to attend Horse Guards."

"I trust it is nothing too serious."

"A missing gentleman." Major Tenterchilt began walking away. "But come, tell me when you returned."

"Today, sir," Fotherby began. "But I am obliged to tell you that I am no longer a lieutenant but a captain. I suspect," he continued as they stepped into the great building, "that the two cases are linked."

"How so?" Tenterchilt asked, his eyes narrowing.

"I am not generally a gambling man, but I would wager the gentleman who vanished was the same man who caused my promotion."

"And four years ago I may have accepted your wager. But I made a vow to Mrs Tenterchilt that I should never do such a thing."

"How is Mrs Tenterchilt? And the three misses Tenterchilts?"

"All well, Captain. They have adapted well to Scotland and enjoy the landscape for its own sake. Although our eldest daughter is still lamenting her absence from London. But come, your comment needs to be expanded upon." Major Tenterchilt ushered Fotherby to sit beside a fire. "Captain Peters is gone then?"

"Indeed. But it is John Johnson that I believe you are missing."

"John Johnson?" Tenterchilt asked. "J.J.? How do you know of him?"

"He was Captain Peters, sir." Fotherby took the major's letter from his pocket and handed it to him. "I admit that I hoped you would know the outcome of Captain Peters' departure, for he left me no indication of why he was leaving."

"That sly devil," Tenterchilt laughed. "He planned all this so carefully."

"I do not know what it is he passed on to me, but I should warn you, sir, I am a poor person to correspond with."

"Peace is coming, Captain," Major Tenterchilt said softly. "Our armies are returning home and the French threat is abating. Let John Johnson fade with it."

"You cannot know how eagerly I have wished to hear those words, sir," Fotherby began, with clear appreciation. "I trust you heard of victory at Seringapatam?"

"I did. I was present at the return of the 73rd and 74th Highlanders."

"Did you hear, too, of Lord Barrington's fall?"

"All of London and England has heard of it, Fotherby, and the scandal that surrounds him."

"Scandal?" Fotherby asked softly.

"Indeed." Tenterchilt quickly shook his head as he saw the expression on the surgeon's features. "No, not the gentleman you knew. His brother, I believe it was."

"Harris?"

"Yes. Executed for treason not two months since."

"Treason?" Fotherby choked on the word. "The man did not have the mind for such a thing."

"It would seem that his position in court led him to take liberties with the prince regent's wife. As gentlemen we should not be in the business of handing on gossip, but many believe that his involvement was with Mrs Maria FitzHerbert. I believe debts were also mentioned, for the regent owes many of his courtiers great quantities of money. The end to this war could not come at a better time, for the coffers of state are empty."

Fotherby tried to acknowledge what the man had said but he felt his head could not absorb the information. "Then David is Lord Barrington?"

"David? No," Major Tenterchilt said softly, pouring two glasses of wine and offering one to Fotherby who graciously refused it. "The title was stripped from the family. There is no Lord Barrington now."

The conversation of the two men turned then, discussing all that Fotherby had missed in his absence, most notably the uprising at Britain's back door a year ago as the Irish united against them. But they also talked of Scotland, of their shared experiences in the army, and of India, the land Fotherby found so enthralling.

Their conversation concluded late in the evening and Fotherby stepped out into the London streets, wondering where he could stay in this city where once he had always had a place. He did not wish to travel to the house that had been Lord Barrington's residence but instead walked in the direction of Mayfair. The harsh discovery of his uncle's and Sir Manfred's exploits in the West Indies disgusted him so much that he could not bear to seek a favour from the man, yet he walked to the white house and stood outside for a time. Finally, he wandered around the side of the building and down an iron flight of steps to a black painted door, and knocked lightly.

"A little early for the milk lady," a voice began as the door opened and a young woman, perhaps in her fifteenth year, looked up at him. "You do not look like the milk lady, either," she laughed. "What can I do for you, sir?"

"I am looking for Manny. Is he still here?"

"Well, that depends, sir," she continued, tucking a strand of dark hair behind her black ear. "If he is in trouble again, you should have used the other door, you see."

"In trouble?" Fotherby asked, shaking his head. "Why would he be in trouble?"

"Why would you be here in a uniform if he were not, sir?"

Fotherby smiled and shook his head. "No. He was good to me once and I hoped he might find it in his heart to be good to me once more."

"God in heaven above!" shouted an angry voice. "Shut that door!"

"You had best come in, sir. I shall fetch Manny."

How different the cold dimly-lit kitchen was compared to the pristine white marble of the entrance hall above. Fotherby only stared in amazement at it while five faces, all black, stared back at him. He smiled at each one in turn, bowing his head formally to acknowledge them, before he heard someone clattering down the stairs and beheld the young man he had last seen many years earlier.

"Forgive me, Manny," Fotherby began with a smile. "Only, I recall that you once invited me and I am in great need of a roof over my head tonight."

"Lieutenant Fotherby," Manny began, pulling the white wig from his head and discarding it onto the table. "I never thought you would remember me. Good lord, you look smart enough to be a king."

"I am a captain now, but more through other people's departures than my own achievements."

"You were so good to us, Captain Fotherby, I cannot believe what you say is true." He guided Fotherby to a chair and poured him a drink of rosehip cordial. "Patience makes this," he continued. "But her name is as mismatched as you were with Sir Manfred."

"I learnt, when I was away, what my uncle and Sir Manfred did in the West Indies. And I am sorry for it, Manny."

"But it was not you. I have never had a guest come into this house whose parting I have so often lamented as yours, sir. But we each have our burden to bear, have we not? You seem terribly weary with yours, Captain."

"I cannot compare my hardships to those men suffered at the hands of my uncle and Sir Manfred."

"Some still do," chimed the young woman as she leaned in the doorway, staring at the surgeon critically.

"Quiet, Hannah," Manny snapped, before he turned back to Fotherby. "Miss Chester is married now."

"Indeed. My uncle had a letter informing him before I sailed to India."

"You have been to India?"

"Yes, I only arrived back today. That is why I cannot thank you enough for opening the door to me."

"For you, Captain Fotherby, the door shall always be opened. Have you heard that our cause is strengthening? More and more countries are abolishing slavery."

"I had not," Fotherby said softly. "But it is good news. I only wish Lord and Lady Barrington were here to hear it."

"Enough talk for one night, sir. You are weary and must sleep now. You shall take my room for, since Honest died, his bed has not been slept in."

"What happened to him?"

"He was stabbed two years ago and pushed into the Thames. Washed up a good deal lighter in his pockets than he went in."

Fotherby felt sickened by this revelation and the thought of remaining in the city only disgusted him more. Manny picked up the wig he had discarded and guided Fotherby to a small room which, except for the two beds, could fit little furniture. Taking the captain's coat, Manny hung it on the back of the door and pointed along the corridor to another door.

"That is where we wash. Can you bear to share a room, sir?"

"Manny, when we reached Calcutta I shared a room, and before that a room would have been a luxury whether it was shared with one man or ten."

"But can you bear to share with black men? With savages?" The fire that Fotherby remembered from his previous stays in the house returned to his eyes.

"I do not consider the two things to be the same."

Fotherby pulled the boots from his feet and laid back on the bed, staring at the cracking plaster on the walls and the coarse wooden beams above him. It was all so different from upstairs, but felt far more honest. Manny, not yet having completed his tasks for the evening, had left him alone with his thoughts. Although the straw mattress was far from comfortable, it felt strange to be lying on a bed after the months of boat travel. Without even noticing that his consciousness was drifting, he had fallen asleep.

He awoke with a start as his candle extinguished and he looked across to find a figure at the door who, upon realising that the surgeon had awoken, muttered an explanation.

"Candles are costly, sir."

"Sorry, Hannah," he replied sleepily.

"Sorry?" she whispered and stepped to the foot of the bed. "I have never heard the word from a white man."

Fotherby sat up and looked across at her. "That is all going to change, Hannah."

"It is true, then? All the great things Manny has told us of? He said that your coming so many years ago marked the change for us. But I was only ten, sir, I do not remember you."

"It is not I who will make the change," he began, blushing as he felt weighed down by her words.

"Manny speaks so highly of you, sir." She did not speak again, until she turned and looked back. "He incurs the rage of Sir Manfred for trying to secure the change you speak of. I hope it comes soon."

"As do I," Fotherby replied, but it was to himself only, for Hannah had left the room, closing him in the dark.

Fotherby slept surprisingly well and rose the following morning feeling almost prepared for the task the day held in store. He was offered the same breakfast Sir Manfred ate upstairs but took only a bread roll and a cup of coffee, not wishing to trouble the staff, nor certain he could stomach so much food after being on rations for so long. Manny would not allow him to leave, however, until his boots and coat were cleaned. When the footman was content with the figure that the surgeon cut, he nodded approvingly and reached up to straighten the coat over his shoulders.

"Now you are ready to find her."

"Who?" Fotherby asked quietly.

"The woman who has the other half of the ring that you wear." Manny and the other servants laughed as Fotherby blushed. "You cannot hide anything from a servant, sir."

"I am beginning to realise. But I am afraid that the news I carry to Miss Simmons is not the news she will want to hear."

"You must come back tonight, sir, for we wish to know how you fare today."

Fotherby assured him that he would and stepped out into the streets of Mayfair. The early morning sky was still dark, and the streets were quiet. The dawning of the new century seemed to have been missed by many but, for some, their business would not permit them a holiday. Fotherby walked on, forming the words in his head that he longed to say to Miss Simmons but, as he reached the door to the small house, they all fled from his mind. He stepped forward and knocked lightly on the wooden panels. He received no response and walked backward looking once more at the illuminated window and frowned slightly to himself.

Feeling foolish as he stood there, he turned and began walking away, but stopped as he heard the steady creaking of hinges as the door opened behind him.

"Henry?" asked the gentle voice he had waited so long to hear.

"Miss Simmons," he began, turning to face her and offering a sorry smile. "I trust you are well?"

"Come inside, Henry," she said quickly, looking up and down the street as though she expected to find someone watching. But they were alone. She allowed him into the house and, closing the door, she stared expectantly at him. "What has happened to you, Henry?"

"To me? Nothing, Miss Simmons. But I have so much I must share with you."

"Of course."

He watched her as she led him to the sitting room and invited him to sit before she hurriedly prepared a drink for him. "It is a funny thing," she mused as she returned. "I had never thought to have any servant but, now Lizzie has gone, I can scarcely remember how to pour a drink."

"You are alone here, Miss Simmons?"

"Indeed. I could not afford to keep Lizzie any longer." She sat opposite him. "Papa sent no money to me and I should not have afforded the rent had one of my friends not assisted me." She straightened the skirt of her dress and sighed. "It is a strange thing, Henry, but two months ago people stopped entertaining me. And some even scorn me on the street. I never knew ladies could behave in such a way. And I thought often of your return and, now you are here, you simply sit and stare. What do you stare at, Captain Fotherby?"

"Forgive me, Miss Simmons," he muttered. "I had, as I walked here, decided all the words I should say to you, but now I cannot bring myself to say them."

"Oh, Henry," she began, trying to hold back tears. "Have you a wish to terminate our engagement?"

"No," he replied quickly, setting the untouched cup on the table and reaching across to take her pale hands. "Kitty, you have been the one thought that has brought me safely home, I am sure of it." He watched as she dried her eyes. "But I must relate bitter news to you. About your father."

"Papa?" she whispered.

"I am truly sorry to be the one to tell you, but your father perished in India."

"Papa is dead? When?" The tears she had sought to conceal spilled from her brimming eyes. Fotherby lifted her hands to his face and kissed them.

"In July. He," Fotherby paused as he tried to consider the gentle way in which he had decided to share the news with her but, at the image of despair and sorrow before him, his words failed him.

"What?" she demanded. "What happened, Henry?" She snatched her hands back and glared at him.

"He was-"

Kitty rose to her feet and looked down at him. "Tell me, Henry. Please tell me."

"He was court martialled, Miss Simmons." He rose, too, but bowed his head, reluctant to meet her gaze. "He was executed for insubordination. He had an argument with an officer and struck him."

"And because Papa was not a gentleman he was condemned?" She leaned against Fotherby and wept onto his coat. "That is not justice."

"No. It is not," he agreed gently, wrapping his arms about her.

"Was this what you wrote to me of, Henry? Why did you not tell me?"

"I was certain he would be acquitted. I did not want to worry you."

"Did you not support him?" She leaned back to look into his face.

"I tried. But Sutton discredited me for, somehow, he discovered our engagement."

"Thank you for trying," she whispered, stepped away from him. "You have been so good to me and my father, Captain Fotherby."

Despite knowing that the words he had shared with far more grievous to her, he felt stung by her formal address. "I hope you understand why I did it, Miss Simmons."

"You have believed far more in me than anyone else had before. Even my father." She smiled across at him, melting his concerns. "And I love you for it. You must know that to be true."

"Does it seem improper to talk of marriage in the same conversation?"

"No," she began, placing her hand on his cheek. "For that was the past, and we have a future, have we not?"

"I believe so, Miss Simmons."

"But how will society accept me? The daughter of a disgraced soldier?"

"You are the daughter of a wronged man. But you shall be the wife of a gentleman. And any man who would not accept such an understanding is not a gentleman at all." Placing his hand into his shirt he pulled out the ring that hung there. "I would proudly walk out with you, Miss Simmons, and have words with any who thought to challenge us. I have been true to my promise, Kitty. Where should we marry?"

"It seems only right to marry at Wanderford. For that is where we shall live."

"Then, tomorrow I shall return to Derbyshire and we will be married as soon as I can arrange it."

Fotherby left the house of Miss Kitty Simmons shortly afterwards, kissing her hand and promising to return as soon as he was able, with the news they both longed for. He was anxious about leaving her alone in the house and asked her whether she would consider staying with her friend until he could return.

"Oh no," she laughed lightly, blushing. "Miss Allen lives with her brother. It would be most improper. I shall wait here for you, Henry."

The premature night was closing in around him by the time he stepped down the iron staircase and knocked on the door, which was opened by Hannah.

"You have come at an opportune time, Captain," she began, ushering him indoors. "Manny has need of you."

Fotherby felt the smile that had accompanied him back from Miss Simmons' house slip from his face as Hannah guided him to the kitchen. Manny stood leaning over the table, wincing each time one of the serving maids wiped a cloth over his bleeding back. A look of disgust reached Fotherby's face, before he thought to check himself.

"Yes, sir," the maid said sharply as she looked across at him, "it is not just our hands and faces that are black."

"Enough," Manny said sternly, before Fotherby could answer. "Patience, hold your tongue." He straightened to stand up and met the surgeon's gaze.

"Get me a bottle of brandy," Fotherby said sternly, never turning, but Hannah ran off at once to do as he ordered. "What happened?"

Patience stared at him and watched in confusion as Fotherby shrugged out of his coat and rolled his sleeves up. Manny held his hand out.

"You do not need to do this, Captain."

"I have a great respect for you, Manny. But you are wrong. Some of these abrasions are infected. You are lucky not to have been poisoned by them. Perfect," Fotherby continued, as Hannah handed him a small applewood cask. "Now a beaker, please, Hannah, and a fresh cloth."

Pouring half the brandy into the beaker, he set it on the table before Manny, before he ran more of the brandy over the cloth and began cleaning the wounds on the young man's back. Hannah stood at the door and watched thoughtfully as Manny drank from the vessel before him, trying to dull the pain.

"What happened?" Fotherby repeated.

"I had a mind to host a lecture," Manny mumbled. "They are quite common now and, at each one, we raise more support. A gentleman asked me to talk at the next lecture, but Sir Manfred discovered it."

"So he beat you?" Fotherby asked.

"No. He had Thomas beat me. He has never delivered punishments himself. He has not the stomach for it. Still," Manny laughed sleepily, "at least Thomas is only half the size that Honest was. He does not deliver such heavy blows."

"This is barbarism."

Manny placed his head on the table and Fotherby rose to his feet, looking down at the gashes on the man's back. He was confused between the two worlds that existed within the one house. How could the opulence and wealth of the upstairs be allowed to exist while such poor conditions downstairs strove to enable it? He collected his jacket after washing his hands.

"The rosehip cordial was wonderful, Patience," he said as he walked past her. "Have you enough to spare a bottle for my wedding?"

"You are getting married?" she asked, placing her hand on his chest.

"Very soon."

"I hope she understands how fortunate she is."

"To marry a captain?"

"To marry a good man."

"You all pay me too many compliments," he muttered, feeling suddenly uncomfortable. "I do no more than my duty dictates. I cannot leave a man wounded when I can help him, any more than you can."

He shut himself in the room he had occupied last night and lay back on the bed, falling asleep quickly. He did not awake until the next morning, when he walked into the kitchen to find that he was greeted by sixteen smiling faces, inviting him to the table. He took the empty seat and listened as conversations began to be shared, all with him as the topic.

"I am afraid I am leaving today," he began. "And, yes, I am going to arrange my marriage."

"It is bad luck for the groom to organise it," Hannah said. "Your wife should sort it."

"Enough, Hannah," Manny said. "I am certain the captain does not hold with luck."

"I try not to. I have witnessed too many men whose luck has run out."

After they had all breakfasted, Fotherby excused himself and collected the bag of belongings he had brought from India. He thanked each of the servants for their hospitality and walked up the iron staircase, with a lightness in his step that he could not have believed possible a week ago. He turned as he put the bicorne on his head, at the sound of his name.

"Captain Fotherby!"

"Manny?" he began. "What is it?"

"Will you take my hand?"

Fotherby clasped the outstretched hand. "Whatever for?"

"I have shaken hands with a white man I respect."

"We are not white or black, Manny. We are men. The change that you seek, that Lord and Lady Barrington fought for, that we all deserve, it is coming. One day you will leave this house as a free man, and not just in name."

"Godspeed your journey, Captain," Manny smiled. "For no man deserves it more."

## Chapter Twenty-Two
*An Unacceptable Match*

The new century was a week old when Fotherby finally stepped down from the coach three miles from Wanderford Hall. The road was carpeted in snow and Fotherby had to coax his feet to continue walking as he trudged on, finding the journey almost unbearable. At times he had to think back to India and the endless sunshine that had poured down an inexhaustible heat, inspiring him to walk on. The snow was not deep but it was enough so that the soles of his boots made a squeaking crunch with each step he took.

The midday sun, a perfect disc beyond a shroud of cloud, was shining down on the snowy lawns before Wanderford Hall, and the water in the fountain was glazed with shards of ice which floated in the pool. At the sight of his house before him, he hurried forward with a renewed drive. He did not knock, or ring the small bell that hung beside the door, but pushed it open and walked in. The majestic image of Bosworth Field stared down on him and he took a moment to try and imagine what it must have been like to battle in such a primitive time, when medicine had scarcely progressed beyond the knowledge of the Ancient Greeks.

At the smell of woodsmoke coming from his father's study he knocked on the door and walked in. His breath caught in his throat as he beheld the view before him and he rushed over to the old man who stood at the window, his back turned and unaware of Fotherby's presence.

"Father?" Fotherby placed his hand on the bent fingers of his father's where he leaned against the stone ledge.

"Your hands are cold," came the reply, as his father turned to him. "No, no," he began. "There is only one man I know so tall." He lifted his two hands to his son's face, running them over the thin features and creating a picture in his mind as he did so. "Henry?"

Fotherby kissed his father's cheek, forgetting all the sorrows and elations the past year had thrown at him, as he clutched his father's hands.

"Henry, when you had not returned by Christmas, your uncle and I were anxious you might not return at all." He began leading his son to where the chairs sat before the fire but, after helping his father to a seat, Henry knelt beside him. "I am afraid my sight is almost as poor as my hearing now. I see only the light of the fire and the shapes of those things before it. And I hear nothing. Have you been in England long?"

Fotherby, who had not relinquished the old man's hand, spelt out on his father's palm as he said aloud, "One week."

"We were sorry to hear of Lord Barrington."

Fotherby nodded slowly but ventured no words either spoken or formed. He stared into the fire as he contemplated the fall of the Portland family, feeling that he was in some way responsible for all that had befallen them. Could he have predicted, seven years ago, that he would have become so attached to the family of the foolish man who had allowed his own man to strike him? At once he recalled the bitter events of that summer when Cullington had hanged himself, and considered for the first time the fate of Miss Margaret Webb. It made him think of the curiously calm acknowledgement of the youngest, and now only, Portland upon finding the hanging groom. From there his thoughts turned to Second Lieutenant Keith, to whom he had entrusted the task he knew he should have executed himself.

His father, content with the silence that encircled his very existence, placed his free hand on Fotherby's shoulder. He needed no words to know the degree of thoughts that filled his son's head, but to have his only child sitting beside him once more gave him cause to smile. He stared at the glow that was the fire, as his son did the same, and it was in this way his brother found them as he opened the door and stepped in.

"Good God, Henry!" his uncle began. "You are home."

Fotherby rose quickly to his feet, causing his father to turn towards the door.

"Paul?" the old man asked.

"I could be Caesar and he would not know. Welcome home, Henry."

"I feared Father would be dead on my return," Fotherby began, helping his father to his feet. "I am only so pleased to find you both alive and in good health."

"Good health?" his uncle asked as he walked to his nephew and embraced him warmly. "I do not consider being blind and deaf as being in good health."

During the afternoon, Fotherby sat with his father and uncle around the fire in the Drawing Room. He did not relinquish his father's hand but used it to share the conversation with him. He spoke of India, the beauties, the drought, before at length his uncle asked,

"Will you go back?"

"No," Fotherby muttered reluctantly. "I have a duty here to fulfil and Miss Simmons has no wish to travel to India."

"Miss Simmons?" his uncle asked.

"Yes, I am to arrange a date for our marriage while I am here." He lifted his chin slightly, awaiting his uncle's harsh response, but the older man only nodded. "Is that where Charlotte's ring went?"

"Yes." Fotherby shifted awkwardly on his chair at the casual manner with which his uncle named his mother. "Do you object so much?"

"Should I not? Your mother was a lady. You are a gentleman. What has Miss Simmons to recommend her to you?"

"What had Miss Chester? What had Mrs Gardener?"

"Both of them had money," came the short reply. "Money may make a lady in this age, almost as surely as birth. But it is you who must make the decision."

"Henry?" his father began. "Where is the army sending you next? Will you be staying with us for a time?"

Fotherby spelt out the word "marriage" on his father's palm, which he was pleased to find raised a smile on the old man's features.

"To Miss Simmons?"

Fotherby nodded, the blurred movement visible to his father, whose smile deepened.

"She was a dear girl, Henry. Is she ready for life at Wanderford?"

"I doubt it," his uncle interrupted.

"She will be. But I do not want you to die, Father," he said as though he expected his father to hear. "This will be your house for many years to come."

Fotherby excused himself, then, keen to wash before supper and to collect his thoughts regarding his uncle. He considered the discovery that Portland had revealed to him on the day of his death, that his uncle was a man who traded in the lives of others, and he considered the story his father had told him about one of his uncle's friends being beaten to death. He tried to understand the man, but at every turn found him only more infuriating.

He descended the staircase two hours later, sparing a second to look out over the lamplit courtyard and on to the snow-topped hills, which seemed to glow in the distance. The Dining Room was set with three places, although a fourth chair rested beside his father's seat. Three candlesticks, each with five candles, were placed along the table and a fire burned in the hearth, but the gaslights were not lit and the room danced in the flickering candlelight. Fotherby felt a sense of trial as he sat down and awaited his uncle's further criticism of his choice of wife, but it was not this which made the meal difficult. The full extent and impact of his father's condition had not occurred to Fotherby until he witnessed him being fed like a child by one of the servants. Upon seeing tears within the younger man's eyes, his uncle drew away his attention.

"Do not think on it, Henry. Your father is happy in the world he exists in. And it is not a sight to fill your gaze with. Tell me, for when I last visited London the streets were awash with the news, is it true that Lord Barrington's brother lost the title?"

"I understand so. Though I heard it only from another man, and it was little more than gossip."

"And did you meet this brother? Was he inclined to attacking women?"

"I did meet him. But I did not know that he was accused over attacking anyone. Rather, I thought, he had recommended himself a little too highly."

"And did he do it, would you say? Or was it simply spite for his sister-in-law?"

"I cannot understand why any man would take quarrel with Lady Barrington."

"Only that you had your arm slit open for her."

"But he loved himself more than any other soul, perhaps save his brother, and so I think he could have believed others should love him with equal enthusiasm."

"What else happened in India, Henry?"

"What do you mean?"

"You have been unable to hold a comprehensive conversation, and only answer questions. You seem greatly distracted by something."

Fotherby looked down at the dogs sitting on the floor between him and his uncle. "I have to prepare to be married. It is a commitment larger than any I have ever taken, and my mind is filled only with this."

This statement was true to an extent but the image of his father, a man Henry had admired and respected all his life, being brought low gave him cause to question his place in Wanderford Hall and, indeed, society. Was it right that he departed from his father to join a cause overseas? Could he leave the estate in the hands of his uncle after the man had, on several occasions, announced that he did not want Wanderford? And, finally, was he prepared to leave his post to accept the responsibility that the house demanded?

When the meal was over, Fotherby rose and excused himself from the room. He walked out of the Hall and into the snowy night. There were clear skies that made him shiver as he walked towards the fountain and sat down on its rim, rubbing his arms to try and keep warm but unwilling to return inside. He had so much he wished to consider without the interruption and distractions of his father and uncle. But, as he sat there, staring up at the dancing stars, all he could think about was Miss Simmons and he questioned the words she had spoken about society. Had he been cruel to lift her into a world where she did not belong? Had his uncle spoken the truth that birth and money were what made a lady? And, for the first time since he was a child, Fotherby found himself wishing he had known his mother.

He walked back to the house after a time and retired to bed without a word to anyone. His own bed in his own room was always welcoming to him, and the staff in Wanderford Hall always left his belongings exactly as he had arranged them. It was peculiar to lie in his room and question whether this could remain his own, as it had been for as long as he could remember.

These questions and thoughts lulled him to sleep and the sun was rising in the winter sky before he finally awoke. His arms and legs ached from the cold of the night before, but he rose with the excited anticipation that today he would be securing a date with the parson to make Miss Kitty Simmons his wife. He dressed and rushed down the stairs, meeting his uncle in the hall as he walked in from his morning ride.

"You have a certain spring in your step, Henry," he remarked.

"I am going into the village to hire the services of the parson."

"The village? My boy, that church holds no more than twenty people. You should be going to Buxton. Get married in the church there."

"But Father and Mother married in Wanderford."

"And look how it ended for them. Your poor mother died and your father was reduced to the life of a beggar in his own home."

"Do you think they failed in their marriage, uncle?" Fotherby demanded.

"No," came the gentle reply. "But with more friends around you, you can go much further."

"But I cannot think of more than twenty people who I should invite."

"But a marriage is not just about you. I expect Miss Simmons has fifteen cousins alone."

"I want her to invite whomever she wishes, but she has less family than I."

"Only her father?"

"No one," Fotherby whispered, a sorrow at his own words.

"But we met her father, Henry," his uncle began. "A fine man who I taught to behave like a gentleman."

"Yes. But he is dead now. He died in India."

"Poor child," his uncle said softly. "No wonder she is eager to be married at once."

"It was my decision, uncle, not hers."

"Were you there when he died? What happened?"

"No." Fotherby turned from his uncle and studied his hands. "But I tried to stop it. I should have done more."

"Henry, you saved so many lives, but some men are beyond curing."

"No, it was not that." He turned to face his uncle once more. "He was court martialled and shot."

"Good lord, Henry," he said quickly. "Whatever for?"

"Insubordination."

"And you defended him?" His uncle scowled up at him and shook his head. "Do you want the revolution here in England? King George may struggle with himself but that is no reason to guillotine him."

"I defended him because he was wronged," Fotherby replied, as calmly as he could. "He was not able to consider his actions."

"You cannot do it, Henry."

"Do what?"

"Bring that into Wanderford Hall."

"What do you mean?" Fotherby whispered, staring at the man before him.

"I tolerated your engagement to a woman of no birth and no money. I accepted her and her father into this house. But you cannot take the daughter of such a man and make her the mistress of Wanderford Hall."

"It is not your house to tell me what I can and cannot do. I say that Miss Simmons shall be a fine mistress of Wanderford Hall. How can you judge a woman on the actions of her father? I should not care to think that I were judged on your actions simply because I am your nephew."

"Yet you would be happy to be judged on your father. Because you are a part of him. As she is of her father."

"Have you ever been in love, uncle?"

"Do not talk to me of love, you foolish boy," his uncle snapped. "You are not at liberty to fall in love. You have a responsibility to this place, and the daughter of an executed revolutionary is not going to secure the future of Wanderford Hall. No one will respect her and no one will respect you. Is that what you want for your future?"

"I did not want Wanderford Hall to be my future," Fotherby replied pointedly. "As you did not."

"We do not all have an alternative, Henry. You have no brother. You have no son, and your father will not survive long enough for any son you may have to take over the responsibilities of Wanderford Hall. You can hate me if you wish, but you will not bring that woman into this house."

"If Wanderford Hall shall not have Miss Simmons as its mistress, it shall not have me as its master." Fotherby walked past his uncle and stepped, once more, into the snow. But this time he did not stop at the fountain, nor the end of the long drive, but continued down the road until he reached the crossroad. He had no notion of the time, nor of how long he should have to wait for a coach, he only knew that he had to be away from Wanderford Hall and all it contained. He walked ten paces down each of the five roads trying to coax warmth into his legs. The memory of the winters he had spent in Flanders flooded back to him and, with that, came the memories of his departed friend, his former captain, and the simplicity of a life that had seemed so cruel at the time, causing his eyes to water. The dark was closing in now and the low temperature only dropped further. Still no carriage lights appeared and Fotherby began to stumble as he walked backward and forward, no longer sure that he could feel his feet, but knowing that he could not cease walking.

Presently, he heard the sound of hooves on the snow and he turned to look down one of the roads to find a rider approaching him. He felt his heart sink as he realised it was his uncle. The older man dismounted and guided his horse behind him as he walked over to his nephew.

"You will freeze to death here, Henry. Come home."

"I do not know where home is, anymore," Fotherby muttered, his jaw trembling with cold and causing his teeth to chatter.

"Get on the horse," his uncle commanded. "Your father is worried, Henry."

"I am going to go to London," he replied, hearing the words he spoke as though they were someone else's. "I am going to find Miss Simmons."

"Write her a letter, Henry. It is far easier." He snatched his nephew's wrist and pulled him over to the horse.

"I hate riding," Fotherby muttered as his uncle held the stirrup for him. "I do not trust horses."

"Do not let them know. You are talking quite candidly, Henry."

"I am so cold," he mumbled in reply. "I do not think my head can hold my tongue."

They began the three-mile journey back to the house with Fotherby passing comment on any thought that occurred to him but, before they reached halfway back to Wanderford, he felt his head drop down against his chest and sleep overtook him. His uncle continued to guide the horse on, their journey taking an hour to complete before he assisted Fotherby from the horse and tried to lead him indoors. Eventually, he guided his nephew into the Drawing Room and sat him down in one of the chairs before pulling his sodden boots from his feet. He stood then for a time watching the sleeping figure of his nephew, through deep eyes that might have concealed any emotion, before he left the room, returning some minutes later to help the young man out of the coat he wore and wrapping two heavy woollen blankets about him.

When Fotherby awoke the next morning it was to find himself staring into his father's face, and it took him some moments to establish where he was. He did not recall the journey back to Wanderford Hall but his clarity on what had driven him from it was complete. As he moved on the chair, rubbing the back of his neck which stung terribly, his father sighed.

"You gave me quite a cause for concern, Henry. I thought you had left me." He reached out his hand, which Fotherby took, before he continued. "Your uncle told me what happened. About Miss Simmons and her father."

"Do you agree with him?" Fotherby asked, before realising his father could not hear him and he spelt out "agree" on the old man's palm.

"Henry, it should not fall to you to carry such burdens. If Paul had settled in Wanderford and had a son of his own, things would have been so very different. But he did not, and Wanderford will be your duty."

"My duty is to help people," Fotherby muttered, but his father could not hear and continued to speak the words Fotherby wished he could not hear.

"It is not a duty Miss Simmons should carry. It is not a duty I believe she can carry."

"I did not want Wanderford Hall," Fotherby muttered, knowing his words fell on deaf ears. Instead he spelt out "London" on his father's hand.

"Yes," he whispered in reply. "You must tell her."

Fotherby would have left at once to find Miss Simmons, but the snow began again that afternoon and it was a further three days before his father had their own, somewhat modest, carriage readied for his son to journey to the capital. The snow made the trip slow and wearying, and it took him four days to reach London.

There was no snow here and, after Fotherby directed the driver for a time, they stopped outside Miss Simmons' residence. Fotherby had not spent the carriage ride idle. He had decided on what he deemed to be the best course of action, irrespective of the views of his uncle and father. He intended to marry Miss Simmons immediately in London, but to conceal the marriage until Wanderford Hall became his own. Thus he had neither broken his promise to Kitty, nor given his father cause to worry.

He stepped down from the carriage and walked up to the door, knocking and waiting for it to be opened. Finally it was opened by a woman he did not know and she stood looking critically at him.

"Is Miss Simmons home?" he asked, trying to ignore the icy glare she gave him. The woman did not respond, but sniffed disdainfully before stepping back to allow him entrance. Fotherby followed her as she walked into the sitting room where Miss Simmons sat, an expression of angry confusion on her face.

"Why are you here, Captain Fotherby?" she demanded.

"May I speak with you in private, Miss Simmons?" he asked softly, turning slightly toward the woman who stood behind him.

"Miss Allen is my good friend," Kitty replied. "Was it not you who suggested I stayed with her? Was it to prepare me for the news you wished to share that our engagement was to be terminated? That, because of my father's death, I am no longer suitable to be your wife?"

"What are you saying?" Fotherby asked, confused by how the woman knew of his predicament. "I came to marry you, Miss Simmons."

Kitty's face faltered and the anger cracked to reveal a sorrowful expression. "I cannot marry you, Henry," she whispered. "You and I, we do not belong together. You have a life you must uphold in Derbyshire, a duty to your estate, and I have nothing."

"You wish to be released from the engagement?" he muttered, staring down at her as she handed him a letter. Opening it under the heavy, judgmental gazes of both women, he read the words that flowed in his uncle's hand.

"Dear Miss Simmons, I write to you concerning your engagement to my nephew, Captain Henry Fotherby, whom I understand you had hopes to marry shortly. While I acknowledge and appreciate the affection you have for him is sincere and deep, I must beg you to consider the duty that Captain Fotherby has to his position and estate. I am certain that, should your love be as deep as Henry has assured me, you will understand why, in light of the events surrounding your father, you must relinquish your claim on my nephew. It brings me no joy to divide you and he, but I have a duty to safeguard my family's interests. Yours in anticipation, Paul Fotherby."

Fotherby watched with a numbness that seeped through each bone in his body as Miss Simmons pulled the ring from her pocket and placed it into his hand, closing his fingers about it.

"He does not speak for me," Fotherby insisted, as he looked into her eyes.

"But he speaks for me, Captain Fotherby." She stepped back from him. "Still, I want you to know that I do not regret a moment of our engagement."

"Very well, Miss Simmons," he muttered, smiling in a manner so false that it failed to convince even himself. "I release you from our engagement. And, truthfully, I wish you every happiness the world can give you. For you deserve it. I am only sorry it could not be with me."

He walked from the house in a daze and did not notice whether Miss Simmons or Miss Allen followed him to the door. He ignored the carriage that waited for him, feeling the need to walk away from everyone and everything that he knew. He deliberately turned down alleyways where the carriage could not follow and where he felt sure he should swiftly lose himself in the city. How could his uncle take such a decision? Perhaps because he knew his nephew would contrive the solution he had done.

When he was content that he did not know where he was, nor how to reach anywhere he knew, he sat down against the wall of a large warehouse. Putting the two parts of the ring together, he opened them to look at where the heart should have been behind the two hands, but that third lay half the world away, buried in the pauper's grave of a condemned man. He put both halves onto one of his thin fingers and dropped his head into his hands. He remained like this for several minutes until he rose and, once more, walked into the city, as lost physically as he was in his soul.

## Chapter Twenty-Three

*A Missing Surgeon*

After spending a night in the open air of London, unsure where he was or where he was going, Fotherby sat on the low window-ledge of a house and watched the comings and goings of the city people. Some were wheeling carts through the streets but, as they called to him, he dismissed them with a wave of the hand as Captain Peters had so often done to him. Others were hurriedly walking to work, or to the shops. None of these people even looked at him, until one came and requested he left as he was infringing on their custom. This Fotherby did dutifully and proceeded to walk on, his eyes falling closed as he stumbled and on one occasion he was almost struck by a cart.

He came to places he knew and stared at them with sorry eyes, remembering better times and lighter responsibilities. Duty had become a millstone about his neck, weighing so heavily he felt his back would break under the strain. The first place he visited was Chanter's House. It was empty and the windows were shuttered. It looked so unwelcoming that he was not at all unhappy to move to the next place, which was Lord Barrington's club. He could not help but wonder whether the men inside continued with the same vigour without Portland, or if the spark he had placed in Fotherby's life had also been extinguished for them. Next he walked to Horse Guards, surprised to find how close it was, and on past the college until his feet guided him to Portland's house. Without thinking about what he was doing, he walked up to the door and knocked upon it.

"Captain Fotherby," Chilvers announced as he opened the door, "I forget so many faces, but I shall never forget yours."

"I cannot tell you how glad I am to see you, Chilvers," Fotherby began. "I was beginning to believe that no one was left of the London I used to know and I began to hate it even more."

"Captain Fotherby, come and sit down. Can I get you a drink? Something warm for you look perished."

"Coffee, please, Chilvers. Coffee would be gratefully received."

Chilvers guided him into the room where the tapestry hung and Fotherby sat down before the fire. Almost at once this acted as a catalyst for sleep and, by the time Chilvers had returned with the coffee, Fotherby was already asleep in the armchair.

He awoke to the sound of whispering voices but felt too tired to open his eyes, only listening to the two men who spoke to one another.

"I have not seen him in years," one continued, his tone one of laughter. "But, poor man, he deserves to sleep."

"I shall leave, then," the second said, sharply but not unkindly, in an accent that made his words strange. "Besides, I do not think that he will have any interest in seeing me once more."

"But tomorrow," the first said. "I still need a hat."

"Tomorrow," the other agreed and Fotherby listened as, having shared parting pleasantries, the door closed.

Footsteps, confident and light, walked into the room and Fotherby opened his eyes, rubbing them to try and steady his vision. What he saw was a young officer who stood, his back turned, warming his hands by the flames of the fire.

"Forgive me, sir," Fotherby began. "I knew the gentleman and lady who used to live here."

"What a coincidence, Fotherby," laughed the other man as he turned to face the captain, "for so did I."

Fotherby rose to his feet and looked at the officer through startled eyes, taking in his neatly clubbed hair, his strong gaze and the evident pride in his eyes. "David?" he whispered.

"Indeed, Captain," came the reply, accompanied by a laugh once more. "But I am Second Lieutenant Portland, now. I bought my commission in November and am now a military gentleman in all but a hat." He pointed to his head, before he took the surgeon's forearms and looked critically at him. "But you, Captain Fotherby, you seem in poor health and spirits. You cannot let the winter so affect you."

"I am sorry to have intruded into your house, Portland," he began, stumbling over the name as he considered how strange it was to say it to Lord Barrington's youngest brother. "I had no idea you lived here now."

"Not for long," Portland said softly. "Harry's death created quite a hole in our family's bank so I am selling the house."

"I am sorry."

Portland relinquished the surgeon's arms and shrugged his shoulders. "It is only a house, Fotherby. But I shall treasure my memories of it. I recall visiting once with my father, and then when I stayed with Philip before he journeyed out to India. Poor Chilvers shall have to come home to Cornwall with me, and I know he hates the sea."

"I was sorry to hear of Harris' fall."

"Fall?" Portland repeated as he sat in the other chair and encouraged Fotherby to retake his seat. "That is a very gracious word for it. He shot himself in the end. Mother could not bear the fact our priest would not allow his body to be placed in the mausoleum, so he is buried in the grounds at Barrington Manor."

"How is your mother?"

"Grieving. Harry was her pride and joy. Philip and Cassandra were always Father's children, and Harris was hers. But I could not stay with her, Fotherby. Is that not terrible? I could not witness her bringing Barrington Manor down about her, for she blames herself for the deaths of Harry, Cassandra and Rosie. Philip, thankfully, she does not feel guilt for, as it was Father who bought his commission and he who asked to travel to India. And, Henry," he added, smiling with such sorrow that Fotherby felt his heart would break, "thank you for seeing him safely home."

"I wish I had known of his plan. I wish I had tried to stop him."

"No. He did what he wished. He died a hero's death, I heard."

"Then the lieutenant told you what happened?"

"Yes. Indeed, Second-Lieutenant Keith has become a good friend. He has helped me learn what it is to be an officer, and tomorrow we are to find me a hat. You must come too, Fotherby. You know London better than either of us."

"In truth, I do not think I would be good company."

"What has happened, Captain?"

Perhaps because he was exhausted and could not stop himself, or perhaps because David so clearly wanted to offer his support to the man who had become almost a brother to him, Fotherby told Portland all that had happened in India. He spoke of Lord Barrington's fall; of Captain Peters' departure, although he did not mention John Johnson; of Lieutenant Kitson's attitude towards him; and of Sergeant Simmons' court martial. Finally, he relayed the events of yesterday and how he had spent the night walking through the city.

"There is little wonder you are exhausted," Portland said softly, as Fotherby concluded the tale. "You wish to leave London at once? You cannot. Winter is cruel to travellers, and I suspect that your carriage will not have waited for you in London. You must stay here for a time."

Portland would not accept a refusal and instructed Chilvers that Captain Fotherby was not to leave London, and that he should have every care attended to. Chilvers, whose memory so often slipped, was as diligent in care as he could be and, subsequently, Fotherby spent two months in the company of Second-Lieutenants Portland and Keith. The three men shared the house, for Keith had nowhere to stay in the city but, although the company was welcome, it could not shake the bitter disappointment from the surgeon's heart.

Portland, however, loved the company and actively sought ways to discourage buyers from taking his house.

"You will not believe what I heard today," Portland began, as the three of them sat at the long table.

"Enlighten us," Keith began, drawing a pipe from his breast pocket and filling it with tobacco.

"A gentleman asked me if I had heard of an army surgeon by the name of Fotherby."

"What?" Fotherby asked sharply, leaning forward in his chair. "Who was he?"

"A gentleman named Shipton," Portland replied, smiling across. Keith watched this exchange with barely-concealed amusement as he lit his pipe. "I told him that I had, of course, though I believe he already knew. He told me he met Lord Barrington once."

"That was a long time ago," Fotherby said softly. "I am surprised he remembered."

"I did not know that you went to such great lengths to secure Rosie's honour. I have heard quite a story about you today, Fotherby. But I told Doctor Shipton that I would ask you to meet him tomorrow at Westminster Bridge."

"Will you go?" Keith asked. "Who is this man?"

"Yes, I shall go," Fotherby replied. "He is a gentleman who assisted me a great deal in the past. He is a physician from Buxton."

Fotherby lay awake that night, questioning repeatedly why Doctor Shipton had travelled to London to find him. He left early in the morning and walked down to Westminster Bridge, continued backward and forward across it, studying his feet as he paced, and reluctant to meet the gaze of the other people who hurried on their way. He stopped to look up as a man stood in front of him.

"Captain Fotherby?"

"Doctor Shipton? What has brought you to London, sir? Surely it cannot be me."

"It is you, Fotherby," he said quietly. He turned and began walking away, still talking so that Fotherby felt obliged to follow. "Your uncle came to see me at the start of March to find out whether you were working with me."

"Is he well?" Fotherby asked, feeling unsure whether he wanted to hear the answer.

"He is worried. Almost as worried as your father. For the last thing that was seen of you was when you marched away from your carriage into the city. When the driver returned to Wanderford a week later, no one knew what had happened to you."

"I shall go home," Fotherby said flatly.

Doctor Shipton smiled slightly, an expression of pride clear in his features, as though he had expected nothing less from the man beside him. "There is something you should do before you leave London, Fotherby."

Fotherby wanted to ask what the doctor wished him to do but he continued in silence. Shipton did not stop until they stood outside a familiar looking building and Fotherby smiled slightly, shaking his head.

"Captain Fotherby, please listen to me. Today you can enlist for your final exam and be qualified in a week. I have never seen a surgeon with such commitment or care as you have. I want you to qualify. Then, if you choose to leave the army or there are no wars to fight, you can continue in your calling. And you can manage Wanderford Hall at the same time."

"Very well, sir," he muttered, feeling at once cornered by the sense and logic of the man and privileged to have secured such a high regard. Shipton gestured toward the door and waited until Fotherby reluctantly stepped towards the building. Despite the passing of six years, nothing seemed to have changed, and he felt the same nervousness he had experienced then. Shipton waited in the hall, listening to the younger man's voice as he addressed the clerk in the room beyond, and turned a grateful smile to Fotherby as he stepped into the hall once more.

"Have you registered, Fotherby?"

Fotherby nodded before he walked out into the early spring morning and sighed. "You must come back to Portland's house, sir. You need not stay in an inn."

"Thank you, Fotherby. But I think Lieutenant Portland may not thank you for letting out his rooms."

"Of some men that would be true, but David Portland is an open-hearted gentleman. He would be most happy to welcome you, I am sure."

The old man returned with Fotherby and, although he regaled the young men with stories of the past, he did not stay for long. Portland and Keith both enjoyed the older man's retelling of the adventures and work of Fotherby, who refuted every time he was praised in the story and shook his head through much of the telling.

"Tell my uncle I shall be home as soon as I have taken my exam," Fotherby said softly, as he saw the surgeon into a cab. "But there is one visit I must make before then."

"I have heard it said that we all consider our own burdens to be the heaviest any man can bear. But I have never seen that in you. Until today."

"I have no right to feel the self-pity I have," Fotherby agreed.

"Whatever your business was in London, Fotherby, see it is completed swiftly so you can return home. You are needed there, whatever you may believe."

They parted then, and Fotherby returned to the house, where he was met by Keith's intent gaze.

"You have the look of a man who has been forced to play his hand, Captain. What are your intentions?"

"I am returning to Derbyshire," he said, as Portland nodded. "I have enlisted to take the final examination at the beginning of next week. Then I shall go home."

"We shall miss you, Fotherby," Portland began. "But, in truth, I can scarcely afford to keep the house any longer."

"Indeed," Keith muttered. "Perhaps we should all depart. I assured my sister I would be present at her wedding in eight days' time."

"Then I shall return to Cornwall for a time." Portland forced himself to smile as he looked at his two friends. "I must admit to having found a gentleman who wanted the house two weeks since, but I have been unable to part with it. Would you see to it, Fotherby? If Keith is to leave at once, then I shall stay until you have a mind to leave, but I find I cannot bear to be the one to relinquish the key."

"I have four days until my exam, so shall leave on the fifth. But I am happy to convey the business for you."

The following day, Keith departed in order to reach his sister's wedding in Scotland, wishing the other two gentlemen well before he journeyed north. Portland reluctantly sought Mr Kildare, who wished to purchase the house, leaving Fotherby to walk out into London and, finally, go in search of Miss Simmons. He could not reconcile with her swift acceptance of his uncle's wishes and he felt that, if she would only hear him, he could make her understand the hopes of marriage that he still held. But upon arriving at the house, he found it was empty and, although he beat repeatedly on the door, there was no one to open it.

"Is it Miss Simmons you are looking for, sir?"

Fotherby turned to face a woman who appeared from the house opposite. "Yes," he replied. "Does she no longer live here?"

"She has moved west, sir. Out toward Westminster."

"Thank you," Fotherby whispered, unsure whether he was truly grateful. He walked away, feeling almost as lost as he had the last time.

"You look like a man with great purpose," Portland remarked when Fotherby returned to the house.

"Great purpose but little direction," he replied, sitting opposite the younger man. He felt his brow furrow at the image of his friend before him, for he held a bottle of wine in one hand and a large glass in the other. "How have you spent today?"

"In the company of Mr Kildare, a charming gentleman who informs me he knows my uncle rather well. How happy my uncle has been since Harris' disgrace, for it has proved him right in every degree."

"Is that the gentleman who wishes to purchase the house?"

"Indeed. No doubt my uncle will find great enjoyment in walking through my father's halls."

"The hour is late, Portland," he said gently. "Perhaps we should both retire."

"But you, Fotherby," Portland said quickly, setting aside the glass and the bottle. "What have you done today?"

"I sought Miss Simmons, but she was not to be found."

"Are you certain that was wise?" Portland seemed to sober at once and he looked across at his friend with great pity. "You have chosen your course and she has chosen hers. Is it not better that you part amicably?"

"I cannot allow her to think that my uncle's words were in any way my belief."

"But you cannot undo what he has done, Fotherby. However much you may wish it."

Fotherby nodded his agreement, but it convinced neither of the men. Indeed, as Fotherby prepared to leave in the morning, Portland remarked on the point of his venture.

"You look prepared for Fleet Street, Fotherby."

"Fleet Street? What is on Fleet Street?"

"A bookseller," Portland replied as though nothing were more obvious. "He has his name on the door, I believe."

"Who does?"

"Mr Allen. That is where Miss Kitty Simmons is residing."

"How do you know?"

"When I came home to find you here, and you told me your story, I had a mind to help you. I followed Miss Simmons' progress." He walked over to Fotherby and looked him in the eye. "But that was when I realised that you were better leaving the matter, so I also resolved to do so."

"Miss Allen is her friend," Fotherby said softly. "It will be as her guest that she resides there." He turned from Portland and stared out of the window. "I failed her, Portland. I failed her by forcing her to wait to marry, by being unable to save her father, and by allowing her to be cast aside so easily."

"You have not failed her, Henry," Portland said softly. "But I see you must discover that for yourself."

They took breakfast together in silence, each considering the events of the next few days. Portland had already requested that the house should be emptied, and the servants had begun stripping the walls of paintings and the enormous tapestry, leaving an empty space both visually and in the young man's heart. The quiet of the house clung to Fotherby as he stepped out and adjusted his hat before walking in the direction of Fleet Street. He was unsure whether he was grateful for Portland's words regarding Miss Simmons, but felt certain they were well-intentioned.

Fleet Street was a busy road with traffic coming and going in both directions, filled with noise and so different from Portland's address that Fotherby felt he had travelled the length of the country instead of a short distance in the city. He found the black door of Mr Allen's shop with great ease, for his name was painted at the top as Portland had told him, but he could not bring himself to walk into the shop. He continued the walk to the end of the street before he turned and walked back once more. Three times he past the shop door before, at last, he stepped inside and looked about him.

It was dark, the window being so full that there was little light could penetrate, and he was met almost at once by a gentleman a little older than himself. He wore spectacles as he read from a small book that he held in his hand, but pulled them off to regard the tall surgeon.

"Can I be of assistance, sir?"

"I am searching for a lady who I believe lodges here," Fotherby began, and watched as the man's face altered, curiosity turning to concern before the surgeon added, "Miss Simmons."

"It is true, she does lodge here. But who are you, sir?"

"My name is Fotherby, sir," he began, but stopped as the door opened behind him. He turned at the sound of laughter, which stopped abruptly as his presence was noted by the two ladies who had stepped in.

"Good lord, Henry," Kitty whispered as she handed two boxes to Miss Allen. "What are you doing here?"

"Miss Simmons," Fotherby began, feeling his breath catch in his throat at the sight of the woman before him, "I desire only a few minutes of your time to speak alone."

Kitty looked torn before, at last, she nodded and guided him into the room at the back of the shop and up a flight of stairs that led to the rooms above. She showed him into the Living Room and closed the door, leaning against it so no one could enter, but maintaining her hold on the handle so she could leave quickly.

"Why are you here, Henry?" she asked softly, watching as he removed his hat and lowered his head, reluctant to meet her gaze for a time.

"I had to ensure that you knew," he faltered before he stared across at her. "That you knew my uncle wrote only of his own feelings and not mine."

"That is not entirely true, is it, Captain Fotherby?" Her voice was hard and set as she added, "It was also the view of your father, of Wanderford, and of society."

"I still intended to marry you."

"Through charity, no doubt. I have never known a man so committed to helping outcasts as you." She shook her head as she gazed across at him. "You have no duty to me anymore, Captain Fotherby. You served it, and I do believe you tried to assist my father, but it was never more than a duty and, since we parted, I have seen that. I was foolish to believe we might marry, but you were similarly foolish to believe such a thing was possible. You and I, as I have told you, do not belong together. There is nothing further to discuss."

"I have to know one thing," he whispered as she opened the door. "If my uncle had not written to you, when I arrived that day, would you have married me?"

"I would have married you years ago," she replied. "But that day, after the death of my father and the disgrace I carried as a result of your failed testimony? No, I would not."

"Then I shall trouble you no further, Miss Simmons. Indeed, I travel north in three days' time, so will be away from London."

"Henry," she said quickly, placing her hand on his arm to stop him from walking through the door. "Do not rebuke me for this. It is of your doing."

"You have no need to tell me, Miss Simmons. The guilt I carry is sufficient, I assure you."

"For my father?"

"For it all."

"You truly believe that by carrying the cares of the world on your shoulders no one else can feel them. There has never been a man so committed to martyrdom that they fail to live their life. Suffering is not exclusive to yourself." She allowed her hand to drop and stared vehemently at the man before her. "You and your friends have taken more from me than I ever knew I had, and now all I ask is that you leave me to build my life once more."

"I am sorry," Fotherby whispered.

"Do not call on me again, Captain Fotherby. It is too distressing."

Fotherby did not speak a word but left the building, ignoring the proprietor, with his long strides carrying him out into the spring morning. He walked down the street with great purpose, but stopped as he felt someone take his sleeve.

"It is difficult to keep up with those long strides," Portland announced. "You were not well-received, then?"

"No," Fotherby muttered, as they began walking at a more leisurely pace. "Have I been cruel to her, Portland? Should I have never mentioned her name to Lady Barrington? For then she would never have been at the dinner party, and I should never have known her beyond as a sergeant's daughter."

"Rosie had such terribly romantic ideas," Portland laughed. "She truly thought the world would be a better place if we all could love someone. But she was a woman, Fotherby. We men know differently. And have we not seen the bitterness and obsession that love can cause?"

"What became of Miss Webb?" Fotherby asked, realising what Portland meant.

"I do not know. Harry sought her, I believe he would have wrung her neck himself, but I do not think he found her. Though there were reports of her boarding a ship in Bristol, bound for America." Portland rushed to stand in front of Fotherby so the surgeon stopped in his tracks. "Margaret cost Rosanna her life, Fotherby. In turn, it led to Philip's death. Do not let Miss Simmons cost you yours. I cannot bear to lose anyone else."

"I recall being told that Miss Webb held a spell over Lord Barrington," Fotherby muttered. "I do not believe in such things."

"That may not protect you from them," Portland said sternly, but stepped aside.

The two men continued their journey back to the house, discussing any topic that took their minds. Fotherby was pleased to have company for, if he found his thoughts returning to the bitter conversation with Miss Simmons, Portland was always on hand to offer a new discussion. They stepped into the empty house and Chilvers greeted them, explaining that all the servants except the cook, himself, and one maid had departed. The remaining occupants took their own sorry thoughts with them through the rest of the day, communicating nothing with the others but retreating into different rooms.

## Chapter Twenty-Four
*The Service At Saint Bride's*

Finding his place after Miss Kitty Simmons' cruel words had seemed an insurmountable obstacle for Fotherby. However he excelled in his exam and, after settling Portland's affairs with Mr Kildare, returned to Wanderford Hall. Leaving the London house only confirmed Lord Barrington was truly dead, and the guilt he had laid at his own feet caused him to stumble as he stepped out of the coach in Buxton. He had made a decision to visit Doctor Shipton before he journeyed on to Wanderford Hall, for he owed it to the gentleman after all he had done for him.

The doctor could not have been happier to find the king at his door, and this welcome gave Fotherby the strength he needed to face his homecoming. He boarded in Buxton for three nights before travelling on to Wanderford Hall.

As he walked down towards the house, he tried to recall that this was where he belonged. His uncle had truthfully spoken that this was his duty, but never had the cruelty of Miss Simmons addressing him as a martyr seemed more appropriate. He had not reached the house before the door opened and Fotherby saw his uncle standing before him. His four dogs leapt towards Fotherby, each jumping up at him.

"I am glad you are home, Henry," Paul began, as his nephew walked over to him. "Where have you been all this time?"

"Staying with Lord Barrington's brother." Fotherby stepped over the threshold and inhaled the air of his future. "And I visited Miss Simmons, as I left intending to do so."

"I am sorry, Henry," his uncle said softly as he closed the door.

"Well," Fotherby laughed bitterly. "There is a word I never thought to hear you say." He never took his eyes from the picture of Bosworth field and frowned as he stared at the clash of the two sides. "It is odd, is it not, that our family found its feet in society in a war against their own kin?" He turned his dry-eyed gaze back to his uncle and smiled slightly. "I understand why you did it," he continued, handing the folded letter his uncle had sent to Miss Simmons back to the man who had penned it. "I understand, but I cannot reconcile with it."

"I did not expect you would. But, in time, when you become the master of Wanderford Hall, you will."

"As you are its master?" Fotherby asked sharply.

"Yes," his uncle replied, his face becoming angry at his nephew's attitude. "You are more of a fool than I could believe possible if you do not see that, with your father's condition, I have run Wanderford Hall." He sighed and turned away. "We have all made mistakes in our pasts, Henry, but we are defined by how we live the present. I did not want Wanderford Hall any more than you do, but we have a staff and tenants numbering more than fifty. That means fifty lives depend on this estate running as it should. Perhaps more when you consider their families. Wanderford Hall has to succeed, or all these men that you save will be for nothing, as you are condemning so many others. There is more duty on you than on the farmer, although he complains of his work and hours. Or the farrier, although he is never content with his heavy labour."

"That, and that alone, is why I came back."

"Doctor Shipton informed me that you were to take a further examination. Did you qualify?"

"Indeed, I did."

"I know you do not wish to hear this, Henry, but I am so proud of you."

"Thank you," Fotherby said, feeling guilty for his anger towards the man before him. "Where is Father?"

"In his room." His uncle watched as Fotherby walked to the door of the study before he shook his head and continued. "No, Henry, not his study. His room."

Fotherby turned to his uncle but did not say anything. Instead, he rushed up the wooden stairs, taking them two at a time, and along the landing. He did not spare a glance for his beloved view but walked to his father's door. He knocked, although he knew he could not be heard, and entered. His father sat at his desk, running his fingers over the pages of a book of sermons as though he could feel the words talking to him. He turned as the door opened, feeling the draught on his back, and beckoned Fotherby into the room.

"This is a message to you, Paul," his father began and, before Fotherby could correct him, the old man continued. "Does this not tell us we should consider our own actions before rebuking others for their own?"

"It does," Fotherby muttered, as he walked over to his father and stared down at the book.

"You are not Paul," his father said, his face lighting up. "Have you come home?"

Fotherby only lifted his father's cold, bony hand to his face and kissed it.

"Henry, I am so glad you are back. I was anxious for your safety." He clutched his son to him as he rose, uncertainly, to his feet. "I have been confined to this room for so long," he sighed. "Can you believe, I miscounted the steps and stumbled down the stairs?

- 582 -

How many years have I lived here? Yet still I made such a mistake."

Fotherby did not talk but guided his father to the window of the room and opened it wide, spelling out the word "April" on his palm. He watched as his father took in deep breaths of the early spring air as though it were an intoxication. The old man's skin was thin and pale, and his cheeks seemed to sink deep into his face. His grey hair was unkempt, and his swollen hands struggled to grip the window's frame.

This image was to haunt Fotherby as the days turned to weeks, and he felt reluctant to leave his father for any length of time. Each morning, he walked out into the gardens or through the meadows beyond to pick flowers to take his father, bringing something of the landscape he loved into his small prison. It is true that he put aside the anger and disappointment he carried regarding Miss Simmons for a time while he tended his father and even resolved to accept his uncle's apology. As summer arrived and his father's health and spirits became stronger, Fotherby began journeying into Buxton to offer any support he could to Doctor Shipton.

As September dawned, all the talk to be had in the town was of Mr Thomas Garton, a staunch abolitionist, who was to hold a lecture in Buxton the following month. Everyone had an opinion on the upcoming lecture, as many in favour as against, and Fotherby found that all the memories of Lord and Lady Barrington resurfaced, bringing him sleepless nights and pensive days. He was grateful to receive a letter, then, on his return to Wanderford Hall.

"I am leaving," he announced to his uncle that evening.

"But, Henry, you have only just returned from Buxton. Are you not attending chapel tomorrow? Who will tell your father what messages Mr Wesley is sending from heaven? I know I shall not."

"You may have to," Fotherby replied calmly, ignoring the flippant scorn of his uncle. "I am ordered to the Mediterranean. And I shall have to leave at once."

"I shall be sorry to see you go, my boy," his uncle said gently. "It has been good to have someone to talk with."

"I shall be sorry to leave, too. But I hope to be back within the year. Keep Father safe for me."

"As long as you keep yourself safe, Henry."

Fotherby left as swiftly as he had promised, although he spared enough time to pen a letter to his friend, Portland, informing him that he was briefly returning to London before travelling to war again. He arrived in London as October overtook September, and the city was basking in the last rays of summer as he stepped down from the coach. He had intended to stay with Manny and the other servants at Sir Manfred's house in Mayfair but, as he walked towards Westminster, he found himself on a familiar street.

He stopped across the road from a shining black door and frowned slightly. The conversation that had been shared in the upstairs of Mr Allen's shop had been one he had desperately sought to forget, but now the memory struck him like a hammer.

"Captain Fotherby," called a voice from a little further down the street.

Surprised to be recognised in the city, Fotherby turned to face the gentleman who had called out to him, and shelved his self-pity as he smiled across.

"Keith," he began. "Why are you in London?"

"I have been transferred to another regiment, Captain. I am based here now."

"But what coincidence you are here on Fleet Street," Fotherby said with an expression that spoke of disbelief. "You were to attend a wedding when last I saw you. I trust your sister is well?"

"Indeed," Keith laughed. "And a child already on its way, she tells me."

"The blessing of having a lady to correspond with," Fotherby replied. "I only ever discover things when I stumble across them. But why are you truly on Fleet Street?"

"To search for you."

"But how did you know I should be here?"

"Portland asked me to come and find you. He seemed quite sure that you would be found here. He spent almost all of yesterday pacing this road, so I volunteered to spend today doing the same thing."

"I am to meet with my lieutenant."

"Egypt?" Keith asked.

"I believe so."

"Two days, Fotherby. Why not wait for two days before you seek out Lieutenant Kitson? You know you wish to see him as little as he wishes to see you. I scarcely remember him except as a grey cloud over everyone with his poor attitude. Come, we are in a billet south of the river."

Fotherby could not understand Keith's reluctance for him to find Kitson, but he did not mention it as they continued toward the rooms that Keith and Portland had been staying in. Keith had been in London for two months now, and was living in a collection of rooms in a tall three-storey house. From the outside it looked dingy and ramshackle, and the staircase indoors seemed as poorly kept. However, as Keith opened the door to his rooms and invited Fotherby to enter, the warmth of the fire in the grate greeted him. Portland was sitting on one of the low armchairs, but at once rose to his feet as they walked in.

"You found him, Keith," he laughed. "Well done."

"Well," Keith replied, barely hiding his amusement. "He is not a difficult gentleman to find in a crowd, for he stands a foot taller than everyone else."

"Fotherby," Portland said quickly, as he saw the surgeon frown at this exchange. "I knew you should make your way to Fleet Street, even if you meant not to. But I hope you do a more efficient job of avoiding it in the next few days."

"I am only here for a few days. Then I am travelling to the Mediterranean."

"I know, and I have something I wanted to give you." Portland held his hand up to the tall man, silently ordering him to stay where he was, while he walked to the corner of the room and returned with a long sword sheathed in an elegant black scabbard with a silver buckle and tip. "This is for you, Fotherby."

Fotherby took the weapon from Portland's outstretched hands and studied it, feeling overcome by the generosity of such a gift. "Thank you. But why?"

"Because I owe you a great deal, Fotherby," Portland said, as though it was obvious. "And when I heard Doctor Shipton discussing the duel you fought for

Rosanna, I realised just how loyally you had stood by the Portland family. I appreciate it beyond words."

Keith closed the door and walked over to the corner of the room where he poured out drinks for the three of them, wine for Portland and himself and a blackcurrant cordial for Fotherby.

"Then let us drink to the good captain's health," Keith ventured as he lifted his glass. "That you have a safe trip to Egypt, Captain Fotherby. May you find success and good health,"

Fotherby thanked them both as they drank his health and success, feeling wholly uncomfortable with such attention, before the three of them sat down on the armchairs before the fire.

"I must go tomorrow and meet Lieutenant Kitson," Fotherby began, as they discussed their plans for the next few days.

"No, Fotherby," Portland said quickly, sitting forward on the chair. "Keith has only two days before he has to travel to Suffolk. Can you not wait until then?"

"Suffolk?" Fotherby asked. "Whatever for?"

"It is not such a bad place," Keith laughed. "There has been unrest surrounding some of the abolitionist rallies. The army has been ordered to maintain peace."

"We have one in Buxton in two weeks," Fotherby explained. "I cannot understand why a lecture should inspire such violence and unrest."

"Philip would never have had it so," Portland agreed. "But the cause is old now. Old and bitter to those who have fought it for so long."

Talk of the army ensued, and Keith and Portland both expressed their relief at not being called into Egypt, but their disappointment at having to police such events as the rallies. Fotherby, by contrast, was pleased to have the chance to leave England once more, although he remained concerned for his father's health.

There was insufficient room for the three gentlemen to sleep in Keith's lodgings, so Fotherby announced his intention to leave and find a bed elsewhere, but neither Portland nor Keith agreed to this.

"You cannot go out, Captain," Portland began. "You and I shall sleep on these chairs. They are comfortable enough are they not?"

"You outrank us both, Fotherby," Keith agreed. "Why do you not take the bed?"

The surgeon stared hard at the two younger men who had carefully positioned themselves between him and the door. "Why are you both so anxious about my leaving? I am quite accustomed to London by night, and it does not worry me."

"Even so, Fotherby," Portland said, glancing sideward at Keith. "It would be rude to turn down Keith's invitation, would it not?"

Feeling suspicious of the two men's behaviour yet accepting Portland's argument, Fotherby agreed to stay, but turned down the offer of the bed and instead slept on the floor of the antechamber while Portland slept in one of the armchairs. The following morning, however, Fotherby arose before dawn and, upon finding Keith's door closed and Portland still asleep with his head on the arm of the chair, he belted his new sword about his waist and left the apartment. He walked out into the crisp October morning and tried to remember how to reach Westminster.

For a time, he became lost, until he reached the river and followed it until he found a bridge that would take him across. He watched as his breath steamed before him in the chill air as he walked over the river and began searching for the inn where Kitson was to meet him, but he despaired of this as he once more lost himself in the thin streets and twisting alleyways of London. The sun had risen now and struck the earth, burning away the queer fog that had settled along the river and encouraging him as he walked on.

He stopped outside the towering spire of Saint Bride's Church and looked at the open door. Perhaps he would never have noticed it on any other day, but this morning there were voices to be heard from inside, and it was towards these voices that Fotherby walked. There were a small number of people inside, certainly no more than twenty. All of them wore smart clothes and hats and there was little wonder for, as he stepped further into the church, he realised there was a wedding taking place before him. He began turning to leave, for he had no place in such a ceremony, when he realised why he had entered.

Before the priest, stood two people, neither of whom were strangers to him. Neither of them noticed his presence at the back of the church, but he felt his legs tremble beneath him as his gaze rested on Mr Allen and Miss Simmons. He stumbled out of the church and leaned against the wall of the mighty building, taking a moment to realise that he was not alone.

"I thought I might find you here," Portland said softly, as he offered his hand to the captain. "You were meant to stay in Keith's chambers."

Fotherby took his outstretched hand and laughed, causing the young man to frown. "That is what she meant."

"What is that, Fotherby?"

"That the army had ruined her. And it has ruined me, too."

"What are you talking about?" Portland asked as he followed Fotherby, who walked down to the river once more. "You spoke of your work as a calling."

"To try and save those who were responsible for this situation? I do not wish to help them anymore. I have spent ten years in the service of men who have rewarded me with what? With seeing my friends slain, innocent men executed, and my fiancée marrying another man. Look," he continued, unfastening the leather cord that he still wore around his neck and opening the two parts of the ring. "There was a heart there. My heart." He swung the cord round his head before letting go, so that the ring disappeared into the River Thames. "Please, Portland," he continued as he pulled the epaulets from the shoulders of his coat. "Take these to Lieutenant Kitson. He is staying at The Crossed Keys in Westminster."

"What are you doing, Fotherby?" Portland whispered. "You are hurt, that is all. Do not be so rash."

"Then I shall take them myself."

"You have defaced the King's uniform," Portland began, as he took the epaulets from Fotherby's hand. "You could be flogged for that."

Fotherby shook his head, remaining silent, but walked away from his friend.

"Where are you going?"

"Back to Derbyshire," Fotherby replied. "It may be the last place I wish to be, but it is where my true duty lies."

Portland, confused by such an outburst from the quiet gentleman, stared down at the epaulets, before he shook himself awake. He turned back to his friend, but the man had gone.

Fotherby had not wasted a second, but began the journey back to Wanderford at once. He walked a great distance, leaving London behind and sleeping in the open for two nights before, at last, he boarded the stagecoach, stopping in Peterborough and disembarking in Buxton two days later. He was lost in his dark thoughts as he walked towards Doctor Shipton's house, but he stopped as he reached The Sun Inn. He stared thoughtfully at it before he continued to the doctor's chambers.

"Captain Fotherby?" Shipton began as he saw him standing at the door. "I heard you were journeying to the Mediterranean."

"I decided against it, sir. And I am no longer a captain."

"Fotherby, what has happened."

"I could no longer do it," Fotherby said. "Captain Sutton might have bled to death if I had not cauterised his wound. And how did he repay me? He had the man, whose daughter I was to marry, executed. I cannot do it anymore."

Doctor Shipton guided him further into the house, but Fotherby shook his head.

"I have made terrible mistakes, sir. I cannot undo them."

"Stay here tonight, Fotherby. Tomorrow you can complete your journey to Wanderford Hall, for you are in no fit state to travel tonight."

Fotherby accepted the offer, feeling certain that the other gentleman would not accept a refusal. He spent the evening staring into the flames of the fire, tears burning in his eyes but remaining unshed. He studied the sword that Portland had given him and tried to recall the young man who had earned such a fine weapon.

His father, for as long as he could remember, had always told him that tomorrow was the greatest gift man had, and that it was his responsibility not to waste it. But, as the following morning dawned, Fotherby could not bring himself to make anything of it. He assisted Doctor Shipton during his work of the day but, at the end of the evening, he walked with great purpose to The Sun Inn and, buying a bottle of wine, sat at a table in the corner of the room staring at it. After several minutes he poured its contents into a beaker and drank heavily, instantly topping up the vessel and drinking until the bottle was empty, whereupon he called for another.

His head was spinning as he watched a gentleman sit down opposite him and it took him a moment to realise that it was his uncle. The older man folded his arms and surveyed his nephew critically.

"I have waited a long time for you to come to your senses about alcohol." He poured out a beaker, before he drank straight from the bottle. "This was not how I imagined you would do it. You have upset a good many people, Henry."

"I am sure the list is not as long as your own."

"Then this is about Miss Simmons?"

"She is Mrs Allen, now," he replied harshly. "But she and I are not the only people on your list, are we? What of your friends in Haiti or Saint Vincent? What of all the men, women and children you shipped and you sold as though they were cattle? I know exactly how you made your money, and it was in cotton not wool. I would wager your list is so long even you do not know the number of names on it."

"Did I not tell you that we all have a past, Henry?"

"So many people tried to tell me about you and your deplorable friend, Sir Manfred, who believes he still owns those people."

"As he does, Henry. You are too drunk and too immature to understand what you are talking about."

"How young were the children you sold?" he demanded, trying to rise to his feet but finding he no longer had control over his limbs, causing him to stumble.

"They did not know how old they were, and it is true that I did not care. But it was a profession, Henry."

"With lots of money."

"Yes. But remind me once more why you did not marry Miss Simmons when you first fell in love with her?"

Fotherby swallowed hard and glared across at the man before him as he felt the full impact of his words. His uncle walked away and Fotherby sat with his head in his hands, staring at the empty bottles and feeling so much disgust in himself that he could not stand it anymore, so he walked out of the inn, having to lean on the wall. His uncle stood outside and held the door to the carriage open.

"Get in, Henry. You have the length of the journey to Wanderford Hall to sober yourself. I believe it would kill your father to know you had been in this state."

Fotherby climbed into the carriage and sat on the floor while his uncle climbed in after him. At once, the carriage began moving forward and its motion made Fotherby nauseous.

"When you were twelve," his uncle began, as he watched him pale. "When you should have been doing this, you were reading journals and copying pictures of severed arms. Why have you chosen to do everything backwards, Henry? I am much too old now to be chasing across the county to find you."

Fotherby did not answer, but remained silent on the long road back to Wanderford Hall. He felt he had not only failed, but embarrassed himself, his father and his uncle, and wished beyond anything that he had not so rashly abandoned his post in the army, for it had granted him the only freedom he could gain from the suffocating duty of Wanderford Hall.

## Chapter Twenty-Five

*The Fire Of Abolitionist Passion*

Although Fotherby's uncle did not tell his brother about the events in Buxton, Fotherby could not bear the deceit of concealing it from him. His father seemed unsurprised to discover such behaviour and this only deepened the young surgeon's feeling of guilt. He sought for any form of penance, but he could not free himself from the disappointment he had brought upon the other two gentlemen in the house. It came as little surprise to any of them then, when four days later, Fotherby announced his intention to return to Buxton to hear Thomas Garton's lecture.

"Be careful, Henry," his father muttered as he held his son's head in his hands. He was still confined to his room and seemed more uncertain about leaving it now.

Fotherby kissed the old man's hand and left the room, rushing down the stairs, where his uncle was standing at the open door. "Keep your head down, Henry," he said softly. "These lectures have been turning to riots across the country. People feel passionately about this topic and men, from both sides, are intent on stirring this fire into a blaze."

"Will you not come, too?"

"I am afraid I shall be neither safe nor welcome."

Fotherby nodded and parted from him, walking up the broad drive and on to the crossroads, before he boarded the coach on to Buxton. The town was filled with people, areas were so crowded that he could not walk through them. The lecture, that had been to take place in the assembly halls, had been moved to the open air of the parkland opposite The Crescent. Fotherby could not hear what was being said by Mr Garton for, despite standing on a podium, he was a short man and his voice did not carry in the open air.

"They do not look the same," someone shouted from close to where he was standing. "How can they be the same?"

Fotherby tried to find who had spoken, but the numbers were too great to be able to tell.

"All men should be equal," someone else replied.

This remark was met with calls of revolution and at once the crowd began to scatter as men in the red coats of the army appeared from the edge of the park. Fotherby tried to calm the men around him but there was panic amongst the crowd as a volley of shots was fired as a warning into the air. Someone tried to run past the soldiers, but they were struck by the butt of a musket.

In the few seconds in which this all happened, Fotherby tried to understand the events that had led from peace to pandemonium so swiftly. He moved over to the man who had been struck and carefully guided him away from the violence that erupted wherever the soldiers stood. Wasting no further time, Fotherby snatched the sleeve of a young man and ordered him to fetch Doctor Shipton, and to warn him of the confused riot that was ensuing.

Fotherby had never been in the thick of battle before, always being on the periphery, but he could not believe that it would have been any worse than what he was witnessing here. Unarmed men attacked soldiers, who had little choice but to respond. There were no further shots fired, but the unprepared abolitionists were beaten back with the blunt edges of the guns. As the minutes turned, the grass around the shrine of Saint Anne's Well became red. The violence did not end here but, as the men ran, it spread throughout the town.

Doctor Shipton assisted Fotherby in tending to the wounded men and women, pleased to have his young apprentice returned to his usual calm and patient self. The inns took in the wounded, and it was here that the two surgeons established their temporary hospital. Despite the lack of shot, the day was not without fatalities and Fotherby felt the haunting chill of failure seep through him at the deaths of twelve men and two women.

"You could not have saved them," Shipton whispered, as he offered the younger man a beaker of wine. "Come, I heard you had shaken your abstinence. And God knows, Fotherby, you deserve a drink."

Fotherby took the beaker and stared down at it, before he took a sip, feeling almost at once the benefit as it relaxed him.

"That cannot be wine," a voice expressed as the door to the inn opened. "Fotherby, I am surprised beyond measure."

"Not as surprised as I," Fotherby began, rising to his feet at the sound of the man's voice. "Portland? Why are you here?"

"Keeping the peace," he announced, easing the man he was helping down to the floor. "Do not look so surprised, Fotherby. You knew it was our company's orders to maintain the peace."

"I am a little surprised to find you partaking."

"I am a supporter to the cause of freedom, as strongly as you are, even more so perhaps. But the way to achieve equality is not through behaving like animals. We must reason."

"Why ever did you enter the army, Portland?" Fotherby muttered. "You should have been a politician."

Portland only laughed at this statement before he turned and walked toward the door. "Derbyshire is a nice place, Fotherby," he mused. "I can see why you chose it."

The night was deep when at last Fotherby and Shipton left the inn and went their different ways. Although he had politely refused Doctor Shipton's offer of a bed, Fotherby had not considered where he was to sleep that night, but walked down the road, lost in his bleak thoughts. Could it be right that men fought one another in an attempt to find equality? And how far could one go before equality became revolution? He sat against the trunk of one of the trees in the parkland opposite the inn and stared down towards the island that had been the site of his duel many years ago. There was a thin curtain of rain that seeped through the jacket he wore and down to his skin as he stared into the darkness, shivering suddenly as though he had only just felt the cold. He rose to his feet and walked back to the inn, joining the wounded men, who slept on tables, chairs, stools and the floor.

He awoke to the sound of someone setting a plate before him, and looked up to find Second-Lieutenant Portland smiling across.

"That was quite a display yesterday," Portland said happily. "Is Buxton usually this busy?"

"No," Fotherby replied, rubbing his neck. "Generally, it is a place where the most newsworthy occurrence is if a lady wears a bonnet that does not match her dress."

"You handled it all remarkably well, Fotherby. There is little wonder you were indispensable on the battlefield."

"Your brother was too generous with his compliments," Fotherby laughed.

"I agree with you," Portland conceded. "But Captain Kitson is not."

"Kitson said that?"

"Is it so surprising after how you managed yesterday?"

"Any praise from Kitson is surprising." Fotherby looked down at the warm bread roll and the cloth-covered butter. "Thank you for this."

"I was not happy with the way we parted last time. I know I should have been honest with you and told you at once about Miss Simmons' marriage."

"I appreciate what you tried to do," Fotherby whispered. "I might even have tried to do the same, had our roles been exchanged."

"Let us make a promise to one another, Fotherby. I shall be honest with you from this moment on, for I know I cost you your profession and your happiness by withholding the news of Kitty Simmons' wedding."

"And I shall be honest with you, also," Fotherby promised as he smiled across.

"I have to be at the Drill Hall by nine o'clock," Portland said quickly as he rose to his feet. "But I should like to see more of Derbyshire. Have you plans to leave Buxton before this evening?"

"No," Fotherby smiled. "I suspect that the work of yesterday shall fill today. We can journey to Wanderford Hall this evening."

"I shall meet you then," Portland said, patting the surgeon's shoulder as he walked out of the inn.

Fotherby's assumption concerning the employment of the day was correct, and he checked on each of the injured men. There had been one man who had needed to be stitched after being attacked with a knife but, for the most part, the men were able to return to their homes. There were three people in the rooms of the inn with head injuries, and he divided his time between the three until each of them had awoken from unconsciousness. Fotherby did not leave the inn until the sun was setting, when he walked towards the Drill Hall, unsure where else to find his friend.

There were lights still burning inside and Fotherby stood outside, listening to the sounds of the Hall and recalling a time he might have entered. Portland came out several minutes later and smiled across at Fotherby.

"Have you a horse?" he asked jovially. "For I have been inquiring and it seems that Wanderford Hall is some ten miles away."

"I have been known to walk it," Fotherby laughed. "But we can borrow Doctor Shipton's carriage. He assured me he had no use for it this evening."

He guided Portland through the streets of Buxton and stopped as they reached the doctor's chambers, where they had a drink before the two young men prepared to leave.

"Thank you for your help, Doctor," Portland said quietly, while Fotherby climbed into the carriage. Doctor Shipton only smiled across at the two men and watched in silence as they began the journey to Wanderford Hall. Inside the carriage, Portland and Fotherby talked happily.

The coach slowed after a time and Fotherby frowned slightly, leaning out of the window. They were in the small village of Wanderford that rested in the valley below Wanderford Hall. The carriage stopped and, without offering any explanation to his friend, Fotherby climbed out and looked about him. People were standing in the road, which was why the horses had stopped, and Fotherby frowned slightly as he thought he recognised some of the men who were gathered there. But his memory seldom recalled faces, and he shunned it as just confusion. Portland stepped out from the carriage and immediately, as his attire was noted, the street began to clear.

"What is it, Fotherby?" he asked, his voice shaking slightly.

"I do not know," came the equally confused reply. He walked back to the carriage and was about to open the door when someone rushed up to him and took his sleeve. It was a woman from the village, and Fotherby recognised her at once as she clutched at his arm, tears forming in her eyes.

"Sir, they have done such things, sir."

"Who?" Fotherby asked quietly, exchanging a puzzled look with Portland. "What things?"

"They said they heard a raised voice a week since, back in Buxton." She took deep breaths of air to try and steady her crying, and Fotherby took both of her hands in his own.

"Carry on."

"And with the horrors of yesterday, with the soldiers and all, they have become blinded."

"You are not making sense," Fotherby said, calmly but not unkindly. "Begin again."

"One man heard a conversation in The Sun Inn at Buxton, not a week since, about slaves and freedom. And since yesterday, when those that wanted freedom and equality were beaten, someone made a call to find the slaver."

"My uncle?" Fotherby began, his face paling.

She nodded quickly. "Lord, sir, they left with fire, and swearing justice and equality, up to the house."

Fotherby relinquished her hands and began running at once toward Wanderford Hall. Never had the distance seemed so great, nor the hill so steep, but he ran on. He did not spare a thought for Portland, nor the woman, but continued to run. If he had not known the way or became lost amongst the trees, he had only to follow the beacon atop the hill. As he crashed through the trees and charged across the lawns of the Hall towards the fountain, he gave a cry at the enormous flames that were visible through all the windows, and the thick billowing smoke that rose from the structure. He flung himself against the timbers of the door, but it was to no avail for they had been locked. It took him several minutes before the door gave beneath his blows and he collapsed into the building.

He coughed into his sleeve as he beheld the aggressive fire consuming the interior of the house. The huge painting of his ancestors blistered and burned before him, and he looked about for a moment before calling out to his father and uncle. But, as he did so, the smoke caught in his throat and he began coughing violently. Henry froze as his gaze rested on his uncle's body beside the door. He forced himself over to him and dragged the man to the safety of the night air beyond, but there was no breath left in his lungs, only the smoke that had suffocated him. Fotherby could not allow himself the time to weep but rushed back into the house, calling his father as though he expected the old man to hear. He rushed towards the stairs and began climbing but, three steps from the top, the timber structure collapsed beneath him and he plunged to the floor below.

The next thing Fotherby knew was that someone was struggling for breath close to where he lay. They were coughing and wheezing as they tried to steady the air they needed. Forcing his eyes to open, he looked beside him to find Second-Lieutenant David Portland, who was the source of the terrible noise.

"Portland?" he tried to say, but his voice was harsh and his throat unable to coax a sound. He forced himself to sit up, leaning heavily on his left arm for support, and stared with tearful eyes at the burning remains of Wanderford Hall, from where he sat beside the fountain in the middle of the driveway.

"Fotherby," Portland spluttered. "Thank God. When you crashed through that staircase," he paused to cough further. "I thought you would break your neck."

It was apparent that Portland had not wasted a second after Fotherby had left the carriage, but he did not know the terrain and had become lost trying to find a gap in the thick hedge. He had seen, as he ran forward, Fotherby pulling one man from the fire before the surgeon had returned into the blazing inferno. Without considering what he was doing, only that he knew it was right, Portland had run into the house in time to witness the staircase cascade in a shower of burning splinters. Carrying Fotherby from the building would have been difficult in ordinary circumstances, for the man was so much taller than him, so Portland had been forced to drag the unconscious surgeon out of the house. His chest was tight and each step his legs took seemed to tighten the clench of the smoke on his lungs, but he had not stopped dragging his friend until they reached the fountain where, having laid him on the ground, Portland collapsed in a fit of coughing, unable to breathe through the smoke he had inhaled.

"Why did they do it?" Fotherby muttered, trying to steady his thoughts and his breath. "Why would they do it?"

"It seems," Portland coughed, "we are never quite able to lose our past."

"He left it behind. And my father," Fotherby began as he struggled to his feet, but he could not remain standing. "He was as strongly opposed to slavery as any man alive."

Portland quickly rose to his feet and supported the surgeon as best he could, encouraging him to be seated on the edge of the fountain. "I am no physician, Fotherby," he muttered as he glanced into the soot-stained face of his friend. "But I do not think you should be walking." He began coughing once more before he continued, his voice harsh as he tried to clear his dry, burning throat. "You could do nothing more, Fotherby."

"I should have done less. It was I who shared the angry, drunken conversation with my uncle in The Sun Inn. He had left that life behind, buried it in honest industry, but I made it public. He is dead because of that fact alone. My father for the same reason." Fotherby allowed the silent, heavy tears to fall from his eyes, creating clean streaks on his ash-covered cheeks. "He could not hear. He could not see. Can you imagine it, Portland? They locked the doors. They locked him in. A blind, deaf man is as helpless as a child."

"We will find the men who did this, Fotherby. They will face justice."

People were arriving from the village now, rushing down the long drive. They formed a chain from the fountain to the house, trying to extinguish the fire with buckets of water, but the books of the library, the timber structure and the thick tapestry furnishings had taken such a hold that the water made no difference. Fotherby stared at the building before him all that night, lost in the dark thoughts, imagining the horrendous fear that must have claimed his father and the great injustice of his death. Portland sat by his friend, but did not volunteer any further words. He was far from silent, however, as he continued to cough all night.

As dawn arrived it was to the appearance of rain, which eased the burning of the house and quashed the angry flames. One by one the residents of the village left, some sharing words of sympathy for the young man who stared with glazed eyes at the remains of his home. They had placed Paul Fotherby's body on a cart, leaving the vehicle in the broad driveway. It was a reminder to Fotherby that there were other bodies to reclaim from the smoking shell of Wanderford Hall. Portland rose to his feet to offer support to the surgeon as he stumbled toward the house once more.

"I have to do it," Fotherby muttered. "I have to find my father."

"You cannot go in there, Fotherby. Firstly, you are injured, and secondly, you will get yourself killed. Tell me where to find him."

"There is a flight of stairs at the back of the house," Fotherby muttered. "Then he will be in the room at the end of the landing."

Portland nodded and, after helping Fotherby to be seated once more, he ran toward the back of the house. The door was locked, but the charred timbers gave way easily beneath him as he pushed himself against them. Smoke rushed out at him and he began coughing once more before he lifted his sleeve to his face and walked in. He stared numbly at the bodies of five servants, each lying close to the door, where they had fought to their dying breaths to be free. The building was little more than a shell now, the flames having destroyed almost all the interior. Parts of the peeled boards still smoldered, but most of what remained was the suffocating smoke that Portland endeavoured not to inhale. Recalling his promise to his friend, he found the stone stairs and climbed them. The corridor opened from the top as Fotherby had told him it did, and he cautiously stepped onto the timbers of the landing. Covering the short distance took great time, for the young officer would not tread where he was uncertain the floorboards would support him. There was less smoke here, for the open door in the hall below and the huge hole in the roof where the burnt joists had collapsed created a chimney. He reached the door that Fotherby had told him would open onto his father's room and pushed the timbers back.

The old man sat on the chair at the desk, his head tipped forward and his eyes closed. One hand rested on an open book and the other hung down at his side. Portland stepped forward, feeling curiosity drive his step, but snatched out at the door as he felt the floor tremble beneath. Flames became visible as the floorboards collapsed into the room below and Portland quickly rushed forward, grabbing the chair that the old man rested on and pulling him towards the doorway. He stepped into the landing, holding the lifeless body to him, in time to watch the floor of the chamber fall down to the room below.

Twice, as he carried the body across the landing, his leg penetrated the charred wood of the floorboards, until he reached the stone stairs and inhaled once more the sickening black smoke. He could not conceal his face as he carried the old man, but he tried to hold his breath until he reached the bottom of the stairs. Laying his burden down, he clutched at the collar of his shirt, feeling that he was being strangled by the tendrils of smoke. He could not cease coughing as he looked across at the body of the man who had suffocated, as he was so close to doing.

Presently, the room became black, and Portland felt someone take his wrists, but it was too dark to tell who it was. He rose to his feet, limping as his leg throbbed from where it had penetrated the timbers of the landing.

"Wait," he began, choking on his breath. "I have to get his father."

"I will return for him," announced the calm voice of his friend and, as Fotherby guided him outside, Portland watched as the surgeon, with considerable difficulty, walked back into the building and carried his father out.

"Thank you for finding him, Portland," Fotherby began, as he placed his hand on his father's still chest. "And thank you for finding me."

Portland could not answer but suddenly felt lightheaded. He knew his legs had buckled beneath him, but his body was too numb to feel the impact of the ground as he collapsed.

## Chapter Twenty-Six

*To Whom We Owe So Much*

Portland's collapse had awoken Fotherby to his senses. He left his father's lifeless body and struggled the short distance over to his friend, lifting his head and willing the young man to breathe. Rebuking himself for allowing the man in his arms to enter the building, he snatched his wrist to find a pulse. A relieved smile caught his lips as he felt the frantic beat beneath his thin fingers, and he turned as he heard the sound of cartwheels on gravel.

"Doctor Fotherby?" he heard a voice call. "Henry?"

"I am here," he tried to call back, but his burnt throat would not allow any volume.

It did not matter for, within seconds, Doctor Shipton rushed into view and took in the sight before him. Fotherby was seated on the ground, his back against the blackened stone wall and his legs stretched out before him. At the open doorway to the kitchens lay the body of his father, while beside the young surgeon was his friend, the officer's head resting on Fotherby's thigh.

"I came as soon as I heard," Shipton began, as he walked forward.

"They are dead," Fotherby muttered, as his gaze met with the older man's eyes.

"And Lieutenant Portland?"

"I think he is alive."

Shipton moved over to them and knelt down. He looked at the shredded leg of Portland's britches and eased a long splinter from this side of his shin. Portland made scarcely a move but gave a muffled whimper.

"Yes," Shipton said softly, "he is alive." He called out to his driver and ordered him to carry Portland back to the carriage, before he offered his hand down to Fotherby. "And you, Henry? Are you hurt?"

"No," he said, as he accepted the man's outstretched hand. "I fell, but I am quite sure I have only cuts and bruises."

The servants were placed on the cart alongside Fotherby's father and uncle, and Shipton guided Fotherby to the carriage. They journeyed on to Buxton, stopping first in the village to arrange the funerals with the undertaker. The next few days passed Fotherby by in a peculiar daze of endless faces and voices, without being able to recognise any of them or anything that they said. Portland remained weaving in and out of consciousness for a further two days, during which time Doctor Shipton had stitched his leg, and Fotherby sat beside him.

Now, Fotherby stared blankly at the two mounds of earth that marked the final resting places of his parents and uncle. There was rain pouring from the heavens and none of the other mourners wished to remain in the graveyard longer than they had to. Fotherby ignored them all, staring at the turned earth and considering all that he could have done to lead to a different ending. Rain ran down his face and the back of his neck, but he barely noticed. He held his hat in his hand, reluctant to show disrespect before the graves of the two men. They were buried in the churchyard of the small church in Wanderford, the same church that, less than a year ago, he had believed would hold his wedding. What disaster this century had brought, and it was only in its initial ten months.

It was this thought that caused Fotherby to frown as he considered the self-pity he was granting himself. He knelt down on the wet, muddy earth, placing his hand on the mound that covered his father and sighing firmly.

"No more, Father," he said sternly. "I shall not waste time or energy in such frivolous thoughts. I shall have no self-pity. I shall live my life for all those things you taught me."

"Sir?" Fotherby turned to face the speaker, a woman perhaps ten years younger than him. "They have found the three men, sir."

"Where are they?" Fotherby asked in a calm tone, as he struggled to his feet.

"In Buxton gaol, sir."

"Thank you." Fotherby turned to look once more at the graves before he walked silently alongside her to the lychgate, where two gentlemen in uniform sat on horseback.

"Doctor Fotherby?" one asked in a clipped voice.

"Yes."

"We were to fetch you at once, sir, for the men have been found."

"In Buxton?"

"Indeed, sir. They were in the cellar of a house."

Fotherby looked at the saddled horse that the other soldier held steady. He hated riding but, given the situation, climbed onto the horse before he turned back to the young woman.

"Thank you," he whispered.

"I hope you get justice, sir," she whispered. "It was a cruel thing they did. God shall not forgive them."

Fotherby considered this statement as he joined the two soldiers on their way to Buxton. They reached the gaol in the middle of the afternoon, and Fotherby dismounted at once and walked into the building. He was shown to the cell, where three men sat on the floor, each of them turning to face the surgeon as he stood at the iron door. The soldiers stood back a short distance and discussed the prisoners with the guards.

"I know all three of you," Fotherby began. "Do you know me?"

None of them answered, but two of them lowered their gaze.

"I tended each one of you after the clashes with the soldiers. I found a safe place for you to rest, though I grant it was not comfortable. I was on your side. I want abolition."

"What has this to do with our charges?" one of them asked bitterly.

"Those men who you locked in Wanderford Hall were my father and my uncle. Allow me to simplify this for you." He rested his head against the bars and stared down at them. "I saved your lives and you robbed me of the lives which mattered most to me. I spent this morning burying my kin. You will receive no sympathy from me for your treatment today."

"He was a slaver," one of them said quickly. "A man argued with him on such a topic."

"I was that man. But he had forsaken his years in the trade to become an honest man." Fotherby took a step back and shook his head. "I do not wish to see you hang," he said calmly. "I have seen enough execution. But, before you celebrate your lives, I must caution you. The other gentleman who was caught in your fire was their officer," he pointed to the soldiers. "Another abolitionist. It is from them you now need mercy, and loyalty is what holds the British Army together."

Fotherby walked out of the gaol, tipping his hat to the soldiers and guards on his way out. He did not look back at the three arsonists but continued through the streets until he reached Doctor Shipton's house. He knocked on the door and waited to be admitted by the footman who explained that, following the funeral of the two Fotherby gentlemen, Doctor Shipton had gone to visit an elderly gentleman beyond Wanderford.

Fotherby relinquished his sodden coat and hat, before he walked up the stairs and silently opened one of the doors on the landing. He peered in to find Portland as he had left him that morning, except that his head had fallen to one side. Closing the door, he stopped as he heard Portland's voice.

"Fotherby?" he muttered. "I have discovered why Philip loved laudanum."

"What are you talking about?" Fotherby laughed as he stepped in and walked over to the bed, sitting down on the hard chair beside his friend.

"I think Doctor Shipton gave me some laudanum, Fotherby. I cannot feel any of the pain I remember being in."

"Do not get a taste for it," Fotherby cautioned, smiling across at his friend. "There is little point in asking you whether you are well for, if the laudanum has dulled your senses, you will not know."

"How long have I lain here, Fotherby?"

"Three days. But your officer has been advised of your situation."

"I am so sorry about your family," he murmured.

"They were buried this morning," Fotherby replied, his voice trembling only slightly. "I am going to sell Wanderford Hall, such as it is, and my uncle's mills, too. I have no interest in being a mill owner and I cannot bear to remain in Wanderford."

"But it is your home, Fotherby," Portland said softly.

"But not my duty. I have no skill but for being a physician and surgeon, and I will not assist as many people here as I did in war."

"Are you rejoining the army?"

"No," Fotherby said flatly. "I have a mind to establish a hospital."

"Do you never think of yourself?" Portland laughed, sitting up so that he was leaning on his arm and staring across at Fotherby with a drunken expression. "You have a life here."

"But one that benefits no one. Not even myself." Fotherby rose to his feet and smiled down at his friend. "I cannot thank you enough, Portland. I hope you will never think that if I cease thanking you aloud I have ceased being grateful. You truly are the very best of friends."

The following day saw Doctor Shipton removing the stitches from the young man's leg before Portland returned to London with the rest of his company. As November stripped the trees bare, Fotherby could find less and less cause to remain in Derbyshire. He had successfully sold the seven mills to a gentleman his uncle had known, although he had been advised to maintain shares in them and, when he had a buyer for Wanderford Hall estate, he announced to Doctor Shipton his intention to leave the county.

"I shall be sad to see you leave, Fotherby," the old man confided, "but I must assure you that it comes as little surprise to me. You have nothing to tie you here any longer and, besides, Second-Lieutenant Portland told me of your wish." Shipton lifted his hand and smiled across. "Do not rebuke him for it. Poor boy was so drugged that I suspect he had no control over his words."

"Then you know my hopes? I wish to establish a hospital where I can treat those men injured in war, for I have seen the poor care that they receive on their return. And I shall establish it in the city."

"I wish you every luck, Fotherby. No man has given so much to so many ungrateful souls, as you. I hope you are treated with more kindness in your selfless venture."

Fotherby thanked him, unsure how to accept such a compliment. The following day he packed his few belongings and made his farewells before he journeyed south to the capital. He found humble lodgings in a small room above a shop in the crowded streets of the city, and began to search for a building in which he could establish his hospital. After walking through the streets searching for the venue for countless days, he finally decided upon what had been a corn exchange. It was a vast hall that he could easily imagine dividing into wards with a series of offices upstairs.

With a new purpose, he began enquiries to learn from whom he might purchase his new investment but, as he was passed from lawyer to lawyer, he began to feel foolish for ever believing such a project might succeed. He had, furthermore, discovered that he was unable to stay away from Fleet Street, as he lived on one of the roads that ran adjacent to it and, each time he witnessed Mrs Allen walk out with her husband, he began to fall under the hand of self-pity that he had promised his father he would avoid.

It was the last day of November when he received a letter asking him to attend a meeting at the corn exchange. More through curiosity than hope, he walked to the building and stood before the great steps, imagining the hospital he wished to open. He turned as he heard someone addressing him and found a thin-faced gentleman wearing a suit of complete black and a wide brimmed hat to match. He was impossible to age, for his looks were youthful but his expression was stern and severe.

"Doctor Henry Fotherby?" he began.

"I am Doctor Fotherby."

"It has been brought to the attention of a lady and gentleman that you have intentions for this building."

"Pardon, sir," Fotherby stammered. "But who are you?"

"A lawyer, sir. I represent the interests of the aforementioned lady and gentleman. They have a will to support you in this venture."

Fotherby frowned at the man beside him, before he looked at the exchange once more. "I have sought the owner of this property, sir. I do not believe he wishes to be found."

"Mr Grassford has moved his interests out of the city, Doctor. And as you see, he no longer has call for this property. My client wished me to offer you the detail and address of Mr Grassford, that you might purchase this building if you had a mind to." Here, the lawyer handed Fotherby a letter, before he tapped his hat in a brief farewell and walked down the steps to the carriage that awaited him.

Fotherby looked at the familiar writing, that simply stated his name, before he tucked it into his pocket and walked down the steps, returning to his lodgings. He stepped aside quickly to allow two ladies to walk along the pavement, bowing his head slightly as they walked on. He watched as Miss and Mrs Allen continued down the road, laughing with one another and never looking back. It was a strange feeling to be not only snubbed but utterly unnoticed, and he continued to his rooms in a sorry state of bewilderment.

When he reached the house, he sat down, staring at the letter the lawyer had given him in one hand and the portrait of Miss Simmons in the other. He had never ceased carrying it with him and, each time it emerged from his pocket, he felt the guilt for all that had happened to the young woman. As the days had turned, he found himself more unable to apportion reason and blame to anyone but himself and this, in turn, drove him to only more determination to achieve the life he had chosen. Returning the portrait to his left breast pocket, he opened the envelope and read on in curiosity.

"Doctor Fotherby," it opened formally. "We have been so very sorry to hear of your losses and wish to offer our condolences in wake of such tragic news. At such a geographical distance, it is difficult to offer the assistance that my wife and I wish to provide after all that we both owe to you. However, it has come to my attention that you have a mind to continue in your military work with the intention of establishing an army hospital and, furthermore, have found a most suitable venue. For reasons relating to my own foolish history, the owner of the building, one Mr Grassford, has become reluctant to deal with property, but I have assured him of your intentions and I believe he will now sell. In this way we hope, perhaps, to repay a little of the debt we owe to you and trust that, despite your choice to leave the army, we may remain in your friendship. Your servants, Josiah and Elizabeth Tenterchilt."

He stared at the letter, trying to understand what had inspired such an offer from a gentleman to whom he owed far more than the major would ever accept. Yet it had given him a new hope that he might succeed in his wish to establish the hospital.

"I beg pardon, sir," a small voice began, as the door behind him opened. "Shall I lay the fire, sir? It is terribly cold."

"No, thank you," Fotherby said quickly. "I am not ready for fire yet."

She curtsied before leaving and, at once, Fotherby walked to his desk and began penning an appreciative reply to the Tenterchilts, and a letter of intent to Mr Grassford, using the address that Major Tenterchilt had written on the back of the letter.

Fotherby never heard from Mr Grassford, although a week later his lawyer appeared at Fotherby's dwelling. He was a large man with a sagging face and a serious expression, and he regarded Fotherby with a calculating gaze.

"I imagined you would be older," he said, after announcing his name as Mr Hilton and his role as Mr Grassford's lawyer.

"Twenty-eight, sir," Fotherby replied apologetically. "Does that matter?"

"I expect not." Mr Hilton wrapped his long coat tighter about him in a pointed way. "Young blood is clearly not so thin as mine. I trust you will tend your patients with more warmth than yourself, or they shall die through cold alone."

"Then Mr Grassford has accepted my offer?" Fotherby said excitedly, standing back to allow the lawyer in to his immaculate but freezing rooms.

"Indeed," he stated, taking the glass of wine that Fotherby offered him. Hilton watched as Fotherby looked at his own glass for a moment before he took a sip from it. "In fact," he continued, "work has already begun on clearing it ready for your enterprise."

"How is this so well known? I have told no one of it."

"In London, sir, one gentleman's business becomes the business of the whole of society. It seems that certain persons wish to support you."

"Major Tenterchilt has been truly loyal to me," Fotherby muttered, feeling once more indebted to the charismatic man.

"For certain," Hilton replied cryptically as he handed Fotherby the heavy ring of keys to the corn exchange. "But I doubt he would soil his hands with the jobs that are being done. Would you lay your signature to this, sir? I shall arrange payment with your bank. I understand you have work to attend at once."

Fotherby took the document that Hilton had produced from his pocket, and carried it over to the desk. It detailed Fotherby's permission for the lawyer to remove two hundred pounds in exchange for the property. He dipped the fine silver pen into the inkwell and wrote his signature, his steady hand forming the perfect image of his future.

"And the deeds, sir?" Fotherby asked as he rolled the blotter across the document, before folding and returning it to Hilton.

"I have handed them to Major Tenterchilt's lawyer, much beyond my better judgement, for he is even younger than yourself." He returned the document to his pocket after setting down the empty wineglass and shook Fotherby's hand. "I wish you the very best, sir. As does Mr Grassford."

Fotherby showed him out, before snatching his own coat and the ring of keys, and rushing out through the streets to his new property. He stood before it and gave a contented sigh. It may not have been as grand or inhabitable as Wanderford Hall, but it was an industry and a chance to do what he had wished for all his life.

"Learning to love London, Fotherby?" asked a clipped voice and he turned to smile at the two gentlemen who stood behind him.

"Lieutenant Keith," he began. "I trust you were more successful in Suffolk than Portland and I were in Derbyshire?"

"That is not fair," Portland laughed. "I did manage to save a great man."

"It was with far less incident," Keith agreed. "But I would declare today's events a great success that would not have arisen without the tragedy in Derbyshire."

"What a price to pay," Portland whispered thoughtfully. "I had the strangest feeling this morning that Delphi was talking to me, Fotherby. About you."

Fotherby stared at him as he walked up the steps and pushed the doors open to reveal a shining clean room with polished panelling and stripped wooden floors. Fotherby stared in amazement at the vast space and stepped in, uncertain to whom he owed thanks for the repaired doors and the tidy appearance. There were three long folding-screens that divided the room and, as Keith stepped inside and watched the surgeon with keen eyes, Fotherby rushed through the door that led to the offices upstairs. They were as spotless as the wards below, although one had no floor laid, for the rotting timbers had not yet been replaced. The offices were whitewashed, so fresh that it made his eyes sting. He walked back downstairs to where Portland and Keith were talking and laughing with one another.

"Is it not amazing what sixteen people can do in two nights?" Portland asked, as he beheld Fotherby's astonished expression.

"Who did it?"

"You have no idea?" Keith laughed.

"You have touched so many people, Fotherby," Portland said, his tone incredulous in his respect for the understated man before him. "They all want to support you. And I include myself in that, for your loyalty to my family and the pain you bore for them, I feel you are as much a brother to me as ever Philip or Harris were. And I loved them both dearly."

"Then you did all this?"

"No," Portland laughed.

"Sixteen free men and women walked out of slavery. You taught them they could be free and, in their hours of freedom, they did this." Keith looked levelly across at the surgeon and shook his head. "I am not a political man, whatever my father may believe, but what you have inspired from these men and women through your own politics is a loyalty as strong as any I have ever seen. Manny?" Keith questioned, turning to Portland who nodded in reply. "He would follow you to hell and back, Doctor."

The three friends stood for a time, considering the past and the onset of their brighter futures. There was a silence in the great room that each was comfortable to maintain as the minutes ran by them. Finally, Keith placed a hand on the arm of both his friends.

"Let us retire and drink to the success of Doctor Fotherby's hospital. For certain," he continued, turning to Portland, "you and I may yet have need of it. And Fotherby," he added, looking into the surgeon's contented face, "I hear you have broken your abstinence and I have a very fine, very small, case of whisky I have kept since my sister's wedding. We shall go and open it."

They left, then, Fotherby turning the heavy key in the great lock while his friends watched on with the pride and contentment, which he shared. The three men walked down the steps and through the oppressive city, each with a smile on his face, eager to embrace the futures which lay before them.

Also by **CROWVUS**

*Day's Dying Glory*

by **Virginia Crow**

*The sequel to Beneath Black Clouds and White.*

*Share the adventures of three sisters living in Highland Scotland during the Napoleonic Wars.*

*£9.99*

*Get 35% off your first order by subscribing to the Crowvus Call-Out Newsletter.*

www.crowvus.com/subscribe

www.stompermcewan.com

Lightning Source UK Ltd.
Milton Keynes UK
UKHW011819010819
347227UK00001B/1/P